SECOND [...]
As a Hollywood stuntw[oman, Beth follows in her dad]'s footsteps. But can she [measure up] as a private eye, as well? When Lucas Hallam is away, it falls to Beth to solve a case of attempted murder—on a cat! It's her first case, and she has a lot to learn, but she's never admitted defeat—and she's not about to start now!

SHOES, SHADES, AND FAERYDUST—DEBORAH MACGILLIVRAY
When Dominique won a pair of red leather Gucci pumps at a Halloween festival, she felt like she had put on Dorothy's ruby slippers. Little did she know those shoes would carry her to where her heart wanted to be—to sexy Bran MacKenzie. But dare she hope the girl everyone shunned could win the love of the most popular guy in town? Take red shoes, a pair of sunglasses and sprinkle liberally with golden faerydust, and you have a magic spell in the making…

MR. FRED'S TREASURE BOX—CHERYL PIERSON
Lovey Villines has mysteriously died, with only her cat, Mr. Fred, as a witness. As her greedy siblings squabble, Brady Rowe, a veteran police officer, tries to keep the peace and learn what truly happened. The key to Mr. Fred's Treasure Box is hidden in a most unlikely place, and Officer Rowe must have it to solve what could be murder—and find out what will become of Lovey's feline companion, Mr. Fred.

CAT'S CRADLE—MOLLIE HUNT
When cat lady Lynley Cannon discovers a stray kitten trapped in a gym bag, she finds herself pursued through Portland's warehouse district by gun-wielding thugs. Lynley has no idea what the shooters want, but she's not about to give up the kit to those crazies, so the race is on.

THE NERD IN SHINING ARMOR—ISABELLA NORSE
Abby needs a hero. Ryan needs an assistant. Can a battle-scarred tabby with a penchant for quoting from *Star Wars* bring them together?

THE CAT ON COOGAN'S BLUFF—ROCHELLE SPENCER
A Harlem detective delves into the mysteries surrounding his neighborhood in this intriguing tale about baseball, cats, and murder.

Will he be able to solve the mystery of an old-time baseball celebrity's death in a fall that wasn't accidental? The clues are scarce, and hinge on Harlem's mysterious residents, a blue-eyed Persian, and an old love gone bad.

MISSING LYNX—CLAY MORE

It is 1926 and the world mourns silent movie heart-throb Rudolph Valentino who has suddenly and tragically died at the age of thirty-one. His secret lover, the movie star Kay du Maurier, is bereft, but must keep her secret hidden from the world and especially from her husband, the famous adventurer and big game hunter, Colonel Fenton Carlyle. Rudolph's death is only the first in a series of tragedies in this supernatural feline murder mystery tale from the silent movie era.

DREAM WEAVER—C.A. JAMISON

Mary Lynn Price moves to California to take a job as a secretary for a screenplay writer she has never met. On her first day at work, she has a chance encounter with an unforgettable stranger she can't put out of her thoughts. Given the impossible task of reading three romance novels in three days, Mary is in disbelief when her newly-adopted cat has her dreaming the actual outcomes of the stories—and taking part in the books. The handsome blue-eyed stranger is the hero in each novel, and Mary has no idea she is falling in love with her new boss.

CLAWS FOR JUSTICE—MARIAH LYNNE

Two spunky shelter cats, Shurlock and Wattson, learn their time at the shelter is up. The furry duo finds a clever way to escape their fate, only to find their caretaker, Robby, dead. They now must make it their mission to find Robby's killer and bring him to justice before they get caught again.

WHO LET THE CATS OUT?—FAYE RAPOPORT DESPRES

When a mysterious fire tears through the main house of the Jane S. Dooley Cat Shelter, Adalyn, the shelter's director, vows to keep the shelter open. Thankfully, the cats who were housed upstairs got out and escaped the fire. Now, Adalyn has two mysteries on her hands: Who set the fire, and who let the cats out?

THE CALICO—BRANDY HERR

After Larry's wife walks out on him, the sudden arrival of a mysterious calico cat appears to be just what he needs to lift his spirits. But appearances can be deceiving.

ANGEL—ANGELA CRIDER NEARY

An enchanting cat named Angel and a series of suspicious fires has a Colorado sheriff wondering if cats really do have nine lives—and trying to figure out who the next victim will be.

THE EASTER CAT—BILL CRIDER

When Hollywood private-eye Bill Ferrel gave a ride to the Easter Bunny, he thought he was just doing a friend a favor. How was he to know he'd wind up chasing a cat through the jungle and trying to prevent a murder?

NINE DEADLY LIVES

An Anthology of Feline Fiction

Livia J. Washburn
Deborah Macgillivray
Cheryl Pierson
Mollie Hunt
Isabella Norse
Rochelle Spencer
Clay More
C.A. Jamison
Mariah Lynne
Faye Rapoport DesPres
Brandy Herr
Angela Crider Neary
Bill Crider

Nine Deadly Lives by Fire Star Press
Copyright© 2015 Fire Star Press
Cover Design Livia Reasoner
Fire Star Press
www.firestarpress.com

All rights reserved.
ISBN-13: 978-1517535421
ISBN-10: 1517535425

This is a work of fiction. The characters, incidents, and dialogues are products of the author's imagination and are not to be construed as real.

No part of this book may be used or reproduced in any manner whatsoever without written permission of the publisher, except in the case of brief quotations embodied in critical articles and reviews.

Second Nature Copyright © 1994 Livia J. Washburn
Shoes, Shades and Faerydust Copyright © 2013 Deborah Macgillivray
Mr. Fred's Treasure Box Copyright © 2015 Cheryl Pierson
Cat's Cradle Copyright © 2015 Mollie Hunt
The Nerd In Shining Armor Copyright © 2015 Linda Ward (w/a Isabella Norse)
The Cat On Coogan's Bluff Copyright © 2015 Rochelle Spencer
Missing Lynx Copyright © 2015 Keith Souter (w/a Clay More)
Dream Weaver Copyright © 2015 Cynthia A.Moore (w/a C.A. Jamison)
Claws For Justice Copyright © 2015 Mariah Lynne
Who Let The Cats Out? Copyright © 2013 Faye Rapoport DesPres
The Calico Copyright © 2015 Brandy Herr
Angel Copyright © 2015 Angela Crider Neary
The Easter Cat Copyright © 1996 Bill Crider

Table of Contents

Second Nature by Livia J. Washburn 1

Shoes, Shades and Faerydust by Deborah Macgillivray 19

Mr. Fred's Treasure Box by Cheryl Pierson..33

Cat's Cradle by Mollie Hunt..49

The Nerd In Shining Armor by Isabella Norse...................................63

The Cat on Coogan's Bluff by Rochelle Spencer................................80

Missing Lynx by Clay More..98

Dream Weaver by C. A. Jamison 124

Claws For Justice by Mariah Lynne...151

Who Let the Cats Out? by Faye Rapoport DesPres..........................170

The Calico by Brandy Herr 186

Angel by Angela Crider Neary 201

The Easter Cat by Bill Crider..220

Second Nature

Livia J. Washburn

Can Beth Hallam make the cut as a private eye?

Beth Hallam took a deep breath and tried to ignore the fear in her belly. Then she stepped out into empty space, fighting off the impulse to close her eyes against the terrifying nothingness beneath her. She had to keep her eyes open so she could see where she was falling. Otherwise, she might miss the net stretched out beneath her.

The wind of her fall tugged at the cap secured tightly on her head. The cap had to be tight, or it would have come off and let her long red hair stream up and out around her head. Since she was doubling for a twelve-year-old actor—a boy—having her hair come loose would have ruined the gag. In the ragged shirt and baggy pants she wore, the curves of her body were well hidden, and she and the kid were within an inch of each other in height. Beth had doubled for him in his last picture, too.

The net was hidden in a cluster of large boulders at the foot of the bluff, where the cameras couldn't see it. Beth hit it cleanly, perfectly, knowing that the director would be shouting, "Cut!" right about now. The net gave under her, then sprang back up, tossing her into the air. A wave of exhilaration swept through her, as it always did at moments like this. In all of her twenty years, she had never experienced anything like the feeling of a dangerous gag that had gone just as planned.

She bounced up and down a few times in the net, then rolled to the edge and swung down from it. The second-unit director, an old-timer who had spent a quarter of a century staging stunts like this since coming to Hollywood in the early Twenties, hurried over to her and clapped a hand on her shoulder.

"Great job, Beth," he told her. "I never saw your daddy do any better."

Beth tugged the cap off, letting her hair spill free. There wouldn't be any second takes. She looked up at the rim of the bluff, which was a good three stories above her. "Lucas never jumped off a cliff like that," she said with a laugh. "Not even with a horse under him."

"Well, that's true. Not for the camera, anyway. I don't know what he might've done back when he was just a young buck. I'll have to ask him about it someday."

"Don't get him started," Beth said, and laughed again. "Not unless you've got plenty of time to listen to his stories."

"Speak of the devil." The second-unit director pointed toward the road that wound along the canyons of this rugged area that, for all its seeming isolation, was only a few miles from the intersection of Hollywood and Vine.

Beth looked where he was pointing and recognized the car bouncing along the road. Her father had driven a black flivver for years, and he was still of the opinion that all cars ought to be painted black, even in this modern day and age. And Lucas Hallam was nothing if not stubborn, as Beth knew from long experience.

"You need me for anything else, Yak?" she asked the second-unit director.

"No, you go on ahead. Say hello to your dad for me."

Beth waved at him and moved off through the hustle and bustle of a movie company on location. There were quite a few trucks and cars parked around the area, and trailers had been set up for the stars to use as dressing rooms. The army of flunkies that went hand in hand with moviemaking hurried here and there, seemingly aimlessly. Beth knew it all made sense if you knew what you were looking at. She had no desire to get that well acquainted with the process. She knew stunt work, and that was enough. It was second nature to her, something that was in her blood. And she came by it honestly, since her father was Lucas Hallam, who had performed gags and worked as a riding extra all through the Twenties and well up into the Thirties.

As Hallam stepped out of the roadster that he had parked by some of the equipment trucks, he looked like he could still swing up into a saddle and gallop off with a make-believe posse after a gang of celluloid owlhoots. He was a big man, his frame shrunken a little by age but still powerful. His leathery face had been craggy and lined as far back as Beth could remember, and as the years passed, the lines just seemed to get deeper. The mustache drooping over his wide mouth was iron gray, as was the rumpled thatch of hair under the broad-brimmed brown hat. He leaned against the fender of the roadster and crossed his arms as he watched his daughter come toward him.

"Elizabeth, you look like some sort o' hobo," he greeted her.

She glanced down at the ragged outfit she was wearing. "I'm supposed to. The kid's playing a tramp in this picture. Of course, he's really the heir to a fortune and doesn't know it, or some such claptrap." Beth jerked a thumb toward the bluff behind her. "I just jumped off that cliff for him."

"Yeah, I remember you tellin' me about the gag you had lined up. How's he supposed to get out of it?"

Beth shook her head. "He doesn't. He's already done his death scene. They showed me the rushes of it before I did the stunt." She grinned. "It's a corker. There won't be a dry eye in the house."

"Any problems with the gag?"

"No, it went fine." Beth frowned a little. "What are you doing out here, Lucas? I thought you were going to be in the office all day."

Ever since his bones had finally gotten too brittle to do stunt work or stand up to the constant pounding of long days in the saddle, Hallam had concentrated on the one-man private detective agency he had built up over the years. He thumbed his hat to the back of his head and said, "I got a call from a feller over in Palm Springs who wants to see me about a case. He's promised me a thousand bucks just for hearin' him out, so I reckon I'll drive over there and see what he's got to say. Just wanted to let you know where I was goin' and make sure it won't be a problem."

"You could have left me a note," Beth said.

Hallam shrugged his wide shoulders. "Yeah, I reckon."

Beth smiled slightly to herself. Her father wasn't the most demonstrative man in the world. But she knew him well enough to realize he had come out here to the location just so he could say goodbye in person.

Beth had never known her mother. Lucas had raised her from an infant, somehow juggling the responsibilities of parenthood with his busy career. And Beth loved him dearly. She stepped over to him, came upon her toes, and brushed a kiss across his cheek. "You go on to Palm Springs," she told him. "I'll be fine."

"All right," Hallam said. "I'll give you a call and let you know how things are goin' and when I expect to be back. You got a ride back into town?"

"Sure. I came out on one of the trucks."

"Well, I'll see you in a day or two, more'n likely."

Beth watched him get back in the roadster and drive away. As fathers went, he was a mite unusual, maybe—but that was all right with Beth. She liked to think she was a mite unusual herself.

oOo

She got back to the apartment she shared with her father on Fountain Avenue in West Hollywood not long after dark. The telephone was ringing as she unlocked the door, and Beth muttered to herself as she hurried across the living room to answer it. She scooped up the receiver and said, "Hello?" as she tossed her purse onto a chair.

A woman's voice said, "I need to speak to Lucas Hallam, please." The words had a brisk, businesslike tone.

"I'm afraid he's not available right now," Beth said. "Could I take a message?"

"Well, hell. I really wanted to talk to the old coot."

Beth blinked in surprise. She'd had the caller pegged as a potential client. "I beg your pardon?"

"Oh, don't mind me, dearie. I knew Lucas back in the old days. My name is Delores Banning. I called his office and his service gave me this number. I need to see him right away."

"I'm sorry, but—"

"It's a matter of life and death."

Beth wanted to stare at the phone. She had never actually heard anybody say that before—except in the movies. She wondered if Delores Banning was an actress.

If so, she was probably a good one, because there was a definite note of urgency and sincerity in her voice. Beth hesitated only a moment, then gave in to an impulse she had felt before.

She said, "I'm Mr. Hallam's associate. Perhaps I can help you."

Well, why not? she thought. She had been around while Lucas was working on some of his biggest cases. It wasn't like she didn't know *anything* about the detective business.

"You're a gumshoe, too, sweetie?" Delores Banning said.

"That's right," Beth said. She felt a little nervous about lying like that, but Lucas was out of town and Delores Banning sounded *really* troubled about something...

"Well, come on out to the house. It's on DeMille Drive, over in Los Feliz." Delores Banning gave Beth the number and told her how to find the place. "Make it quick, before something else happens to Chester."

"Chester?"

"That's right. Somebody's trying to murder him."

That made Beth's eyes widen. Delores Banning hadn't been kidding about it being a matter of life and death.

"Maybe what you'd better do is call the police."

"I tried that, honey. They don't care." For the first time, Beth heard something besides brassy self-assuredness in the woman's voice. "Nobody cares about Chester but me."

What would Lucas do in this situation? Beth couldn't remember him ever turning his back on anybody who was really in trouble. In the Old West that Lucas Hallam came from, a man just didn't do that.

She was nothing if not her father's daughter, Beth thought. She took a deep breath and said, "I'll come right out there."

"Thank you, sweetie," Delores Banning said. "By the way, what's your name?"

"Elizabeth."

"Well, you hurry on out, Liz. I'll be looking for you."

Beth hung up and looked at the phone for a long moment. *Liz.* That was what Lucas had called her mother, although he hardly ever talked about her. He had never called his daughter by that name, however. To him, she had always been either Elizabeth or Beth.

Well, there would be time enough to set Delores Banning straight once she got there, Beth thought. For now, there were more important considerations.

Like murder and somebody named Chester.

o0o

DeMille Drive was a narrow, winding street named after the director, whose mansion was located in the hills of Los Feliz, until recently one of the most exclusive residential areas in Los Angeles. Lately, many of the stars who lived in the neighborhood had been moving southwest to Beverly Hills, but there were still quite a few celebrity mansions in Los Feliz. Delores Banning's was one of them. It was a sprawling pile of stone and white stucco perched atop one of the hills and surrounded by acres of lawn. Now, as night was settling down over the city, it was brightly lit. Beth wheeled her cream-colored Ford through an arched stone gate in the fence and started up the hill on a curving drive that led her to the house.

As the car's headlights swept over the lawn, she saw that it could use cutting. The flower beds dotting the lawn were unkempt and full of weeds. Beth frowned. Delores Banning wasn't keeping the place up very well. Not only that, but the wrought-iron gate had been wide open, and the intercom set into one of the stone pillars at the entrance hadn't seemed to be working at all.

Beth hadn't been able to get a squawk out of it.

She brought the Ford to a stop in front of the house, and the double doors opened before Beth could get out of the car. A tall, rawboned woman with obviously dyed black hair swept out of the house and came toward the car carrying a cat in her arms. The woman wore an expensive silk gown that was as rumpled as if she'd slept in it for a week. She said, "That you, Liz?"

"My friends call me Beth, Mrs. Banning. Or is it Miss Banning?"

"Oh, it's Missus, dearie. I was married to Hubert Banning for thirty-five years."

Beth recalled Hubert Banning's name. He had been an executive at one of the studios, and her father had mentioned him several times over the years. Banning had died several years earlier, Beth seemed to remember.

"Come on in, Beth," Delores Banning said. "I don't like standing out here in the light like this. You never know when somebody's spying on you."

"Wait a minute," Beth said, uncertain whether she wanted to go inside with this woman or not. "You said on the phone that someone named Chester was in danger?"

"Well, of course he is. That's why I want to get back inside the house. The poor dear's already been bushwhacked once." Delores Banning held up the cat. "See?"

There was a bandage on the shoulder of the animal's left front leg.

o0o

Chester was a big orange tomcat, nothing fancy about him. He sat in Delores Banning's lap and licked the woman's hand almost constantly, the rough tongue making a faint rasping sound against her skin. Beth thought that licking would have driven her crazy in a matter of minutes.

"He got sick from the poison," Delores said, "but the vet was able to save him. Then he came home with his hind leg all scratched up and Dr. Hubbell said it looked like somebody tried to catch him in a trap. And then there was the gunshot wound." Delores shook her head, her strong but attractive features set in a mixture of sadness and anger. "Someone is definitely trying to kill Chester. And I can't imagine why anyone would want to hurt him!"

Beth sat in an overstuffed armchair with a lace doily over its back. The whole room was furnished like that, chintz and foofaraws everywhere you looked—except for the walls, which were covered with red velvet. Beth could almost imagine what her father's reaction would have been to this place. He would have said it looked like a cross between a preacher's parlor and a Kansas City whorehouse. Obviously, Delores Banning had rather eccentric tastes.

Beth already regretted giving in to the impulse that had made her tell this woman she was a detective. She figured Delores Banning was a little off in the head.

"Are you sure you're a private eye, honey? You look awfully young to be doing work like that."

"I'm older than I look," Beth said.

"I was just the opposite. Looked older than I really was. The boys liked that just fine, though. I was playing supporting roles as grown women when I was barely seventeen. That's how I met your boss; he was working on a Tom Mix picture I was in, back around '28." Delores shook her head. "A long time ago."

Beth nodded. She hadn't told the woman that Lucas was her father, and it might be best to keep it that way. She said, "Let's get back to Chester."

"I want you to find out who's trying to kill him. Whatever your agency's regular fee is, I'll pay it. Money is no object."

That was another saying Beth had never heard anyone use in real life. But Delores had been an actress, and she was probably used to saying things like that in scripts. Beth glanced around at the room with its air of genteel poverty, and Delores went on, "Oh, don't worry about how the place looks. I know it's getting a little rundown. But I can pay you. I promise you that. I can give you cash—"

"No, that's all right," Beth said. "A check made out to Mr. Hallam will be fine. Now, do you have any idea at all who might want to hurt your cat?"

"Told you I didn't. It doesn't make sense. I—"

The front door opened, and there was a quick patter of footsteps in the hallway. A woman's voice called, "Aunt Delores! Are you here?"

A blonde woman appeared in the doorway of the room where Beth and Delores Banning had been talking. She was in her early twenties, well dressed, and undeniably beautiful. She said, "Oh, there you are. I was worried about you." Blue eyes flicked over to Beth. "And who is this?"

The coolness in her tone betrayed dislike, and Beth figured she could learn to return the feeling pretty easily. Delores said, "She's a detective, dear. She's going to find out who's been trying to hurt Chester."

The blonde looked away from Beth, already dismissing her in her mind. "I told you nobody's trying to murder your cat, Aunt Delores. You've been imagining things, just like always."

Delores Banning flinched a little, as if somebody had struck her. Beth felt a quick surge of anger. She said, "That gunshot wound isn't a figment of anyone's imagination. And I want to know who *you* are."

Delores said, "This is my niece, Nicolette Banning. Nicky, please try to be polite to Elizabeth."

All of the aging actress's previous self-assurance seemed to have drained away in the presence of the younger woman. Nicolette Banning gave Beth a haughty look and said icily, "How do you do."

"Pretty good most of the time," Beth said, her own tone cool. "What do you know about the attempts on Chester's life, Miss Banning?"

Nicolette frowned. She was wearing an expensive gown and a fur stole, despite the warmth of the evening. She said, "I don't like the sound of that. You don't think I had anything to do with bothering the cat, do you?"

The animal in question was curled up in Delores's lap, purring and sleeping soundly, his claws working slightly back and forth. Delores said to Beth, "Nicky wouldn't hurt Chester, Liz. She's the only relative I have left. She takes care of me."

"I *try*," Nicolette said, her self-appointed martyrdom apparent in her voice. "I called earlier and didn't get any answer. That's why I came over."

"I was up in the screening room, watching one of my old pictures. You know there's no phone up there, sweetie. Hubert never wanted to be disturbed when he was watching a picture."

Nicolette slipped off her stole and tossed it carelessly over the back of a sofa. "You could hire a servant to answer the phone when you're busy. You could certainly afford that."

"I know. It just seems like there are so many better ways to spend my money."

The younger woman's lips pressed together until her mouth was a thin line. Beth saw the reaction and figured she knew what Nicolette Banning was thinking. Delores had said that Nicolette was her only relative; that meant Nicolette stood to inherit whatever estate Delores left. Beth wondered just how much money they were talking about, but there was no way she could ask tactfully.

Of course, tact had never been Lucas's strong suit as a detective, and she had learned from him, after all...

Nicolette opened her purse, took out a gold-plated case, and shook a cigarette from it. As she lit up, she said, "I've got to be going in a minute. If you want to waste your money on some sort of detective, Aunt Delores, that's your business."

"Yes," Delores said, "it is."

"But I won't be any part of it." Nicolette picked up her stole and looked at

Beth. "Don't try to take advantage of my aunt."

"I don't intend to," Beth said.

Nicolette gave a little ladylike snort of disbelief and walked out of the room. A moment later, the front door opened and shut.

"I'm sorry, Liz," Delores said. "I wouldn't let anybody else run over me like that, but what the hell, she's family. She and Chester are all I have left."

"I understand," Beth said, although she really didn't, not completely. "Can you keep Chester inside tonight?"

"Well...I suppose so. He enjoys his roaming, of course, all cats do, but if you think it's safer..."

"I think it would be best. I'll start asking some questions around the neighborhood tomorrow morning. Maybe I can find out something."

"All right. As long as you get results."

"Now, that's something I intend to do," Beth said.

o0o

Beth didn't have any stunt work lined up for the next day. She probably could have scrounged up a gag if she had tried, but at the moment, she was more interested in helping Delores Banning. Beth liked the older woman. Like Lucas, Delores was a survivor of another era in Hollywood. This was a town that tended to forget anything older than last week, but Beth had never been that way. She knew that Hollywood never would have grown into what it was without the efforts of Lucas and Delores and thousands more like them.

She figured it might be better to start by talking to the servants who worked in the neighborhood around the Banning house, rather than the owners of the other mansions. By the middle of the morning, she had learned that Chester was a far-ranging little varmint. More than one groundskeeper reacted angrily when Beth mentioned him, and she knew they would have cursed had she not been a woman. She supposed it was pretty annoying to labor over a flower bed for hours and then discover the next morning that not only had the plants been chewed up, but that Chester had left some other little presents to be cleaned up as well. The cooks looked on the cat more kindly, and a few of them admitted that they fed him scraps.

None of which really helped Beth any, because everyone she talked to seemed surprised when she told them that someone was trying to get rid of Chester. No one had seen or heard anything unusual in the neighborhood. As far as Beth could tell, they were all being truthful. She wished she had her father's ability to read people and know whether or not they were lying. That was something that might take years to develop, though, and she wasn't sure she would ever be investigating another case. Lucas had always tried to keep her at a distance from this part of his work.

She worked her way down one side of DeMille Drive and then back up the other. She was at the house directly opposite the Banning estate when she rang the bell at the servant's entrance and found herself facing a woman who was definitely not a servant.

The woman was wearing a dress that looked expensive enough to have come from one of those swanky shops springing up over on Rodeo Drive since movie stars had moved in droves to Beverly Hills. She was in her mid-forties, with chestnut hair. She was carrying a fluffy, extremely fat white Persian cat. The cat blinked stupidly at Beth.

The woman was anything but stupid. She said, "Yes? Can I help you?"

Beth didn't know what the mistress of this mansion was doing answering the back door, but since she was here, she might as well go ahead and ask her questions. "My name is Elizabeth Hallam. I'm a private detective." That little fib was beginning to sound like the truth to her. "One of your neighbors has been having some trouble, and I've been hired to help her find out about it. Do you know Delores Banning?"

"Of course I do. Delores and I have been friends for years. My husband and I entertained her and Hubert many times. By the way, I'm Carolyn Hawes. Won't you come in, Miss Hallam? I'm afraid it's cook's day off, but I was about to have some coffee. Would you like some?"

"All right. That would be very nice."

Carolyn Hawes seemed like a nice woman, pretty down to earth for somebody who was obviously so rich. She put the cat down carefully on the highly polished floor of the kitchen and gestured for Beth to have a seat at a heavy wooden table.

The coffee was already brewed, and it was quite good, Beth discovered as she sipped from a fine china cup that was probably worth more than what she got paid for jumping off cliffs.

"What sort of trouble has Delores been having?" Carolyn Hawes asked as she sat down on the other side of the table with her own cup of coffee.

Beth decided to try a slightly different tack this time. "Do you know anyone who might want to harass or frighten Mrs. Banning?"

"Certainly not. Delores is a lovely person. A bit...strange, perhaps, but I can't imagine anyone wanting to cause problems for her."

"Strange?"

"Well...she let all her servants go after Hubert died, and there's simply no way she can keep that place up by herself. If you've been there, you've seen for yourself what it's like."

"Maybe she can't afford to pay servants anymore."

Carolyn Hawes shook her head. "I happen to know that Hubert left her very, very well-off. My husband and I use the same law firm, and well, one hears things." She bent down to pet the white Persian, which was rubbing around her ankles and purring. A frown appeared on her face as she went on, "You know, I *can* think of someone who might not be happy with Delores. That niece of hers."

"Nicolette Banning?"

"That's right. Have you met her?"

"Briefly," Beth said.

"That was probably enough for you to know that she's not a very pleasant person. I remember Delores told me she was upset about the provisions of the will Delores had drawn up."

Beth tried not to look excited as she said, "Will?"

"Yes, that business with Chester." As she spoke the cat's name, Carolyn Hawes grimaced slightly.

"You're talking about Mrs. Banning's cat?"

"Of course. Delores's will leaves—"

Beth jumped the gun. "Everything to the cat!"

Carolyn Hawes stared at her. "Certainly not. That would be ridiculous, and Delores...well, she's a bit dotty, yes, but she's not insane."

Beth felt a little ridiculous herself for having leapt to the wrong conclusion. "I'm afraid I don't understand."

"Delores's will does leave a sizable bequest to be used for Chester's care as long as he lives. That responsibility falls to Nicolette, of course."

"How sizable a bequest are we talking about?"

"A hundred thousand dollars," Carolyn Hawes said offhandedly. "The rest of her estate will be placed in a trust, and Nicolette will earn the income from it until Chester dies, then inherit the entire amount, providing that, in the judgment of Delores's executor, she has taken good care of the cat." Carolyn smiled and shook her head. "Perhaps dotty isn't quite strong enough. Now that I've explained the situation, I'm afraid Delores does sound a bit more than eccentric."

"A bit," Beth said. "But what if something happens to Chester before Delores dies?"

"Then everything goes to Nicolette immediately." Carolyn leaned forward and went on in a conspiratorial tone, "Please don't tell Delores that I've been discussing her affairs. I shouldn't even know these things, of course, but my husband hears gossip from his attorney and from other men at the studio. He and Hubert worked together for years, you know."

Beth nodded. "I won't say anything."

"You never did tell me what sort of trouble Delores has been having. I hope it's nothing serious."

"No, probably not. She was worried enough to hire the agency I work for to check out a few things."

"I understand. You have to be cryptic about the details, of course. Client privilege and all that."

Absently, Beth nodded again. Actually, she was anxious to get out of here now that she had stumbled onto a possible motive for somebody to want Chester dead.

She was about to stand up when the Persian suddenly sprang up into her lap. Beth leaned back in surprise as the cat stuck its face up to hers and sniffed.

Carolyn Hawes beamed. "She likes you," she said. "And you must like cats."

Beth scratched the Persian behind the ears. "Sure."

"Edwina can tell that. All cats can tell when someone likes them. They're quite intelligent, you know. They can tell when someone doesn't like them, too."

Now that Beth thought about it, she supposed Carolyn was right. She had owned a few cats over the years, and all of them had taken to her without any trouble. On the other hand, she remembered having friends over who didn't like cats, and the animals had always reacted with either aloofness or outright hostility.

That had nothing to do with her present problem, though. She wanted to talk to Delores Banning again as soon as possible and find out if Nicolette had been around any of the times when Chester's near-fatal mishaps had occurred. Beth would have been willing to bet that Nicolette had been there, all right.

Gently, she lifted the heavy Persian down from her lap. Carolyn Hawes took the cat before Beth could put it on the floor. "She's my precious," Carolyn said. "She's a magnificent creature, don't you think? She's won shows all over the country, and I'm so proud of her."

Beth had never gotten that slobbery over any of her pets, and besides she had to get over to the Banning house as soon as she could. She stood up with a smile and said, "Thank you for talking to me, Mrs. Hawes. You've been a great help."

"I'm not sure how, but if I have, I'm glad. Here, let me show you out."

oOo

Beth went straight to her car and sent it down the driveway to the road. It took her several minutes to reach DeMille Drive, then climb the hill on the other side of the road to the Banning estate.

That was long enough for her to think through her suspicions. As far as she could see, Nicolette was the only one with a real reason to hurt Chester. Not only would the cat's death increase the estate she would inherit by a hundred grand, but if Chester wasn't around, Nicolette would get the whole thing as soon as Delores died, rather than having to wait for the cat to die, too.

Judging from what Beth had learned this morning about Chester's nocturnal habits—more than one of the servants in the neighborhood had talked about what a feline Lothario the cat was—he was in the prime of his life and might live a long time yet if nothing unforeseen happened to him.

And once the cat was dead, who was to say that Nicolette might not try to hurry along Delores's demise, as well?

As Beth pulled up in front of the house, she frowned at the sight of a small, sporty coupe parked there. Even though she hadn't seen what Nicolette was driving the night before, the little car struck Beth as the sort of car the blonde might have. Quickly, Beth got out of the Ford and started toward the door.

Before she got there, the sound of a raised voice drew her to the side of the house. She recognized it as Nicolette's as the blonde called, "Chester! Where are you, damn it?"

Beth's pulse kicked into a higher gear, just as it did before she attempted a risky stunt. She broke into a run, circling the house and spotting movement in an overgrown garden between the mansion and a large pool. Nicolette was there, wearing pants and a silk shirt today, and as Beth approached, she saw Nicolette suddenly lean over and grab at something. She lifted a squirming ball of orange fur by the nape of the neck and said, "Now I've got you!"

Beth left her feet in a flying tackle and crashed into Nicolette before she could wring Chester's neck—or whatever other violent end she had in mind for him. Nicolette yelled in surprise as the impact knocked her off her feet. Beth sprawled on top of her as Chester pulled away and bounded off, disappearing around the front of the house.

Nicolette was still yelling and struggling. Beth got hold of both of her wrists, and with the strength she had developed in her stunt work, she had no trouble pinning the other woman to the ground. "You thought you'd kill

Chester so you could inherit everything right away, didn't you?" Beth said, panting for breath from the exertion and from the adrenaline coursing through her.

o0o

Nicolette stopped fighting and stared up at Beth in confusion. "What are you talking about?" she demanded.

"I know all about your aunt's will—" Beth began.

Delores Banning's voice said sharply from behind her, "Liz! What the hell are you doing, girl? What's this about my will?"

Beth twisted her head around and saw that Delores had come out of a side door. The older woman was looking on anxiously. Beth said, "I think Nicolette's the one who's been trying to hurt Chester."

"Nonsense! Nicolette adores Chester, just like I do, even if she doesn't always show it." Delores sounded utterly convinced of that.

"I'm afraid you don't know your niece as well as you think you do, Mrs. Banning. Nicolette's the only one with any reason to harm Chester, and just now I saw her grab the cat and try to break his neck!"

"I did no such thing!" Nicolette said. "Chester got out of the house, and Aunt Delores wanted him inside so he'd be safe. She asked me to look for him!"

"That's true," Delores said. "I did ask Nicky to find him. I know she wouldn't hurt him. Why, many's the time I've found Chester curled up in her lap, sleeping peacefully. He only does that with people he can trust."

Beth blinked and tried to make some sense of this. She looked down at Nicolette and said, "Then...you *didn't* try to murder Chester...?"

"Of course not!"

"Oh, shoot," Beth said softly.

Between clenched teeth, Nicolette said, "Now will you please get *off of me!*"

Quickly, Beth stood up and helped the other young woman to her feet. "I...I'm sorry," she said. "When Carolyn Hawes told me about your aunt's will, I just thought—"

"Carolyn has been gossiping about me again, has she?" Delores cut in. "It's hard to believe that woman was once my best friend."

"She's not anymore?" Beth said.

Delores shook her head. "She's been very cool to me lately, and for the life of me, I can't figure out why. I certainly didn't do anything to offend her, at least, not that I know of."

As she brushed off her clothes with curt, angry gestures, Nicolette said, "Mrs. Hawes told you I wanted to hurt Chester?"

"Well, not in so many words, but I just thought..."

No, she hadn't thought at all, Beth realized suddenly. But she was thinking now, and she turned and ran as hard as she could toward the front of the estate.

oOo

Chester had been going in that direction when he fled. Beth had no idea how to go about tracking a cat—Lucas might have been able to do something like that, but she couldn't—but she knew she had to find the animal before something else happened to him.

She threw herself into her car, backed around, and took off down the drive. Delores and Nicolette probably thought she had completely lost her mind, but she couldn't take the time to worry about that now.

She headed straight toward the house where she had spoken to Carolyn Hawes, keeping a close eye on the shrubbery on both sides of the drive, watching for a flash of orange fur.

By the time she reached the house, she had seen no sign of Chester, but that didn't mean he wasn't over here.

As Beth got out of the car, she heard a sudden squall from the other side of the house, loud enough to carry plainly to her ears.

She ran again, her long strides carrying her around the large, sprawling house. She could still hear the squalling.

As she rounded the corner of the house, she saw that Carolyn had Chester backed up into a corner of a flagstone patio. The woman didn't look so cool and elegant now as she lifted a croquet mallet over her head and said, "All right, you lecherous little beast! You'll never ruin any more of your betters!"

"Mrs. Hawes!" Beth called, only a little out of breath from her run. "Don't hurt him!"

Chester let out another squall. His fur was puffed up all over and his teeth were bared in a snarl as he faced the woman he instinctively knew was his enemy.

Carolyn's head jerked around. "Go away!" she said to Beth. "This is none of your business!"

"Yes, it is," Beth insisted, trying to stay calm. "I know what happened now. When are the kittens due?"

"It doesn't matter. I'm going to destroy them immediately, of course. Edwina will be devastated, but it can't be helped." The woman looked at

Chester again. "But at least he won't ever force himself on anyone else's precious little darling. He'll be dead!"

"You knew why I was here this morning," Beth said. "You tried to point me at Nicolette Banning by telling me about that will. It almost worked, too. But Delores told me how Chester trusts Nicolette enough to sleep in her lap, and I can see for myself how he reacts to you. He remembers the other times you tried to kill him, doesn't he?"

"He doesn't deserve any less. Now, get off of my property, or I'll call the police."

Beth swallowed hard. She didn't know how the police would react to this situation, but she had a hunch they would frown more on her trespassing than they would on Carolyn's attempts to kill Chester. Protecting a cat wouldn't rank high on their list of priorities.

"Let me take Chester with me," she said. "I promise you he won't ever bother Edwina again."

"He certainly won't, the low-bred little monster. I'm going to kill him."

"Maybe I can talk Mrs. Banning into having him fixed." Slowly, Beth moved closer as she continued, "And Edwina will be okay, she really will. Lots of cats have had kittens."

"Not Edwina. She's high-strung. She'll never be the same. She'll never win another show."

Beth kept edging closer, and she was almost near enough to make a grab for that croquet mallet. Then Chester let out a howl and tried to dart past Carolyn. The mallet swept down with surprising speed.

Chester was faster. The mallet smacked against one of the flagstones. Beth leaped toward Carolyn, and the older woman jerked the mallet around, backhanding it at Beth's head. Reflexes honed by stunt work allowed Beth to drop under the swing and lower her shoulder as she ran into Carolyn. Both of them went down.

Out of the corner of her eye, Beth saw Chester taking off toward home.

She wrenched the mallet out of Carolyn's hands, rolled a few feet away, and stood up. She flung the mallet off to the side. "That's enough!" Beth said. "I'm going to tell Mrs. Banning everything that's happened, and I hope if you hurt Chester that she sues you!"

Carolyn pulled herself up on her knees and glared at Beth. "I told you once to get off my property," she said coldly.

"I'm going. But you'd better remember what I said."

Beth went back to her car, trembling with anger. She had solved the case—such as it was—but she hadn't done anything to protect Chester from further harm. Abruptly, she stopped and turned around, striding around the house to face a still-fuming Carolyn Hawes.

"This whole affair is a secret, isn't it?" Beth said. "Nobody in your fancy cat-show circles even knows that your cat is going to have kittens. Maybe they'd like to hear about it—including who the father is."

The pallor that swept over Carolyn's face told Beth her shot had struck its target. "You wouldn't dare," she said.

"Sure I would. The rivalry in those shows is pretty fierce, isn't it? I'm sure a lot of your so-called friends would love to hear about how Edwina was rutting with Chester like a common alley cat."

For a second, Beth thought Carolyn was going to pick up the croquet mallet and come after her again. But then the woman pointed a shaking finger at her and said, "You just keep your mouth shut. I...I won't do anything else about Chester. But tell Delores Banning to keep him away from here!"

"I'll tell her," Beth said. She felt a little better as she went back to her car and drove away from the Hawes estate.

o0o

On the way back to the Banning house, she spotted Chester sitting in some flowers and chewing happily on their leaves. She stopped the car and called him, and after a moment's hesitation, he sauntered over to her.

His instincts must have identified her as an ally, because he allowed her to pick him up, put him in the car, and drive him back home.

Delores was overjoyed to see him, and even Nicolette seemed happy. The blonde rubbed Chester's ears as Delores held him, and she said to Beth, "My aunt and I don't agree on everything, but I hope you understand now that I would never hurt Chester."

"I know," Beth said. "It was Carolyn Hawes who was after him."

"Carolyn!" Delores said. "But why?"

Beth explained, feeling a little foolish as she did so, and concluded by saying, "Once I realized that Persian cat I saw over there might be pregnant instead of just fat, I figured out what could have happened."

"I should hope so," Nicolette said. "I mean about why somebody else might want to hurt Chester. It seemed a little far-fetched, but..."

"You're the detective, Liz," Delores said. "I suppose I'll have to have Chester...well, fixed so that he won't roam so much."

"I think that would be a good idea."

"I hate to do that. He was just following his instincts, you know. It was second nature to him."

Beth nodded. She thought about how Delores had said she was the detective. Beth liked the sound of that. What Chester had been doing was second nature to him...and Beth suddenly realized that, just like stunt work, this private eye business might be second nature to her, too.

After all, she was Lucas Hallam's daughter.

For *Scruffy*

About the Author—Livia J. Washburn

Under the names Livia J. Washburn and L.J. Washburn, Livia Reasoner has been writing award-winning, critically acclaimed mystery, western, romance, and historical novels for more than thirty years. She began to write in collaboration with her husband, author James Reasoner, and soon branched out into telling her own stories. She received the Private Eye Writers of America award and the American Mystery award for her first mystery, WILD NIGHT, and was nominated for a Spur by the Western Writers of America for a novel she wrote with her husband, James Reasoner. Livia recently won the Peacemaker Award from Western Fictioneers for her story "Charlie's Pie".

Shoes, Shades and Faerydust

Deborah Macgillivray

True magic can happen on Halloween night under the full moon...if you only believe...

Dominique Meacham reached toward the cardboard box hidden at the very back of the closet, but then hesitated. Disappointment was rule of thumb in her life. Was it silly to hope after all this time? To think a pair of red leather shoes held magic?

She glanced to her black cat Pye Wackett. "Oh, once upon a time I had believed, Pye."

The long haired cat climbed down from his perch by the laptop, and came to do a dance next to where she knelt. The silly beast then head-butted her arm, almost seeming to push it forward. So strange, the feline seemed to be able to read her mind, and appeared almost as eager as she to see the cardboard container opened.

"It's not kitty treats, if that's what you think." She scratched his soft black fur that held a strange mahogany cast to it. "Being a cat you probably just want the box to sit in."

He meowed loudly as if to say, *get on with it, coward.*

Carefully lifting the shoes from the box, she stared at them, recalling a Halloween night three years ago when she'd won them at a high school fair...

o0o

The box was covered with red foil paper, the type used at Christmastime; rather odd, since no one else had bothered to wrap their donations. No thrill, surely? Something discarded, unwanted by its owner. She'd won a prize in the cakewalk–time to pick what she wanted. So strange, it was as though she couldn't focus on anything but that box. She climbed up the wooden bleachers, the glittering foil beckoning, lured as the Sirens had Ulysses. Something *extraordinary* was inside. In her vivid imagination, she almost could believe her faery godmother left it there for her to discover.

All the music, laughter and chatter in the gymnasium receded to mute, as she raised the lid.

Nestled within black tissue paper was a pair of fire-engine red heels. Again, why trouble to wrap the box and shoes? Just a pair of heels someone had worn once or twice and then contributed to the festival as a prize. Other prizes were stuff you'd give to a church bazaar—secondhand toys, clothing or baked goods—pies, cookies or cakes. Obviously expensive, the soft leather called out to be stroked. As she held them, she wondered if Cinderella had felt the same when she'd put on glass slippers and waltzed with her prince.

Instantly, Bran Mackenzie's face shimmered in her mind. He was so heart-stoppingly beautiful, with wavy blue-black hair and pale grey eyes—and, oh, she had danced with him last Valentine's Day, underneath white crepe streamers and red paper hearts! Oh, what she wouldn't have given for him to kiss her! Her mama warned her against him—*a bad boy*—fussing about how he was never without his sunglasses. *What was he hiding?* she forever complained. Despite all the maternal forbiddings, Dominique wanted her first kiss to be from Bran. *Only Bran.* No matter how pointless the wish, it wouldn't die within her heart.

Rushing through the double doors to the outer lobby, where no one lingered, she kicked off her tennis shoes and slipped on the pumps. They fit as if fashioned for her! Buckling the straps about her ankles, Dominique stared down at the shoes she'd won, pondering if they were magic. She *felt* different, suddenly, no longer a child, but transformed by the Gucci heels.

Born on the stroke of midnight on Halloween, she would turn eighteen in two hours. "Time to put aside childish things and embrace the night." She laughed, and stepped away from the school's entrance, and into the warm autumnal darkness.

She had a bit of trouble gaining her balance, never having worn heels before. Never owned a pair. Mama didn't approve. When she reached the hill, the yellow harvest moon broke from behind the clouds, flooding the nightscape with an eerie gold, as if kissed by faerydust. Once more, she paused to glance down at her new shoes. This was insane! They were just a pair of heels someone had discarded, put up as a prize for the carnival. Only...she'd known as she opened the lid on the box, they were special somehow. Once she'd put them on, all had changed.

"Do you grant wishes, *Ruby Slippers*? I could use a little magic in my life." She closed her eyes, and then clicked her heels thrice. Instead of Dorothy's mantra of *there's no place like home...* words fell from her lips, born from the unrequited hope in her heart, "There's no one like Bran...there's no one like Bran."

How dumb is that, her mind taunted. Bran little noticed her. All the people of the town shunned her, whispered hateful taunts like *witch*—or worse. Some hated her with an evil passion she could not understand. Some feared the jeerings of *witch* were true. Why should Bran be any different? Putting on a pair of second-hand shoes and uttering a wish wouldn't alter anything. Life was simply *not* that way.

As she reached the bottom of the hill, she nearly stumbled.

Bathed in the golden rays, Bran Mackenzie sat, half-reclining, on the stone bridge that spanned *Goblin Close Creek*. Next to him, stretched out as if they were old friends, was her cat Pye Wackett. Bran's hand absently stroked the feline's long body. An artist's study of light and shadows, Bran was majestic. "Handsome" was too feeble a word to describe this Celtic prince who seemed to have materialized from the preternatural moonlight.

Her heart stopped. She couldn't breathe. When it finally *did* beat, the rhythm was erratic, pounding, bruising against her ribcage. *Don't fall off the heels and tumble down the knoll*, she silently admonished herself. A hundred feet or so she walked to the bridge, the space more like a mile—all the while, questions running through her mind.

He was sitting all alone, save for the kitty. The corner of her mouth quirked up as she noted he had on his shades. Her mama's words arose to mind—and just as quickly, she pushed them from thought. Was he waiting for her? *Stupid girl*, her mind mocked, *Bran Mackenzie—the most popular guy in town—would have no reason to wait for you.* She was as far from his orbit as Mars was from Pluto.

She glanced down to the red heels, appearing almost black under the moon's rays. The odd thought once more flitted through her mind...had her *Ruby Slippers* carried her where her heart wanted to be? She only had seconds to decide what she'd say, how she'd act, but reasoning was beyond her.

She saw the flare of his cigarette, then the stream of smoke he blew into the air. He appeared to be chuckling to himself...or the black cat. He tilted his head down and shook it, as if saying he didn't believe what he saw.

As she drew near, she thought she heard him singing words from an old song by Gary Puckett: *My love for you is way out of line. Better run, girl. You're much too young, girl.* Surely, her mind played tricks? This golden faerydust was infecting her mind! Maybe this was nothing but another dream, and she'd awaken in her bed. It wouldn't be the first time she had dreamt of Bran.

Self-doubt rose. Was he finding humor at the little girl playing dress up? Maybe he was only making fun of her. He knew of her crush—*hell, the whole town did*—thought it amusing, and was teasing her.

Bran looked up. His deep voice queried, "Left the school fair early, Dominique?"

Nervous and trying to hide it, she shrugged. "Everything seems so…childish."

"It *is* childish. Why'd you go? You're no longer a child."

She swayed in the pumps, unable to stand still. "Not much else to do…I'm too old for Trick-or-Treating. Why are you sitting on our bridge?" The bridge *was* on her land.

"I'm not sitting—I'm leaning." He smiled, so sexy he should be outlawed.

"Okay, why are you *leaning* on our bridge?"

"Waiting…for you. Or should I say, *we* are waiting for you. I take it this mangy beast belongs to you?"

Waiting for you. The simple statement rocked her. Oh, she'd love for those words to be true; only, she wasn't brainless enough to set herself up for that humiliating disappointment. "Pull the other one, Mackenzie. And yes, Pye is my cat. Or rather, I am his human. I don't think anyone can ever be the master of Pye Wackett."

The cat rolled over and exposed his belly for scratches, and promptly rumbled when Bran complied with the silent command. "I know…you named him after that old Kim Novak-Jimmy Stewart movie. The one with the brother who was a warlock. He went around turning street lights off with his powers. I'll think of the title in a minute."

"*Bell, Book and Candle*. Wonderful movie, and I always wanted to look like Kim Novak, but that's not why I named the cat Pye. It's an old witch's familiar name. You would see it in old manuscripts about the *Burning Times*."

"Gruesome stuff. I figured you for a romance reader," he teased.

"Why do you think that?" She was curious what he assumed about her. The idea that Bran did think about her at all was novel. Oh, she was constantly mooning about him, but she never really considered he might have opinions about *her*. Maybe she didn't want to know, but it was too late to take back the words.

He looked her over as if really taking time to study her. "Oh, I don't know. You just seem to have stars in your eyes. As if you have one foot in this world and another off someplace magical."

"I guess that is a polite way to put it." She wasn't sure whether to laugh or cry. "So what are you doing here being a slave to my cat?"

"Seriously—I was waiting for you. The cat just popped around to introduce himself. I thought he might be waiting on you, too."

Pushing the shades down to the tip if his nose, he looked over the frames, taking in her long hair worn loose, the red square-neck sweater, tight white shorts and dichotomic high heels. Flames roared through her, ignited by the path of those pale warlock eyes.

"I dropped my sister off at the carnival earlier. I saw you go in and figured you'd walk home. There's trouble tonight. I deemed it best that I made sure you got safely to your front door."

"Mason, Lee and Dewey," she guessed, disgust clear in her tone. "Sir Mason the Monster and his shit-eating toadies. Wonder if the Stuarts removed the glass globes on their bridge lights? The Three Stooges toss rocks at them every Halloween."

"No rocks this time. They have .22s. Sheriff Tate's patrolling, on the lookout for them."

She gave another derisive laugh. "Big comfort there. He won't do anything to the town psychos, and you know it."

"Dominique, they *are* psychos. Golden boy is sick—a socio-psychopath. The day will soon come when they will be forced to do something with him. You walking home alone is putting a target on your back. I thought I'd hang around and see you got home. Remember the time Mason tried to set your hair on fire?"

"Not something one on the receiving end forgets. I was only six. He terrified me. My hero! You ran him off," she teased, touched Bran considered her welfare; surprised he recalled the incident from years ago.

"No one has ever called me a hero before." He reached out and picked up a strand of her hair, rubbing it between his finger and thumb. The cat swatted at him, perturbed to lose the tummy rubs. Dropping the lock, Bran took another drag on the cigarette. He looked her over again and gave a quirky half-smile. "Love your Halloween costume."

"Just shorts and a sweater." She shrugged, suddenly feeling vulnerable. "I didn't dress up."

"You could've fooled me." The corner of his mouth tugged a bit higher. "Little girl playing woman."

She frowned, suddenly peeved. A child playing dress up was the last thing she wanted Bran Mackenzie to see her as. Sliding her hands under her heavy breasts, she bounced them a couple of times. "These aren't fake, boyo.

Despite Nancy Lawson going around telling I stuff them with toilet paper—they're real."

Bran tilted his head back and howled with laughter. It caused Pye to jump to his feet, not sure what was going on.

Oh, he had a sexy throat. A lot of men didn't, but Bran's throat was a perfection that should be captured in a sculpture. She wanted to kiss that throat, lick it. She almost shook her head to dispel the golden moondust from clogging her brain and feeding these fantasies.

"Being male, I think we are born with a bullshit meter, and can tell the difference between extra soft *Charmin* and the real thing. It never crossed my mind they were anything but *all* Dominique. You always struck me as shy, so tongue-tied around me. You mostly stared. You stare at me a lot." Taking another pull on the cigarette, Bran glanced away from her and at the landscape, thrown into gold monotone shadows by the half-hidden full moon.

"Can I have a puff?" Dominique reached to swipe the ciggy from his fingertips.

As she tried to take it from his hand, Bran swung his extended arm away from her and to the side, making her follow. His longer arm kept the half-smoked cigarette out of reach. So busy leaning, trying to snatch it, it took an instant to realize the position brought her body against Bran's.

She stilled, her eyes traveling the length of his arm to his face, mesmerized by those pale grey eyes, watching her over the rim of his shades. She swallowed hard.

"Why do you watch me so, Domino?" His voice was a whisper, his breath fanning over her face.

Flames rolled through her veins, her body awakening to the pains and hungers of being a woman, of wanting so desperately what she couldn't have. She felt dizzy, swaying to him, craving him with every pore of her body. She drank in his breath, leaned to him, hoping, praying he would kiss her.

"Hmm…gone back to being shy, Domino?" It was a challenge.

For an instant, he faintly tilted toward her, as if caught up in this strange magic. The spell shattered as a car sped down the hill, the headlights illuminating them. Bran put a hand to the back of her head, pulling her to the safe harbor of his chest and neck, shielding her face against prying eyes. The Corvette zoomed past them and then accelerated up the steep incline, disappearing.

Locked in the spell of being so close to Bran, Dominique felt heat rolling off him. *Intoxicating.* His male scent drew her, filled her brain until she was drunk. He smelled *so good.* They stayed motionless, their eyes locked, breathless, neither one able to move.

"Your heart's beating like a wild bird. I feel it against mine." He said in hushed awe, his eyes studying her face intently.

She chanted in her mind *kiss me and set me free,* over and over, and for a shard in time, she thought he might. Suddenly, Bran shifted and pushed away from the edge of the bridge. *A fledgling witch's magic just isn't potent enough,* she sighed.

"Ow!" he cried, turning around to look behind him. "Your damn cat just took a plug out of my back."

Whimsical, she sighed. "Pye gets to have all the fun."

His head whipped back around to stare at her. "Did someone give you anything to drink... like punch? Brownies that tasted funny?"

"No. Want me to stand with my feet together, then bend my arm and touch my nose to prove it?"

"Well, something's gotten hold of you tonight. You're not the shy Domino I've watched growing up."

"Maybe I'm just drunk on moonlight and faerydust," she laughed. Then she blinked, not accustomed to her own laughter.

She so seldom had anything to smile about, let alone laugh over. Why, Pye Wackett had been such a blessing when he turned up sitting outside her window one stormy night, demanding she let him in! She finally had a friend, someone to talk to, so she wasn't alone in the night.

Trying to regain her mental footing she asked, "Why do you wear shades all the time?"

He shrugged. "Light tends to hurt my eyes. They're gradients, so not that dark. Besides, the moon's quite bright. Bright enough to see more than you think."

Maybe see too much.

"Come on, let's walk you home before I do something foolish." His tone was slightly angry. Pushing his glasses back up his nose, he took her hand and started up the hill, nearly dragging her behind him.

She resisted. Not now. *Oh, please,* her mind screamed. This was as close as she would ever to be having her dream coming true. It was painful to think of letting it go. "I don't want to go home." She locked her knees and set her weight against him.

Pausing, he turned around. "Didn't your mama warn you it's not safe to be out with men?"

"Regular sermons on it. '*Rough, hairy beasts. Eight hands. And they...they all just want one thing from a girl,*'" she said.

"Your mama is Jack Lemmon?" He asked incredulously, then laughed. "I've seen *Some Like It Hot*. I am beginning to think you are an old movie buff."

"I do spend a lot of late nights watching TMC. Not much else to do." She felt the shroud of sorrow that was her life trying to wrap itself around her, to blot out these new, magical feelings. It often felt as if something in her life seemed determine that she should never experience happiness. "Mama says I should …especially…" Dominique swallowed back the truth before she made a fool of herself.

The cat came pussyfooting up, meowing for attention, distracting him. Bran's head slanted to the side. With the shades on, his pale eyes were hidden from her. "Especially what, Domino?"

Looking down, she gave a pretense of petting Pye when actually she was trying to prevent him from seeing her face. It was unfair he could see her emotions all open for his inspection, while he hid behind the shades. Even so, she couldn't stop the words from coming. "When she catches me watching you."

She recalled when she was thirteen, riding her bike past the park. Bran was there playing tennis with some others from his class. She had stopped, just outside the green chain link fence, pretending she was merely watching the match. To this day, she barely recalled the two girls and the other guy who were his partners. She had stared, mesmerized in a breathless spell as she observed him toss up the yellow tennis ball and serve it. He was so handsome in the white shorts and shirt that it made her heart ache. People would laugh and call it a crush, but she knew with a certainty that she had fallen in love with Bran Mackenzie that day—and nothing since had caused the longing to fade.

"Your mama's smart. You should run home as fast as those red shoes will carry you."

She wavered. This was the first time she'd spoken more than a few words in passing to him, more than a hello at the *Dairy Queen*, or a smile and wave as he passed by in his shiny black Jaguar. He always waved at her, and likely had no idea how important that small gesture was to her, how it filled her heart to soaring. His smile kept her on a cloud for a week. She wanted to stop time, and savor these precious moments, cherish them later in the dark of night when she lay in bed and thought of him.

"It's not late. Besides…it's my birthday—or will be, in a couple of hours." Dominique bit her lower lip. Just to spend a little time with Bran would mean everything to her, the best birthday present ever.

"Domino, it's *not* wise to be out with me."

"Haven't you heard…*that Meacham girl* isn't too bright?" She smiled through crystalline tears, threatening to fall.

"Ones who aren't bright don't see how sharp you are. How special," he said softly.

"I *hate* pity, Bran."

Looking up the dark, winding drive toward the house hidden from view, she felt so *empty*. Something inside her would die if she returned to the old manor and had to welcome her eighteenth birthday with only Pye to share the moment. If she couldn't have Bran's friendship, she sure as hell didn't want his pity. Trying to force the tears down her throat, she dropped his hand and stepped back.

"Come along, Pye." She was having trouble swallowing; her throat was so choked with unshed tears. "Thanks…for being concerned. That was most kind of you. There's no need to see me home. See you around…sometime, Bran."

Have a happy life, her mind whispered. Stepping past him, she started up the long, winding drive with the overgrown yew hedge lining each side. Pye was right at her heels.

Catching up to her, Bran reached out and snagged her arm. "Dominique, I said I'd see you to the house. I don't want Mason and his toads to jump you."

"I'm a big girl…" *I don't need a knight in shining armour*, her mind cried. But she did. Desperately.

He laughed, "Domino is all grown up, eh? Precisely, why I don't want those creeps near you." Letting go of her, he fell in step beside her, slowly going up the long driveway. The cat ran circles around Bran's legs, meowing.

Ancient oak trees lined each side, blocking out moonlight. The trunks were thick from age, enough to hide someone if they were standing behind them. Suddenly, she shivered, her mind conjuring images of Mason and his blond Dorian Grey beauty stepping from behind one. Mason scared her, so despite her words, she was comforted with Bran beside her.

"Why are you wearing shades at night?"

"I told you, the full moon's bright." He lifted them up and to the top of his head. "There? Better?"

"It's hard to see your eyes with them on…see if you're serious…or laughing at me."

"I promise you…I never laugh *at* you, Domino." As they reached the end of the double row of trees, Bran swung around to block her path. "Why do you watch me so much, Domino?"

Because she loved him. Oh, how she loved him.

He'd laugh at her if she told him that, but it was the truth. She had since the first time he'd stepped between Mason and her, saving the bully from setting her hair on fire. Mason had been chanting, *burn the witch, burn the witch*. But that seedling emotion came into full bloom that hot summer afternoon by the tennis courts. She couldn't elucidate the feelings. It wasn't puppy love—of that, she was sure. Her stupid heart whispered *destiny* when she looked at him. Regardless of knowing that love would never be returned, she'd contented herself with worshipping Bran from afar. Now, he was so close she'd never be satisfied with that small crumb of life ever again.

"I cannot explain," she admitted in a whisper. "I don't dare say it aloud."

"I'm too old for you, Domino, by nearly five years. I will graduate college come spring. After that I am going to England to stay with my grandfather, do some graduate work over there. I likely will be gone for some time."

Dominique could feel her heart shattering into a thousand pieces. Her blood turned to ice. She knew she could never have Bran. He was much too good for her. But to never see him again? She felt her world turning black. Words swelled, trying to break free, to tell him all the precious feelings she held inside. Instead, too used to life's disappointments, she just nodded understanding. She'd been a fool to hope even for a fleeting moment. A tear trickled over her cheek and fell down onto the red leather shoe. Even *Ruby Slippers* couldn't give her what she wanted.

"Come on." He took her upper arm to guide her toward the towering antebellum mansion, looming ahead of them. In the unearthly golden moonlight, it appeared in grace and perfection, as it must have been in its prime. The shadows hid the shabby, rundown condition revealed by the harshness of day.

He walked up the steps and onto the portico, all the way to the front door. She smiled faintly. No one used the front door. She couldn't recall the last time someone had ever come to call. She didn't fret about anyone spotting them. No one was home. There'd be no one to celebrate her birthday with her. She hadn't expected it. She took the key from the pocket of her shorts and fumbled with the ring.

Bran reached out and stroked her cheek with the back of his hand. "Happy Birthday, Domino. If you were celebrating your twenty-first birthday, this night would be ending a different way. For your eighteenth, you'll just have to settle for a kiss."

He leaned toward her and brushed his lips across hers. So fleeting, she wanted to grab his arms and hang on forever. Instead, he pulled back. For a long moment he stood staring at her face bathed by twinkling faerydust and moonlight—his hidden by the shadows, unreadable. "Goodnight, Domino."

Emotions were flying around in her, wild, frantic, so many things she needed to say to him, to ask him. Instead, she stood there accepting Bran was walking away from her. Walking out of her life. Come spring, he would leave for England. He began whistling an old tune by a singer named Bobby Vee, *Come Back When You've Grown Up, Girl.*

Choking back the tears, she called after him, "Go ahead! Run, coward! Someday, you'll regret not giving me a proper kiss on my birthday."

Pye stood, dancing back and forth on his feet. Confused, he wanted to go inside with her, and also felt the urge to follow him.

Bran's laughter rolled softly through the night. "Oh, I regret it already." He moved farther down the driveway, but he turned around and kept walking backwards. "Tell you what, Domino—how about a date?"

The question jumped out of her throat. "A date?" Hope exploded in her heart.

"Yep. What say you? Three years from now—meet me at the bridge, wearing those red shoes, and I'll give you a proper birthday kiss."

She nearly strangled. "Bran Mackenzie, I *hate* you!"

"No... you...don't." Haunting, mocking words.

She wanted to call those hateful words back, but he took off, jogging back down the darkened driveway, not looking back.

o0o

She rubbed her thumb over the red leather, debating if she should put them on. "Once a fool, always a fool, I suppose." Pye yawned in boredom.

Three years and no word from Bran. For all she knew, he was still living in England with his grandfather. No postcards, birthday wishes, no jolly St. Nick on a Merry HoHo card. His mother had closed down their house and joined her son overseas, not wanting to ramble about in the huge mansion by herself, once his sister had gone to college. Drawn like the stupid moth to the flame, she had walked by at twilight, hoping to see a light on the old Victorian manor.

Yesterday, with the bite of autumn in the air and leaves falling covering the ground, she had ventured up the winding driveway of his family's estate, out on her daily walk. Somehow, her steps had carried her to the gates of the old manor. She hadn't meant to go there. She never had before, but something drew her. No lights were on inside, nothing showed signs of anyone about. Casting a last glance over her shoulder, she had gone on home.

Shoes, Shades and Faerydust

Now, torn by the compulsion to put the red shoes on once again and the nagging voice saying she was setting herself up for another disappointment, she finally gave in and slid them on. "Well, if he isn't there, then no one's about to witness me being a total sucker for believing in faerytales," she told the cat.

With Pye following along, chasing dry autumn leaves, she was halfway down the darkened driveway when doubt began to win the battle with common sense. Feeling slightly sick to her stomach from following the foolish folly, she almost turned back. However, as though the shoes had a will of their own, her steps carried her onward. She broke free of the inky shadows at the mouth of the drive. The bridge loomed ahead, the grey stones pale in the moonlight.

No one was there.

Had she really expected anything more? For a girl who had found life rarely smiled upon her, disappointment was expected. Oh, why hadn't she stayed in the house where her heart couldn't be hurt again? Approaching the bridge, she reached out and touched the stones where Bran had once sat. It felt warm, as if someone had recently been sitting there. Her hand jerked back. Where the heart wants so desperately, it has the power to play tricks on the mind.

She sighed, afraid to touch the stones again. *If one didn't believe, didn't reach for that hope, then nothing would ever come true, would it?* Placing her hand flat to the stone, she held it there. It *did* feel warm.

"Well, here goes, Pye." she said, the words laced with self-mocking, "You're no Toto, but Judy Garland has nothing on me."

Closing her eyelids, she clicked the heels of the red shoes together three times. For several heartbeats she was loath to opening her eyes. Finally, she lifted the lids. *Nothing had changed.* Scattered clouds passed over the moon, throwing the landscape in deep shadows. Darkest despair welling up in her chest, she swallowed the hard lump back.

"Dumb, dumb, dumb! Pye, how stupid can one girl be?" Dropping her hand, she took a step back and spun to go.

"Do you always talk to your cat, Domino?"

The haunting words floated from the blackest night at the mouth of the drive. Her heart stopped, and she felt faint, unable to draw air. *Domino.* Only one person called her that.

Bran.

That fist of disillusionment inside her released, morphing to hot pleasure, which flooded through her body. It sped to her heart, where it felt like it might burst. Cautiously, she walked toward the disembodied words.

"I've heard most good cat owners do," she replied. "It's when they start talking back that you begin to worry. They say highly imaginative children talk to imaginary playmates. Having a cat to natter to is probably the grown up version."

Pye's eyesight handled dark better than a human's. He dashed into the blackness, where Bran materialized from shadows. Slowly, he walked into the moonlight. "As I told you the last time we stood here, you are no longer a child."

Bran. Looking a bit older, more mature…but he was still wearing his shades. Bad boy to the core!

She couldn't help it. Laughter burst out. It was either laugh, or cry.

In his hand was a long-stemmed white rose. He held it out to her. "Happy Birthday, Domino." When she hesitated to accept it, he asked, "Did you think I wouldn't keep my word to you? We had a date, remember?"

"Yes, I remember. I wasn't sure *you* did. You've been in England for a long time. You even have an accent now. You could've sent me a postcard to let me know you were alive."

"I did. And birthday cards…Christmas. I had a feeling you weren't getting them when you never answered me."

She closed her eyes against the pain. "Mother. She was dying of cancer…"

"And afraid you might leave her alone. I assumed as much." He stepped close and brushed a butterfly kiss to her cheek. "But nothing was going to bar my way from keeping our date. Did you never wonder how I knew you watched me so much? Well, I was watching you, too. There was always an odd sense of *Fate* when our eyes met. I was too old for you. But a voice whispered, '*Someday, when she grows up.*' Well, you're twenty-one now, or at least you will be on the stroke of midnight.

She shook her head. "Don't you know what they whisper about me, Bran? Nothing has changed. I am still that crazy Meacham girl who they fear is a witch."

"Fear? I know you *are*. How else could you have stolen my heart all those years ago…one hot summer day, when you stood clinging to a fence watching me play tennis?"

"Bran—" Buffeted by wild emotions, she couldn't find words.

"I love how you say my name." His long, elegant magician's fingers cupped her chin, tilting it up. "In fact…I love you, Domino. And have, for a very long time. I just had to wait until the time was right."

He kissed her gently, then not enough. Domino stepped into his embrace and relished the kiss she had wanted so desperately three years ago.

She couldn't help it…the heels on her red shoes clicked thrice once more setting the seal on her final wish—*to be Bran's wife.*

Pye, reading her mind again, let out with a *"Meeeeeeeeooooow!"* of agreement.

About the Author—Deborah Macgillivray

Deborah Macgillivray, Award Winning Author with Montlake Romance/Amazon Publishing; Kensington Zebra Historicals; and Dorchester LoveSpell. Her books have been translated by publishing houses around the world including Random House Kodansha Ltd. (Japan); Romance Nova Cultural (Brazil); ACT (Russia); Knaur (Germany) and Ediciones Pamies (Spain).

Scottish Medieval Historicals (Dragons of Challon series) and Contemporary Paranormals—on the quirky side—(Sisters of Colford Hall series), novellas that features cats as characters, and Regency novellas.

Member of: RWA; Authors Guild; Host of The Haunt @ PRN

She is winner of the prestigious Gayle Wilson Award of Excellent for Best Contemporary Romance for RIDING THE THUNDER (2008)

Mr. Fred's Treasure Box

Cheryl Pierson

Mr. Fred's treasure was the love of his mistress.

How can you measure the kindnesses of a lifetime? The gentle pats and sweet words; the special treats—my favorite was warm nacho cheese; and the companionship…No value can be placed on that!

My owner—my companion—is dead. Mrs. Roberta Villines. But everyone called her Lovey.

They say she died peacefully in her sleep, but I know better. I was there with her when it happened. There was nothing peaceful about it—not at all.

I believe—I'll just say it. I believe she was murdered. I don't know how, but I have a good idea of *who*.

"I hate that damn cat. Look at him staring at me."

That's Lovey's younger brother Allen. Wish I could talk. The feeling is mutual. I hate him, too. Can't tell you how many times I've had to run for my life when he's been here visiting.

He's a master at kicking, trying to slam the door on my tail as I'm leaving, and just being a rude jerk, in general. As Lovey always said, "Allen was born on third base and thought he'd hit a triple." She didn't like him much, either.

"Allen, the cat doesn't care about you. He's probably afraid with all these strange people in the house. Oh, I wish the coroner would get here!"

Ah. Let me tell you about the baby in the Villines family, Amelia. She pretends to be very close to Lovey…at least, she *did*, before Lovey died. Amelia has always been kind to me, when she's visited. But lately, her visits have been few—and far between. And Lovey has missed her so.

Amelia has a special place in my heart, just because of her dislike for their brother. Amelia always wanted kids, but couldn't have them. Brother Allen? As luck would have it, he never wanted any, but has three. It took three illegitimate children to convince him to use condoms. Not only is he a mean cuss, he's not very smart, either.

Now, Allen just sits and glares at Amelia as if he's mad that she's let him know I'm not interested in him, after all. He's used to being the center of the universe. It pains him when he finds out he's not.

Since it aggravates him so much, I think I'll sit here a while longer. And ignore him.

I've lived with Lovey almost all my life. I feel like I belong here more than her sister and brother…I don't know what will happen now that she's …dead.

"Well, the old girl was getting on up there," Allen says now.

Amelia and I both stare at him.

"Allen, sixty years old is not 'getting on up there'. You'll be sixty in six years, yourself."

Amelia gives a self-righteous sniff. Probably thinking that it's only another ten years for her. She's a vain one.

"Just sayin'…her time had come."

Now, I glare. Lovey was not old. Her "time" had not "come"… More and more, I'm convinced someone has killed her. She felt fine yesterday. She and I sat together and she petted me. She did all the things she always did.

Lovey has made me a special lunch every Thursday ever since I came to live with her. She always told me that was a special day—Thursday was adoption day—the day she and I became a family.

Day before yesterday was our last Thursday together. My last special day with Lovey. She bought me a can of salmon for my very own. And I ate every piece of it.

Lovey gave me a smile. It always seemed to make her so happy when we had our special Thursdays. Fifteen years of Thursdays.

I'd lived on the streets for the first few months of my life. My mother and sisters and I were rescued, and then Lovey came, and my life changed.

Now, Amelia puts up her hand. "Allen, I don't want to hear any more. Lovey's gone. Can't you have a shred of sympathy for her? She was your sister, too!"

If only Amelia knew—but, I suppose she does. Allen has no sympathy, because he has no soul. I knew about the things he did to Amelia when she was a little girl. Lovey had told me about the way he made fun of how she talked; how he held her at arm's length; and the tears in little Amelia's eyes at her revered big brother's relentless taunting.

She'd learned to turn it back on him now, but I could see he still had some ability to hurt her.

"Yes, of course, Amelia." He put on his fake comforting voice.

But I knew what a snake he was under it all. And in the next instant, Amelia did, too.

"Wonder who'll inherit the old gal's money?" He tried to ask it casually, but couldn't manage to keep the burning hope out of his voice. He shrugged. "Should be me—being the eldest, now, and with three kids—"

Amelia leaps to her feet, taking a step toward him. "If you think, for one second, that what Lovey has worked so hard for her entire life is going to support your three 'baby mamas', you have another thought coming, Allen Davis Villines! And how you can even think of money at a time like this—"

"Now's as good a time as any, sister, *dear*," Allen sneers.

He's very good at curling his lip, but it gives him a harsh, unattractive look—for a human.

The low-pitched conversation between the two police officers upstairs in Lovey's room has ceased. The older policeman, Officer Rowe, comes down the stairs and pauses just for an instant at the heated exchange between Allen and Amelia. He wipes the revulsion from his features, making his face a blank slate. Then, he comes on into the room.

I get up and move to an out-of-the-way corner of the living room where I can lie down. I've had a rough night myself. I was there when Lovey breathed her last. She tried to say something, but couldn't get it out before she collapsed.

My eyes were the last thing she saw before she died. I wanted to let her know how much I loved her, but how? She was gone so quickly.

For so long, she'd joked about living to be one-hundred-and-one.

"Fred," she'd say, "don't you worry. I'll be gone long before you. You'll have a good place here as long as you live. I know you had a rough start, but hopefully, you've forgotten those days. We're both going to live to a ripe old age—I don't plan on going until I'm at least a hundred-and-one, and you can't go until after I do."

That was how Lovey talked to me all the time. With love.

Now, I relaxed in the corner, where I could hear everything.

"Allen…Amelia." The officer acknowledged them, and the way he looked at them let them know what he thought of their squabbling at a time like this.

Truthfully, I didn't see it as squabbling on Amelia's part. She knew her sister well enough to know Lovey would never want to see her fortune go to her brother's foibles and mistakes.

"Would either of you like to come say goodbye to your sister before the coroner comes? We got word he should be here in the next half-hour or so."

"Of course," Amelia said, starting for the stairway.

"Oh—uh—yes." Allen follows her, as if he hasn't yet realized he has a dead sister lying upstairs, after all.

"They're coming up, Peterson," Officer Rowe calls out, and Amelia turns to him in surprise.

"Really? You have to announce us and our movements?"

He gives her a long, unblinking "cop stare" and then says, "Really."

Amelia turns back to climbing the stairs in a huff, and Allen rolls his eyes at Rowe as if to say, "Dumb broad."

But Rowe doesn't crack a smile at Allen's antics, which offends Allen—as most everything in the world does.

Oddly enough, Officer Rowe turns and walks over to where I'm lying on the floor.

Lovey bought me a comfortable bed, and I use it sometimes during the day, because it pleases her. She always smiles and pets me when she sees me in the bed, and usually she'll say something like, "There's my good boy! Are you enjoying your bed?"

Can't tell you how many times she's asked me that same question, just like she's never asked it before. And I used to always answer her with a "meow", but in the past few years, it seemed enough to just look up at her and close my eyes when her gentle hand came across the top of my head in a loving caress.

Lovey never missed a chance to pet me.

Officer Rowe stops in front of me and squats down, putting a hand out for me to sniff. Then, he pets me. Procedurally correct, as a police officer…

"I bet you've had a rough day, ol' pal," he says.

I want to tell him he doesn't know the half of it. Those two always bicker like children— and now, Lovey won't be here to stop them anymore.

He goes on. "I went to school with Allen. He was always horrible to everyone. And I dated Amelia for a while…" A pained look crosses his face, and I know that means she must have cheated on him.

"I wasn't such a good judge of character back then," he says.

You got that right, Officer! But love can be blind, they say.

"Don't worry. I'll see you get a good home," he tells me.

I get a lump in my throat. People think animals don't have feelings—but that isn't true. This man's offhand kindness is unexpected. I rub my face against his knuckles.

"Might just take you home with *me*." He laughs. "Two bachelors'd do well together."

I meow and lick his finger, and he gives me an ear scratch.

"Sure wish you could talk. I bet you could tell us what happened, here. Something isn't right. I keep wondering—well, I don't believe this was a 'natural causes' check mark on the death certificate."

I don't either, I want to say. But I can only meow again.

"I take that as agreement, mister," he says with a smile. "I gotta go upstairs. Rescue the rookie. He won't know what in the hell to do with those two in the same room. Wanna come?"

I am not *about* to let him out of my sight!

I jump up and trot along at his side. The stairway is getting harder to climb, I notice. Usually, Lovey carries me up and down the steps, tucked safely under an arm, the other on the banister.

We walk into Lovey's bedroom to find a strange tableau before us, for sure. My dear Lovey is covered, neck to toe.

Her face looks peaceful. I want to believe it is because I'd been there with her when she—well, when she passed.

The "rookie", as Officer Rowe had called him, is Officer Peterson. He's a young one, all right, with not much "command" about him yet. He stands uncomfortably at the end of the bed, scratching his neck.

Amelia methodically searches Lovey's jewelry box, and Allen, her dresser drawers.

Officer Rowe's face clouds. He glances at Peterson, who puts his hands out in a "Well? What can I do?" gesture. Officer Rowe is about to show him.

"What are you two doing?" His voice is like thunder.

Allen turns, like a thief caught in the act—which, of course, he is. Amelia gives a funny nervous laugh and keeps right on looking for whatever it might be she's looking for. She makes the mistake of pocketing something.

In two long strides, Officer Rowe is on her like a duck on a June bug.

"Empty your pockets, please. Both of you." With a sharp nod at Peterson, he lets him know to take over with Allen. He will see to Amelia himself.

Sighing, Amelia turns toward Officer Rowe, trying on her twenty-years-past high school aren't-I-the-cutest-cheerleader-ever smile.

I know this policeman won't go for it—and, he doesn't.

"*I said*," he begins in a frost-covered voice, "empty your pockets. Both of you. And I'm not asking again."

MR. FRED'S TREASURE BOX

They both begin to lay the items they've pinched on the bed beside their dead sister.

A ruby brooch. A diamond-and-emerald ring. A wad of "emergency" cash. *Ugh. Allen had gone through Lovey's underwear drawer!*

I feel a hairball working its way up. *Sick bastard.*

"That last thing you *stole*..." Officer Rowe says to Amelia. He nods at the bed where everything else is laid out. "Put it there."

She fidgets, and her lips thin for a moment but she understands Officer Rowe is not going to be cajoled into anything.

Frustrated, she lays the key she's taken onto the bed beside the brooch. She heaves a deep sigh.

"Why, you little witch!"

Allen always turns red when he gets mad. And he's livid right now. The key is important...*they think.*

But I know better.

"Allen, I told you it was here and one of us would find it."

"You knew where to look! And you were going to keep it from me!"

"No—no, I wasn't!" She puts her hands out. Shades of childhood. She's flashing back, not wanting any confrontation. "I was going to tell you—honestly!"

"Honestly?" Allen sneers. "You don't know the meaning of the word."

"What does the key go to?" Officer Rowe says, interrupting this lovely family discussion.

I sit down and lick my front paws. *I haven't washed my face today!*

They look at each other, but neither of them answers.

"We're not leaving this room until you answer me."

This policeman is becoming my favorite human, now that Lovey...has gone. I can't bear to look at her. I keep washing my face.

"It's a key to her 'treasure box', as she called it," Allen finally mutters.

"And...what's inside this 'treasure box'?" Officer Rowe asks.

They both shrug, and young Peterson flexes his muscles a bit.

"Oh, come on! You know, or you both wouldn't be looking for the key."

"We really don't know *everything* that's in it," says Amelia. "But it's where she kept her will." She glances nervously at big brother, who rolls his eyes at her as if she's just given the policemen a piece of incriminating evidence that could lock both of them away forever.

"Where is the box?" Rowe puts out a hand to forestall the lies and denials. "Save us some time, here, please."

Allen heaves a sigh. "In her closet."

Amelia whirls to face him. "Oh. My. *God!* You already scoped it out? I can't believe you!"

This is why I despise Amelia, almost as much as Allen. Her voice irritates me...times like now, she sounds like a true Valley Girl.

But from what Lovey said, *"Amelia only left Oklahoma long enough to find herself in the 'family way' and come back home from California looking like something the cat dragged in..."*

But Lovey apologized for that last part, not wanting to hurt my feelings. Then, she'd hugged me and said, "Fred, that's one thing I love about you. You never *do* drag anything in. You never bring me gifts of dead birds or rats. You're a present every day to me—just yourself, and your love."

My eyes are watering now. Must've gotten something in them. More washing.

Allen takes the treasure box out of Lovey's closet and puts it on the cedar chest at the end of the bed. He picks up the key and glances at Officer Rowe, who gives him a quick nod.

But when Allen tries to fit the key into the lock and give it a twist, it doesn't work. It won't turn.

"Dammit!"

Officer Rowe—"Brady", I see on his nametag—holds out his hand. "Doesn't work. It's not the right one. But I'll take it with me for safekeeping."

Peterson opens an evidence bag, and as Allen hands Brady the key, he slips it into the bag. Peterson collects the jewelry on the bed and bags it, as well.

"Where's the real key, then? To the treasure box?" Amelia's eyes narrow as she gives her brother the "once over" from head to foot. "If you knew where the box was—how do I know you don't already have the key?"

"Why would I have it?"

He's red again. Sputtering. Reminds me of a Shakespearean quote: 'Methinks thou doest protest too much.' Lovey read Shakespeare to me a lot. He was one of her favorites, because she said, "He understood the human spirit, both good and evil, as no other person who ever lived did." Which must be true—because my dear Lovey believed it.

But, I digress. Allen doesn't have the key. And I don't have a way to let Brady know where it is. Now might not be the best time for that, anyhow, with the "evil twins" standing in the same room. I need to let him know secretly. The fight continues.

"How would you know where the treasure box was kept, either, unless you were in here snooping around, Allen?"

Mr. Fred's Treasure Box

"Look—she-she *told* me where it was!" Allen glances at Brady. "In case—you know—something like *this* ever happened!"

"Oh, right! I don't believe that for one minute! If she told you where it was, she'd have given you the key—which she obviously did not do, and—"

"*Enough!*"

Brady's had it with them...and I have, too. Poor Lovey's lying up in the bed, dead, and her younger siblings stand there arguing about a damn key to the stupid treasure box. Who cares about that? Lovey...she's gone forever, and they don't seem sad about it. All they care about is what she might have left them.

"Hello?" a voice calls from downstairs. "Coroner."

Peterson walks from the room, obviously relieved to have a reason to get away from the discord.

Now that the coroner's here, I know I have to tell Lovey goodbye. I've watched enough detective shows with her to know that the coroner is the one who removes the body. I run around, past Allen and Amelia, and jump up onto the bed.

I realize I will be saying goodbye to this room, and the bed, too, where Lovey let me curl up beside her and sleep. Every day, she woke up and smiled at me, first thing.

"Hello, Mr. Fred," she'd say, and give me a good ear scratch before she got up. She never forgot that.

Now, I rub against her one last time. I'm going to miss her, so much. Looking at her still, pale face, I hope I was always good. I hope I was—*worthy*. She was everything to me.

I glance down at her, past her...to the small wastebasket beside the bed...and see a half-finished muffin...

And suddenly, *I know what killed her*. She was eating the muffin just before she had her "spell" that led to her death.

And those muffins were not brought over by her brother; I knew that much.

"Reeow!"

Amelia lifts me off the bed—a bit roughly—and it startles me. She's not normally rough, but in her touch, I feel nervousness and tension.

She sets me down on the floor and Allen tries to give me a kick. But I expect that from him, and run under the bed. I know where I'm headed, and what I need to do.

I come out on the other side of the bed, right beside the small wastebasket.

Lovey never let me eat chocolate. She said it was bad for dogs, so it might be bad for cats, too. The muffin is chocolate, and it smells wonderful, but...there's another smell there, too. One I don't know.

But the coroner will...

I put a paw on the trash can and pull it toward me. When it tips over, the partially-eaten muffin rolls out onto the floor.

Officer Rowe notices it and stoops to pick it up, just as the coroner and Officer Peterson come through the bedroom door.

Amelia's eyes get big. "Oh, you bad cat! Here, Brady, let me—"

But the policeman wasn't born yesterday—and I'm so glad he is the one nearby instead of the rookie.

Brady pulls the muffin away from Amelia's grabby fingers.

"Hi, doc," he says to the coroner, taking a step back away from the bed.

The doctor steps closer to Lovey and nods.

Amelia doesn't even acknowledge the coroner. She's still trying to figure out how to get the uneaten half of muffin away from Officer Rowe.

He looks right at her. "Evidence," he says. His voice is steely, and he stares directly into her eyes.

"But—it's just trash—"

"We haven't finished this investigation, Mrs. Spaulding."

Oh, he's gone all formal, now. Amelia doesn't know how to deal with that. She puts on her pouty look—the one she used on him in high school, her glory days in this small town.

"Now, officer...I just want to help clean up the mess this bad kitty has made." She makes another grab for the muffin.

I see in Officer Brady Rowe's face he knows he's found the first piece of the puzzle to how my Lovey was killed. *He knows she was murdered.*

"Well, then." Amelia squares her shoulders. She tries to hide her anger, but it's impossible.

Brady's eyes tell me he's quickly putting this all together. Before he can say anything else, the coroner straightens and walks to the door, and into the hallway, looking over the banister to the living room. He's left the front door open, and now he motions to the paramedics who've had nothing to do but wait until he could get there and conduct his business before loading my dear companion into the ambulance.

"I'm sorry for your loss," the coroner says, looking at Allen first, then Amelia. Allen nods and mumbles a thank you. Amelia....Amelia is more composed. She meets the coroner's eyes and says, "Thank you," directly to him, rather than to the floor, as her brother does.

Mr. Fred's Treasure Box

As they take Lovey out, my eyes start to feel prickly again. She was the only one who loved me. No more old John Wayne movie-watching together. No more warm nacho cheese in a Styrofoam cup. Ah, what a treat that was...No more love.

I have no illusions. I'm not a cute little kitten anymore. And I'm black—almost completely—except for my paws.

Lovey decided not to name me "Boots" or "Socks" or something "cutesy"— as she called it. I'll be forever grateful to her for that. She knew, someday, I'd grow up. No one remains cute and cuddly forever, you know.

"You look like a 'Fred' to me," she'd said. "I think I'll call you that, mister." Then, she smiled, and rubbed her cheek against me gently. "Mister Fred. Perfect."

The room empties out. The coroner, his assistant, who'd arrived late—the paramedics, Officer Peterson...and Lovey.

I walk over beside Officer Rowe, and sit down close to him. He will not step on me. He is aware of everything around him.

I hear Officer Peterson locking the front door as everyone exits.

Brady—Officer Rowe—looks at Allen, then Amelia. "This is the scene of an ongoing investigation. The house will be secured with police tape that will not be breeched. Understand?"

Allen nods. But Amelia gets her back up.

"You mean—you mean we're being locked out of our sister's *home*? We can't come in?"

"It's a possible crime scene."

"What?" Amelia screeches. *Makes me shiver.*

Allen looks up quickly. "You believe someone k-killed our sister?"

"It's possible."

"But—"Amelia starts to protest again.

"Just get your handbag, Mrs. Spaulding, and you and your brother head for the door. We'll be in touch with you. Don't either of you leave town—I may have some questions."

"But—what—*Brady!* Are you insinuating that I or Allen might be a suspect? A *murder* suspect?"

"I'm not sure yet, Mrs. Spaulding. That's why I'm asking you not to leave town."

Amelia tries a different tact. She moistens her lips, takes a deep breath, and...

"All right," she says, in her calm little acquiescent voice. The one that she uses to get her way.

"Don't load up your pockets on the way out," Brady says.

Amelia huffs.

Brady nods at Peterson to escort them out. Allen goes meekly, with no comment, trailing after his sister.

"Don't come back," Brady calls. "I'll be in touch." He follows them out and watches from the hallway as Peterson ushers them to the door.

Amelia turns and looks up at him. "What about the cat?"

"I sure as hell don't want him," Allen says with a smirk. "I hear cats taste a little like chicken."

Amelia gasps. *"Allen!"*

Brady does not laugh. He doesn't even smile. In fact, he looks like he'd like to take a fist to Allen's smarmy grin. "Animal cruelty is a felony," he says. Allen sobers quickly.

"I-I don't have a place for him," Amelia says, trying to placate everyone. "Poor Mr. Fred. Lovey loved him so much."

"I'll take care of things," Brady says.

"Oh, good. I hate to have him put down, but—well, he's old, anyhow."

I see revulsion cross Brady's face. Amelia is one cold human. At least, Allen is honest about it. He doesn't like me. He never has. Amelia pretends, but I've always felt her resentment.

Brady says nothing else as Amelia and Allen go out the door, followed by Officer Peterson. He's probably making sure one of them doesn't steal the new bird bath Lovey bought last week.

Brady reaches down and puts his hand close to my face, then picks me up.

"Ah, don't worry, boy. You're coming with me. Don't pay them any attention, Fred. You're safe." He strokes my head.

My heart is so grateful. There's no way Brady can know what his kindness means to me. *And I'm going home with him!*

He scratches under my collar. I used to be a little embarrassed about that collar. Lovey bought it for me, and she said it was fit for a prince. It's red, with sparkly red rhinestones. She put my rabies vaccine tag on it along with…the key. She said it was the key to her heart, but *I* know it goes to the treasure box.

I look at Brady. I lift my head so he can see the key, but the tag is in front of the key.

He scratches my ears, and I courageously lift my head higher, baring my throat. I don't ever do that, but it's necessary. He has to notice the key!

"What's this, buddy?"

He found it! Oh, if I could talk! I wish I could tell him—but, he knows.

Mr. Fred's Treasure Box

He puts me on the bed and unfastens my collar to get the key off.

It only takes him a second to get it. When Lovey put it on my collar, she said she'd never lose it, because she'd always have me.

"I bet I know what this goes to, Fred." He turns toward the treasure box. He inserts the key, and turns it. The tumblers click and he lifts the lid.

I'm curious, of course. I've been wearing that special key on my collar for many years now. Now that Brady has the treasure box open, I just have to know what's in it. You know what they say about cats and their curiosity.

Lovey called it "Mr. Fred's" treasure box sometimes when she talked to me about it.

"Mr. Fred's treasure box," she'd say, giving the ornate wood box a pat as she turned the key and put it back on my collar. "Everything is in order, dear boy."

Brady pulls out a few old pictures. I'm surprised to see that many of them are of me, or of the two of us—Lovey and me—together.

I give a startled meow, and Brady rubs my head.

"I know. You miss her, don't you? She thought an awful lot of you. Just look at all these pictures...wait a minute..."

Brady turns one of the pictures over to read on the back of it. I'm glad he reads aloud. I *can* read, but it's tedious.

"Me and my dear Mr. Fred at our beach house in Port Aransas. Fred loves car trips and he loves the beach. World's largest sand box! Deed enclosed."

Brady reaches quickly for the next picture. It's one of me eating up that wonderful Thursday luncheon dear Lovey always thought to prepare for me.

"Mr. Fred looks forward to our special Thursday lunches. He loves a can of salmon—I usually buy one of the better brands—the big can. Thursday was the day I adopted him—a very special day. So, we celebrate."

Brady smiles. "Well, today's Saturday, Fred. Guess we'll have to have us some salmon *twice* a week from now on, huh?"

The next snapshot is of me in the bed Lovey had bought.

"Fred loves his bed," Lovey had written. "But he'd rather sleep in my bed where we can watch old movies together."

Brady's grin widens. "I'm kinda partial to those ol' black and whites myself, Fred. This lady sure did love you."

His face changes. "What's this?" He reaches in to pick up a folded piece of paper. It isn't in an envelope, or anything. He unfolds it to read it.

"Last Will and Testament..."

His eyes scan across the paper quickly. And then—he *laughs*. Not a soft chuckle, but a deep belly laugh.

He laughs so hard the tears almost come.

I find myself getting cross. "Fun is fun for everyone," Lovey would say. *Maybe I'd like to know what's so damn funny myself!*

As if he hears my thoughts, Brady turns and looks right at me.

"It's all yours, Fred. Almost every last penny of what Miss Roberta Laticia Villines owned is yours—according to her will. Oh, Allen and Amelia will both receive one dollar. You won't mind, will you? Keeps them from being able to say she must've forgotten them."

He sits down on the cedar chest beside the treasure box and shakes his head. His smile fades. "It's enough to make a person wonder—"

Just then, we both hear the front door open once more.

"Brady!" Officer Peterson yells from the just inside the living room.

"Wait here, Fred." Brady heads from the bedroom. "Whatcha got?"

"A murderer."

I can't stand it. I have to follow my new master.

Looking down through the banister railing, I see Officer Peterson, his hand gripping Amelia—and she's wearing handcuffs.

I knew it! She was worried about the muffin. Brady had sensed it, too.

"Amelia?" Brady questions, but he's not really surprised, either.

Officer Peterson stands just behind Amelia in the doorway, as if he thinks she might try to make a break for it.

"Brady, I can't stand it. I—I put something in that muffin."

The tears begin to flow down her cheeks, but I can't feel sorry for her. Not at all.

Cats are sensitive to many things. I feel Brady go tense beside me—and I feel his aching sadness. Nat King Cole sang one of Lovey's favorites—This Is the End of a Beautiful Friendship. It's about a couple's friendship turning to love. But in Brady's case—I know he's saying goodbye to the last little smidgeon of emotion he might have felt from years past...when he'd been a football hero, and Amelia had been the prettiest cheerleader ever. No, I didn't know them quite so far back. But Lovey had proudly—and lovingly—showed me pictures of her younger siblings through the years.

Brady nods. "I figured. Why, Amy?"

All the lost love of the past, his aching disappointment in her, and the confusion he is experiencing mingles in his tone.

"I-I got greedy, I guess."

Brady meets young Peterson's eyes.

"I read her her rights already," Peterson assures him.

She nods. "Yes. He did, Brady. Turns out, I *do* have a conscience. I brought the muffins over yesterday evening. You'll see when you check the phone records that I tried to call her last night. We talked briefly. She—she thanked me for bringing the muffins. Said she was planning on having one for breakfast."

"Which she did," Brady said. "No wonder you and Allen were over here so quickly after it happened. Nothing like precise planning, is there?"

Bitterness drips from his tone, and I know it's not just Lovey's death he's talking about.

Amelia shakes her head, her eyes filling with hurt. She must still care for him, too—just a small bit. Her heart is softer than she realizes—in both instances.

"I-I needed a new car. Mine is on its last legs," she explained.

"You couldn't just *borrow* the money? Like everyone else does?"

"I don't have any credit."

Brady stands and stares at her. There's more, and he is forcing her to admit it.

"I—well, I have kind of a gambling problem."

Finally, after a few seconds tick by, Brady says, "So, it's not really that you need a new car, it's—"

"It's everything! I need a new car, but I need to pay some of my gambling debts, too. Whatever Lovey has in that damn treasure box of hers would be enough to get me out of trouble."

I remember when she came to talk to Lovey about a car—a brand new one. Lovey had smiled and said she'd be happy to help her out with a smaller amount for a used car. I had sat and let the sun warm me in the window sill as they talked.

"A car is just a glorified wheelbarrow to move your trash from one place to another," Lovey had told her.

How wise was my dear Lovey!

Brady fixes Amelia with a cold stare—one I imagine she's never seen before.

"Your sister was one of the kindest, most generous, loving people in the world. She most likely would have given you whatever you needed—if she'd had it."

Amelia nods. "I know. But what she had wasn't enough. Only her life insurance would give me enough to do it all."

"It never is 'enough' for you, is it, Amy?"

No answer. She just looks down. In a moment, she says, "I have to know. Did you find the key? Did you open the treasure box?"

Brady hesitates, then gives her a curt nod. "Yes."

She looks up at him. "Oh—what was in it?"

Here, I see Brady debating with himself. "Her will."

"How much do I get?"

A slow smile crosses Brady's face. "Murderers can't profit from their victims' deaths. So it doesn't matter."

"But...how much would it have been?"

"Not enough, Amelia. Not enough for you."

Brady nods to Peterson. "Why don't you take her down to the station and get them started processing her, then come back for me? I need to make sure everything's locked up tight and secure the entire area around the house."

Amelia looks up, still disappointed in Brady's refusal to tell her about the contents of the will. "Don't forget about Fred. He needs to be dropped off at the pound."

Again, Brady bends a steely gaze on her. "He's not *going* to the pound. He's coming home with me."

She looks at him, horrified. "But—*why*? He was Lovey's cat. She doted on that mangy old thing—"

"And you want no reminders of what you did, do you?" Brady shakes his head, this time in disbelief at his own memories. "My God, you are one cold fish. How could I have ever thought I was in love with someone like you?"

"My good looks?" She smiles. "I *am* still beautiful, aren't I, Brady? And high school wasn't all *that* long ago."

Peterson takes a step back out the doorway, a disgusted look on his face. He hauls her with him.

"Be back in a bit," he calls to Brady.

"Be careful," Brady responds, then shakes his head again. "Why'd I say that, Fred?" He looks down at me. "She's more dangerous than I ever realized. Amelia killed her sister for—nothing." He rubs my head.

My Lovey was an exceptional person. And so is Brady. He wanted me before he knew Lovey had left everything to me. I know I can trust him. And we'll get used to each other, in time.

But right now, I hate Amelia even more than I despised Allen. And suddenly, those special Thursday lunches don't seem as important as they had before. As much as I appreciate Brady taking me home to live with him, that wouldn't be necessary if Amelia hadn't murdered dear Lovey.

Lovey had done her best for me during her life, and now—her death.

I didn't want the things Lovey had left for me in her will—I only want *her*. Who is left to remember her, and to love the memories of her laughter, her sweet voice, and the small things she did for so many every day? From her boss at work, to her family, down to me—her cat.

I am all that is left.

And I vow to remember, until the day I die. I will be all that she thought I was—more human than her own family has been.

Lovey has been the only treasure I will ever need.

About the Author—Cheryl Pierson

Cheryl is a native Oklahoman with eight novels to her credit as well as numerous short stories and novellas. Founding Prairie Rose Publications with Livia Reasoner is a dream-come-true for her—there's something new every day. Helping other authors is at the top of her list, and she enjoys every minute of it. Cheryl is the current president of the Western Fictioneers writing group. She has two grown children and lives with her husband and her rescue dog, Embry, in Oklahoma City.

See Prairie Rose Publications' website for more of Cheryl's work: **www.prairierosepublications.com**

Amazon link: ***www.amazon.com/author/cherylpierson***

Facebook: **https://www.facebook.com/cheryl.pierson.92**

Cat's Cradle

Mollie Hunt

Lynley Cannon vows to do whatever she must to protect a kitten from gun-wielding thugs.

It all had to do with the kitten, you see. Kitten of wonder; kitten of danger; kitten of things to come.

My name is Lynley Cannon, and I admit it—I'm known in some circles as a crazy cat lady. I suppose it's because of my slightly obsessive involvement with cats: aside from my clowder of five, I volunteer at a cat shelter, foster sick cats, and help at the Spay and Neuter Center at least twice a month. I am often sought out to give catly advice such as *Why does Babie sleep all the time?* (Because he's a cat.) or *How can I get Pepper to stop licking my ankles?* (You probably can't). I do not, however, go in for kittens. I have nothing against the young of the feline species, and I'm certainly not immune to their round-eyed angel cuteness. It's just that everyone loves kittens. I prefer the lost and abandoned; the lop-eared FIV-positive; the scruffy-coated elderly; the malcontents; and yes, even the hospice cats whose days are counting down toward the Rainbow Bridge. Those cats need me. Kittens don't.

Still, there is nothing quite so forlorn as the sorrowful mewl of a kitten in distress, and when, on a walk by the riverside, I heard that sound, instinct took over like a magnet. Before I knew it, I was down a rabbit hole of my own making, lost in a labyrinth of surprise.

Portland's Eastbank Esplanade isn't my usual territory but I'd promised myself I would check it out one day. I'd made that promise years ago when the eclectic Willamette River walkway was built, but these things take time. Though I'm retired and edging toward sixty, I always seem to be busy. Then, one day while cleaning litter pans at Friends of Felines, my shelter buddy, Frannie, asked out of the blue if I'd like to go. Of course I said yes, and just

Cat's Cradle

like that, we'd set a date for Saturday.

Today.

When Frannie called at the last minute to say she was stuck at the shelter with a batch of intake cats and couldn't make it, I was already there.

With a shrug witnessed only by a herd of bikers and a jogger or two, I figured I might as well continue with the plan. I strolled solo up and down the wide concrete landscape. I stared across the glimmering ripples of the river. I checked out the public art and the interpretive panels describing the rich history of the area. I admired the lights of downtown that were beginning to flicker on in the summer twilight. For a while, I worked at picking out the place they had filmed the intro for *Portlandia*, our local television show, and the sleeping scene from the cult movie, *What the Bleep Do We Know?* It was all very entertaining, though I wished Frannie had been able to come along.

Frannie DeSoto, with her perfectly blonded hair and meticulous make-up—despite the rigors of shelter work—had been a true friend for years. We'd shared many experiences, both happy and sad, and mostly cat-related. Of an age, we saw the world in a similar fashion, and enjoyed each other's company. Though I had no problem being on my own, I admit I missed her. When the third bout of melancholy hit me, I decided it was time to go.

The sun was creeping down toward the west hills, which meant it was getting late. I didn't want to be caught out after dark; the esplanade was probably safe enough, but I had some iffy territory to cross to get to the bus stop for home. Behind the gentrification, the lofts, diverse cafes, and bistros, Portland's lower east side was a warehouse and industrial district. Beneath the bridges, buildings older than my grandmother still crouched, moldering and dark. Who knew what went on there? Signage read "Boxes", "Storage", "Wholesale Paper", and "Tile", but as I stared up at those grimy windows, gray with age, I had to wonder.

That was when I heard the kitten. She was mewling her little heart out in total abject anguish, which with a kitten could mean anything from pissed off to hurting to hungry, lonely, or lost. Being a cat advocate, it was my duty not only to discover the problem, but to right any wrongs as well.

I turned from Water Street up Madison under the Hawthorne Bridge and was instantly plunged into dusk. I could no longer see the sky—only buildings, and the ribs of the old on-ramp above. To my right was a three-story brick edifice decorated with a colorful filigree of graffiti, and to my left, a delivery dock fronting a concrete warehouse. The warehouse was dark and vacant. I stopped and listened, trying to pinpoint the plaintive mew. I was close, but more than that, I couldn't tell.

I located a set of steps, and up I went onto the dock. Once there, I took another look, another listen. Was it my imagination…or was the wailing just a bit more feeble than it had been before?

A huge bay door with an antiquated pulley sat opposite the stairs, and beside that was a human-sized entrance. With surprise, I saw it was open a crack. Moving swiftly, I pushed it a bit farther and stared into gloom.

"Hello? Anyone here?"

The only answer was the renewed vocalization of the kitten. It was a call for help and I had no choice but to respond.

With a creak of oil-starved hinges, I swung the door open all the way. It hit me that if I entered the premises I was crossing a line, but what could it hurt? It was only a warehouse, a place of business. And it wasn't like I was breaking in. If they didn't want visitors, they should have locked the door. In spite of my rationalizations, I gave a furtive glance around the outside. No vehicles. If anyone besides little Kit were in the building, they had parked elsewhere.

As I eased into a lightless hallway, the kitten squall increased. My heart sped and my mind told me this might not be such a good idea. What if there were someone bad with the cat? An abuser, kidnapper, or thief? But it was much more likely that Kitten had merely got herself stuck somewhere. She would probably get herself out again without any help from me. Cats were good at that. It really wasn't any of my business, and exploring front street warehouses without an invitation could be asking for trouble. I almost turned to leave, but then there was another series of tiny "*Help me's*", and without a thought, I was down the hall and halfway into the bright room at the end.

It was more than a room; it was the warehouse itself, a huge, lofty chamber that could have been transported through time from the nineteen-twenties. What I had mistaken for electric lighting was the sunset glow shining through a massive bank of small-paned skylights. It was not nearly as lucent as I had first imagined; the edges of the room were in shadow and darkening by the second as the sun edged toward night. Large wooden crates were stacked against the walls several feet high, looming like stocky giants in the dim. The center of the room was empty save for a gym bag sitting on the wood plank floor. The meows came from there.

The bag was squirming with a life of its own. I rushed forward. Kneeling, I saw a little spotted nose poke out from a nearly-closed zipper. Then the nose disappeared, replaced by a sharp, reflective eye as the kit stared up at me, yowling like a baby lion.

"Oh, sweetie," I whispered, petting the tiny black and white head through the hole. "What have you got yourself into?" Kitten didn't answer; or maybe she did and I just couldn't translate *mew mew mew* into anything enlightening.

Had someone left her, closed her in that bag? Had she crawled into it on her own? If she belonged to someone who was planning to come back for her, then it really wasn't my place to set her free. On the other hand, who would leave a kit in a bag with no food or water? Depending on the amount of time she had been a captive, it could be considered animal abuse. If Kitty were lost, she needed an ally; if she had been dumped by her owner, I was liking them less and less all the time.

"Let's get you out of there," I said, pulling the zipper tag to set her free. It traveled a quarter inch, then stuck. I closed it, then opened it again with the same frustrating results. I fiddled at it, then felt around underneath to see if I could find what was binding, but no luck.

Sitting back on my haunches, I stared at the enigmatic bag. Kit was going a little crazy now that her freedom was at hand. She struggled to push through the small hole. If she kept it up, she would tear her spotted face on the hard plastic teeth.

"*Crap,*" I hissed. I poked her head back into the bag and pulled the zipper closed. Instantly she calmed down, but now she was completely trapped in the bag.

I thought about taking her, bag and all, to someplace where I could see better, where I could finagle that crusty zipper into opening. She was small, and just needed another inch or two. But it wasn't my bag, and decades of etiquette were telling me it was not polite to mess with other people's stuff.

I wondered what else was in the bag. I began to feel around the edges. It was by no means empty. Something squarish and heavy, papers or books, lined the bottom; above that was a layer of soft, squishy stuff—like clothes. At least Spot had somewhere to rest in her isolation.

I'm not sure when I'd made the transition from Kitty to Spot, something resembling a real name for the tiny baby in the bag. Granted, I hadn't seen much of the cat—a nose, a forehead, and an eye—but of those, only the golden eye lacked the distinctive black and white freckles. Spot was a good name. At least until something better came along.

Suddenly, I heard heavy footfalls approaching from the hallway. I went rigid, guilty trespasser that I was. I began to stand and turn, face my accuser and attempt to offer the explanation of my presence without sounding like a blithering old bat, but I never got the chance.

A duo of deafening blasts jumped me out of my skin. Something whizzed past, splitting the air, then impacting a wooden crate behind me, splintering wood.

"What the—" I spit without thinking, but I didn't need a reply to grasp what was happening. I grabbed the gym bag and scurried, half-bent, toward the far wall. Though it was not within the realm of my previous experience, I had no doubt whatsoever someone was shooting at me.

I dodged behind the stacks of crates just as a few more bullets flew. Not stopping to see where they landed, I bolted down the narrow passage between the wall and the boxes as fast as I could go. Footsteps slammed across the planks in my direction. I glanced backward. Though the makeshift passage gave good cover from the main part of the room, once the gunman got there, I'd be an easy target. I needed to get around the crates and back outside again.

That plan fizzled when I saw the wall up ahead that transformed my corridor into a dead end. For a moment, I was frozen with fear. Then, a thought came over me—a thought which changed everything.

There must be some mistake.

The revelation sent harp chords and rainbows leaping through my panic-amped system. *Why would anyone want to shoot at me, Lynley Cannon, beloved cat lady?* There had to be some mistake.

I turned, calm now, to face the person who had so cruelly confused me with someone else. I guess I didn't see the obvious, that even if he weren't shooting at *me*, he was still shooting at *someone*—which didn't make him a very nice guy. I missed that part as I took a step toward the shadow that wavered ever closer. With a bravery that was both unfounded and absurd, I confronted him.

"Excuse me, sir, but I think you've mistaken me for someone else," I said in my sweetest voice. "I don't know you, have never met you. I didn't mean to come here at all. I heard the kitten, you see."

The man actually paused and I had a moment to study him. Though all detail was lost in the near-night blur, he looked big as an ogre and as buff as The Terminator. I'd caught him off guard, but what I mistook for acceptance was probably shock at my audacity. He said nothing; then, slowly, he began to raise the gun.

My second revelation—that he was going to kill me anyway—was not so pleasant as the first, but got me moving a lot quicker. I'd noticed that some of the boxes forming the wall of my corridor were not set square, creating giant steps. Could my aging body still climb?

The gym bag was equipped with a wide, padded shoulder strap, so I slung it across my chest and proceeded upward. Fear pushed me, and as another bullet cracked, I made it to the top in record time.

Once there, I crouched, out of breath, wondering where to go next. "I don't suppose you can fly," I asked Spot in a muted whisper. She gave a tiny mew in response, but we didn't take off toward the ceiling, so I guess her answer was no. I was getting silly. I knew it. I didn't care. I'd go back to acting like an adult when I was once again safe and sound.

I heard the footfalls start up again, but was surprised to note they were heading in the opposite direction. Maybe he wasn't going to shoot me, after all. He came into view and I watched him slink back across the warehouse, a shadow in classic bad-guy black. He looked angry. He had a gun. I had no idea why he was after me but was way past my plan of trying to find out.

He stopped by the door and seemed to be listening. I shrunk closer to the warm plywood, the bag cradled under me, kitten quiet inside. Then, as my heart did a giant flip-flop, the man swung around and began to return. He was hesitant, searching. Though he'd seen me climb up the other side, he now looked uncertain. That was a point in my favor. If I stayed silent, maybe he would give up and go away.

A sudden wail cut loose from the bag, and that option winked into the dimension of *things that might have been*. Peeking over the edge of the crate, I saw the man staring back at me. Time to move. I had two options, aside from throwing myself on his dubious mercy: I could shimmy back down the way I had come, back to the dead end corridor—or I could go up. Above me, a balcony ringed the warehouse beneath the peaked glass skylights. The crates were piled high, and I thought I could reach the railing if I really really tried.

I really really tried. It took some effort to pull myself up and over, but I managed it. As I lay on the dusty ledge, congratulating myself on my accomplishment, I heard running steps and what sounded like a pig-snort from down below. The chase was on.

I grunted to my feet and began to sprint around the balcony. There was a fire door at the west end of the building where the antique green exit lamp still burned. I made for it, praying it wouldn't be locked. The man had found the stairs and I could hear him crashing like a troll behind me. I got to the door and pushed through to the roof. I was greeted with a panoramic view, far superior to that from the esplanade, but I barely noted it as I hurled myself forward. For whatever reason, the man was coming for me. He'd be through that door at any moment, and when he got there, I needed to be gone.

It wasn't hard to find the fire escape. Old and rickety, it couldn't have been more welcome had it been a marble staircase, and I took the wrought iron treads with angel wings. I didn't know I could still run that fast. Hell, I didn't know I could still run *at all*.

The zig-zag flight ended in a straight vertical ladder with a six-foot jump from the last rung to the ground. Someone had conveniently ditched an old mattress underneath. Normally, I loathe litter, but I made an exception. I jumped, rolled on the spongy filth, and took off at an arthritic jog.

Once back on the street, I looked for a place to hide. I was getting winded and wasn't sure how much longer I could keep this up before the inevitable old lady heart attack overcame me. Down the block, I caught sight of an all-night bistro and made for it, slowing to a nonchalant stroll to mingle with the patrons out front. It seemed to be a popular hangout. I wasn't dressed in six-hundred dollar jeans or a designer dress, but in the dark, I hoped no one would notice. This was Portland, after all, and we can, with the correct attitude, keep it weird.

The door was open and I ducked inside. I wanted, oh so badly, to peep behind me and see if the man was still following; but I didn't, just in case he was.

"Do you have a reservation?" asked a slight dark girl in a print dress so skimpy I could see her breasts.

"No, I just need...I just want..."

She looked at me quizzically, then smiled. "There's still a few places at the bar. Let me know if you change your mind about a table and I'll put you on the list."

I uttered a heartfelt thanks and headed in the direction she was pointing. Through a brick archway was the cocktail lounge, a cozy space resembling a wine cellar with a mural of an Italian street scene painted on the stucco wall and fairy lights cascading from the high-beamed ceiling. Though filled to bursting with loud, happy drinkers, sure enough, there were a few empty stools and a tiny booth someone had recently vacated. I slipped onto hard wooden bench and breathed; just breathed.

"Water?" I called to the server when he brushed by to take my order.

"What kind?" he answered without missing a beat.

"Cold," I said, and closed my eyes. He got the point.

Much as I would have loved to sit quietly, happy to be alone and alive, I knew I needed to keep alert. I pulled my cell phone out of my pants pocket and dialed Frannie. Frannie and I had been friends for long enough that I knew I could count on her not to ask stupid questions like *Why are you being shot at?* She would just take my word that I needed help and be there for me.

As I waited for my water, I explained everything I knew about the events of the past half-hour. "I need to get out of here and I don't trust the streets. He might still be out there. I know you're busy, but—"

"Not another word, Lynley," came the reassuring voice. "Tell me where you are and I'll come pick you up."

"It's a bistro on the waterfront." I looked around for a name and came up with a napkin. "Webster's."

"Okay, hang tight. I'll be there as soon as I can. But I'm at the shelter so it might take a little while."

My heart sank, but I said, "No problem. I'm sure I'm safe here."

I scrunched the phone back into my pocket and took another deep breath. The kitten had been quiet for some time and I was thankful, but now a terrifying thought hit me. What if something were wrong with her? What if one of my clumsy maneuvers had knocked the bag against a wall or a rail and hurt her? Or what if she were sick or injured to begin with? I hadn't exactly had time to check her out. Instantly, I was pulling at the heavy zipper. "Spot?" I urged. "Hey, sweetheart, you okay in there?"

The zipper still caught at the inch-and-a-half mark, so I forced in a finger, wiggling it around to get her attention. For a scary moment, nothing moved, then there she was, little nose pressed up against my touch. I tried to feel over her body, but all I could reach was face, sideburns, and ears, fluffy and unharmed. When Frannie came, I'd have her take us straight back to the shelter to get little Spot checked over by the doctors there. Until then, I couldn't do much but wait.

The server came with my water. "Thank you," I told him as he set down a green bottle, an ice-filled glass, and a check.

"Anything else, ma'am?"

"No, that's it. Thanks." I gave Spot another scratch on her sideburns and withdrew my hand. I had intended to take a much-needed drink of the very expensive H2o, but Spot thought otherwise and began to cry. It was amazing how loud such a small thing can be when she put her feline mind to it.

The server turned in his steps and stared at me. "Is that a cat?"

"Well, um, it's a kitten, actually."

"Sorry, ma'am, but animals aren't allowed in this establishment. You're going to have to leave."

"My friend is coming to pick me up. She'll be here any minute. Can't I just wait for her?"

Spot kicked it up a few notches, sounding as if she were being tortured, or worse. Patrons turned their heads and a small crowd was gathering. I shoved my fingers back in the bag and tried to calm her, but this time, she wasn't falling for it.

"I'm sorry, health department rules."

I took a gulp of my water, flung a few bills on the table as I hefted the bag, and left. "Haven't you ever heard a cat before?" I grumbled to the onlookers as I brushed by.

Outside, I hunkered near the wall behind a little cluster of smokers feeling very sorry for myself. I was mad. Mad as hell, but mostly because I was scared. It wasn't the server's fault the health department was shortsighted about cats in restaurants; it wasn't Spot's fault that she was frightened and probably hungry; and it certainly wasn't my fault I was being chased through lower Portland by a creepy *person unknown*.

I peered around for any sign of him, but beyond the lights of the café, the streets were empty. Then, my mind cleared, and suddenly I knew what to do. How had I been so blind? Fear and adrenaline might help make the body move fast but not so much for the mind. In my attempt to run and hide, I had missed the obvious.

I took my phone out one more time and started to dial 911. How simple! I would tell the police what happened and let them deal with it. Shots had been fired, after all. That was the sort of thing they liked to know about.

A hand touched my arm and I whirled around. There he was, the man in black. For a moment I saw his face, charcoal baseball cap low on his forehead. He was young, white, scruffy, but built like a brick outhouse. As his grip tightened, I jerked away and ran.

He was after me in a heartbeat. I swerved around a crowd of well-dressed young people, pushing a willowy redhead into his path.

"Sorry," I yelled over my shoulder, then added, "Help!" and "Call the police."

I'm pretty sure they didn't take me seriously because their only replies were, "What the—" and "Watch where you're going, lady!"

I didn't want to leave the area, because Frannie was on her way—so I turned the corner at the end of the block and made to come back around from the other side. I held to the shadows, this part of the neighborhood being strictly old school, warehouse and factory—closed up tight for the weekend. It was full dark now, and I strove to be silent as I ran on tiptoes. No one pursued. Maybe I'd been wrong about the man. Maybe it wasn't the assailant at all, but someone else who wore black clothing. That wasn't exactly rare in a city of Grunge and Goth. I turned the second corner, then the third. Up the street was the bistro again, a bright sparkle in the night. Jogging from a run to a walk, I breathed heavily. I hadn't got this much exercise in as long as I could remember. I'd be sore tomorrow, I laughed to myself.

Behind me, a chunk of gravel crunched on the sidewalk. I turned—and there he was. Damn, it *had* been him after all! I saw him look out across the street and followed his gaze to a second man. White ball cap, white tee shirt, tight gray jeans, but the same hefty build. They could have been a set of wrestler twins.

Man in Black nodded to Man in White and they began to converge. For a moment, I stood petrified. I knew I could never outrun them both. Now would be a good time for Frannie to come driving by, I thought to myself, but as I scanned the sparse traffic finessing its way across the cobblestones and railroad tracks of the waterfront district, there was no sign of her little car.

For lack of a better idea, I shoved my hands in my pockets and kept moving toward the bistro. If I could make it back there, I had a chance. I could try to convince the half-drunk clientele I needed assistance; I could go back inside and maybe, if nothing else, they would call the cops on me.

Man in White was heading straight for me now, Man in Black, still moving up from behind. It didn't take a strategist to see I was never going to get near that peopled oasis of light.

Glancing around for alternatives, I discovered a wrought iron gate barring a narrow passageway between two buildings. With a sprint, I ran for it. Footfalls behind me let me know I wasn't alone. It was déjà-vu all over again, except now, there were two of them and I was dog-tired, feeling every year of my age.

The gate was chained, and my heart fell—until I realized the padlock hadn't been clasped. I flung it aside and hurried through, pushing the iron bars shut behind me. The alley was little more than a footpath, hard clay and garbage. I didn't want to guess what those slimy shopping bags contained, nor did I care to look any closer at the piles of multifarious debris. I know what it smelled like, and was glad when, in another few yards, I burst out the other side. It was a courtyard, once a garden of sorts but now just dried weeds and more garbage. The building backs abutted the dreary square, windows barred and security doors locked and padlocked. A few folding chairs were scattered haphazardly on the cracked dirt where workers came for a break, a smoke, a sandwich. No one was there now, the metal seats abandoned. All was dull and dark except where a string of colored lights hung like Christmas in June—the rear of the bistro.

The pathway continued through the block, and an alley crisscrossed in the other direction. A truck was parked there and without thought, I made for it. I tried the door but it was locked. I don't know what I'd expected—that it would be open, keys in the ignition, my magic ride to freedom? God, how much more of this could I endure? My knees buckled. I sank to the ground, utterly defeated.

The men were in no hurry now. They loomed over me, making no attempt to do anything more.

"What do you want from me?" I whimpered, sounding a lot like the kitten.

"Give us the bag and we'll leave you alone," said Man in Black.

"The bag," I laughed. "You can have the bloody bag, but please just let me take the kitten." I hugged the bag to me, feeling Spot squirm inside.

The men looked at each other as if I were crazy. "Give it over," commanded Man in White. He reached out and I shrunk back. There was no way I was delivering Spot into those menacing hands.

With a slap that sent me sprawling, he grabbed the handle of the gym bag, but it was still slung across my shoulder so even as he pulled, I slid along with it. I screamed and he jerked even harder.

An explosion split the night. Both men whirled, then bounded for cover. With one last bone-jarring yank, Man in White let go the strap and I was free.

Free, in the middle of a war zone.

Shots were coming from all sides, though I couldn't see the other shooter. I didn't care. Low and fast, I crab-scrambled behind the truck. Farther down the alley, a mere half-block away lay Water Street, the esplanade, and the clear glitter surface of the Willamette River. Zombie-like I staggered for it.

With a screech of gravel and a blinding blaze of headlights, a vehicle flung itself into my path. It blocked the alley and with it, my only escape. I crouched against the wall. I hunkered down, shut my eyes, and waited to die.

Powerful arms pulled me to my feet. I fought but there was no fight left in me. Another set of hands guided me into the van, and a familiar voice, thick with concern, spoke quietly.

"Lynley, it's okay. We're here." It was Frannie, and as I gazed up into the face of my captor, I saw not a stranger but Special Agent Denny Paris, humane investigator for the Northwest Humane Society. He was a cop, but his job was to save abused and neglected animals. I gave a prayer of thanks he was here to save me.

The strong special agent hefted me into the investigations van and Frannie pushed in on the bucket seat beside me. Special Agent Paris threw himself in the driver's side and took off in reverse, spinning tires all the way to the street. He was great! He didn't ask me what had happened and I don't think I could have told him. All I managed was to point at the bag in my lap and whisper, "Kitten!"

Frannie raised an eyebrow and then slipped the strap from my neck.

Gently feeling the length of the bag, she pulled the zipper. Like before, it caught at the one-and-a-half inch mark, and then, miracle of miracles, opened like a song. The kitten jumped soundlessly into her lap and nestled in her arms. The van hit a pothole and down went the bag onto the floor—but it didn't matter, since Spot was safe. In the light from the passing street lamps, I gazed at my little beauty.

Spot was the perfect name for her. Unlike any domestic cat I had ever seen, she was freckled black and white like a baby leopard. I stroked her tiny back and head. The sound of her purr rivaled the van's big motor.

"Look!" Frannie exclaimed, pointing to the floorboards where the gym bag had spilled its contents.

"Damn," exclaimed Special Agent Paris as he glanced at the miscellanea littering his carpet: a towel; a silk paisley shawl; a few suspicious baggies full of fat, white capsules...and numerous shrink-wrapped stacks of paper money.

I reached down and picked up something round and sparkling. "Cat toy. Yours?" I asked the kitten.

Spot extended a speckled paw and gently touched the plastic ball, making it rattle. I dropped it into Frannie's lap and Spot curled around it like a potato bug.

Frannie picked up a packet of money and held it up to the street light. "I think I see the problem," she said slowly. "These are hundreds."

Paris glanced over and gave a whistle. "Looks like it's got a currency strap. That would make them $10,000 each, and there are at least twenty."

"What now?" asked Frannie.

"It's time to go to the police."

We pulled around a corner and were suddenly head to head with a light show of red and blue. A tactical-vested officer with a bullhorn shouted, "Stop your vehicle and get out of the car, hands where I can see them."

Frannie grinned at me, her eyes wide. "I'd say the police have come to us."

o0o

The sun was rising over the fir-treed dome of Mt. Tabor, slanting warm rays through my kitchen window. Frannie, Special Agent Paris, and I were having much-needed cups of coffee, and Spot was burying her face in a bowl of feline stew. There was a chorus of disgruntled meows coming from the other side of the kitchen door—my own cats. I had explained as I gave them their breakfast at an impromptu feeding station by the television that they couldn't see the kitten until after she'd been cleared by the vet.

It had taken a little convincing to persuade the officer at the barricade that I was not a criminal absconding with the drug loot, but luck was with us. It turned out Special Agent Paris knew the man's partner, and when they heard my story, they took the bag with its assorted contents, sans kitten, and ran off after the real criminals, leaving us in peace. We still had to make a statement or six, but that was later–for now, I was off the hook and blissfully out of danger.

"Lynley, what did you get yourself mixed up in this time?" Frannie was holding my hand. She had barely let go since she found me, and I hadn't wanted her to.

"I have no idea," I sighed, pressing an ice bag to a bruise on my face where Man in White had whacked me. Now that I was safe and in the comfort of my own home, the leftover adrenaline was making me bold and a little giddy. "I gave them a good run for their money, though! Whoever they were."

"Yes, I'm sure you did," she indulged. "But who were they?"

When I didn't answer, Franny turned her gaze on Denny Paris.

"I gather from Jake—Officer Roland—they're presumed to be drug dealers from somewhere south. There are a few new gangs in town, and law enforcement wants to stop them before they can establish here."

"It looked like somebody else wanted to stop them too," I muttered. "Back in the courtyard, someone was shooting at them."

"Could it have been the police?" Frannie asked.

"Wouldn't police have identified themselves? These guys just started firing. Caught the wrestler twins by surprise."

"Rivals. Drug wars." Special Agent Paris shrugged. "You don't think about Portland that way, but we're as susceptible to those elements as any other growing city."

Spot had finished her food, licked the bowl sparkling, and was now batting at a piece of lint on the floor. Frannie rummaged in her pocket and came up with the plastic toy from the bag. "Maybe she wants this."

I took the ball from Frannie. It was weightier than I had expected. I jiggled it in my hand, creating a satisfying rattle, then tossed it down where it skittered on the floor. Spot was on it in a flash. She volleyed it about until it rolled under the refrigerator and she lost interest. With a leap that defied gravity, she was in my lap, snuggling and mewing.

Spot must have been between two and three months old, and though hungry, she looked clean and well fed. "I wonder where she came from? How she got herself into the gym bag in the first place?" I petted her thoughtfully. "I don't imagine she belonged to the drug dealers."

"You know how kittens are," said Frannie. "They can get into the smallest of places."

"But if that's true, then why couldn't she get out again?"

Frannie sipped her coffee thoughtfully. "Theory? The bag was unzipped when she first jumped in. She began to play with the zipper and it got stuck on loose a thread."

"Or maybe whoever made the drop didn't know she was in there when he zipped it closed," offered the special agent.

"Maybe they can tell more when we take her in for her check-up," said Frannie.

I looked at the clock. Still only six a.m. and too early to get hold of the doctors at Friends of Felines. I felt around Spot's scruff and found a capsule-shaped lump. "I think she might be microchipped." I wasn't sure whether I was happy or sad that the kit might have real people out there somewhere. I'd become quite attached to her in our short but thrill-filled time together.

Spot had curled herself into a polka-dot circle and was snoring softly, as kittens do. "It's probably for the best," I sighed.

"What is?"

"That she already has a home. Otherwise, I'd want to keep her."

"And how many would that make?"

"Only six," I giggled.

Frannie gave me a mock-stern look. "And you wonder why they call you a crazy cat lady!"

"I'm not crazy." I gave Spot a scratch on her ear and added, "At least, not yet."

About the Author—Mollie Hunt

Mollie Hunt lives in Portland, Oregon with her husband and a varying number of cats. Like her character, Lynley Cannon, she is a grateful shelter volunteer. She also fosters for the Oregon Humane Society and visits hospice patients with her feline Pet Partner, Tinkerbelle. Currently she is working on her Crazy Cat Lady Series, beginning with "Cats' Eyes" (2013) and "Copy Cats" (2015). "Cat's Paw", 3rd of the series is anticipated sometime in 2016. Besides mysteries, Mollie also writes in the cat science-fantasy genre.

Mollie's website: https://lecatts.wordpress.com
Amazon Author Page: https://www.amazon.com/author/molliehunt

The Nerd In Shining Armor

Isabella Norse

May the fur be with you.

"Where's a hero when you need one?" Abby sighed as she looked at the sad remains of her beef and broccoli oozing across the floor just outside of her apartment. "I had my stomach all set for that, too." She juggled the bags, books, and purse cradled in her arms until she was able to twist her wrist just so and slide the key into the lock. There was just one problem. It was the wrong key. "I can hear Granny now, 'That's what you get for trying to carry everything in one trip.' Yeah, yeah. But, why make four trips when one will do?" Biting the corner of her bottom lip in concentration, she fumbled through her keys, feeling for the one she needed. "Let's try this one." The key slid in and turned smoothly, the bolt clicking back with a satisfying thunk. "Ha! Take that, Granny!"

She staggered across the threshold, divesting herself of items as she walked. Keys went in the bowl on the table by the door. She shifted the plastic bag in her right hand to her teeth and hung her purse on the hooks above the table. Then, it was a few short steps into the small kitchen where she deposited bags willy-nilly on the counter. She grabbed a couple of paper towels and headed back to the hall. Halfway to the door she reconsidered, turned around, and grabbed the entire roll.

Stepping over rapidly congealing stir fry, she began swiping at the mess. While the paper towels rapidly soaked up the broth, the stain just seemed to spread, chunks of beef and broccoli as far as the eye could see.

"I'm here to rescue you." A familiar voice sounded from near Abby's elbow. There was a brief pause before it repeated. "I'm here to rescue you."

Recognizing the line from one of her favorite movies, Abby turned to greet her savior. Words failed her when she saw no one except a rather battered brown tabby hunkered down licking the gravy, a look of feline bliss on his face. Her head swiveled as she looked for whoever had spoken.

Then, she heard it again. "I'm here to rescue you." She looked down. There was no doubt about it. The voice had come from the cat. She reached out a cautious finger and stroked the tabby behind the ear. He leaned into her touch while continuing his feast. He paused long enough to look at her with large green eyes, blinked, and said "I'm here to rescue you."

Forgetting about cleaning, Abby dropped to her knees and stared. However, she couldn't help answering in kind. "Fine. I'll play along. Aren't you a little short–and furry–to be a stormtrooper?"

Her hero didn't answer. A deep purr began rumbling through his chest.

The door to the apartment across from hers opened and a harried young man with flyaway brown hair rushed out. "Have you seen…" His gaze fell to the cat and he sagged against the doorframe, resting his head on one forearm while the other hand clutched his chest. "Oh, thank God!" He turned his gaze to Abby, his eyes as green as those of the cat. "I thought for sure Lucas was gone! The folks at the shelter would have killed me." He twisted the old-fashioned cut-glass door knob a couple of times. "That does it! The landlord has *got* to fix this door. It doesn't always close well and this guy—" he nodded at the cat "—is a regular Houdini."

Abby stood and brushed off the knees of her slacks with her free hand while searching for somewhere to put the wad of soiled paper in the other. No community trashcans magically appeared in the hallway.

Her predicament must have reached the newcomer because he ducked back into his apartment and came out with a waste basket which was already just this side of overflowing. "Put your trash in here. I was planning to empty it later tonight, anyway."

"Thanks." She shoved the used paper towels in the proffered bag, then tore off a clean one and wiped her hands before offering her right one. "You must be my new neighbor. Hi. My name is Abigail, but everyone calls me Abby."

"Hi, Abby. I'm Ryan." He placed the trashcan on the floor and wiped his hands on his jeans before shaking hers.

"I'm here to rescue you." Lucas chimed in from his seat at the floor-level buffet.

"So I've heard." Abby smiled at the cat, then turned her attention to Ryan. "Care to tell me what's going on? I feel a bit like Alice standing on the edge of a *Star Wars*-themed rabbit hole."

"Oh, Lucas is part of a project I'm working on for Unconditional Love Animal Shelter." Ryan nodded at the mess on the floor. "Hand me some paper towels. I'll help you clean this up, then I'll show you."

They worked side-by-side until the worst of the spill had been removed. Abby left Ryan to dispose of the paper waste while she ran back into her apartment for a damp mop. Lucas seemed disappointed when the last of his feast was wiped away before his eyes. He chirruped once, sat down, wrapped his tail around his feet, and began bathing.

Ryan scooped up the cat and headed back to his apartment. "C'mon." He used one hand to motion for her to follow.

"I, uh, appreciate the help." Abby followed slowly, clearing her throat. "I'm just not comfortable going into your apartment. We just met. I don't know anything about you." She met his eyes briefly, then looked away. "Sorry. I guess that sounds pretty mean."

"It's understandable. How about this? You can stand here in the doorway and just look while I give you an overview of what I'm doing."

Lucas twisted his head around to look at her. "I'm here to rescue you."

Abby laughed. "How can I resist such a smooth talker?" She propped her mop against the wall outside Ryan's apartment, stepped into the doorway and leaned against the doorframe. His small living room was cluttered with enough electronic equipment to stock a small store. "Wow. This stuff looks pretty serious."

"It is–and it isn't. I've always been fascinated with movies and making them. I've been doing it since I was a kid. My hobby comes with a lot of fancy equipment. A year or so ago, I started volunteering with the animal shelter." He shrugged. "There are so many awesome animals in need of homes–especially adult dogs and cats–that I decided I needed to do something more to help. It dawned on me that I could put both of my passions together. I'm going to make knockoffs of some popular films, using the animals as stars, in an effort to help them find homes. My first project is called *Claw Wars*."

"And Lucas?"

"Lucas will be playing the role of Luke Pawwalker in the film. Look out!" Ryan warned as a black cat darted for the door. "I forgot to tell you—standing in the doorway also means you get to play cat goalie and stop any of my feline guests from escaping."

Abby snagged the black cat and settled him in her arms before noticing something was wrong. She examined him closer. "What happened to this guy? He's missing a foot."

"That's Darth Jellybean, and he was born that way."

"Darth Jellybean?" Abby giggled as she tucked the cat into the crook of her arm. He seemed eager for the attention and snuggled close to her.

"Black cats and dogs are the hardest to find homes for. I remember reading a story about a shelter volunteer who started naming all black cats Jellybean and it helped! The name caused people to stop and look at the cats they would normally ignore and they got adopted." He nodded at the now purring bundle in her arms. "So, this guy is Jellybean. And, since he's missing a foot, he's perfect for the Darth role. But, you asked what happened. When he was born, the umbilical cord was wrapped around his foot. He lost the foot but the leg healed cleanly. He gets along fine with just three feet." He chuckled–a warm sound. "He doesn't realize he is supposed to be any different."

Abby scratched her new buddy under the chin. He pressed his face against her hand, urging her to scratch harder. "What? No raspy breathing from the villain?"

Ryan laughed. "Initially, I planned to make the film and dub the voices in later. Then, I had a 'brilliant' idea. I worked with a friend of mine who is an electronics wizard. He came up with a small recorder for me to put on their collars. That way, I could record the lines for each cat and trigger them as needed with this." He rummaged around on the top of his table for a moment and came up with the smallest remote Abby had ever seen. "Lucas–who was named for George Lucas, by the way–was the first test of the system. As you can hear, there are a few bugs to work out."

"I'm here to rescue you." Lucas leaped onto the table, scattering papers and electronics everywhere. He rammed his head into Ryan's hip searching for attention.

Ryan scratched him behind the ears absent-mindedly. "So, what do you think?"

"I'm impressed." Abby nodded as she took in the equipment, the movie posters decorating the walls, and the comic books–er, graphic novels–scattered across the coffee table. "You're a regular nerd in shining armor."

Ryan's face lit up and he executed a bow. "Why, thank you, madam. I think that's the nicest thing anyone has ever said to me."

"So, why *Star Wars*?"

"Well, it's both an easily recognizable classic *and* my favorite movie."

"Mine too." Abby ducked her head.

"Seriously? I would never have guessed." He nodded at her work attire. "You look so... not *Star Wars*," he finished lamely.

"Then, my disguise is working." Abby threw caution to the wind, stepped just inside the apartment, and leaned back against the wall. "I'm both a bookkeeper and the youngest person in my office. None of my coworkers understand my fascination with *Star Wars* and other stuff like that. So, I dress the non-nerd part during the day, then let my hair down after work. Not that there's been much time for *that* recently. The person I'm replacing left everything in a mess. I've been working a ridiculous number of hours the past few months. I'm just starting to get my life back." She laughed. "My dark purple hair is my one non-conformity. I think the boss would like to tell me to get rid of it, but since I have been kicking butt and taking names job-wise, he hasn't." She jerked her head back toward her apartment and continued. "All of this excitement happened before I had a chance to change." Her stomach growled. "Sorry. It's been great to meet you. All of you," she added, including the cats. "However, since my supper wound up on the floor, I really need to go in search of sustenance." She gave Jellybean one last scratch under the chin before placing him on the couch and heading for the door.

"Abby?" Ryan called. "Would you like to help me with my project? It would go much faster with an assistant."

"What do you need me to do?"

"Well, tomorrow is Saturday. I'm planning to go to the shelter and spend some time with the cats. I need to decide which ones I'm going to cast for the remaining roles. Once that's done, the actual filming can begin."

"I'm here to rescue you." Lucas wandered to the door as if he were planning to leave with her.

"Oh, no you don't." Ryan stopped the tabby before he could escape again. "Since the recording devices are a bit of a bust, you could also help with the voices, if you're willing."

"Really? I've always thought it would be fun to do voiceovers." Abby cocked her head and studied her new acquaintance. "Okay, I'm in. I'll see you in the morning. I'm an early bird, so, just knock when you're ready."

o0o

Abby had just finished breakfast when there was a knock at her door. She looked through the peephole and saw Ryan, as expected. She took a few extra seconds to look him over in private and decided he was definitely easy on the eyes. When he knocked again, she realized she might have been staring longer than she thought. She smoothed her hair and ran her hand over her shirt checking for errant crumbs as she unlocked and opened the door.

"Good morning, are you re—" Ryan's words fizzled as he stared, open-mouthed at her chest. "Holy video games! Is that a *Massive Age of Dragons* shirt?" He raised his eyes to hers. "You're a *gamer*?"

"Yes. I take it you are too?"

"Absolutely. *MAD* is my all-time favorite game."

"Mine too."

"What's your gamer name? We'll have to play together some time."

"No way." Abby held her hands up to ward off the suggestion. "I don't do multiplayer online. I'm a campaign girl only. By the time I get home from work, this introvert has had enough of dealing with people."

"Oh, that's a shame." Ryan drummed his fingers against the leg of his jeans as he thought. "What if we just play campaign together? No online. What sort of character do you play?"

"I'm a spell-slinger. You?"

"I'm a warrior. We'd make a killer combination."

"Tell you what, I've never played with anyone, but I'll at least think about it. So, are you ready to get this party started?"

"Absolutely."

"Let me grab my purse and we'll hit the road."

o0o

Several hours later, they returned to Ryan's apartment armed with blankets, a rough draft of project plans, fast food, and two more cats.

As Ryan unlocked the door, he teased, "So, do you think you know me well enough now to actually enter my apartment?"

"I'll take my chances," Abby responded. "I don't expect trouble, but I know if it manifests, Lucas will be there to rescue me. Or, so I've heard."

"Well, he will be quieter now. I removed the voice unit from his collar. It got to be a little creepy hearing it at all hours of the day and night."

"I can imagine." Abby lifted her arms to display the cat carriers in each hand. "What do you want me to do with these guys?"

"Oh, hang on." Ryan tucked the blankets under his arm and opened the door to his bedroom. Abby watched as he laid the blankets on his bed. He then returned to the living room, picked up Lucas and Jellybean, deposited them in his room, and shut the door before they could dart out. "Now, you can let them out."

Abby set the carriers down and opened the door to the first one. The dainty calico inside stepped to the door, her nostrils flaring as she scented her new surroundings. "Welcome to your new temporary home, Princess Organza." When she opened the second carrier a self-assured gray cat strolled out as if he owned the place. And you as well, Han Pawlo." She nodded toward the bedroom. "What was all of that with the blankets?"

"The blankets are from the shelter and have the odors of the new cats. Lucas and Jellybean can now get used to the scents of Callie and Smokey while the newcomers get used to their smells out here. Tomorrow, I'll open the door and let them meet face-to-face. Hopefully, by then, there will be a minimum of hissing and no bloodshed."

"Sounds like you've done this before."

"A few times." Ryan checked to make sure the newbies were okay and motioned for Abby to join him on the couch. "Let's get started."

"With what?"

"Lunch and research."

"What kind of research?"

"We need to watch *Star Wars*."

"The original?"

"Not *just* the original–the original trilogy."

"Sounds good. When do you want to do this?"

"How about now? Today? We've got lunch and can order in dinner."

Abby cocked her head, grinning as Ryan added, "Pleeease?"

"You're cute when you beg. Okay, I'll stay."

"Yesss!" Ryan pumped his fists in triumph. He patted the couch. "Make yourself comfy. I'll start the first movie."

"The least I can do is contribute some snacks. I'll get them while you get set up." Abby dashed across the hall to her apartment and returned within minutes with a cloth bag full of a variety of salty snacks, candy, and sodas. "Excuse me, Han." She moved the gray cat off of the coffee table and spread the bounty out for easy access.

Ryan plopped down on the sofa, remote in hand, stared at the table, and selected a soda. "You had all of this at your place? How much junk food can one person eat?"

"When that person is me, quite a bit. In addition to being a closet nerd, I'm also a certifiable junk-food-aholic." Abby snagged a snack-sized bag of cheddar cheese flavored potato chips and a diet soda and settled on the unoccupied end of the couch. Callie climbed into her lap before her full weight had settled.

"Ready, padawan?"

"Ready."

When the credits rolled, it had taken them almost four hours to watch a movie that lasted just over two. They stopped the movie often to make notes for the project, and, in true nerd fashion, to debate the relationships between the characters and how they would have reacted in the same situations. Their discussions contained a lot of good-natured teasing and occasional popcorn battles. The cats were happy to dispose of any ammo not consumed by the humans.

"Okay, okay, I surrender!" Abby threw her hands up in defeat after losing yet another round of *Star Wars* trivia. She used the internet search feature on her phone to make sure Ryan wasn't feeding her a line of horse hockey. He wasn't. "You are indeed the master and I will be your student for years to come. But now, Obi Wan, I must go home. My apartment isn't going to clean itself. What's on the agenda for tomorrow?"

"I think we should start filming."

"What happened to watching the rest of the trilogy?"

"We've got enough notes to get started."

"Do you need some help?"

"Sure."

"All righty, then. I'll see you in the morning. Say, nine? Breakfast is on me. Callie, you have to move now." Abby laughed when she looked down at the cat who had been in her lap almost all afternoon. She was now curled into a furry, multi-colored ball, the only distinguishing characteristics were the paw sticking out of the middle of the mass and the golden eye that stared unseeing. "You're kind of creeping me out, you know." Abby laid one hand on the cat's side to make sure she was still breathing. Callie gave a deep sigh and pulled her paw back, covering her eye as if to block out the light.

"That, my friend, is a very happy cat." Ryan leaned back against the arm of the couch, the corner of his mouth quirked up in a grin as he watched the couple.

"Can I ask you a question?" Abby continued to stroke Callie as she turned her attention to him.

"Sure."

"Why do you do this?"

Ryan dropped his head, studying his fingernails. He took a deep breath before speaking. "I know how they feel."

"What do you mean?"

"I lost my family when I was young. They died in a car accident. I was supposed to be with them, but wasn't." He laughed, but it wasn't a happy sound. "Devastating grief and puberty aren't a good combination. I wound up in the foster care system and got passed around a lot."

"How terrible!"

"I don't blame the families. I acted out and pushed everyone away. Not everyone is willing–or able–to deal with that type of behavior. But, I was lucky. Eventually, I wound up with a family who wouldn't let me go. They told me that they would love me, no matter what." When he looked back up, his eyes were filled with tears. "And, they did. As soon as they could, they adopted me."

After a moment, he went on. "So, I know how these guys feel. They just want someone who will love them. They don't want to spend their lives cooped up in a cage or shelter. I found my new family. Now, I want to help them find theirs."

Abby leaned forward and snagged a napkin from the coffee table. Callie grumbled as her human bed shifted. Moving the cat to the cushion she had just vacated, she turned her attention to Ryan, wiping away his tears. She then leaned forward and planted a kiss on his cheek. The stubble of his whiskers was soft and damp against her lips. She wondered what his lips would feel like against hers, and pulled back before she could act on the impulse.

"What was that for?" Ryan raised his hand to his cheek, his eyes growing large in surprise.

"You're a pretty cool guy, Ryan. I'm glad I met you."

A rosy blush touched Ryan's cheeks.

Abby patted him on the knee and stood up. "Now, I really am out of here. I'll see you in the morning."

"Bye."

o0o

"Knock, knock!" Abby sang out at exactly nine the next morning.

Ryan opened the door to find her holding a picnic basket in both hands.

"Come in, come in." He stepped back, giving her room to enter. "You look like you've got enough food for an army."

"I love to cook." Abby smiled and ducked her head. "It's been a long time since I've had a chance to cook for someone else."

"Well, I'm glad I could give you the opportunity. It's been a long time since I've enjoyed a home-cooked meal. What culinary delights await in yon basket, milady?"

"Ham and cheese omelets, pancakes, and bacon. We need to eat up while it's still hot."

"I'll grab some dishes."

"Don't bother." Abby opened the basket, displaying the plates and flatware stored in the top. "My basket comes fully equipped. Well, *almost* fully equipped. Mugs would be good. I have carafes of coffee and hot chocolate. Choose your poison."

"Hot chocolate for me." Ryan dashed to the kitchen, grabbed mugs, and then returned to the living room and cleared the coffee table, which still held snacks from the night before. He then helped Abby set everything out. They piled their plates with foods and balanced them on their knees as they sat on the sofa.

"You do know there are tables designed for the sole purpose of supporting plates while meals are consumed, don't you?" Abby asked, swallowing a mouthful of omelet.

"Ooh, the lady is a smart aleck! If you are referring to a dining room table, what do you think is holding all of my equipment?" Ryan pointed across the room.

"Ah. Point taken. Tell you what, next time I cook for you, we'll eat at my place."

"Next time?"

"Sure. Why not? Even nerds have to eat, right?"

"Uh, yeah. Of course." Changing the subject, Ryan said "Don't look now, but we're surrounded." Four furry faces peered over the edges of the coffee table.

Abby paused in the act of putting a forkful of pancakes in her mouth. "Hey, the whole crew is in one room! When did that happen?"

"This morning. They hissed at each other under the bedroom door last night. I decided to let them meet face-to-face this morning. So far, so good."

"I've been thinking. I think you should change the name of your movie."

"Why? *Star Wars, Claw Wars*. It's perfect."

"Well, claws are sharp, pointy, and dangerous. Paws are soft and warm. Why not use *Paw Wars* instead?"

Ryan stared at Abby thoughtfully. "You might be right. Okay, *Paw Wars* it is." They clinked mugs companionably.

When Abby moved to put her mug down, she noticed a black paw snaking onto her plate, heading for the bacon.

"Hey, Jellybean! What do you think you're doing, dude?"

Jellybean didn't comment, just licked his paw.

Ryan laughed. "C'mon, let's clean up and start filming."

"So, what exactly do my duties as your assistant entail?" Abby began stacking plates as she talked. "Do I escort the guests to and from the green room? Make sure they have bowls of green kitty treats, or what?"

"Nothing that difficult. I'll get a lot of footage of them just doing what they do. But, I'll also need you to stand behind me with toys and treats to help with action shots. Think you can handle it?"

"Point me at the toys and watch me work. You will be ah-mazed." Abby removed a scrunchie from her pocket and pulled her hair into a ponytail.

Two hours later, both she and the cats were exhausted. "Cut!" Abby flopped onto the couch–after moving Jellybean to the side. He pulled himself into her lap and collapsed into a purring pile. "You never told me you are such a slave driver." She glared at Ryan as he pointed the camera at her and continued to film. "Turn that thing off! You have no need for footage of me in a movie starring cats."

"You'll be in the part that shows after the credits. Audiences have come to expect extra scenes."

"Whatever." She began stroking Jellybean who turned turtle, inviting her to scratch his belly. She obliged. "Darth and I have bonded today. He's a really cool guy." Abby turned to Ryan, her expression soft. "Your movie's already found a home for one cat."

"Seriously?"

"Yeah. I want Jellybean. He already has me wrapped around his paw." She stroked the sleek black fur again. "You've got your work cut out for you, playing the role of a bad guy. You're a total softie." She looked back at Ryan. "What do I have to do to make it official?"

"I'll let the adoption coordinator know. She'll draw up the paperwork and you'll have to answer so many questions you'll think you're adopting a human child. Are you sure about this?"

"Absolutely. I'm excited…I've never had a pet of my own!"

"Between your expression and your hair, you look like a big kid." Ryan tucked a strand of loose hair behind her ear. "But, no pets? Wow, I can't even imagine."

"My dad is allergic to almost everything with four feet so, our house was a fur-free zone. I've gotten so used to not having animals around that I guess I've never really considered getting a pet before. I may have to rely on your expertise sometimes."

"Of course. I'll be here whenever you need me. Now, have you got your second wind? We need to start looking through the footage to determine what can be used and what we still need. Excuse me." The *Imperial March* began issuing from Ryan's back pocket. He dug his cell phone out and glanced at the screen. "It's the animal shelter director. I need to take this." He swiped the screen to answer and wandered into the kitchen as he talked. When he rejoined Abby, his skin had taken on a decidedly grayish hue.

"Are you all right?" Abby struggled to move Jellybean, who was sleeping hard. He had gone limp and was about as easy to move as a sack of potatoes–

if the sack was small and covered in slippery black fur. Giving up, she leaned forward and grabbed Ryan by the hand, tugging until he took the hint and sat beside her.

"That was Mrs. Hill."

Abby nodded. "You said the director of the shelter was calling. What did she say that has you so shaken up?"

"She, uh..." Ryan stopped, cleared his throat, and tried again. "The shelter is having its annual fundraiser in three weeks. It's a really big deal–it's even black tie. They have all sorts of auctions and giveaways and all of the proceeds go to the support of the animals at the shelter."

"Okaaaay. So far, I haven't heard anything earth-shattering."

"She wants *Paw Wars* to be the highlight of the night. What if it's not good enough? What if we can't get it finished in time? What if..." Ryan's gaze darted from one place to another and he began jiggling one leg nervously. Abby wouldn't have been surprised if he had gotten up and run out of the apartment.

"Ryan, look at me." He didn't respond, so she tried again. "Hey, you." Abby placed her fingers under Ryan's chin, forcing him to face her. "You need to breathe. C'mon. In and out. In and out. That's right, keep going. Everything will be all right. This is what you wanted, isn't it? You wanted your movie to find homes for these guys. What better place to show it than at the biggest shelter event of the year?"

"But, three *weeks*?" The color that had just started returning to Ryan's cheeks fled as the hunted look returned to his eyes.

"Yes, three weeks. You don't want to let the shelter down so, you work with what you've got. And, it's not like you're in this alone. I'm here, and I'll do whatever it takes to make sure you're done on time. Okay?"

"Okay." Ryan took a deep breath, then reached over, took Abby's hand in his and squeezed. "Thank you for sticking with me—and for talking me off the ledge." He chuckled, the sound cutting off abruptly. "Oh no. It's black tie and I don't have a tux! What—"

"You know, I would've never guessed you were the panicky type. Breathe, Obi Wan. One crisis at a time. We're going to start viewing the footage like you said we should and go from there." She had unconsciously twined her fingers into his when he took her hand. She held their hands up where he could see them. "We've got this. Together."

o0o

"Yoo hoo!" Dale Hill sailed across the crowded floor. A solidly-built, well-endowed woman, her bosom parted the crowd like an ice-breaker on a frozen sea. "Ryan!" She waved to get the attention of the star of the evening. "There you are. I've been looking everywhere. It's almost time to start the movie. I'll go on stage and get everyone to take their seats, and then I would like for you to do the intro."

"Me?" Ryan squeaked, his forehead beaded with sweat. Abby was afraid he was going to pass out. If she had had a paper bag, she would have made him breathe into it.

"Well, of course, dear. You've done all of the work, it wouldn't be right for anyone else to do it."

Abby interrupted, extending her right hand. "Hi, Mrs. Hill. Remember me? Abby Sanders?"

"Of course, Abby! I could never forget young Ryan's sidekick. How is Jellybean?"

"He's spoiled rotten and settling in nicely. I don't know how I ever lived without him."

"Was it your idea to put a bow tie on Smokie and the pearls on Callie?"

"Yes, ma'am. This is a black tie event, so I thought they should be dressed for the occasion."

"It was brilliant! It's been a *huge* hit with the crowd."

Abby placed her hand on Mrs. Hill's arm and pulled her closer. "Ryan is more than a little nervous about all of this. Would it be okay if I do the intro? He'll be on the stage with me, but I'll do the talking." She glanced over her shoulder at her friend. "I think there will be less chance of projectile vomiting that way."

"Oh, dear. You may be right." Mrs. Hill peered closely at Ryan. "I've never actually seen someone turn green before. Why don't the two of you move toward the side of the stage? I'll cue you when it's your turn." She turned to plow her way to the front of the room and stopped. "And dear? You look lovely."

"Thank you." Abby slid her arm around Ryan's waist and pulled him into Mrs. Hill's wake. "C'mon, Obi Wan. It's almost over. All you have to do is stand beside me and look dashing in your tux. I'll do all the talking."

"You…will?"

"Sure. I don't have any problems talking in front of people."

"What are you, some sort of alien?"

"Nope, just a regular girl who is going to pull your rear out of the fire."

"Thanks, Padawan."

"Any time. Oops, there's our cue." Abby took his hand and started up the stairs. "Remember, I talk. You breathe."

"Breathing."

As they stepped onto the stage and into the spotlight, Abby raised her arm and waved to the crowd. "Good evening, ladies and gentlemen. Thank you so much for your presence and your support for Unconditional Love Animal Shelter. My friend here, Ryan McAllister, has a heart for homeless animals and filmmaking. He had a wonderful idea and combined his passions into the film you are about to see. Now, without further ado, I present *Paw Wars*."

As the crowd applauded, Abby steered Ryan off the stage and down the stairs as the lights dimmed and the movie began. They watched from the shadows at the edge of the room.

The crowd laughed as the electric sound of light sabers clashing filled the air. "Well, you were right." Abby leaned in, whispering in Ryan's ear. "I didn't believe that Jedi cats were really a thing. I guess I owe you twenty bucks."

"We'll discuss the terms of your surrender later." Ryan gestured to the crowd. "The important thing is that they're laughing in all the right places!"

"Of course they are! You're a genius." She slid her arm through his and leaned her head on his shoulder as the film continued.

As the credits rolled, Mrs. Hill took to the stage again. "That was wonderful! Please, everyone give a big round of applause to Ryan McAllister and Abby Sanders for this wonderful presentation." She pointed to their location and a spotlight searched them out, blinding them. They squinted and waved as Mrs. Hill continued. "Now, if anyone is interested in adopting any of the stars of our film, volunteers are waiting with applications at the back of the room."

The members of the crowd got to their feet, laughing and talking. A line of well-wishers formed, congratulating Ryan, asking about his inspiration, and what it was like filming with cats. Abby stepped to the side and watched. Unlike when he was on stage, he was in his element, talking about his two great loves.

"But, I couldn't have done it without Abby's help." He turned, searching for her, and smiled when their eyes met. He held out his hand, waiting. When she placed her hand in his, he pulled her to his side. "First, she rescued Lucas, the star of the film."

"Actually, Lucas rescued me—or tried to, at least."

"But, that's another story. I think we'll save it for the blooper reel. Believe me, we have *plenty* of outtakes."

The crowd thinned out and volunteers swarmed the room, beginning the cleanup process. Mrs. Hill bustled over, brimming with excitement. "Ryan, you did it! We've got multiple applications for all of the cats. I'm sure they will all be in their furever homes by the end of the week. Get it, *fur-ever*?" She giggled girlishly, her gray curls bouncing. "I can't wait to see what you come up with for us next!"

"Um, next?"

"Yes, dear. This was what you might call a rousing success and we have a lot more animals that need homes. The directors of several other shelters were here tonight and many of them expressed an interest in meeting with you. I think you might want to get some business cards, hon." She bustled away to oversee the cleanup crew.

"Business cards? Me?" Ryan looked more than a little flabbergasted when he turned to face Abby.

"See what happens when you find–and follow–your passion? I'm proud of you."

"Thanks. Are you ready to get out of here?"

"Sure. Where do you want to go?"

"Back to my place. You still owe me a game of *Massive Age of Dragons*."

"Well, then. What are we waiting for?"

o0o

Two hours later, Ryan crowed in triumph. "Did you see those Unnaturals run?" He turned to grin at Abby. He still wore his tux, but had loosened his tie and unbuttoned his collar. "I told you we would make a great team."

Abby had shed her funky purple shoes with the glittery kitten heels and sat on the all-purpose couch with her feet tucked under her. "Well, don't get ahead of yourself." She motioned to the screen. "These were just low-level flunkies. But yeah, between my spells and your sword, we will rule this virtual world." She held up her hand.

Ryan slapped his palm against hers in a high five, then waggled his eyebrows. "I've got a surprise for you."

"Really? I love surprises. Where is it?"

"Be right back." Ryan went to his bedroom and came back carrying Lucas. The cat opened his mouth in a silent meow of greeting.

"Lucas! Give me some paw." Abby held her hand out, palm up. Lucas patted her hand and chirruped. Abby scratched him behind the ears. "What's he doing here?"

"I decided to keep him."

"I'm so glad! I'm sure Jellybean will be, too. Is this my surprise?"

THE NERD IN SHINING ARMOR

"Only part of it. The rest is in here." Ryan held out a small white box. "It's from both Lucas and me."

Biting her lower lip in anticipation, Abby opened the box and removed a delicate gold chain with a small box-shaped pendant.

When Ryan reached over and pressed a recessed button, a familiar voice issued forth. "I'm here to rescue you."

"It's perfect—thank you! Would you mind?" Abby gestured toward her neck and turned her back toward Ryan, inviting him to put it on her. The brush of his skin against hers as he hooked the clasp and smoothed the links sent a shiver down her spine.

"Um, Abby?" Ryan placed his hands on her shoulders, turning her to face him. "I've got a question for you."

"What's up, Obi-Wan?"

Ryan ducked his head, looking up at Abby through his lashes. "I couldn't have finished this project on time without your help. You know that, right?"

"It was fun. I'm glad I got to be a part of it." She placed her hand on Ryan's knee and leaned forward so she could look him in the eyes. "I'm glad I got to know you."

"Same here. That's... sort of where my question comes in. It's been fun working with you and getting to know you. I've grown to treasure your friendship. I was wondering if you might be interested in taking our relationship to another level." He paused and swallowed. "I was wondering if you would like to be...my girlfriend?"

"Girlfriend, huh?" Abby sat back, grinning. "I don't know. Mrs. Hill called me your sidekick–that position probably comes with a cape. What do I get with the girlfriend gig?"

"How could a cape possibly compete with *this*?" Ryan stood and gestured from the top of his wavy hair to the soles of the sneakers he insisted on wearing with his tux. He gave her the lopsided grin she had come to adore. "What do you say?"

"Well..." Abby got to her feet and faced Ryan. She liked the fact that they were almost the same height. "I thought you'd never ask." She grabbed him by his collar and tugged, stopping his forward momentum with her lips. After a moment, she pulled away and looked him over with a newfound respect. "My, my. You have been hiding your light under a bushel, dear sir. You are quite the kisser."

"Well, I don't want to brag, but I *am* a man of many talents."

"Such as?"

"I can't just tell you all of my secrets. Where would be the fun in that?"

"True. But, don't worry. I'll get them out of you. Now, kiss me again."

"You sure about this?"

"Yes." Abby clutched the front of Ryan's shirt with one hand while sliding the other into his hair. "These are *definitely* the lips I've been looking for."

About the Author—Isabella Norse

Isabella Norse scored major "cool mom" points by playing the same video games as her sons and their friends. In these virtual worlds, she's slain demons and destroyed machines bent on galactic extermination while simultaneously wooing cocky assassins and sexy aliens. She fell in love with the make-believe worlds and rich characters that inhabited them and now writes her own tales of love, romance, and adventure.

Still a gamer–and still cool–Isabella lives in Georgia with her husband and a herd of rescue cats.

The Cat on Coogan's Bluff

Rochelle Spencer

A cranky detective uncovers secrets about baseball, Harlem, and cats.

All I wanted was a fish sandwich. I woke up hungry but didn't get time to eat until late—about four-thirty. After waiting so long, I needed something to saturate my arteries, so I went over to St. Nicholas and waited fifteen minutes while Fat Larry fried up lunch. By the time I'd found a park bench and unwrapped my sandwich, I was ready to chew my arm off.

"You Malik?" she stopped me mid-bite, in a voice that *told* me who I was instead of asking. The way she dressed matched the way she spoke. You'd glance at her, think: flowing skirt, locked hair—a free-spirited, bohemian sister. Then you noticed she'd coordinated everything. The cream-colored toe nails matched the cowrie shell in her hair; the handwoven purse went with the straw-colored weave in her sandals. She'd put time into her appearance, so if she looked carefree, she'd made an effort to appear that way.

"Yeah?"

"I need your help." The woman stared at a kid, about nine, smacking a half-deflated basketball with his palm. You could look at this woman and tell she didn't approve of the kid, somehow disliked his awkward dribbling, the flat, un-rhythmical thud of his hand meeting the ball.

"You don't know me."

The woman waited until the kid stumbled away before she answered. "I know your people. My family lived here before the neighborhood got gentrified. You went to school with Aeisha—my cousin. She told me all about you and the Island Kings."

"Which Aeisha?"

"Nelson."

I nodded, remembering. Aeisha Nelson had been a track star in high school, a member of the debate club. I'd heard a while back she'd become a lawyer and was raising money to run for state rep. But she'd never make it, smart as she was—too honest.

On the basis of the Aeisha connection, I asked the woman the code. She gave it to me without blinking.

"For adultery, petty theft, anything like that, twenty-five per hour." I wiped crumbs from my mustache with the one napkin not covered in fish grease. "No checks. No IOUs. No barter and no money orders, either—they just make people suspicious. Cash only. Most cases solved within forty-eight hours. Fee includes documentation—photographs, tapes, all the physical evidence you need to win in court. If he's cheating with anyone in the five boroughs, I'll track her down so you can beat her ass yourself."

"My man's not cheating. And don't you go worrying about money, I got plenty."

"I need the first five hours—one hundred twenty-five—upfront."

"There's a branch of my bank right around the corner."

"You're for real." I put down my newspaper and the remainder of the sandwich, and opened space for her to sit. "What's your story?"

"My name's Natalie Walker." Natalie tucked her skirt around her tightly, as though the bench could bite. "My grandfather passed away eight weeks ago."

"Condolences."

"Don't start. I don't need pity. I need help, and you're good at what you do. Also, you're discrete."

"Try to be."

"That matters, because no one in my family knows I'm here. Not even Aeisha." Natalie paused like she was waiting for me to disagree, warn her of the dangers of going up against family. "Nobody wants to talk about Granddaddy's death. They keep saying it's hard, but I need to go ahead and accept it. But some things, people shouldn't accept. Understand?"

I looked not at Natalie, but across the park, to where thick oak trees made the air cool and damp. A man my age walked from the park's shady side to the spot where concrete stairs soaked up sun. As he walked, the kid with the worn-out basketball ran toward him, his legs wobbling left, then right, in a shaky zig-zag. The man laughed, scooped the kid up under one arm. Something about the whole scene made my head hurt. I closed my eyes for a second.

"You heard what I said? I'm trying to give you a compliment." Natalie stared at me, and I wondered how long she'd been talking. She had eyes like Nadine's, my wife. Dark brown, and so narrow and slanted, it looked like she squinted at you.

"Do that after I solve the case." I returned her stare. Once again I was sharp, present, back to my old self. "How old was your grandfather at the time of death? What'd the coroner list under 'official cause'?"

"Granddaddy died just two weeks shy of his eighty-fifth birthday."

"So, natural causes?"

"They say old people have less balance, so they fall more easy. The coroner claims Granddaddy fell—hit his head a few hours before his death, and the internal bleeding caught up with him."

"But you don't believe him?"

"Since when do our people believe everything some random white man tells us?" Natalie shook her head to show how idiotic she found this idea. "I haven't been in my grandfather's life much in the past couple of years, but he was my heart, and I know something's not right. Aeisha's always going on about you, saying you're Superman, the way you cleaned this neighborhood up—"

"That was back in the day."

"People still remember what you did. And the truth is, I know who killed Granddaddy, but I need evidence. You can get it."

She paused and turned to me again with her upturned eyes, stared at me so hard I couldn't look away. At that moment, I realized just how much she reminded me of Nadine; she had that way of looking at you so it felt like the whole world was trapped behind her irises. "I respect you, but this neighborhood has had more than one hero. My grandfather was the type to make everyone realize how strong they could be. But our people get jealous of that kind of power. So just because Granddaddy was old, don't mean he didn't have enemies."

"Seriously? You really believe your grandfather was murdered?"

Natalie didn't answer, but reached into her bag and took out a yellow newspaper clipping from the *Amsterdam News*. Her grandfather was in a baseball uniform. The words "Rube Walker Brings Championship to New York" hung over his face. Rube Walker may have been trapped inside a fading picture, but you felt power emanating from him just from the way he held his bat.

"My grandfather was a star player for the New York Cubans, one of the old Negro league teams. And yes he was murdered—murdered by his old rival and former teammate."

o0o

It'd been a long time since I'd had a murder case. But I couldn't tell Natalie no. Besides, while I'd always been more of a basketball than baseball fan, this case was about more than a game. It was about preserving something left behind, something in danger of being forgotten. That's why Natalie had come to see me. And that's why, two hours later, I found myself back in my office, creating spreadsheets and googling the hell out of the New York Cubans and the Cleveland Buckeyes, their main competition.

Nadine walked in during the middle of the search. She brushed her tongue against my ear, laughed when I jumped.

"Hey." I pulled her into my lap.

"Who stepping out?" Nadine nodded at the spreadsheet.

"Not that kind of case. Woman says her grandfather's been murdered."

"Mudah?" Nadine's surprise made her accent slip out. When I'd met her ten years ago at the Royal Peacock in Atlanta, I'd wondered where she was from. It wasn't Trinidad, Barbados, or Jamaica. I couldn't place her accent, which frustrated me because that was one of my talents—I could locate people by voice. You could tell me you were born and raised in Brooklyn, and I'd tell you the exact neighborhood. So, after five dances and a couple of rum punches, I finally broke down and asked. Maybe it was the rum punch, the fact that dancing so tightly together had made us both a little woozy, but when she answered, "Nevis, an island so small you can walk it in a day," I not only believed her, I felt like I'd lived there my entire life.

"Her grandfather was Rube Walker, a player for the Cubans, New York's Negro League team," I explained. "This guy, Terry Bunch, played against him on the Cleveland Buckeyes before getting traded to the Cubans. When Bunch joined the team, Martin Dihigo, the Cubans' best player, was considering retirement, and Bunch and Walker, being young and ambitious, competed for the fans' attention. They ended up with a sort of old-school Jeter and A-Rod competition going on. Natalie—that's the client—thinks Bunch killed her grandfather."

"Rivalry to last more than fifty years? Nuh, don't believe it."

"Happens. Just last week I read about two old men, how anthropologists wanted them to have a conversation. Now, these two the only folks left on earth still speaking this ancient language, but they hate each other so much they won't talk to each other. Same with Bunch and Walker. They hated each other all their lives. They both played for the Cubans, and briefly, for the Giants. They never got paid much, but their reputations opened up financial opportunities. So, Bunch and Walker competed to have the best stats and the most fans."

"What you say make sense. But after they leave baseball, what good it do to keep competition going?"

"That's the problem. More animosity developed when their careers ended, because, literally, they no longer played for the same team. After they retired, they used name recognition to start almost identical businesses. Bunch sold hamburgers on one thirty-sixth. A couple of blocks over, Walker opened a BBQ joint. They even had kids around the same time. Their kids kept things going by having children—granddaughters—born the same year."

I paused because Nadine had wrapped her face in my shirt, her body erupting in a sound that could have been a laugh or a cry. I patted her back, considered for the hundredth time whether her small size had something to do with the way I could never read her. Because a smaller person's body is more physically visible to others, they find new ways of hiding themselves. With Nadine, she's developed this way of looking as though she could, at any moment, take off and fly. Like you could be having a conversation with her, blink, and suddenly she wouldn't be there.

"You alright?"

Nadine didn't answer but leaped from my lap.

"You making plans to solve this?" She spoke with her back to me, and then I knew for sure she'd been crying. And though I knew she'd been asking about the Walker case, it was like she discussed us, the one thing that kept our five-year marriage from being perfect.

"Headed there first thing tomorrow," I answered. "Got to find out what Bunch has to say."

"Not a lot of new clients coming in, so Jina say she give me some time off," Nadine said softly. "Tomorrow, you finish up early and we meet for lunch? A picnic?"

"I want to, baby, but I got forty-eight hours. There's not enough time."

"You're right. There's not," Nadine said. "There never is."

She walked inside the bathroom, shut the door behind her.

o0o

My business has to be run a certain way. If you're the neighborhood detective, not everyone can know who you are. In fact, the fewer people who know what you do, the better you do your job. That's why I operate on referrals and why the 48-hour turnaround policy is for my clients as much as it is myself. Clients like it because they get useful information quickly. I like it because the longer a case drags out, the more questions get asked. In my line of work, you don't want too many people asking questions.

I've got to be especially careful because of how I look. People never believe there's a reason for a six-two, two hundred pound black man to just hang out in their neighborhood—and that includes other six-two, two hundred pound black men. So, if I know I'm going to hang out somewhere for a while, I wear a disguise. When I say disguise, I don't mean funny mustaches and glasses. I'm talking about the ability to adapt a persona, make people think you are whoever they want you to be. I've lived in this neighborhood for years, but with the right prop, I won't get recognized. Ever read Ellison's *Invisible Man*? If so, you understand what I'm saying, and realize Ellison got at least one thing right: every once in a while, being invisible has its advantages.

The morning I started the Walker case, I threw on a Yankees hat that made it hard to get a feel for the exact shape of my face. Then, I put on glasses, because glasses make it hard for people to see the person wearing them. The final touch? A camera, a small but useful item, in my car trunk. These days, when people see cameras and think there's even a possibility of their picture being taken, the person holding the camera gains instant invisibility. All people can think about is their own image being projected. Cameras are the closest thing in the world to an invisible cloak.

But useful as cameras can be, I needed a ruse for carrying one in this neighborhood; Manhattan doesn't get many tourists past 96th street. Bunch lived just a few blocks away from me, and the neighborhood's faded glamour—all kinds of notables (W.E.B. DuBois, Ella Fitzgerald, Malcolm X) had lived on the same street—loaned itself to the film industry. So, I posted flyers around the street corner about a film shoot. "Scouting locations for a new film by Spike Perry," the flyer read. "Will pay small fee if your home is chosen." The flyer listed a number that redirected messages to my voice mail. And as people, some in suits and others in uniforms, trickled out of their apartments, they stared at those flyers and smiled. People, no matter who they are, see their lives as big and inherently cinematic. No one thought it strange that Spike Perry, whose films were all based in Atlanta, had decided to shoot in Harlem.

Also, I hadn't lied to Nadine when I told her I was going over to Terry Bunch's first thing in the morning. I parked across from his apartment at 5:00 a.m., two hours before morning rush began. People up that early are the industrious—morning runners whose feet pound pavement while the rest of the city snores, commuters who fight sleep as they force themselves to be on time for jobs that will hopefully lead to a better life. If you want to hide, the best time is early in the morning, when people are too concerned with their own lives to ask a lot of questions.

A couple of individuals came and left, but nothing interesting happened until a woman walked out of Bunch's building at half-past six. She was different from the others who'd walked out of the squat, grayish-blue building. Like the other residents, she moved not briskly, but determinedly, carrying her bags as though they'd already grown heavy but she knew there was no way of lightening her load. What made her different was she had a sharpness—a *meanness*—they hadn't possessed. Sleepiness had wiped all anger from the early morning commuters' faces and replaced it with just one emotion: exhaustion. But that wasn't true for this woman; you could look at her, at her thin hair pulled into a tight, greasy ponytail, and tell she'd started the day with a chip on her shoulder.

I wondered if I had seen this woman earlier, when I'd first noticed a fluttering in the window of the sixth floor of Bunch's building. The curtain had opened and closed quickly, but the feeling someone was watching me hadn't left. The woman—who stomped, rather than walked, down the street—had a thin, almost athletic body. I mentally replaced her white nursing uniform with a baseball one and wondered if she could be Bunch's granddaughter. Natalie had told me her name was Taneika.

If Taneika had been watching me, I had to get out of there pronto. And even if this woman wasn't related to Bunch, I'd been stagnant for too long. Now was a good time to get coffee somewhere nearby.

I stopped at a place a block from Bunch's building. "Jake's Coffee" had a sign hanging in the window that read "Special: egg and cheese on a roll 1.50" but Jake's interior smelled of bacon more than coffee. Only one person ate; the other customers clutched their coffees as though the best bagel in the world couldn't get them to let go.

There were a couple of tables, but most folks sat at the counter, copies of the *Amsterdam News* or the *Post* unfolded in front of them. I picked a stool and ordered coffee and the special. When the waitress set my egg-and-cheese down, I asked the guy next to me for ketchup.

"You like ketchup on your eggs?" The man looked as amused as a person could be before seven a.m. He wore a threadbare, ill-fitting gray suit. With his lined face and close-cropped hair two shades lighter than the suit, he looked retirement age, too old to be heading in for work. I wondered why he was up so early.

"Must be from the south. That's how people do down that ways." The man on my left wasn't any younger, but was also a working man. He wore a light blue uniform, the logo of a company I had never heard of—"Bretson"—on the chest.

"Just moved up from Atlanta, College Park area," I lied.

"That near the airport?" The man in the Bretson uniform sized me up, looked like he tried to see past my baseball cap and thick glasses. For a moment, I wondered if he recognized me. In any case, I continued with my lie, pretended it hadn't been ten years since I'd left the south.

"Yeah," I nodded. "I'm staying with family now, but I want my own place. Maybe even in this neighborhood. They say rent's cheap at the Chavet. Heard of it?"

The Chavet was the name of Bunch's building. It'd been on the street for years, and even though these two men were twenty years or so younger than Walker or Bunch, if they'd lived in the neighborhood for any amount of time, they knew something about it.

"Nice building, good super but—" the Bretson man stopped talking and looked like he didn't want to continue. I sipped and nodded, creating enough pause in the conversation that someone had to fill in. The man on my right did the job.

"Otis here don't want to say," the man spoke slowly. "And don't neither of us know how bad your family's been working your nerves, but dealing with them's better than heading to the Chavet. A man died there a couple months back."

"So what? People die. Life happens," I said.

"Not like this," the man in the gray suit continued. "Twenty years ago, when the city was at its worst, violence happened on the street, never inside somebody's home. Not how it happened this time around. They saying this guy Walker—he the one lived over in the Chavet—died of a bad fall. But I don't believe it."

"Me, neither." Otis nodded so vigorously his coffee cup shook with the movement.

"What do you think happened?" As soon as I asked the question, three other men came in. They were young, my age, the age a person should be working, but it was as obvious that they weren't as it was that the two men I talked to were. But if they weren't going in to work, why get up so early? Where were they headed? From the corner of my eye, I watched them bellow their orders to the waitress and sit down at one of Jake's few tables.

"Back in the day, Walker owned this neighborhood." As the man in the gray suit spoke, he also watched the men, much more obviously than I had. The moment they walked in, his whole demeanor had changed, from mild amusement at seeing me pour ketchup on my eggs to something that could almost be described as fear.

"Now, Frank, get the story straight," Otis interrupted.

"Well, alright." Frank made an effort to focus back on the conversation with Otis and me. "It was him and another fellow named Bunch. They played ball together. They'd been neighborhood heroes ever since the New York Cubans won the Negro Leagues Championship in '48."

"'47," Otis corrected. "But go on."

Frank ignored him; his eyes were focused on the table in front of us. The waitress had brought back the orders, and as the men ate, they were getting rowdier and more relaxed.

"I said, go on, Frank."

"I'm not your boy. I don't got to take orders from nobody, 'specially you." Frank's words to Otis were more irritated than angry, and it was clear his heart wasn't in anything he said to us. He was a computer, relaying information; he'd directed his real attention to the table in front of us.

"Couple of years ago," he continued, "the baseball commissioner decided to honor some of the old Negro players like Bunch and Walker. For a while, there was all kinds of fuss. People got interested in these men again and what they had to say."

"Saw them all over the local TV," Otis nodded.

"That, and they got big plaques in their honor. Some big-time writer wanted to write a book about their lives. And people in the neighborhood got to talking about all the investments they'd made over the years," Frank paused, and for a few seconds, diverted his attention from the table and back towards me. He gave me a long, searching look. "Wouldn't surprise me if some young-gun decided to break in and steal Walker's stuff, hurt him when he tried to fight back."

"Even at his age, he the type wouldn't go down without a fight," Otis agreed.

Something about Otis's words brought Frank out of whatever trance he'd been in. He got up abruptly, shoving his plate and a couple of dollars at the waitress.

"I got to head on in. Nice talking with you," he told me. "And, you, I'll catch on up with you later on" he nodded at Otis and gave one last parting glance at the table, which had gotten so loud, it had made the half-empty restaurant sound crowded.

"Don't mind him," Otis told me after his friend had left. "He had a bad scare a couple of years back. A couple of these youngsters held him up, jumped him. A hold-up can make any man feel powerless, but it's worse when you get to be our age, and you start to losing your strength, your desire for women, all those things that make you feel like a man."

I thought of the woman I'd seen earlier this morning and decided to broach the subject. "Did Bunch have any children or grandchildren? What kind of people were they?"

"Maybe I shouldn't be saying this, but since you walked in, you struck me as an alright fellow. So here it is—Bunch's granddaughter ran with a rough crowd. She's got a temper, and that boyfriend of hers can't be trusted. Seems the police need to pay more attention to the possibility of theft."

What Otis said wasn't surprising—when I'd researched the case the night before, I'd found some recent press coverage. If Natalie was right about her grandfather not dying from natural causes, then one possibility was that someone had recognized the value of Walker's rare baseball memorabilia, broken in the apartment, and injured Walker along the way. The only problem with this theory was there'd been no reports of a break-in and Walker's injury supposedly happened between five and seven p.m. Who'd steal from a place in the early evening, in a small building where most residents knew each other and would be coming in from their jobs?

"I better get headed to work," I said. I started to stand, but sat back down as though considering a new possibility. "But thanks for the information. Don't know if I want to move to a place with a lot of break-ins. Don't need the stress...In any case, you sure about the break-in? Anyone tell you about Walker being robbed?"

"No one said a durn thing. But something's missing—that baseball plaque they gave him. Could be worth a few thousands."

The table behind us got quiet and looked up at the word "thousands." When they looked up, I saw how young they were. They weren't my age, as I'd first thought, but a good eight or ten years younger, and only seemed older in the harsh early morning light. As they looked at us, I realized it was the first time they seemed to be aware that someone else existed in the restaurant other than themselves, and the waitress who they saw as someone whose purpose in life was to serve them. That was the problem with this generation—with most people, really. It wasn't that they were necessarily bad, but they were self-involved. Nothing mattered except for their own needs.

"You sure about that?" I spoke softly, but now that the table was quiet, the place was so quiet that if a pin had dropped, it would have had an explosion-worthy echo.

"Listen, years after Walker retired from baseball, that plaque was all he talked about. Last I saw him, he said he wanted to be buried with it, but that wasn't the case when he was put to rest. I know, because I was there. And the only way he would have been buried without that plaque is if somebody stole it."

o0o

I went back to my car and took out the camera, before walking into to Bunch's building. I managed to slip inside the building as a well-dressed woman was leaving. My camera made her turn around.

"You—you with *la caméra*," the woman said. Her "you" sounded like "ooh," and her pronunciation vaguely French. "I am Lela Cécile Michèle Thérésa Monet. I see flyer. You look to shoot *le film*, no?"

"I'm in the process of looking—" I began, but Ms. Monet grabbed my wrist. She dragged me into to the elevator and began talking nonstop.

"You visit *mon appartement, oui?* You like. Of course you like. I danced with Mademoiselle Josephine Baker. Also Dunham! *Appartement es magnifique!*"

Ms. Monet's apartment was *magnifique*. Plush rugs thick as fingers and everything in it—couch, walls, chairs, tables—a glaring white. In the brightness of Ms. Monet's apartment, I got a good look at her. She appeared to be in her late sixties with sand-colored skin and a wig that was too "poofy" for her head. Her satin dress, tied tightly at the waist, was the same glistening white as her apartment. But, with one movement, she loosened the belt, and the dress collapsed to the floor. Ms. Monet stood in front of me in a white slip.

"Lady, I'm married."

"*Oui?* Your wife has good taste." She nibbled on my ear, Nadine's signature gesture. Very pleasurable from Nadine, but disturbing from a woman *not* Nadine. "The place—you like? Me? You like?"

Ms. Monet's skin was wrinkled, but she'd maintained the bone structure of great beauties. Her cheekbones arched up towards her eyes, which sparkled with intelligence.

"You're a nice-looking lady. But like I said, I'm married."

"True filmmaker recognize talent," she pouted and sank onto her couch. "You not real filmmaker."

"And you're not really French."

"How you know?"

I explained that something about the way she spoke French reminded me of the odd way some people spoke Spanish. "If I had to guess, I'd say you were from the D.R."

Ms. Monet sighed. "Alright, yes, I'm Dominican. When I lived on the island, I picked up French from my Haitian neighbors. But for years, I told everybody I was from the south of France. Life sounded more romantic that way. Can you really fault an old lady for trying to distinguish herself with a bit of French flair?"

I nodded, finding her intriguing and a bit silly all at once.

"And you? You know my secrets, but who do *you* pretend to be?"

"I'm not a location scout," I admitted. "I just want to find out more about Terry Bunch. He may be able to tell me about Walker's death."

Ms. Monet didn't react the way I thought she would. I thought my confession would make her more forthcoming, but instead, she reached for her dress. "I should put my clothes back on," she muttered.

"You know something, don't you?"

"Go talk to Terry. He lives right below and he's most likely home—he doesn't go out much, anymore. That's the life of an old man. Not that'd you know about that. You can't be much older than thirty, if you've made it that far."

"So, he's home a lot. What else do you know, Ms. Monet? We're two people who like to pretend with other folks, so we might as well be real with each other."

Ms. Monet slithered back into her dress before sitting down again. I noticed a small golden locket around her neck. In the locket, instead of a picture of a sweetheart or a child, was a beautiful snow-white Persian with bright blue eyes.

"Roquefere," she said, after she noticed I was watching. "He died a few weeks ago."

I nodded, waiting.

"Roquefere—probably the only male who ever loved me, and he couldn't talk," she began. "I had an affair—with Rube, and later, with Terry. Don't look at me like that. Both affairs went on for years, but it was never about me. It was their stupid rivalry. I see that, now."

"Was Rube with you the day before he died?"

"No. Rube lived a block away. He'd come over once a month for an afternoon poker game against Terry, and some of their friends. Twenty years ago, Rube took his second wife, and things slowed down with him and me."

"Did Rube's wife know of the affair?"

"How could she not? She knew what it meant to marry a local celebrity. I remember she met me once, at a party. It was obvious she didn't like me. I was wearing a yellow dress Rube had bought me, and wearing it well—in those days, I was something else. Fifteen years younger than Terry or Rube, and quite a beauty. You know, the dress was far from the only thing Rube got me—for years, they competed with gifts. They competed so well, I really thought it was all about me."

"What happened that night?

"Come." Ms. Monet walked over to a large window that overlooked the street. Ms. Monet's apartment wasn't very high—the entire building was only six stories tall—but the window was so wide she had an expansive view of Harlem. I could see my car, Jackie Robinson Park, Jake's Coffee Shop, and most importantly, all the people who entered and left the building. "Rube had a quiet, almost peaceful, nature. He was much less competitive than Terry, who kind of spurred the whole thing along. That afternoon, Terry won a lot of Rube's money in the poker game. And because Rube didn't have much left, he ended up gambling away his plaque."

"The one given to him by the commissioner?"

Ms. Monet nodded. "It was identical to Terry's, but that didn't matter. It was the principle of the matter. Terry made Rube walk back home, pick up the plaque, and bring it to him. On his way back to Terry's, Rube was so upset, he rang my door and asked if I would speak to Terry, try to get him to change his mind. I was trying to listen to Rube, but I got a call from my sister. And because I hadn't spoken to her in weeks and was worried about her, it wasn't like I could hang up as soon as I picked up the phone. But when I took my sister's call, Rube got angry and left my place in a huff. He slammed the door behind him and scared little Roquefere so bad he fell out the window."

"That's what killed your cat?"

Ms. Monet nodded. "Three weeks ago—that was the last time I saw Roquefere *and* Rube. From here, I saw Rube stumbling out of the building. He was being followed by a bunch of young hoodlums."

o0o

It was still early, about nine-thirty, when I left Ms. Monet's apartment and headed to Bunch's. I knocked on the door. It took three knocks for him to answer.

When Bunch finally came to the door, I saw why he and Rube Walker had carried on with mistresses and poker games like men decades younger: the agility they'd achieved as former athletes hadn't quite left. When Bunch answered the door, his back was straight and he didn't shuffle; though from the way he peered at my face, it was obvious he couldn't see well.

"What you need, son?" The door cracked open, and you could smell the dusty, closed-in scent of his apartment.

"Heard about the movie shoot?"

"Can't say that I have."

"There's flyers posted all around the building."

"I ain't been down yet." Bunch started to close the door, but I blocked it with my shoulder.

"I'm scouting locations for a new Spike Perry movie. Alright if I come in, have a look around? I promise not to take too long."

"No," Bunch began pushing the door again. "Them films a disgrace to the race."

I tried one last tactic. "Your friend Ms. Monet doesn't think so. She said your place has good light."

"Lela recommended you?" Bunch smiled for the first time. "Guess I can let you in a while."

"Mind if I take your picture?" I set up my camera in the far end of the room, the one closest to the window. "See how this light looks against an actual body?"

Bunch sat down on a ripped, leather couch. I noticed that while Monet's apartment couldn't have been more maintained, Bunch's had a shabby look—newspapers piled in corners, a grayish-green curtain draped over a window as though it'd been placed there by accident. "Been over a year since I had my picture taken."

"Why's that?"

"Baseball commissioner decided to honor some of us old ball players. We was in all the local papers."

"How long did you play?" I tried to look nonchalant.

"Started when I was nineteen, right before the majors got integrated. Played with Satchel Paige, and my team—the Cubans—won the Negro World Series in '47. I like to think I had something to do with that." Bunch smiled, then kneeled down next to my camera, inspecting the tripod. "Can't be easy carrying this thing along, 'specially in this heat. Care for some water?"

"That would hit the spot," I said.

Bunch nodded and walked into the kitchen.

"Heard about one of your teammates—a Ray Walker? He just passed away?"

"Not Ray, Rube. That old son of a gun!" Two cups of ice water shook in Bunch's hands. There was anger there, but something else, something I couldn't place until finally, it came to me. *It was pride.* The rivalry, the memory of it, was what was keeping Bunch alive. I saw how much he wanted to talk about this, and I felt bad for bothering him, bad for deceiving him.

Bunch handed me the water and watched as I drained the glass.

"I'd better get on," I said. "Go through the rest of these locations before it gets too hot."

"I like talking to you. Come back," Bunch said. "On another day when the heat's less."

"I will," I said—and meant it.

o0o

As I walked out the building, I ran into the young woman who'd been watching me earlier. She was wearing her nurse's uniform, but she didn't appear concerned about anyone's health—least of all, her own. She was smoking, and smoking hard.

"You ain't no damn location scout for no film," she said to me. "Don't nobody care about this place."

"You'd be surprised," I paused on the sidewalk. "There's history here."

"You spoke to my granddaddy? That's about all the history left in this building. And that ain't much." The woman blew smoke at the sky.

"What made your grandfather so special?"

"Played baseball. Everybody in this neighborhood knew him."

"You must be proud."

The woman, I now knew, was Taneika. She nodded in response.

"You a nurse?"

"Home care assistant. Not a real nurse. Don't have time for all that. I wash them, clean up their mess. Film *that* with your little camera. Working ten to six every day, making almost no money—"

"Can't be that bad—you get breaks. Looks like you're on one now."

"For what? Five minutes? Ten? Whenever this arbitrary lady decides she'll let me get some air?"

An ice cream truck pulled up in front of the building, and its sing-songy tune interrupted our conversation.

"Too early for some ice cream," Taneika complained, but I realized she sounded wistful, not angry. "It's not even lunch yet."

Early as it was, a few kids clamored around the truck. Only one kid didn't; he was on a bicycle, moving around the truck in wobbly, unsteady circles. His movements reminded me of the little boy I'd seen yesterday with the basketball. But instead of looking carefree like the other kid, this one looked industrious, focused.

"I got to go back and check on this woman. But before you leave here, you make sure you talk to my granddaddy," Taneika said as she put out her cigarette and stomped back down the street.

The moment she was out of sight, I walked over to the boy on his bike.

"Want to make some money, kid?"

"How much? I don't do anything for less than five dollars."

I handed him a ten, scribbled a message, and waited for the sparks to fly.

o0o

Coogan's Bluff is a dim reminder of what it once was. It's hard to believe some of the world's most famous baseball games were played here. Now, sixty years after the Cubans played there, the place is overrun with trees and weeds, and almost always deserted, though it's not exactly a wildlife refuge. I stared at the scattered trash—soda cans, candy bar wrappers— pressed into the overgrown grass as I watched the killer walk into partial view.

The kid on the bike had earned his ten bucks. It was all falling into place now, with the message I'd given to him to deliver.

"How did you know?" she asked simply. She was close enough to me to be heard, but her face and body were obscured by a few tall trees.

"I didn't want it to be you, but you made it easy, Ms. Monet." I stared at her closely. From the shady place where she was standing, it was hard to tell if she had a gun in her hands, but she was definitely holding something. "I could tell from the way you described Rube's personality that you were in love with him, even though his passion had slowed over the years, and he wanted to break it off with you. But, you're a bit of a narcissist, and you couldn't take it.

"When Rube came over to tell you it was over, you were livid. I suspect that you didn't lie about your sister calling—she did—but that wasn't the reason Rube walked out of your house in a huff. When your sister called, she spoke with you in Spanish—your native language—but Rube had played with Dihigo, who was Cuban, and Satchel Paige, who had played in the Dominican Republic, and other players who spent years playing in the Dominican Republic. I think you told your sister— in Spanish—that you were going to harm Rube's wife. But he understood enough of what you were saying that he got upset and left your house to warn her. You were angry that not only was Rube breaking up with you, but he was also protecting his wife, so you banged him on the head with his plaque just as he was leaving."

"You think you're so clever," Ms. Monet said, and as she spoke, the sun moved from behind a cloud. I saw the black steel in her hand.

"These were all just guesses until I thought about what you said about the cat. You said when Rube left your apartment, his loudness disturbed your cat so much that it jumped out the window. I'd read that white cats with blue eyes are usually deaf, but then I thought it was possible your cat felt the vibrations, and again, I wanted to believe you—until I realized there was no way your cat died from that fall. Cats have a terminal velocity that's different from humans."

"What does that mean?"

"Their bone structure allows them to fall more slowly, and from a short building like this one, your cat would have survived. When Rube left your apartment, he was stunned and bleeding from the head, and he stumbled around a bit outside, probably sat down on the ground somewhere. Your cat was the feline Lassie, and fond as it was after years of seeing Rube, jumped out to comfort him. In the process, the cat got Rube's red blood all over its white fur. When you came down to check on your cat, you realized that Rube was in bad shape. But rather than help him out, you picked up your cat and decided to get rid of him as efficiently as possible—and because you knew that there was a risk of getting the blood from the cat all over your white apartment, you went to the nearest animal shelter and claimed to have found an abandoned cat.

"In the meanwhile, Rube stumbled home and died a couple of hours later, and the coroner attributed the head injury to the kind of falls that happen to a man his age. But that's not what happened, is it Ms. Monet?"

She shook her head. "When I looked at the message that you sent to me—when I saw that the number from the animal shelter was the same place where I had dropped off little Roquefere—I knew you knew. So, how much do you want? I don't have much, just little trinkets that Rube and Terry gave me over the years. But you can have all of that. Look, it works for you: you can either forget what you know and get paid, or remember, and get killed."

Ms. Monet raised the gun towards me, but before she could shoot, one of New York's Finest grabbed her. In the second before she tumbled to the ground, she somehow looked more glamorous than ever as she held the black gun in arms covered by a snow-white coat.

After the police carried Ms. Monet away, I called Nadine. Summer was almost over, and there wouldn't be many warm days left.

"Nadine…hi, honey. About that picnic? Will you meet me for lunch—right over at the Jackie Robinson Park? No, don't worry about packing anything—I'll stop by Fat Larry's. He makes the best fish sandwiches anywhere.

"What about your case?" she asked, still a little miffed.

I smiled, thinking of the ear nibbling Ms. Monet who I'd caught in the end, and felt a deep satisfaction in a job well-done, once more.

"I wrapped it up. Now, it's time for us." I couldn't wait to tell her all about the cat on Coogan's Bluff…and how he'd helped catch his mistress who'd murdered a baseball star.

About the Author—Rochelle Spencer

Rochelle Spencer is co-editor of *All About Skin: Short Fiction by Women Writers of Color* (University of Wisconsin Press, 2014) and her work appears in several publications including *Poets and Writers*, *Callaloo*, *The African American Review*, *Publishers Weekly*, *The Rumpus*, *The Ascentos Review*, *Mosaic Literary Magazine*, and the *Crab Creek Review*, which nominated her nonfiction for an Editor's Choice Award and a Pushcart Prize. Rochelle is a former Board Member of the Hurston-Wright Foundation, a founding member of the Harlem Works Collective, and a member of the Wintergreen Writers Collective and the National Book Critics Circle.

Missing Lynx

Clay More

A supernatural feline murder mystery tale from the silent movie era.

1

Manhattan, New York
August 24, 1926

Her whole life changed when Rudolph Valentino died.

And judging by the throngs of people who had lined every spare foot of the streets along the way and the mountain of roses that were strewn about the bier as the cortege made its slow progress up West 49th Street in Broadway, it was clear that thousands of other women also felt that their lives had been irretrievably changed. They sobbed and wailed at the knowledge that the light had gone out of those magnificent sultry eyes that they had seen so often on the silver screen. They felt robbed of the love that could never be, of the caress that could never be felt or the kiss that would have stolen their hearts.

Valentino, the Latin Lover was gone at just thirty-one years of age, struck down with peritonitis and taken from the world of his adoring public.

Kay du Maurier was there for the funeral mass at Saint Malachy's Roman Catholic Church along with her husband, Colonel Fenton Carlyle and her sister, Blanche Fleming. In any other gathering, the three would have stood out; yet, here at Rudolph's farewell, they were but three among the glittering firmament that had gathered to pay their respects. Clara Bow, Douglas Fairbanks, and Irving Berlin were there, along with an entourage of lesser stars, all standing shoulder-to-shoulder with Rudolph's family, offering what comfort they could to them. Most visible, however, dressed in black with a felt capeline hat and the cleverest of gossamer veils that highlighted rather than obscured her weeping face, was the distraught Pola Negri. She wore a blood-red rose, which matched the thousands of others that surrounded the white blooms that spelled out POLA, that she had arranged to travel in the hearse with his coffin.

Everyone had heard how she had collapsed over his coffin at the funeral home and had to be helped to her car by one of the four men in black uniforms, supposedly sent as a guard of honor by Benito Mussolini, the prime minister of Italy, his land of birth. And then, on seeing his coffin at the actual mass in church, she had fainted again.

Kay watched the fuss being made of her this time, and felt a wave of nausea almost overcome her. Her heart started to race, and she reached out and clutched her husband's arm. He responded by patting the back of her hand and giving her one of his sympathetic smiles. He raised an eyebrow quizzically.

"I am fine," she whispered. "I just…just feel a little queasy."

He nodded, sure that it was simply the emotion of the event.

Fighting back the sickness, Kay pursed her lips in scorn. Pola's faints could not have been any more melodramatic if Cecil B. DeMille or George Melford had been shooting a scene with her.

"She's sticking to her story," Blanche whispered at her side.

"What story?" Fenton asked, craning his head slightly toward his sister-in-law.

"I told you, darling," Kay said, wafting her face with the collar of her lynx fur coat. She was aware that fur in August would be hot, but she felt she had to wear it that day. "She's telling everyone that not only had they made up, but Rudolph proposed to her last week."

"She's staking her claim on his fortune," agreed Blanche, looking directly at him with her good eye, as she adjusted the jewel-encrusted eye patch that she famously wore over her right eye. "She has told the press that she was going to be the third Mrs. Valentino."

Fenton's moustache bristled. "Humph! When I was in Africa, I read an article in a week-old copy of the *Chicago Tribune* about Pink Powder Puffs. All that make-up he wore—they say it's making men effeminate. Apparently, some public men's room had a face-powder dispenser installed, because chaps want to look like him. And I read another article that said his two marriages were 'lavender marriages', meaning he was covering stuff up. Apparently, he loved cats and let them run free in his apartments."

Missing Lynx

Kay unconsciously stroked her lynx fur and felt another wave of nausea.

"Are you sure you are all right, darling?" Fenton asked. "You look flustered. Do you want to take that cat fur off?"

She shook her head. "I'm fine, really."

Blanche leaned toward Fenton. "And did you read that he challenged the reporter, who hadn't the courage to name himself, to a boxing match?" she whispered.

"That's right, darling," Kay added, forcing the nausea down. "He was having boxing lessons from Jack Dempsey, the world heavyweight champion."

Fenton shook his head. "I never heard about that. You don't always get the American newspapers in Kenya."

"Well, he didn't fight the reporter," Kay went on, "but he *did* fight Buck O'Neil, the sportswriter, on top of the Ambassador Hotel. He knocked him down and O'Neil apologized for an article he had written."

Fenton clicked his tongue. "So, maybe Pola Negri wasn't going to be just another lavender wife."

They saw the actress in question sobbing loudly, her shoulders heaving up and down theatrically. Doug Fairbanks laid a comforting hand on her shoulder.

Kay hated Pola Negri more than anything at that moment. There she was, playing the role of the tragic widow—or the tragic *nearly* widow. She had no doubt that Pola would capitalize on Rudolph's death to further her career, just as she had used her first marriage to a Polish count to boost her pedigree.

Pola was famously allergic to cats, so if she had her way and somehow inherited Rudolph's fortune, his beautiful cats would go; which meant that Kay wouldn't see them or his apartment again.

She thought of Alfonso the Persian beauty that Rudolph had secretly given her just three months ago, when Fenton was off on one of his big game hunts in Africa. And a week later, he had given her the lynx fur coat. Both were tokens of their very secret love affair. A love affair that no one could ever know about.

Her heart ached for him, but at least she would always have those links with him.

The noise of the wailing crowds of mourners outside the church filtered through, threatening to drown the voices of the choristers.

"Well, he certainly seems to have had his fan club," Fenton remarked.

"Everyone loved him, Fenton," Kay whispered, aware of the quaking of her voice.

"That's right," said Blanche, closely watching her sister. "We *all* loved Rudolph."

o0o

Kay du Maurier and her sister, Blanche Fleming, were born in Massachusetts to Scottish immigrant mill-workers, called Finlay and Flora McDonald. Morag, who would, in later years, change her name to Blanche, was the eldest by two years and was always the practical one. Their father died from lung disease when Blanche was ten, only to be followed six months later by their mother, from a broken heart. From that moment, Blanche became the mother hen to little sister Isabel, who would also later have her name changed to Kay.

The girls worked in the mills and dreamed of escaping from the life of drudgery to become actresses. It was only when Blanche reached the age of seventeen and tragically lost the vision in her right eye in an accident at the mill that she seriously planned to change their lives.

Once her eye healed, they used their meager inheritance and all that they had managed to scrimp together over the years and boarded a train for New York. There, both being strikingly good-looking despite the eye patch that Blanche took to wearing, they managed to get jobs in vaudeville, first as background dancers, then as a song and dance duo, the McDonald Sisters.

Fortune smiled on them when they were spotted by Florenz Ziegfeld who hired them to become Ziegfeld girls in his famous Ziegfeld Follies. Under the tutelage of Anna Held, Florenz's Polish-French wife, they became skilled and admired showgirls. Both could dance well, but Kay with her copper locks and green cat-like eyes had that extra something—timing. Blanche also stood out, on account of her pirate's eye patch and her blonde hair, but it was her sister who attracted the most attention.

The break came for Kay when Edwin Thanhouser saw her at a performance and gave her a screen test for a part in a western movie his company was shooting at Scott's Movie Ranch in Staten Island, New York. Her name of 'McDonald' had to be changed, however, since Thanhouser felt a leading lady needed a name that sounded vaguely exotic. One of the camera crew was a Frenchman by the last name of du Maurier, so Thanhouser suggested adopting the name, and Kay readily acquiesced.

Within three more one-reelers, he had made her a rising star of western motion pictures, and before long, she was able to diversify and became the much sought after romantic interest in comedies, melodramas and swashbucklers.

Missing Lynx

As Kay's star rose, Blanche gave up her own aspirations and became her assistant, her housekeeper and manager. And she travelled with her when she signed with Mack Sennett at his Keystone Studios in Edendale, California.

It was on the set of *Tarzan and the Lost Treasures of Opar*, playing Jane alongside Elmo Lincoln as Tarzan, that she met Colonel Fenton Carlyle. The famous English adventurer, big game hunter, and animal trainer had been commissioned to procure and train the two lions used in the movie. No one, it seemed, had such an affinity with large cats as did he. He showed her how to treat them to make them do her will. Because of her athleticism and daredevil attitude to execute whatever stunt was asked of her, she became the star of a series of adventure films about *Diana the Lion Queen*.

Throughout it all Fenton was there, watching every scene, just in case he was needed. Their closeness made it inevitable that he would pay her court. It was a whirlwind romance that resulted in their marriage a mere four weeks later at the Catholic Church of the Good Shepherd in Beverly Hills.

Blanche, by this time, had married, but separated from a movie producer, after finding him canoodling on a studio couch in his office with a would-be starlet. Yet she kept the name Fleming, which she too felt suited Hollywood more than the rustic name of McDonald. And so the newspapers announced to the world that Blanche Fleming, Kay du Maurier's inseparable sister, was the matron of honor at the wedding.

Ironically, it was the same church where Rudolph Valentino's second funeral would be held two years later, prior to his interment in the Hollywood Memorial Park Cemetery.

2

Beverly Hills, California
August 9, 1927

Alfonso the Persian cat with eyes of pure sapphire blue sprawled languidly on the bank of silken cushions decked across the chaise longue that had been gifted to Kay on completion of the biblical epic *Salome*, the last film that she appeared in before her pregnancy became obvious to everyone. The drawing room, which overlooked the tennis court, swimming pool, and the carefully tended lawns and herbaceous borders, was vast, with chandeliers, curtains, drapes and furniture in the art deco style. The whole mansion was not as ostentatious as Charles Chaplin's sprawling Breakaway House next door, yet with its décor and trappings, including the framed publicity posters from Kay's movies, the Chinese screen that concealed the marble-topped cocktail bar that Fenton kept stocked with malt whisky and the mixers and spirits needed for any cocktail imaginable, and the odd trophy head on the walls from Fenton's big game expeditions, it oozed money and Hollywood glamour on the grand scale.

"Shoo, cat!" Blanche snapped, as she clapped her hands upon entering the room.

Alfonso rolled over, stared at her for a moment, before standing and stretching. Then he jumped down and disdainfully pattered past Blanche to exit the room.

"That darned cat shouldn't be allowed in here," she said as her sister followed, cradling her baby, young Finlay, in her arms. "It's not–*hygienic* having cats near babies."

She flounced down on the chaise longue and swept cat hairs from the cushions. "Or safe!" she added. "They have claws, remember."

Kay laughed. "Oh, don't be such a worrier, Blanche. Finlay is just fine, and besides, Alfonso is the most perfect of cats. He loves my little Finlay."

The baby started to cough.

"You see, Kay? He's been coughing all morning. I'm sure it must be something he caught from that cat. What will Fenton say about it if we just ignore it?"

"Fenton is away in Europe until next week."

"Exactly! Which is why I'm going to call Doctor Kennedy to come and check him over."

Kay shrugged her shoulders resignedly as her sister left the room, her high-heeled shoes beating a rapid retreating staccato on the Italian tiled floor of the huge two-story tall hallway. She heard her pick up the phone in the recess and place the call. Almost immediately, Alfonso reappeared and leapt up onto his favorite place on the silk cushions.

The actress smiled down at Finlay and as his little face looked up at her with those beautiful eyes of his, her heart quickened as it usually did when she looked at him. With his beautiful olive skin, he was going to be the image of his father; of that, she was sure.

"Your daddy loves you, Finlay, I just know he does."

Oh, how she would have loved to name him after him! But that would have been impossible. The second best option, she had decided was to name him after their father. That had satisfied Blanche. Fenton had seemed ambivalent, but agreed.

And as she thought about it, she started to sob.

From the chaise longue, Alfonso began to purr.

She looked over at him and smiled into his deep blue eyes. At least, she had been able to name the cat after Finlay's father's second name.

o0o

Doctor Roger Kennedy was considered the best and most exclusive doctor in Beverly Hills. He was probably also the most expensive. He had only a small practice, which effectively included only the major stars, directors and producers in Hollywood. He was tall, dark and handsome, and would have looked good on the silver screen had he chosen a different profession. Many had thought he had the look of John Gilbert in *The Big Parade*. Apart from his medical skills, his personal charm mattered to the cognoscenti of the motion picture industry, for they knew the power of panache, veneer and charisma.

He had looked after Kay during her pregnancy, and treated her for depression after Finlay's birth. Her low mood in the last trimester of her pregnancy he had attributed to the stress of her work in the motion picture business.

He was used to dealing with the egos and nervous dispositions of the rich and famous of the silver screen.

"Is...is Finlay ill, Doctor?" she asked as he straightened up from her son's cot after having examined him, The cot had been set up in the bay window of the drawing room.

He wound his stethoscope up and replaced it in his black bag. He shook his head with a reassuring smile. "He is quite well, Kay. He has a virus, nothing more."

"It isn't the influenza virus, is it, Roger?" Blanche asked, inserting a green cocktail cigarette into her amber cigarette holder.

The doctor was well aware of the anxieties that people had about influenza, ever since the pandemic of 1918. So many families had lost relatives from it.

"It is a common cold virus, that's all, Blanche. But I understand the concern, and I will prescribe a good cough mixture for him."

"And it isn't anything that Finlay could have caught from Alfonso, is it?" Kay asked.

"Alfonso? Who—"

"Her cat!" Blanche explained. "I have told her again and again that they are not good animals to have around babies."

Doctor Kennedy placed a reassuring hand on Blanche's shoulder and his face crinkled into one of those smiles that his patients felt was worth every cent of his considerable fees. "The common cold has nothing to do with the cat, Blanche. If Alfonso is that elegant Persian cat that I've seen sauntering around the house on past visits, then I wouldn't worry. Cats are the cleanest of animals. They spend half their lives grooming and cleaning themselves."

He smiled at Kay as he snapped his bag closed. "I hope that settles your mind. I'll make up this prescription and I'll drop it round in a couple of hours."

Blanche lit her cigarette and let out a ribbon of pale blue smoke.

"Well, that is all a relief," she said. "But, I was also concerned about stories I heard of cats sitting on babies faces and smothering them."

"Nothing but a myth, Blanche. I have never come across that in all my years of practice."

Blanche's hand went up to adjust her jeweled eye patch and she seemed about to ask something, then simply shrugged her shoulders.

"I guess that settles it, then. Thank you, Roger. I will show you out."

When they had gone, Kay picked Finlay up and sat down on the chaise longue. She was joined a moment later by Alfonso. He rubbed his head against her hand and then against the bundle that surrounded Finlay. Then, he purred before settling down on the silk cushions.

"You are such an exotic thing, aren't you Alfonso. And here you are protecting little Finlay. Just like–"

She stopped herself from talking out loud, just in case one of the maids was within earshot.

She liked that word, *exotic*. It summed up everything about Rudolph. Like virtually every woman who saw him in *The Sheik*, she had been attracted to him. Yet, as an actress herself, she was all too aware of the magic of the silver screen. The camera could make anyone look glamorous. But seeing him in the flesh for the first time at one of Doug Fairbanks's opulent parties had been different. He was better looking without the makeup; more alluring as he walked and danced without the emphatic movements and strutting that were required by the camera to create those moving pictures on the silver screen. And that voice of his, with the Continental accent, was a revelation. Not only that, but he was intelligent, witty, and full of fun.

Yet, she learned that there was a softer side to him that few knew about. He had a degree from agricultural school in Genoa, and prided himself on his horticultural skills. His apartments were bedecked with exotic houseplants that he personally tended to.

She had never meant to have an affair with him, for she was a married woman. He had been married twice and was in an on-off relationship with Pola Negri. But it had been so exciting, so exhilarating—and so unexpected.

While thousands of women had fallen in love with his screen image, she had fallen in love with the man.

o0o

That evening after dinner, with Finlay settled down for the night, Kay and Blanche sat in the orangery sipping mint julep cocktails. As usual, Blanche was smoking one of her green cocktail cigarettes as she leafed through a file of correspondence and business papers that she had arranged for Kay to sign.

"And I have a whole sack of fan letters that arrived this week. I have arranged them into three groups; the ones you need to see and send a signed photograph to, the ones you might be interested to read, and the ones that I can attend to on your behalf."

"I don't know what I'd do without you, Blanche. Or rather, what we would *all* do without my big sister to take care of us."

Blanche sighed. "Well, actually, my darling, that was one of the things I need to talk to you about. It's about Fitzroy–he wants us to try again. He promises that he has finished with his philandering and wants me to take him back."

"Oh, Blanche, that's...that's good news."

"But, it will mean us going back to the East Coast."

Kay gasped and sat forward, spilling her drink in the process. "But—you *can't!*"

Blanche stubbed out her cigarette and laid the holder beside the tortoiseshell ashtray. "But I think I must, Kay. There is nothing for me here. You have Finlay and Fenton. And you know it is no secret that Fenton thinks I have outstayed my welcome."

"But we need you! If it is security you need, well, you need never worry about money, I've taken care of that, even if–"

"Even if what, Kay?"

Kay bit her lip. "You've always looked after me, ever since Mom and Dad died; even after the accident! Now, it's my turn to make it up, to take care of you. You can't go back to that man. Please, think about it, Blanche."

Blanche leaned forward and squeezed her sister's knee. "I haven't thought about anything else for the past three days. I haven't given Fitzroy my final answer yet. I told him I needed a fortnight to think about it."

She pursed her lips in thought, and then added, "I'm not sure that either of us have been very lucky with men, Kay."

Kay flushed. "Wh-whatever do you mean?"

"It's only the thought of leaving you alone with Fenton that has made me procrastinate."

3

Fenton Carlyle arrived home at the weekend with news of his latest expedition and with news that he had arranged for his taxidermist in Nairobi to prepare a lion and the head of a black rhinoceros that he had shot.

Kay was less than enthusiastic, much to his chagrin.

"You used to admire my hunting prowess," he said after downing two malt whiskies in rapid succession.

"I…I do, Fenton, it is just that I prefer cats to be alive rather than dead."

"Like that damned Persian thing you suddenly acquired?" he asked, picking up one of the silk cushions and tossing it into a corner.

"Alfonso is lovely. Why did you do that?"

He ignored her question. "I can't say I'm keen on the name. Why didn't you give him an English or an American name? Where did you get him anyway?"

"A fan gave him to me as a present!"

"A fan? You mean an *admirer*, don't you? Like the one that gave you that damned lynx coat that you are so fond of, even in the height of summer."

"I don't care for your tone, Fenton. I'm going to check on Finlay. He had a bad cough, but Dr. Kennedy gave him a linctus to settle it down." She glared at him. "You *do* remember that you have a son, don't you? Or were you going to ask about him after you had dinner?"

"My son?" he snapped at her. "That, I'm not sure about. I was hunting in Kenya for two months, remember."

He turned on his heel and stomped out of the room, almost knocking Blanche over as he did so.

"Fenton, welcome home," she said.

"So, it's your home now, is it?" he said over his shoulder. He snorted. "I'll be back sometime."

He did not return until well after four o'clock in the morning, and he slept in one of the vacant rooms.

o0o

On the day before Blanche said she was going to talk to Fitzroy Fleming, her producer husband, the household was woken at seven o'clock in the morning by a scream from the nursery.

Helen the maid found Finlay lying motionless in his cot, his face blue and his body as cold and stiff as marble.

Doctor Kennedy was called and arrived just before the ambulance. He did what he could, but they all knew that it was hopeless.

"I cannot tell you how sorry I am to tell you this," he said at last. "Your son is dead."

"How the hell did it happen, Kennedy?" Fenton bristled.

"I can't be sure Colonel Carlyle. This is an unexpected death, so the coroner will have to decide. That means there will have to be an autopsy on your son, I am afraid."

"No!" wailed Kay, clasping hands over her face and slumping into a chair. "My baby! Finlay! *No!*"

Blanche put a consoling arm about her sister's shoulders. "We'll get through this, Kay. We've gotten through everything else that this crummy life has thrown at us, and we'll do so again. I'm here for you. I'll always be here for you."

"Don't be too sure about that!" snapped Fenton. "My son is dead, so maybe the cement that held this wall together has just gone."

Doctor Kennedy issued instructions to the ambulance crew.

"We will have his body removed for the coroner, and as soon as I have news of the autopsy I will be in touch. I think it would be helpful if you would let me prescribe some sedatives for you all. I have some in my bag and I can leave them."

"Leave them for them," Fenton said contemptuously. "I'm going to have a whisky. Maybe several!"

o0o

Hollywood Daily Citizen,
August 16th 1927

TRAGEDY AT THE DU MAURIER MANSION

Kay du Maurier has had her share of drama, romance and high adventure in her life, as witnessed by the many motion pictures that she has appeared in for all of the main studios on both coasts. Yet, that is as nothing compared to the tragedy that befell her and her husband, the famous hunter and explorer Colonel Fenton Carlyle. Their infant son, Finlay Grenville Fenton was found dead yesterday morning.

Our reporter discovered that an autopsy performed by the

county medical examiner reported that the child had died from suffocation. There were cat hairs in the child's mouth and upon its head, consistent with a cat having lain across the baby's face, obstructing breathing and causing death by asphyxiation.

4

August 19th, 1927

The funeral of Finlay Carlyle took place three days later at the Catholic Church of the Good Shepherd in Beverly Hills.

It was intended to be a small, private affair with family and closest of friends, yet such was the public interest surrounding Kay du Maurier and the tragic death of her infant son that the church was surrounded by well-wishing fans who had come to share the star's grief, as well as a crowd of newspaper reporters and photographers with flash cameras, who wanted to record the event for their respective publications.

As ever, Blanche was on hand to support her younger sister and share her sorrow. Colonel Fenton was there also, yet by his bearing and the lack of physical contact between him and his wife, murmurs of suspicion started to hum around the throng.

Attending Rudolph Valentino's funeral had been the most emotional moment of Kay's life up until then, which she had striven so hard to conceal from anyone. Yet it was as nothing compared with the funeral of her son.

Of *their* son!

Her grief, her tears and her utter desolation touched everyone who saw them. They even seemed to melt Fenton's heart, and he reached out to her for the first time in days and squeezed her hand.

"Our son...has gone!" Kay said from behind her veil, without looking at him.

"He has gone!"

She returned his squeeze, although he did not and could not realize that, in that moment, she was imagining that the hand she held belonged to another.

Afterward, as they left the church they were deluged by a sea of people, who had to be pushed away for them to make it to the waiting Rolls Royce. Amid the popping flash bulbs, Kay realized that she had never felt so alone in all her life. And as she looked at Fenton, still holding her hand, she suddenly felt only one emotion for him–hate.

She was sure that he sensed it, too, for he let her hand slip from his as he pulled open the door for her to get in.

The crowd of people waved and collectively wished them well as the car pulled away, just as a car would in a Kay du Maurier adventure or melodrama. The hero and heroine would be driving off to seek comfort and solace from each other.

But nothing could be further from the truth.

o0o

Doctor Roger Kennedy called on the afternoon of the funeral and again the following morning. Helen the maid let him in and rang through to alert Blanche that he had arrived. Blanche took him through to the dining room where Fenton and Kay were eating in stony silence at opposite ends of the long table. By the thunderous look on Fenton's face and the moistness of Kay's eyes it seemed clear that they had been in the middle of a heated row.

"Damn it, Kennedy, give her something stronger, will you? She won't eat and she can't sleep."

"It is normal, Fenton," Kay said, defensively.

Fenton stood up and tossed his napkin on the unfinished plate of bacon and eggs. "Normal as hell. I'll be in the billiard room when you've finished, Doctor."

Roger Kennedy stood back apace to let Fenton flounce out.

"Is it true, Kay? Can't you sleep?" he asked, as Blanche took a seat on the other side of the table and poured herself a cup of coffee.

"I can't eat, and my mind only sees Finlay," Kay volunteered. "I…I don't know what Fenton expects. I can't just snap out of this with a fanfare of music. This isn't a motion picture."

"Of course not, Kay. The thing is, that Fenton will be hurting just as much as you, and from my impression of him as a man of action, he wants everything to be fixed as quickly as possible. If it is not, then he gets irritable. I suspect that you are experiencing the backlash of that irritability."

"That is exactly my take on this, Roger," said Blanche. "If Fenton can't pull a trigger and get a result, he's cross. He was planning to kill Alfonso, but the cat has just disappeared."

"Alfonso never killed Finlay," Kay said quickly. "He wouldn't. I know he wouldn't. You yourself said that cats smothering babies is just a myth, Roger."

"I did, Kay, but–"

"Please, don't say another word on the matter. Alfonso is innocent; I know it and that is all that matters. But can you help us to feel less tense and help me to sleep?" Kay asked. "Those sedatives you gave us weren't much help."

"They were just the mildest," Roger said. "I'll give you both much more potent ones."

He gave her the slightest of smiles as he opened his bag and drew out his prescription pad. "An odd stiff drink might have helped, if only the government hadn't decreed that they were illegal."

o0o

Kay had never had a great head for drink, so the 18th amendment, which brought about the prohibition of alcohol across the nation, had never been much of a problem for her. She enjoyed the odd mint julep or cocktail with Blanche, but other than that, she had been happy enough without it. By contrast, Fenton had always enjoyed his drink, especially his malt whisky and, like virtually most of the affluent residents of Beverly Hills, he had no problem keeping his bar stocked.

Over the next few days, the stronger sedatives that Doctor Kennedy prescribed for her only made Kay feel suppressed, numbed, and disconnected from reality; yet, they did nothing to stop the agony of grief. The malt whisky that her husband drank made her feel ill, while the mint juleps that she had previously enjoyed drinking with Blanche, did nothing. Gin sling cocktails, however, seemed to produce the slightest of salving effects, albeit never for long. The result was that over the following days, she started drinking a lot of them and virtually stopped eating anything at all.

In this state of torpor she and Fenton got through the next few days, although with fairly minimal contact. It was left to Blanche to organize the running of the house, instructing the staff to give the grieving couple the distance that they needed.

It was the late afternoon delivery of a packing crate from Fenton's taxidermist in Nairobi that brought them out of their state of alcohol-fuelled denial.

As he levered the lid off with a claw-tooth hammer and lifted out the heavy object from its padding of gutta-percha, he found himself laughing. Not just a chuckle, but a deep belly laughter that caused him to jack-knife in hysterical mirth.

Sitting in the drawing room. Kay was drinking a gin sling and Blanche was drinking coffee.

"It's arrived!" he called from the hall as he clumped into the drawing room carrying the large object wrapped in a sheet. "You will both enjoy this," he said, laying it down on a low coffee table.

With a flourish, he grabbed a corner of the sheet and pulled it off to reveal a cat standing ready to pounce, as if frozen in time.

Blanche mouthed an oath and Kay, after staring blearily at it for a moment dropped her glass, which shattered on the floor.

"Clumsy!" Fenton sneered.

"What…what is the meaning–?" Kay blurted out.

"It's a present, my love. You like cats, don't you? This is a caracal that I shot on my last trip. You know, when I was away and you acquired that Persian cat…and when you were given that lynx coat."

"I prefer *living* animals, Fenton," Kay said, standing and walking over to the bar to make a fresh drink. "I told you that."

"That coat isn't living, though, is it?"

She spun round. "What are you trying to say, Fenton?"

"I'm saying that I don't believe you. I don't believe that a fan gave you that cat. And you never did tell me who gave you that coat."

Blanche stood up, ready to move between them. "Kay! Fenton, please, keep calm."

"Calm! I am bloody calm," Fenton said. "But what have I to stay calm about? I've lost my son."

"I have, too," Kay said with a sigh.

"Who gave them to you?" he persisted.

"Who gave me what?"

"The cat and the coat. Who gave you them?"

Kay shook her head, her eyes glassy from the alcohol. "I…don't…remember."

"Then try! It can't be difficult. That coat was worth a fortune. How many millionaire admirers do you have?"

"I can't remember! I don't want to remember," Kay cried, clutching her head. "Just–leave me alone."

"Leave you alone! That would be a delight. And do you know why? Because I loathe you. I don't believe that child was mine. I think the father was your damned admirer–*your lover*!"

He picked up the whisky glass that he had filled earlier, but his hand shook and his facial muscles tightened. Suddenly, he threw it at the bar where it smashed and showered Kay with the amber liquid.

Blanche took a step toward him. "Fenton, you are not being reasonable. You are both getting too heated."

"Too heated am I? Well, tell me this: where is the cat now, and where is the lynx coat? I can't find either of them."

"As for Alfonso, he'll be keeping away from you," Blanche said. "He…he senses that you don't like him. As for the coat–I have no idea."

She looked across at Kay. "Have you put it somewhere, Kay? You haven't been quite so focused lately, have you?"

"No! I haven't put it anywhere." She glared at Fenton and then at Blanche. "One of you has taken it, haven't you? Well, I want it back, and I want it right now."

She picked up the bell and rang it.

Moments later, Helen the maid knocked and entered.

"You rang, ma'am?"

"Where is my lynx coat? I need it now."

"Now, ma'am? I...I am not sure where it is. It is not in your dressing room or in the cloakroom. I...I thought you must have–"

Kay slapped both hands on the bar counter. "Never mind! It doesn't matter! In fact, *nothing* matters any more except getting away from here. I need air. Get Thomas to get the Gold Bug out for me. I'm going for a spin–on my own!"

Blanche protested, but Kay brushed her aside. "I have had enough, and don't even try to stop me."

Fenton folded his arms and sank into an easy chair. "I wouldn't dream of stopping you. You're a woman who does whatever she wants."

Minutes later, the Kissel Gold Bug Speedster's six cylinder engine roared into life and amid a crashing of gears, Kay du Maurier sped off into the twilight.

o0o

Hollywood Daily Citizen,
August 26th, 1927

KAY DU MAURIER KILLED IN TRAGIC ROAD ACCIDENT

A week ago, the famous motion picture actress Kay du Maurier was coping with the sudden death of her baby son, Finlay Carlyle. For the young mother, it didn't seem that matters could get worse. Now, tragedy has struck again and her husband, Colonel Fenton Carlyle, is left to grieve for not just a son, but his beloved wife, as well. Kay du Maurier drove her car into a boulder while driving on one of the snaking roads up in the Hollywood Hills. She died instantly.

o0o

Fenton started drinking in earnest when he returned from the mortuary, after identifying Kay's body. Blanche tried to persuade him to stop, but he would brook no interference.

"If you want to help, then drink with me. If you don't, then just get lost!"

Blanche poured herself a very weak mint julep and lit a cigarette. "I've lost my little sister and my nephew, too, Fenton. How much more can life take from us?"

He drained his whisky and shook his head, wretchedly. After a moment:

"It's all my fault, Blanche. If I hadn't been so dammed jealous, I wouldn't have pushed her so hard. I think…I think she deliberately went out and drove into a rock. I pushed her into taking her own life."

"You can't think that, Fenton. You mustn't. Even if–"

He looked up suddenly.

"Even if what? What do you know that you aren't telling me, Blanche?"

"Nothing," she said, hesitantly. "I don't know anything at all except Kay was in love."

"Who with? Tell me, who with!" he demanded, his eyes wild.

"She was in love only with you, Fenton."

He said nothing for a moment, then his head sank onto his chest and he sobbed.

When he recovered a few moments later, he pointed to the stuffed caracal. "I goaded her with that thing. I was cross about that Persian cat that someone gave her."

As if being given a cue, there was a purring noise from the doorway and then Alfonso sauntered into the room, ignoring both Fenton and Blanche as he walked purposefully to the chaise longue, where he leaped up and then lay down on the silk cushions, as if nothing had happened.

Fenton pointed a trembling finger at the cat, his bloodshot eyes widening in horror as his cheeks suffused with color.

"That bloody thing caused all this, just as much as that darned lynx coat. It's responsible for Kay's death, just as much as it was probably guilty of murdering Finlay. We both know that he smothered Finlay."

"Fenton, we don't know that at all. You need to be calm."

"I'm going to kill it! I'm going to kill it right now."

Blanche stood up abruptly as Fenton dashed from the room. "Don't do anything rash, Fenton. You've been drinking, and you are not thinking clearly."

He returned moments later with the Webley revolver that he had carried on all his expeditions since his days in the British army. He pointed it at Alfonso, who had raised his head and was staring straight at him with unwavering regard. His sapphire blue eyes seemed to enlarge.

"Damn you, cat!" Fenton called, his hand shaking as he took aim with the revolver.

He fired and the shot went wide, but still Alfonso simply sat and stared at him.

"Fenton, stop!" cried Blanche. "You are frightening me."

He aimed again, but this time, Alfonso moved, dashing for the door before Fenton could fire. The hunter gave chase, running into the hall, just in time to see the cat leap up and launch itself out through an open window. He fired at the window, shattering it with a great deal of noise.

Cries of alarm sounded throughout the house as the servants reacted to the noise of gunfire. But Fenton ignored them as he yanked the door open and ran out into the night.

Two minutes later, there was a shot in the dark, followed by a single, high-pitched animal scream of agony. Then, another thirty seconds later, another shot rang out.

The servants became increasingly alarmed when Colonel Carlyle failed to return to the house.

5

August 28rd, 1927

Blanche replaced the earpiece on the cradle of the candle telephone and heaved a sigh of relief. The Beverly Hills undertaker that she had been speaking to had drained her energy, partly because he was so obsequious in his manner.

She sat for a few moments, drumming her fingers on the blotting pad on top of the oak desk. She had begun the arrangements for Fenton's funeral, but would have to wait until the authorities released the body before she could firmly plan the event. She felt as exhausted as Helen and the other servants had sympathetically said she looked.

The whole household had, of course, been shocked at the colonel's suicide down by the gazebo on the far side of the tennis court. Fenton had been a man's man, a hunter and explorer, a man who tamed wild beasts and who, until days before, had seemed a happily married man with a son and everything to live for.

Blanche drew the copy of the *Hollywood Daily Citizen* toward her and stared at the headlines.

BIG GAME HUNTER'S LAST SHOT

Colonel Fenton Carlyle, the husband of dearly loved motion picture star Kay du Maurier, who died in a road accident a few days ago, has taken his own life.

She read the article for the umpteenth time as she reached for the silver cigarette box and carefully fitted a green cocktail cigarette to her amber holder.

"Poor Fenton," she mused as she read on.

The whole of Hollywood shares the grief of Blanche Fleming, the elder sister of Kay du Maurier, who has the sad task of arranging yet another funeral. Her estranged husband, the motion picture producer Fitzroy Fleming, told our reporter that he is planning on taking her away to Europe after the colonel's funeral, so that they can begin to get their lives back on track. He says that it is his belief that the house is jinxed, and that he needs to get her away from it.

Blanche blew a contemptuous cloud of smoke from her lips. Fitzroy had taken a lot for granted in issuing that statement. She would have to talk seriously to him, when the time was right.

There was a knock on the study door and Helen came in upon Blanche's command.

"Doctor Kennedy is here to see you again, ma'am."

Blanche stubbed her cigarette out and nodded wearily. "Show him in, please, Helen."

"Then after he has gone will you be taking some breakfast, ma'am? You must eat, you know. You need to keep your strength up."

"I'll try, Helen. Perhaps a soft-boiled egg and coffee."

Helen beamed and disappeared to get the doctor.

Roger Kennedy looked concerned as he was shown in.

"Thank you, Helen," he said. "No need to show me out after I have finished, but I will probably be calling back later this morning to drop off some medicine for Mrs. Fleming."

Helen nodded with a smile. "Very good, Doctor. The back door will be unlocked. I'm just relieved to hear that madam is going to try and have some breakfast."

Once she had gone and drawn the door closed behind her, they waited until her footsteps echoed down the hall.

Then he took several quick steps and took her in his arms. They kissed passionately and urgently.

"It will soon all be over, my darling," she said, when they parted. "Soon everything will be ours, just as we planned. We will just have to maintain a subterfuge for some time, until I get rid of Fitzroy."

"I love you Blanche. I love everything about you."

"Even my piratical eye patch?" she whispered coquettishly.

"Everything. I love your body and I love your mind. You worked everything out to perfection."

"I have had to manage Kay's whole life since we were children. I am used to organizing things. I created her success and all she ever did was take me for granted. She never knew just how much I have always hated her."

She touched her eye patch. "It was her fault that I lost my eye. The stupid girl distracted me when I was operating a machine all those years ago. It was guilt over that which induced her to make her last will and testament out in my favor, thanks also to some subtle hinting from me. As for Fenton, he just regarded me as an annoying servant."

"You were clever, the way you planted all the right thoughts in her mind–after the deed was done."

An evil look flashed across her face. "She was a fool to have that affair. It jeopardized everything. Having his baby was idiocy, and she deserved to lose it. Doing it was so simple, and her affair gave us the perfect scapegoat in the shape of Alfonso, that revolting cat that she loved."

Her face relaxed and she went on:

"And you put the right thoughts into Fenton's head. The right suggestions during the pregnancy that made him doubt that he was the father. You were superb, darling. He became just like Shakespeare's Othello, eaten up by jealousy. And when he saw Alfonso, he just had to kill him. Then, like Othello, he was wracked with guilt and blew his brains out."

They embraced again and kissed until they had taken up as much time as they could afford without arousing suspicion among the servants.

"I must say, I am starving," Blanche said. "Yet, I have to make them think I can't eat."

"When we are free, my darling, we will feast to our heart's content."

o0o

After breakfast, Blanche went through to the drawing room and lay down on the silk cushions on the chaise longue. The intensity and events of the last few days had been draining, and despite the frugal breakfast, she felt in need of rest.

She dozed and felt herself drifting into a deep sleep. The sort of sleep that unleashed unwanted emotions. Guilt and fear found form in images of her sister, her nephew, Finlay, and of Colonel Fenton Carlyle after he had blown his brains out.

And then, staring at her, she saw those large sapphire blue eyes of Alfonso the Persian cat.

She started awake, only to feel that her body would not move. She could not move a single muscle.

To her horror, the image of those big blue eyes was no figment of her imagination, but was very real. Sitting on her chest, his face mere inches from her face, was Alfonso. The weight of his body upon her chest seemed to be inexplicably increasing and it was hard to breathe.

But how could it be? Fenton had shot him–hadn't he?

"Sh...Shoo!" she gasped.

Instead, Alfonso very deliberately licked his lips and stared at her with those large, hypnotic eyes. Those eyes that now seemed so reminiscent of that recently deceased motion picture star, Valentino.

Then, he inched closer and closer until he was lying on her face, covering her mouth and her nose. She panicked as the suffocative sensation increased.

Yet, she could not move a muscle.

o0o

Two hours later, Doctor Kennedy let himself into the mansion by the back door, as arranged with Helen.

When he let himself into the drawing room, he saw Blanche reclining on the chaise longue. He assumed that she was asleep, like a Sleeping Beauty—and so, with a smile, he laid his bag down and thought he would sneak up on her and surprise her with a kiss.

The kiss of her very own Prince Charming!

He knew when he saw her eyes staring at the ceiling with pupils dilated, that she was dead. The telltale tiny petechial hemorrhages around her slightly bulging eyes told him the truth.

She had been suffocated. She had been murdered!

Fear gripped him as he realized that the murderer was probably in the room with him at that moment.

Yet, before he could react, he felt a heavy thump in the back of his neck that almost made him fall over Blanche's dead body. He felt a lancinating pain on the right side of his face and his neck as a furry shape jumped down from his shoulder and started slashing razor sharp claws over his hand.

Blood flowed freely down his neck and dripped all over Blanche's hands.

It was a cat. That cat!

He struggled to free himself of it, dripping blood over Blanche as he did so.

Then, suddenly, Alfonso jumped clear and darted through the door.

He was about to cry for help, when the sight of his dead lover, covered in his blood made him realize his situation. He needed to get away, dress his wounds and think.

He picked up his bag and ran from the house to his car, then drove straight away to his office.

o0o

Hollywood Daily Citizen
August 29th, 1927

DOCTOR TO THE STARS ARRESTED

Shock after shock has struck at the home of deceased motion picture star Kay du Maurier, who died tragically following the death of her infant son. Her husband, Colonel Fenton Carlyle apparently shot himself, but now Doctor Roger Kennedy, the doctor to half of the Hollywood motion picture industry's elite, has been arrested for the murder of Mrs. Blanche Fleming, the sister of Kay du Maurier.

Lieutenant Nathanial Crosby of the Beverly Hills Police Department arrested the doctor at his office as he attempted to dress wounds he sustained during his murder of Mrs. Fleming. The accused claims that he had found Mrs. Fleming dead, and that he was attacked by the family cat.

The statement of one of the maids, Miss Helen Bordeaux, countered this. She said that she had witnessed the doctor rushing covertly away from the mansion with blood dripping from his wounds. It is believed that these were inflicted upon him as Mrs. Fleming fought for her life as he suffocated her with a silk cushion.

A lynx fur coat was found in the bedroom at the doctor's house. It has been identified as belonging to Kay du Maurier, although the doctor claims that Mrs. Blanche Fleming, whom he alleged was his lover, had worn it and left it when she made one of many visits to his home.

Miss Helen Bordeaux was scornful of the story of a cat attacking the doctor. She told our reporter that Kay du Maurier had owned a Persian cat, but that Colonel Carlyle had shot it before taking his own life, clearly when distraught over the tragic deaths of his wife and infant son.

o0o

Kay du Maurier had purchased a family crypt in the Hollywood Memorial Park Cemetery at 6000 Santa Monica Boulevard a month after Rudolph Valentino died, and her lawyer and executor of her will arranged for her and her son to be interred together in it. Atop the crypt, a marble block from Apulia, Italy, was sculpted into the semblance of a silk cushion, on which was inscribed the message:

For Rudolph and Alfonso, my secret gardener and eternal friend, always welcome.

Rudolph had once told her that the finest marble was quarried in Apulia, near his birthplace of Castellaneta.

oOo

Giovanni Batista, the chief cemetery caretaker, noticed things that others failed to see over his forty years at the cemetery. He did not exactly see spirits of the rich and famous, but he often felt their presence.

Except for the cat. He never knew if it was a spirit, or just an exceptionally long-lived and very fit Persian cat that seemed to spend its time resting by the crypt of Rudolph Valentino, or sprawling on the marble cushion on the du Maurier crypt. He had been a young man of twenty when the great Latin Lover died so tragically and had been interred in the beautiful crypt surrounded by roses. And, like everyone else in the Hollywood area, he had followed the tragedies that befell Kay du Maurier and her family. He had personally prepared her crypt.

He liked to imagine that only he knew about some secret tryst between the great Valentino and the famous Kay du Maurier.

He thought it would make a wonderful tale.

But he was not the sort to tell tales. He would be as quiet as the stars of the silent screen.

About the Author—Clay More

CLAY MORE is the western pen name of Keith Souter, a part-time doctor, medical writer and novelist. He has written about fifty books, some of which have been translated into ten languages. His novels cover four genres, including westerns, crime, historical and young adult. He also writes short stories and has won a couple of prizes, including a Fish Award.

He is a member of the Crime Writer's Association, Western Writers of America and is vice president of Western Fictioneers. He is married to Rachel and lives in England within arrowshot of the ruins of a medieval castle.

Dream Weaver

C. A. Jamison

Mary's cat makes California dreams come true in three extraordinary romance novels.

Chapter One

Working Girl

My story began in sunny California. For me, the fresh start after college came with the excitement of a new job and a challenge this small town girl wasn't quite ready to face. I raised my printed directions to the pouring rain. Yes, I said sunny California, but nothing I do ever goes as planned.

"Hey, cab guy, over here." Puddle slush sprayed on the curb as the cab pulled up. I opened the door, tucked my skirt, and slid across the back seat.

The cabby adjusted his yellow ball-cap and turned his head. "Where to, lady?"

"Umm." The flimsy paper sagged from the rain. I shook the wet map and pulled back on the hood of my raincoat. "Well, it's a..." The ink ran in the corner. The address smudged. "The building is past North Rossmore." I tilted my head. "Toward Fourth and Vine." I turned the paper upside-down. "I think."

"You mind if I take a look?" The cabby held out his hand and, with a quick glance said, "I know the place." He handed the directions back and two seconds later, we were off.

Hollywood, where dreams come true. Palm leaves waved their hello in the wind. A long way from Indiana, but my Uncle Chris had said the job was mine if I applied. His friend, the screenplay writer, looked for fast typing skills and a creative mind. The typing skills—I had. Creative thinking? I couldn't paint or write music, but my thoughts were open to the infinite possibilities of the written word. Would that count? I wasn't sure.

The cabby stopped in front of an old high-rise building where concrete steps surrounded a bubbling fountain.

I reached over the seat and handed him his fare. "Keep the change." I smiled.

I gripped the edge of my skirt, prepared to exit, when a handsome stranger's face peered down at me through the glass. The dark-haired man opened the cab door and held out a courteous hand.

I hesitated, then reached out. His smooth guidance held a gentle touch, as I stepped onto the curb. Under his big, black umbrella, our hands remained clasped. We stood close, and his scent made me want to take a deep breath. His beautiful blue-eyed gaze held me frozen in time.

He uncoiled his fingers and raised the hood of my raincoat. The simple movement had Hollywood sex appeal, and my heart drummed.

"Have a good day." He winked.

"You…you too." Like a backward country girl, I gawked—as if he were an A-list celebrity, but he only waited his turn with the cab. A quiet exhale escaped, as I headed for the building. When I reached the top step, I glanced back and caught him watching me through the drizzle of the cab window.

My phone displayed the time, and I hurried to room 211. Stained glass blocked my view, so I knocked before entering.

A middle-aged woman, with a pencil stuck in her hair and bright red lipstick, sat behind a desk. Her blue shirt matched mine, only her blouse fit much tighter.

Without a glance in my direction, she removed her pencil and used it as a pointer. Her nasal voice blurted the words, "Have a seat."

Three plastic chairs lined the wall. I chose the middle one. After my rush to be on time, I waited for this woman to catch up on her reading.

"I'm the new secretary for—"

She held the pencil in the air and continued to read.

Her paperback book didn't look like an important document, but okay, I'd wait. What choice did I have?

A Writers Guild of America award hung on the wall of the small office, and the door across from me had Mark Randle's name on a gold plate. Mr. Randle—my new boss. I'd never met him in person. Our only link came from e-mail correspondence.

The lady at the desk giggled at something in her book. She placed a marker and looked over her glasses. "Are you Mary Lynn Price?"

"Yes." I stood and held out my hand to greet her. "Mr. Randle is expecting me."

The woman sashayed around the small desk and shoved three paperback books into my outstretched fingers. I steadied the books as the tiny female smiled up at me.

"Mr. Randle had an emergency. He's left for Alabama to see his mother." She opened the door that held his name and motioned me forward.

I hurried through the entrance and turned to face her. "I hope everything is alright."

"Ha, his mother," she complained. "The last emergency was her lost dog. She thought an alligator had eaten the pup. Turned out, the local shelter picked up the mongrel." The short blonde lady shook her head. "That woman cares more about that dog than she does her son's work."

I blinked a couple of times, nodded, and tried not to smirk.

"I'm Gina Gunner. People in the building call me GG." The chain connected to her glasses skirted the edges of her face as she lifted the spectacles to her head. "I don't work in this office. I work for Tom Sanders down the hall. Mark asked me to meet you and give you this week's assignment."

I peered down at the top novel in my hands. The half-naked, American Indian indicated a romance novel. "I'm not sure—"

"You have three days to read those. When Mark returns, he'll expect you to give a full report on which book you would recommend to Cinema Show producers."

"Cinema Show?" I asked.

"You know—" She opened her palms and stuck out her chin. "The movie people. You're in Hollywood, dear."

Had the cuckoo hit the clock in that woman's brains? "Miss…GG, I can't pick one of these for a movie. It's my first day."

"It's *Mrs.*, and of course not." She used a finger to push down on my hand full of novels. "You *recommend* one of these books to Mark. He's the one who will choose which story to format for a screenplay. You're just a *muse* to an end." On her way out, she dropped a set of keys on top of my books. "Don't forget, a fully typed report due by the end of the day, Thursday. I hope you're a fast reader."

"What about Friday? Don't I have all week?"

"He'll be here to discuss your choice on Friday."

"But GG, I can't—"

The door closed. I swallowed and beheld the large workspace around me. "What kind of report?"

I followed GG's trail, but the woman moved fast. The book she was reading had disappeared, and so had she.

That can't be how this works. I looked down at the male model on the cover. Books are recommended in accordance with their sales and distributors. Not by a new secretary dripping water all over the floor. "Good grief in gravy." I removed my rain coat. *What was I supposed to do? Just read—here? By myself?*

The place smelled of lemon polish and needed a makeover. The wooden floorboards creaked as I stepped to a small desk across from me. Books and paper littered the larger desk. I presumed that workspace belonged to my runaway boss.

The weight of the romance novels grew heavy in my arms, and I cleared a spot on the small writing table to stack them. A rip in the cream-colored roll chair pinched my leg as I sat down.

Well. I guess this was it. Not quite the modern California office I expected. I looked at the yellowing walls covered in framed posters of the TV series Criminal Red. Across from me, a large portrait of an elderly gentleman stared with a look of disapproval. It was one of *those* portraits, the ones where the eyes seem to follow you. I turned my head slowly to the right. He stared. Slowly to the left. He stared.

Goosebumps crept up my spine. The plaque at the bottom read, Mark Randle. So, this is my new boss. His distinguished look came from his lifted chin and the touch of silver in his beard. I shrugged. His personality seemed nice enough—over the internet.

I fanned through the pages of the first novel on the stack and returned to the cover. The paper binding reflected the light. *The Untamed Savage.* Book one. *Blood Lust.* It's 2015. They don't make Indian romance movies anymore. Did they ever? I shivered and stood up. That's enough. Uncle has played a terrible joke on me. I scurried to the office door. I should call my mother and tell her—tell her what? I freaked out the first day on the job? California was too much for me?

No way. I locked the office door and returned to my rickety seat. I'd show her and Uncle Chris. I was going to rock at this job. I began to read.

o0o

Two hours later, I sobbed. Is there a tissue in this office? The poor woman in the book had lost her parents in a bogus Indian raid. I spotted a box and wiped the tears from my eyes. She was all alone on the prairie. The town sheriff and his sidekick villains were the true culprits. She merely escaped his evil grasp and fled on her white mustang, Cotton. *Sniff, sniff.* How will she survive on her own?

My boss continued to stare at me from the picture across the room. This time, I ignored him and returned to the book. I never knew a romance novel could be so fulfilling. The characters had worse problems than I did. Once more, lost in the pages, a tap sounded at the door.

I opened the door a crack, and then wider, when I saw GG.

"How did you enjoy your first day?" she asked.

"The book is good." I waved the novel that felt glued to my hand and spoke with pride, "I've read twelve chapters."

"In your first book?" She clicked her tongue and shook her head. "You'll have to read faster than that if you want to finish your report on time."

I stood firm, my chin above her. "I can do it. I'm good with search engines and fast on the keyboard, too."

"Hmm...well, the only thing you'll be searching for is *employment* if you don't get through these books." GG strolled over to the larger desk. "Maybe you should take a speed reading class and reapply?" She tapped on the computer until it came to life.

If this wasn't her office, why was she touching my boss's computer? I glanced at his picture on the wall. His grumbled expression now gawked at her.

"I think I'll manage just fine, thank you." I tossed the book in my bag and moved to stand behind her.

"You have an e-mail here from Mr. Randle." She wiggled the mouse and pointed to a picture of an envelope with my name attached.

"Thank you. I've got it." I covered her hand.

She stood back and rolled her eyes.

The keys to the office were in my reach. They jingled as I held them in front of the snoop. I had been here one day, but this job was mine. My rickety chair. My creaky floorboards. These keys meant the man on the wall trusted me.

"Like you said, GG, no worries. I'll lock up and be back first thing in the morning." I stood by the door with at least fifty questions on my mind, but if Mr. Randle had sent an e-mail, I could send one back. I would find the answers that way. Not from the woman who thought today should be my last day at work.

GG scanned the room before she walked past me. She glanced at my purse. "You can't take anything home."

"I'm not a thief. I assure you, I'll bring the book back tomorrow." *Like I wanted something from this old office.*

She glared for a moment with her pointed nose in the air. "Very well, then. I'll see you tomorrow." She entered the reception area, and the door closed. I set the keys down and hurried to the computer.

The e-mail contained a simple hello and an apology for his absence. No help at all. I read the end of his letter, sent a quick reply and locked up the office.

The Indian romance novel would have to be finished by the morning if I were to stay on GG's schedule. Full knowledge of all three books would be impressive to my new boss when he returned. Besides, the novel had me holding my breath between chapters. The pages were hard to stop reading long enough to take notes.

The tall male Indian, the writer described, had me flashing back to the hot cover. A muscular lean body. Dark skin from his Indian mother and deep blue eyes from a white father. Dancing Fire found Sally by a stream and pulled a thorn from her creamy pale heel. He washed her injured feet in the clear waters of a Kentucky stream. Her heart pounded with fright as he lifted her onto his steed. He had to be taking her and Cotton to his village. I couldn't wait to get home and find out.

"See you tomorrow, Mr. Randle." The eyes on the portrait followed me out the door.

Chapter Two

Indian Love

Hot tea with lemon warmed my throat in the comfort of my living room. A blanket kept my feet toasty as I opened the novel.

I jotted down the word "unpredictable", as Dancing Fire took Sally to a nearby cave instead of his village. He left her alone long enough to gather wood for a fire and berries to eat. The seductive scene pulled at more than my heart-strings as he fed her the sweet fruit, one berry at a time.

As I turned the page, Weaver, my fat domestic cat, jumped on the couch and walked across the book. "Weaver, don't you like hot Indians? I never knew I did until now." I giggled. "Here you go, Weave." I tossed a tiny, plastic ball across the floor.

Weaver pounced. The ball bell jingled as he batted the toy around the room.

The lease on my apartment read, "Small Pets Only," and since a protective Doberman was out of the question, I found my little black-eared Weaver at the local shelter the day after I moved. The cat made the apartment seem less lonely, but I didn't pick him. He picked me. The shelter cats played in a large glass-fronted room, but when I came near, Weaver jumped on a stand in front of the window. His glowing green eyes seemed to speak to me. "Take me home," they said. I didn't name him. He came with a little collar that read, Dream Weaver.

I grew warm under the blanket as Sally and her Indian rescuer bedded down for the night. The story returned to the bad sheriff, and my eyes grew weary. I fell asleep to the sound of Weave's purr as he curled beside me.

"Sally, wake up. Men on horseback."

"What? Huh?"

"Get up. We hurry."

"Oh, I feel like I slept on a rock. What time is it?" I wiggled down into the blanket but freed my arm. "Can you hand me my phone?"

"What is 'phone'?"

A man's voice? I opened my eyes. "Holy moly." I sat up and looked into the eyes of a bare-chested man with a feather in his hair. My scream echoed.

"Sally, no." He covered my mouth. "They will find us."

Find who? Where was I? My eyes took in the dim-lit cave. The smell of ash and horseflesh assaulted my nose. This can't be happening. I've been abducted in the night.

He loosened his grip over my mouth. "If you make noise," he said. "Sheriff will hear."

The sheriff? That's what I needed. The sheriff. I nodded, and he removed his big hand.

"I'm here," I yelled.

The Indian circled his strong arm under my breast and lifted me.

"Stop." I pounded my fist on his biceps as he carried me behind a rock, near the entrance.

"Be quiet, woman. If the sheriff finds you, he will kill us both."

"Bad Sheriff—" I looked down at my long, torn dress. My feet were bare and bruised. "Dancing Fire?"

He ran his fingers through my hair and peered into my eyes. "Have you hurt your head? Do you not remember?"

"I remember." I swallowed. "My name is not Sally. I'm Mary—"

"Shhh. They come." The sound of horses echoed off the cave walls. "Take knife." He held up a large sharp blade. "Kill white man who comes near you." He grabbed his bow and stepped closer to the entrance.

Murder someone? He wants me to kill. I can't go to jail, my mother would kill me.

He took a stance and pulled back on the bow as a man approached the mouth of our cave. His leather-fringed pants gripped tight around his muscles. His body was firm and brown. I'd never seen such a man, and yet...something was familiar.

The arrow sailed through the air with a whisper, and the white man fell to his knees. Dancing Fire fought bravely until all three men no longer threatened our survival.

He held me in his arms. "You are mine now. I will take you with me. Away from the white man's town. You will be wife to Dancing Fire. Live with me at Cherokee village."

"Okay." My heart pounded. This man is not real. I reached out and pinched him.

"Ugh." He spanned his fingers across my hips and pulled me forward. His demanding eyes burned into my soul. Familiar blue eyes. Deep blue-green eyes. No. Iridescent green eyes.

"Weaver." The cat stood on my chest with an intense stare. A dream. Yes, only a dream. *An amazing dream.* The glow of my clock said 3:00 a.m. I lowered Weaver to my side and curled around him.

o0o

The morning came with memories of a night filled with Indian adventure. A western tale that ended with a promise of commitment and abiding love. Never had I experienced such a vivid dream where I wanted nothing more than to remain in slumber.

Get up, girl. I sighed and stretched. My new job awaited, and I had at least twenty chapters to finish before I could start the second book. My cell battery died sometime during the night, and I walked like a zombie toward the kitchen.

"Meow."

"I hear what you're saying. 'Don't forget my breakfast, lady.'" I grabbed the bag of kitty chow from the counter and shook the cereal into his dish. Kitty food overfilled the container and piled on the floor. "Sorry, Weave. Clean that up, will ya?" He seemed to care less for my apologies and dug into the crunchy morsels.

The box by my feet had a sign that read, KITCHEN STUFF. I opened the lid and dug out the clock. "Oh, no." I had a half-hour to shower, dress and find a cab.

On my run to the bedroom, I tripped over a box of unpacked clothes. "Ouch." I rushed into the bathroom. Squish. "Oh, no." I forgot the cat box was in here. "Yuck." Cat moistened granules clung to the bottom of my toes.

I hopped around on one foot until I found the bathroom light. Two bounces back to the toilet to drag the trash over and brush away the mess from my foot. Tick Tock. *I couldn't be late my second day. No time for a shower.* I twisted my plain brown hair into a clip and did the minimum to get out the door.

I glanced around for Prince Charming by the cab line but didn't see him. As a matter of fact, no one noticed my tardiness. I slipped into the office. "Good morning, Mr. Randle." His portrait eyes follow me to the computer where I checked the mail for my name.

Nothing yet. I opened my purse, removed a roll of gray tape, and covered the crack in my rickety chair. That's better. I found the gum wrapper that marked my page. As I read the Indian tale, memories of last night's dreams resurfaced. I flipped forward a few pages. *It can't be.* I turned ahead two chapters. *Am I still dreaming?*

The book matched my dreams. Some of the words had changed, but the events didn't waver. I flipped to the ending and read the last page. The emotion, the actions, all there. My chair rolled backward as I stood.

No way. A trick. I wasn't clairvoyant. I couldn't talk to the dead or read palms.

I carried the book from the room and left the office doors open. "GG," I shouted through the hallway. Which office was hers? "This isn't funny, Mrs. Gunner."

Tom somebody. She worked for Tom Sanders. *Here it is.* I started to open the door when GG walked out.

"Are you out here calling my name, child?"

"Don't pretend you don't know." I held out the book.

She examined the paper cover front and back. Then opened the story and found my marker. "Hmmm, is this as far as you've read? You're not going to last long at this rate."

I snagged the book from her grip. "So you've said. What's really going on here, GG?" I looked around. "Where's the hidden camera?"

She laughed as I glanced at the tall, white cleanings. "I already know what happens in this book," I told her.

"Oh, so you've read this book before. That will give you a head start. Look, Mary, I just wanted to get your butt moving on these." She pointed at the book. "Believe it or not, I like you and think that you'll make a fine secretary for Mr. Randle. I keyed you in on what would impress him and nothing more. I'm not trying to trick you so you'll fail."

Her sincere look made me take a step back. This woman had no idea. How could she possible know I had dreamt the ending prior to finishing the book? I studied her face. How could *anyone* know?

"Are you okay Mary? You look a bit pale." She held my arm as we trailed back toward my office. "You don't have to read so quickly. It's too much pressure. I apologize—"

"No. I'm fine." *That's it. That had to be the answer.* "I've read this book before and just forgot. How silly of me to think you would know this." We stood in the hall in front of Mr. Randle's office. "I'm sorry to have bothered you."

She tilted her head and stared up at me through the corners of her eyes. "Make sure you take a lunch. Go outside, get some fresh air."

"I will. Thank you."

With a nod, she waited for me to go back inside.

In the office, Mr. Randle's portrait stared with those same blue eyes. Why did it seem like he was laughing? GG had a point. I breathed in stale office air all day.

When I pulled the strings on the blinds, dust circled in the light. I coughed and pushed at the window pane next to Mr. Randle's desk. Stuck. I pressed hard until the window opened. I needed to read, but instead I took the next hour to dust and to get more acquainted with my surroundings. More office supplies set outside of the cabinets than in. I hurried to straighten what I could and returned to my desk.

A man with a shield and a blade posed in battle, as a woman in a white gown beckoned at his sandaled feet. *My Fearless Roman.* I filled my lungs with the fresh air from the window and began to read. This time, the tissue box sat on the corner of my desk.

Two hours later, my stomached growled. A reminder of reality, but I couldn't put the book down. Princess Ra had been mistaken for a slave girl and taken hostage on the streets of Upper Egypt. Shackles twisted the skin of her wrist as a guard yanked her up the temple steps.

"*You'll be a tasty offering to Dionysus.*" He laughed.

"*No.*" She pulled back on her bindings.

The guard drew a blade from its sheath and pointed the tip at her chest. *"Come, slave. The priest and his fire awaits. Your sacrifice will bring grapes a-plenty for the master's wine."*

Ra cried out for mercy, but the—

A knock sounded at the office door. "Don't interrupt me now," I whispered. *What's going to happen to the Princess?*

GG's voice sounded from the doorway, "Mary, do you want to have lunch with me?"

Dang. I didn't want to stop reading, but couldn't be rude. "Yeah, sure, just a moment." I grabbed my purse, and we headed out.

Chapter Three

A Lamb in His Arms.

A California breeze blew my messy hair, and I cleared a wild strand from my eye. "Do we need a cab?"

"That depends. There's a quaint restaurant that serves Chinese right around the corner." GG pointed.

I nodded. "I love Chinese food."

Dragons covered the entrance walls as a hostess in a multi-colored blouse smiled. "Two?"

GG nodded, and the hostess seated us next to a large fish tank. The woman handed us the menu, and we ordered drinks. I ordered water because of the low funds in my wallet.

"Order anything you like," GG said. "My treat."

"No, I couldn't."

She reached across the table and patted my hand. "When you get your first check, you can treat me to lunch." She winked and lowered the glasses from her neck chain.

I began to enjoy the sassy lady's company as we relished in our eggrolls and rice. She explained the details of how the book report should be outlined and how Mr. Randle would read my recommended novel. He then would create a synopsis screenplay and pile it on a movie producer's desk with fifty other suggested screenplays.

"Why am I reading the works of other authors when he writes his own literature?"

GG set her chopsticks to the side. "The television series, Criminal Red, is his main focus." She picked up her napkin, wiped her mouth, and smeared her thick lipstick. "Mr. Randle has more friends in the film industry than anyone I know. Publishers are constantly asking him to recommend their books. If he gets an acceptance, he'll sign a deal and turn a novel into a screenplay. He's very good with explosive action."

I thought about his face. "He's good with action?"

She chuckled. "You'll see when he gets back."

I thanked GG for the nice lunch and returned to the office.

Full and comfortable, I focused on the portrait that matched the aging space. Why would the older man bother with love novels? He looked more like the detective story type. I shook my head. Back to Ra and her struggles.

Oh, thank goodness. A Roman soldier to the rescue. He had recognized her princess status, but treated her rough. The masculine hero thrust her into a guarded chariot.

Poor Ra, she would rather be tossed into the fiery pit than go back into the clutches of her sinister uncle. I couldn't blame her. The uncle was a beast.

She dared to ask the soldier's name as the chariot carried them away from her homelands.

Her rescuer, Cyrus, snapped a whip that sent the horses down a barren path. They had traveled under a desert sun for hours before they came upon a large cluster of Egyptian tents.

When Ra pleaded to speak with Cyrus's general, he answered, "*I am in charge.*" He carried her into the cloth shelter. "*One so much like a flower is now my captive. I plan to ransom you for the lands you stole.*"

Ra tried to explain. Her father's death had left her heartless uncle in charge. She had nothing to do with the capture of his lands, and asked not to be blamed for the uncle's barbaric acts.

Cyrus refused to believe that she was innocent. He sent her to a tent where slaves would bathe and scent her for his pleasure.

As the author changed the point of view to Cyrus, I learned of his true feelings for Ra. How he cared for the beautiful princess and had spies who watched over her. He knew she was trapped in her uncle's world, but to show her the weakness of his caring heart could mean death for him and his people. He planned to use her to trap the uncle, but even in his intent, he would never allow her return to the man's ruthless care.

I hummed a sigh. "Just *tell* her already! Ra would appreciate a guy like you." *Okay. Time to go home. I'm speaking aloud to a romance novel.*

I closed a window as the phone rang for the third time today. A pen lay next to my notepad, and I cleared my throat. "Mark Randle's office. Can I help you?"

I had taken messages from colleagues, but this time, the caller claimed to be his sister. Her pleasant voice sounded young. After she had ended the call, I gazed at the portrait. How could he have a sister so young? I studied Mr. Randle's blue eyes. The same blue eyes on the handsome face of the man by the cab door; on Fire Dancer... The matching eyes flashed from one man to the next. I shook my head. *Quit freaking out.*

After returning home, I unpacked a few boxes. Weaver arched his back and massaged his front claws into the carpet.

"I'm with you. An early bedtime tonight."

My pink polka-dot gown smelled like home. A reminder, my mother, would call tomorrow night.

Weaver jumped on the bed. I pooched my lips and said, "Come here, pretty kitty." He strolled up for an ear scratch. A stroke down his back made his tail shake. "It's just us, Weave."

With the desk light tilted toward *My Fearless Roman*, and my pillow fluffed, I let the words sweep me away.

The gold wrist cuffs on Ra's arms were removed. Her headband and blue gown lay tattered on the floor. After a full day in the desert sun, she couldn't remember a more refreshing bath. The slaves dressed her in a simple white frock and left her on the floor surrounded by pillows and a bowl of grapes. She picked at the fruit and pondered her escape.

Cyrus dismissed the tent guards and entered the room. He no longer wielded the shield and sword, but his mere form had Ra gripping the bowl as a weapon. *"You'll claim no reward from my uncle if I'm hurt,"* she cried.

Cyrus laughed. *"My intent is not to hurt, for what pain is there in a kiss?"*

Ra dumped the grapes from the bowl and held it to her side. The pillows hindered her balance as she stood and backed away from his approaching form.

She pointed the golden container like a knife. *"Touch me, and my uncle will have your head for this bowl."*

"Such nasty words from such red lips." Cyrus thwarted her feeble attempt with the bowl and bound her with his strong arms. Braced against his firm chest, the Roman's green eyes burned into the depths of her soul. She refused to cower, and drew breath in anticipation of a hard kiss, but when his soft lips covered hers in tender movement, the tension in her shoulders fell away. *"You taste of sweet wine—"*

I closed the book and tossed it to the end of the bed. *Why did I have to read this stuff? I was single, and this was torture.* I came to California to get away from college-boy flirtation and romance—start a life for myself. Last thing I needed was to be reminded of how good a man's arms felt.

Weaver raised his little furry head, as I ranted. "Long-haired Indians. Broad-chested Romans. I don't want these guys in my brain." I gave Weaver's head a pat. "Do I, baby?"

The TV remote sat inches away. What would be on at 9:00 p.m.? The news, a talk show, maybe a crime story. The masculine form on the book-cover beckoned me. Would Ra give in to Cyrus's lust? I craned back my neck and released an "ugh" into the air. I had to know.

I walked on my knees across the bed and snatched the book. A lick on my finger helped for a quick search. Found it. *You taste of sweet wine...*

Oh, my. Oh, my, gosh, I fell back onto my pillow. *She does give in.* I covered my eyes and read the next two paragraphs peeking between my fingers. The room grew warm with the author's written passion, and I fanned my face through the next chapter. How could Mark Randle add more action to *this* scene?

Ra struggled between the love she felt in Cyrus's arms, and his need to ransom her. At times, he treated her as the queen of the Nile, and other times, a lowly captive. The longer she remained in his care, the more difficult it became to understand his reasons for wanting to be rid of her. She must escape for fear of a broken heart.

With heavy eyes, I turned off the lamp. Weaver purred us to sleep.

o0o

Wait. Wait. Stop! My horse galloped across a desolate plane, under a moonlit sky. With a handful of horse mane, I searched for stirrups. Where was the saddle? "Whoa, baby, whoa." The horse slowed, and I patted his neck. "Where are we going in such a hurry, pretty horse?" A glance over the mare's rump and the answer came in the form of a dark rider on a black stallion. He raced toward me.

The feel of dread wrapped around my body like a blanket. My heels dug into the animal's quarter, but the rider had gained too much headway. His animal stopped the progression of mine.

This country girl rolled a leg over the horse's rump and slid to the ground. "I'm warning you. Stay away from me. I learned karate in the fifth grade." I took a basic stance. "Six full weeks of lessons."

"Nah, Flower Princess. How good is your fight without a fruit bowl in hand?"

"Cyrus." A bare leg showed through the tear in my gown as I crouched and circled.

The red cape of his Roman uniform soared in the wind behind his broad shoulders. He came for me. A twist with a side kick hit him straight in the groin. But it wasn't him who screamed. I hit some metal plate, and my ankle seared with pain.

On the ground in a pile of humiliation, I held my foot and cried.

"Ra, you've brought an injury upon yourself." He knelt on the ground beside me.

I stared into familiar blue eyes. Wasn't he supposed to have green eyes? And that face—Fire Dancer. The cab guy. The portrait. Flash, flash, flash. It's the same man.

Chapter Four

Dream Vision

My lungs filled with air as I awoke with a gasp. Why am I having such vivid dreams of the same guy? I reached for the light and jumped when I saw a set of glowing eyes next to the lamp.

"Meow."

"Oh, you scared me, Weave. What are you doing on the night stand?" The tag on his collar sparkled as I lifted him. Dream Weaver. I dropped him on the blanket, pulled back the sheet and got out of bed. No. A cat can't make you dream.

In all contemplation, the only thing that made sense was a drink. A *real* drink to help me sleep. As I headed toward the kitchen, my ankle gave way. "Ouch. Ouch! What the—why?" My ankle had a blue lump the size of a golf ball. *It couldn't be.* I hobbled back to the bed and searched for my marker in the book. There it was...Ra had fled on a horse. Her ankle hurt from a confrontation with Cyrus.

I limped to the kitchen and found a cork-screw, Uncle Chris's house warming gift. I didn't trouble with a glass, and tilted the entire bottle of wine. The sweet blackberry flavor warmed my throat as I chugged it down. I smiled at the label. *I won't dream after this...*

o0o

But I did dream. I dreamt the entire story. In a field of battle and romance, I played the part of Ra and fell in love with my blue-eyed captor. Cyrus destroyed the vindictive uncle, and we started a royal race of our own by the seaside. Again, love conquered all.

The vitality of the heart-felt dream made it hard to wake in the real world. I stretched across my sheets and touched Weaver's side. "If dreams are the reason your last owner gave you away. They weren't reading the right books." I searched through the pages. Yep, every word. By the end of the book, Ra's ankle had healed, and so had mine.

Up early and on schedule with the books, I used my laptop and searched every link I could find on dreams and cats. There were hundreds of pictures and videos of dreaming cats. How to interpret a dream involving a cat, but nothing on cats that make you dream. The scenario seemed impossible, yet I was sure, Weaver had something to do with my dreams.

My third day at work wasn't unlike the first or second, although the last book on the desk had me wondering what I might dream. The simple red cover read *Seductive Blood*. A mystery, maybe? I turned the book over. Instead of a woman, this time the author was a middle-aged male. I swallowed as I read the blurb. *Vampires*.

Oh no. Would I wake up in the middle of the night, thirsty for blood?

What started out as dread turned to fascination as my eyes scanned the words. The first three paragraphs had me gripping the edge of the desk.

o0o

Devan Carter blew a warm breath into his hands and took careful steps between the graves at old Pike Cemetery. Dusk had settled on the Roanoke River gap, near the edge of the Blue Ridge Mountains. Devan hurried to find his father's headstone before darkness fell. He knelt into a rolling fog and pushed a spiked crucifix into the dirt at the head of his father's grave.

The sound of blackbirds' wings filled the air as they took flight from the branches above. Devan craned his neck at the spectacle and breathed in more than the scent of rotten wood. He smelled death. An army of goose bumps set his hair on end, and an instinct to run battled with the logic in his mind. He started for the exit gate, swung around twice to see if someone followed, then picked up his pace.

The trees whispered the name, *Lenora*, as he rushed through the black iron opening. A sudden gust of wind raised the fog into the air.

Haze encircled his car, and he froze. With near zero visibility, he removed the key fob from his pocket and stepped closer. The chirp sounded mere feet away.

"*Lenora.*" The whisper came once more, but this time, sounded before him. A hand reached out of the mist and gripped down on his shoulder. *"You will bring her to me."* A tall, cloaked figure appeared with red eyes that locked with his own. Devan's legs forbade his command to move.

I rolled back my office chair and rubbed the chill out of my arms. If I dreamt about vampires during the afternoon, instead of the middle of the night, maybe it wouldn't be so scary. And, I would have more time to work on the report.

GG didn't stop by for lunch, so I locked up early and made a quiet dash for home.

Chapter Five

Afternoon Escape

This time, I planned to let the dream guide me. I would say what came to my mind and not interrupt the course.

Like Cinderella, going to the ball, I peered down at my lavender cocktail dress. Hairpins tugged at my scalp and feelings of anticipation beckoned me to the door. There he was. My handsome blue-eyed stranger, standing in a tux. Without thought, I knew his name.

"Come in, Devan."

He handed me a bouquet of red roses.

"Thank you. They're beautiful."

Devan held a hand to his chest. "You're beautiful, Lenora."

I smiled and left the door wide open so he could enter, but found it odd, he remained on the stoop. I tucked the flowers in a vase and twisted the lock on the knob before we left.

Instead of opening the car door, he blocked my path and looked at the ground.

"What is it?" I asked.

His eyes shot up. "Let's leave tonight. Run away from this backward town. I'll show you things you never knew existed."

He took hold of my chin and ran his mouth along my neck.

I giggled and gave him a gentle nudge. "What are you talking about? You know how much this night means to me. Please, let's go. We'll be late for the champagne toast."

The long heels on my white pearl shoes tapped nervously on floorboards as we turned down a back-wooded road. "This isn't the way to the party, Devan."

He stared straight ahead as if in a trance when the car veered to the left and then to the right. "Devan." We headed straight for a tree. "Devan, wake up!"

I gasped and sat up in the bed. My heart pounded. Weaver jumped to the floor and headed for his litterbox. "That scared the pee out of me too," I muttered.

I grabbed the book and thumbed to the last chapter.

After the crash, Devan's vampire blood allowed him to heal quickly. He carried Lenora to the cemetery while she remained unconscious. He laid her on the damp ground near the tombstone of his father. His master, the monster who had changed him, appeared behind the grave.

"*Lenora,*" the creature whispered, standing over her body. His red eyes peered out at Devan. "*You've done well. Now, seek your reward in the freedom I offer.*" He stretched a long, cloaked arm toward the gate. "*Go,*" he commanded.

I made a note. The words the author used to describe Devan's love for Lenora flowed like melted butter over the page. He overcame the master's powers and used the spiked-tipped cross from his father's grave to pierce the heart of the beast.

Lenora had internal bleeding, and Devan had no choice but to turn her into a creature of the night. He sank his teeth into her soft, white neck. A moment filled with sadness and bliss.

It wasn't the exact happy ending that inspired the other books, but the chilling tale made me write the words...My recommendation...*Crimson Red.*

I worked into the evening on a report that was sure to impress my new boss. In the midst of a spell check, the doorbell rang. I looped the front of my robe and peered out the door's peephole. I rubbed my eyes and looked again. It was him.

The cab guy. The hero in the stories. The man of my dreams! I turned full circle. Too late to clear the boxes. I ran fingers through my hair. What should I do?

I straightened my shoulders and opened the door a crack. "Can I help you?"

"Mary Lynn Price?"

I recognized the voice, and the instinct to jump into his arms overwhelmed me. I opened the door a little wider. "Yes."

He tilted his head. "Wait." He blinked. "I recognize you."

Our embrace in Fire Dancer's cave, the kiss in the Egyptian tent, his teeth sinking into my neck all flashed in my mind. "You do? You know who I am?"

"I saw you in the rain by a cab the other day."

My shoulders dropped. "Oh, yeah. The cab."

"And…I'm also your new boss." He held out his hand. "Mark Randle."

I closed the door half way. "No, you're not. My boss is an older gentleman."

He laughed and pulled out his wallet. "We've never been formally introduced." He handed me his card and showed me his driver's license.

I shook my head and handed them back. "I saw my boss's picture on the wall, and you're not him."

His brows wrinkled. "On the wall, at the office?"

I nodded.

"You thought that was me." He tried to cover a grin with his hand. "That's Grandpa Randle. I'm sorry. I see how…" He shook his head. "I just inherited the building a couple months ago. I know the place is a mess. I haven't had time to remodel my office and his picture—"

"*You're* my boss?" I had fallen in love with my boss, and he didn't even know me.

He nodded and smiled.

I opened the door, drew in a deep breath, and stepped to the side. "Come in."

My laptop and vampire book laid on a desk, not far from the door, in plain sight. I looked away and rolled my eyes. *I hope he bites.*

He strolled up to the desk. "You've been working at home. I told GG to have you take your time."

"Yes, GG. Great lady. Mr. Randle—"

"Mark." He nodded. "We're not formal around the office."

"I see." *He was here. In my living room.* "Mark, I feel like such an idiot for thinking that picture was you."

"No." He reached out and touched my hand. "I might have done the same in your shoes."

I looked at my bare feet and doubted it, but I couldn't stop the grin that formed on my face.

He released my hand and stepped back. "I didn't expect to come home this soon and realized there's only one key to the main office door. Apparently, you have it."

He wanted the key. He wasn't here because he'd dreamt of me all week. He needed something from me. Just the key.

"They're in my purse. Be right back." Weaver ran past me.

"DW, what are you doing here, boy?"

I turned to see Mark holding my cat. "You know this cat?"

"Sure, I do. He's mine." He scratched Weaver's chin. "I've been looking everywhere for you." He rolled the collar around his neck to see the inscription. "I had this made for him weeks ago. How did you find him? Did he come to the office?"

"Your cat?" I handed him the keys and took back my cat. "I picked him up at a shelter. There were a lot of cats there. This one can't be yours."

"I'd know DW anywhere. He has a special talent."

Weaver mewed as I held him tight. "You know about his—special gift?"

"I told you. He's my cat."

"You left him in a shelter. Weaver is mine now." I glared at him as though he had a red Roman cape flying from the back of his shirt.

He stuffed the keys in his jean pocket and crossed his arms. "I see you've become attached. I could pay you for him."

I pulled back on Weaver, giving the boss the back of my shoulder. "He's not for sale."

The phone on the desk vibrated on the wood top. I glanced at the screen and ignored my mother's call.

What was I doing? I couldn't make an enemy out of my boss. "I guess I could share him with you now and then. Bring him to the office." The fur on Weaver's head tickled my chin. "Would you like that, Weave?"

"A compromise. I don't know about him, but I like the idea." He glanced at the phone. "I'll let you get back to your evening."

I nodded. "I know you'll think I'm crazy, but Weaver's...special talent—umm..." *Just go ahead and say it.* "Does he make you dream?"

He lifted his brows and stared for a moment. "I've never said this aloud to anyone, but it's the strangest thing. I can be working on a screenplay and dream about my work when DW is in the room. I've locked him out, just to see—it's him, alright. What about you?"

"Oh." I sighed. I wasn't going crazy, and relief filled the air, but could I say more without sounding like a lunatic? I couldn't discuss the heated relationships Mark and I shared through all the stories I'd read. He had no idea. "It's happened to me once or twice."

He smiled. "Maybe we keep *this* conversation our little secret."

I nodded.

The room grew quiet as Mark reached over and petted the cat. There was something in the way he looked at me through those stunning blue eyes.

After a minute, I asked, "How's your mother?"

He turned and picked up the vampire book from the edge of the desk. "She's fine. She lost her dog again."

"Your family can't seem to hold on to animals, can you?"

"I suppose not." He chuckled and held out the book. "Are you finished with this, by chance?"

Right then, a light bulb sizzle-snapped someplace in my head. "Yes. Do you plan to read it?" I swallowed.

"That's why I wanted the keys. Thought I'd pick up the books and read a few chapters tonight."

"You know, I've changed my mind. You keep Weaver tonight." I shoved the cat back into his arms and gave Weave a rub between the ears. *Do your thing, baby.*

"Are you sure?" he asked.

Oh, yeah. "He's probably missed you." I smiled.

Mark left that evening with Dream Weaver in his arms. He dreamt of us that night, and several nights after. A year later, we were married. Our favorite pastime? Reading romance novels...and dreaming.

Three in the bed,
And the kitty cat said,
"Meow."

About the Author—C. A. Jamison

C.A. Jamison holds a certificate of excellence from Romance Writers of America. She loves to create a romantic tale while peering through her window at the blue lake in the backyard. She enjoys wildlife and the peaceful surroundings in her small Indiana town. Some days, she heads to the city to help run the family's high-tech car audio shop—rated in the top 50 in the country—which inspired her science fiction adventure, POLARITY: CHILDREN OF THE ORB. Find her at www.cajamison.com

Claws For Justice

Mariah Lynne

They seem soft and furry, but watch out—the claws will catch you every time!

Chapter One

"Find anything Shurl? The dumpster looks like it's overflowing. Full of good food, I hope. Glad you thought of living near the shelter. Makes life so much easier."

I hissed.

"For you, maybe."

I couldn't believe how anxious Watts was for breakfast.

"Hold your horses; I have to get down in there, first. I'm not real anxious about doing that since there's a strange and not-too-pleasant smell wafting out. Give me a minute to compose myself for the dive."

I'm a furry tabby who detests getting dirty, but when it comes to starving or escaping, I find I'm capable of anything.

Having lived with Watts in the county shelter for so long, I know he's a Siamese who would rather starve then get dirty. So, with that in mind, I held my nose, lifted my tail, and jumped in. I wasn't too worried. Cats always land on their feet—or so the saying goes. Lucky for me, there were some old rags and newspapers that broke my jump.

I looked around, knowing that I had to be careful of any broken glass or sharp metal. I've done this before but this is my first dive since we escaped the animal shelter.

Ah, the animal shelter…Watts and I shared a cage together, seems like forever. Yesterday, we overheard Robby, our attendant, tell a prospective pet parent that if we weren't adopted by tomorrow, our time had run out. He told every human looking for a cat how smart and nice we were, and that he would adopt us himself but he already has four rescue cats at home and his pet bills were getting expensive, considering his salary.

The humans would look us over; one lady even held us, but after all of Robby's pleading, they all said they wanted a kitten. That's the way it goes around here. Nobody wants an adult cat over a kitten.

With that in mind, Watts and I knew we had to act fast. Right before closing that night, we heard the vet tell Robby to leave our cages shut, but not padlocked, since she would come for us first thing in the morning. Watts started to cry.

"We're so lovable. Why doesn't anyone want us?"

"That's the least of our problems right now. We have to find a way out."

I pushed on the door but the clasp kept it from opening. I had to get at that clasp. I scampered over to our claw tower which was on wheels so it could easily be moved from cage to cage and asked Watts to help me push it near the door. If I could climb up high enough, I might be able to move the clasp with my paws.

We pushed and shoved using our back ends until the tower was next to the door. That was a lot of work for a slender Siamese like Watts and a chunky tabby like me. After I took a few minutes to catch my breath, I clawed my way up the tower and came face to face with the clasp. I hung on as best I could and reached out with one paw.

Watts yelled, "Careful, Shurl. I'll try and catch you if you fall."

"Yeah, right," was all I could respond to that idea.

I swatted and swatted until—bingo—the clasp moved. The cats next to us saw what we were doing and cheered meows. They had heard Robby's comments, as well.

"Okay, Watts, I think we got it. Get ready to run."

I dashed down as Watts asked, "Where? They lock the doors at night. I heard there are alarms on them. No matter what we do, we'll get caught."

"I know Robby leaves the empty dog kennels open. They have runs with a doggy door. Once outside, the fence is wire mesh. We'll have to try and climb it, and then jump. Not a perfect scenario, but one we'll have to do if we want to stay alive."

Watts had tears in his eyes. "Hope we make it."

"We will. Positive thoughts. Ready? Let's go."

Watts followed me out and down the long corridor to the kennels. A few of the dogs were upset to have a couple of cats invade their space.

"Hey, get out of here. We'll keep barking until you leave."

I laughed. "No problem. We're just on our way out. Watts, run as fast as you can through the next kennel. Here goes."

We bolted through the empty kennel and out the doggy door to the open run. Once outside, we did not stop, trying to climb the fence by pouncing about third of the way up before clawing our way to the top. Watts got there a little after me so I waited. Friends for life. That's our motto. Watts positioned himself ready to jump.

"On three. One…two…*three*."

We leaped off the fence at the same time and landed on the soft grass below. Even so, I heard Watts meow in pain.

"Oh, my aching tail! I landed right on it."

"Sorry pal, but you'll be real happy to feel your tail tomorrow."

"I know. I just like to complain. Where to now? How will we eat?"

That's my Watts. Always thinking about his stomach—and he stays so thin.

"Before I met you, I lived as a stray in a wooded area not too far from here. At night, you can actually see the shelter lights. If we go there, we'll be near the dumpster where they throw away food and near the roof drain for water. We'll eat before the shelter opens and after it closes to remain hidden. Otherwise, they'll drag our furry butts back there. Understand?"

"Yep. Sure do."

Watts got up and I showed him the way to the tree-filled area. We were fed earlier today, so we weren't hungry. He followed me across the road and down a short hill before we ended up in my old haunt.

"Remember, we have to remain discreet. That's how I got caught. I walked up to a total stranger looking for a hand out or a forever home and he called animal control.

"When the sun comes up we'll go get some grub. I've jumped in dumpsters before. Not pleasant but necessary. Now, find a thick patch of grass and go to sleep. I'll do the same. You were brave to follow me."

Watts purred. "You're my hero. Good thing we live in Florida. At least, we'll always be warm."

Watts lay down and dozed off. I watched Watts sleep, keeping a vigilant eye out for anyone or anything that might hurt us. No one came by our hiding place. Early the next morning, Watts and I headed for the dumpster. That's when we found poor Robby.

I jumped in, even with the bad smell. I moved some papers and cans aside before meowing as loud as I could.

"It's Robby! He's dead. Murdered!"

"Robby? Dead in the dumpster? Why? I can't imagine who would harm him. He always treated all of us animals with such care and love."

Watts jumped to the edge.

"Don't look down. It's too upsetting. Don't try to come down here, either. The whole thing makes me sick."

I could hear Watts crying through his purrs. "Robby is the one who named us. We were always sniffing and pawing at things. He said we're like the famous detectives Shurlock and Wattson and wrote our names on our sign. Poor guy…he was smart, but never got to finish junior high. I heard him tell Amy it was because his Dad left home and he had to go to work. That's when he started at the shelter. Everyone loved him."

Watts started to cry again. I can't lie. Tears were flowing through my fur, as well. I tried to remain stoic.

"We can't just leave him here. We have to get someone's attention without calling out ourselves."

"How, Shurlock?"

"I'm thinking. Wait, I've got it. There's that stray German Shepherd named Bruiser not too far from our hideout. Let's go rattle his cage just enough for him to bark and chase us here. If we can keep him barking near the dumpster until someone comes to work, we might have a shot. In the meantime, before I come out, I'll uncover Robby so the next person who dumps anything will see him—unless he's the killer, that is."

"Great plan, providing the dog doesn't get us first. He must be one mean dude to have a name like Bruiser."

"Used to work protection for some old guy who had mob ties, or so I heard."

I stayed down in the dumpster with the sad task of uncovering Robby. I was as gentle with him as he was with me. I paused for a moment of prayer before telling him, "We're gonna find out who did this to you, Robby. I give you my word."

I jumped out to find Watts on the ground, sobbing.

"Okay. Let's go. Don't think about anything else except finding Robby's killer. Got that?"

"Got it."

We left just before the shelter opened to go to the dog camp and find that Shepherd.

CHAPTER TWO

Watts and I tiptoed around before we came to a group of dogs. No Shepherd in the mix. We looked at some more dogs hiding in the bushes and walked around until Bruiser came out of his lair looking as strong and foreboding as ever.

"Okay. Ready. On three, let's run by him. One…two…*three!*"

I went first. Watts followed not too far behind. That Shepherd came after us like lightning, but we were faster. He chased us all the way back to the dumpster. We jumped up on a nearby bush as he continued to bark at us.

Someone heard him and opened the side door to the shelter. It was Amy. She yelled back, "Thought I heard a dog bark. I'll bring the trash out and check."

I meowed. "Quick, Bruiser. Hide!"

The dog looked puzzled, but when he saw the door open, he moved in our direction and crouched down in some bushes below us.

"Thanks for the chase, Bruiser. We're trying to help a good friend."

Bruiser tilted his head in confusion. He growled.

"How does my chasing you help a friend?"

"We think someone murdered him and dumped his body in the dumpster. He was a kind human who took good care of us. We needed to call attention to the dumpster so someone would find his body."

"How do you two geniuses know he was murdered?"

I looked at him.

"Seriously? And people say you Shepherds are so smart. Who would commit suicide in a dumpster?"

"Maybe he got sick and fell in. Maybe he was so depressed he didn't want anyone to find him. You know we dogs hide when we are very sick."

"Well, that's not what humans do. Besides, he was never depressed. He was happy spending his days with us animals."

"Sounds like a great guy. Wait, I smell someone coming out. Look, she's carrying a bag of garbage."

Amy carried the bag to the dumpster. It was overloaded and heavy. She looked inside to make sure there was enough room before letting out the most blood curdling scream.

"Help! Someone help! Robby's in the dumpster! He looks dead! Hurry…he's not breathing!"

Three more shelter workers including the manager poured out the side door. The manager looked in the dumpster before dialing her cell.

"911. This is an emergency. We have an employee unconscious in the dumpster. He looks dead, but I'm not sure. Please, send help ASAP."

The three of us watched from just far enough away not to be caught. Amy started to cry. The manager held her arm to calm her down

Bruiser saw tears in Watts's eyes. "Don't worry, my new little buddy. If I catch who did this to your friend, I'll bite his leg off."

Looked like Bruiser had a soft spot—if you wanted to call it that.

The paramedics arrived and we watched as one got in the dumpster to check for vital signs.

"Sorry, ma'am. He's been dead about ten hours." He looked at his watch. "It's eight a.m., so that would be around ten p.m. last night. We'll know better when the ME arrives. We can't move him until we get the ME's okay."

We heard another vehicle and a cruiser pull up right after he said that. The cars came to a screeching halt as a deputy and a young man in a white coat got out, respectively.

The young man told the paramedics, "We heard the 911 call and followed when the caller said she didn't know if he was dead. Let me go in and examine the body before you move him."

The ME removed a ladder from the top of his SUV and climbed up to jump in the dumpster. We couldn't see him, but could hear him.

"Odd…no signs of a struggle. Maybe a heart attack or an overdose, but I'll know more when I get him back to the morgue. All right, boys, you can move him—but be careful. Such a shame. He was too young to have this happen."

We continued to watch as the paramedics lifted Robby out of the dumpster and into a body bag before placing him on a gurney. We could hear the three humans sob. I put my paw over my heart out of respect. I looked over. Watts and Bruiser did the same.

The deputy walked over to our shelter manager, Susan.

"Ma'am, my name is Deputy Rooney. You obviously cared for this young man. Mind if I ask you a few questions to help us find out what happened to him?"

Susan shook her head as tears streamed down her cheeks.

"What was his full name?"

"Robert Grancer."

"Thank you. Did you know of any illegal drug use by this young man?"

Susan was emphatic. "Definitely not. We drug test all our employees on a yearly basis. Robby always passed with flying colors."

The deputy wrote her answers in a notebook.

"How about enemies? Or threats from someone denied adoption? Anyone he owed money to? Any girlfriends who felt they were unfairly dumped?"

Susan shook her head negative to all of the above.

"No, no and no. Robby wasn't on drugs, never spent more than he made and was too shy to have a girlfriend. He wasn't the one who made decisions on adoptions."

The deputy smiled.

"It's always the shy ones that surprise us. Well, if you think of anything or overhear anything that might help, please let me know. Here's my card." The deputy handed Susan his card. "Feel free to call me anytime. Sorry for your loss."

"Robby was one of the best employees the Bonita Shelter ever had. We all will miss him."

Susan took the card and put it in her pocket. The three humans went back inside as the Lee County ME and deputy left along with the ambulance. The three of us still in hiding remained speechless. I broke the silence.

"It's our duty to find Robby's killer. I'm sure it was murder. Tonight, Watts and I will hang out outside the shelter windows to see if any of the cats—or dogs, for that matter—heard anything that might help us. Until then, we better head back."

"But, I'm still hungry," Watts replied.

Bruiser growled. "Hey, I dragged a bag of dog food back from my old neighbor's yard. You're welcome to share. I moved it away and out of sight from the other dogs.

Watts let out a sigh of relief as we followed Bruiser back to his lair. He dragged the partially-open bag of food to where we were standing.

"Can you believe someone threw this out because their spoiled little poodle didn't like it? Here, help yourselves."

Bruiser tore open the bag with his teeth and the three of us chowed down.

"Hmm...salmon and chicken. My faves."

Watts had a big smile on his face. I took charge.

"Okay, remember, we have to be alert tonight, so I suggest a little afternoon catnap after our meal...no pun intended."

The three of us lay down in the bushes after Bruiser closed up his bag and went to sleep. We slept like babies until...

"Hoot. Hoot. Hoot."

Thank goodness for Hooty. That owl used to wake me up in the shelter. Never appreciated him then, but we sure need to be awake tonight. Watts was stretching, and Bruiser was already up pacing.

"What do you need us to do?" Bruiser asked.

"We need to go back to the shelter. If any cats or dogs are awake, we need to know if they overheard any of the humans talking about what happened to Robby. Bruiser, you handle the dogs, and Watts and I will ask our old shelter buddy cats. Let's go."

NINE DEADLY LIVES

CHAPTER THREE

We walked out of the bushes and down the moonlit path that led to the back of the shelter. Bruiser went to the runs and whimpered to get the dogs' attention. Four of them came out. Watts and I went over to the cats' screened windows and meowed. Sure enough, the windows filled up with cats, anxious to know what happened to us.

"We're fine. Hey, did anyone hear any more about what happened to Robby?"

"Just that they think his heart failed. He had such a big one, too," Seymour answered.

"I know," I answered. "We sure do miss him. Did the manager find out how he ended up in the dumpster?"

"Susan thinks he must have been cleaning the dumpster like he sometimes did and got sick inside," Bojangles added.

I kept asking questions, even though I was amazed that anyone would buy that explanation.

"Does anyone know what he was supposed to do that day at work?"

"Only something to do with Jinx. Not sure what, but we'll check around tomorrow for you. See you tomorrow night?" Riley asked.

Watts answered, "Sure thing."

We rounded up Bruiser, who later told us that one of the dogs was sick. Amy took him to the vet who does all the county shelter work two days ago, but he was still not any better. Bruiser thought that odd. So did I.

The next morning, Watts and I went back to the dumpster. They had cleaned it out, disinfected it, and hosed it down so there were slim pickings and they were all the way on the bottom. Before I could jump in, I heard a faint meow from around the corner. It sounded like Jinx, an eight-year-old black and white stray. Watts and I went over to where we heard the sound and pounced on the windowsill.

"Hey, Jinx. It's Shurl and Watts. What's wrong?"

"You guys are so lucky to be out of here. Robby took me to the vet, but I never got a chance to see her. He had to take me back, but I still don't feel good. Later that afternoon, he came to my cage and brought me dinner. He picked me up and hugged me. I guess he figured I couldn't understand human talk because he started telling me about his strange day. "

Watts looked at him.

"How so?"

"Well, as he petted me, he said he just came from the accountant's office. He was cleaning the floor near her desk when he knocked over some papers by accident. As he picked them up, he saw there were bills for vet services. One was for me. Since he was the one who took me there twice, he knew I never got any medical attention—not even from a vet tech—and he had to take me back here sick. He told me something strange was going on and he was going to get to the bottom of it so his Jinxy could feel better.

"He then said he was reading my bill when the office manager came in and surprised him. She appeared upset and asked what he was doing. He told me he said he found a bill for Jinx from the vet. He took me there, but no one looked at me, so why would there be a bill?

"He kept petting me and, as he did, said that the accountant told him not to worry about it. She said she would look into the charge, tell Susan, and take care of it. He told me he didn't know what she meant by that, but since she had more authority than he did, he had to trust her.

"He hugged me and told me how much he loved me and wanted me to get better. That was the last time I saw him."

I listened, and watched tears roll down Jinx's black and white face. I looked over at Watts.

"We need to look into this, but I don't know where to start. I guess we could see if any of the other cats went to the vet and received no treatment. Let's go."

We thanked Jinx and pounced over to the other windowsill. Riley was licking his paws. He heard us land on the sill and came right over.

"You guys back again? What brings you here?"

Watts spoke first. "Have you seen the vet recently?"

"I went with Amy two days ago for my rabies vaccine but I never got the shot. They said I'd have to come back next week. They were plum busy. Same thing happened to Bojangles and our social Calico, Queeny...but I could go on and on. Not just for shots. Some needed eye treatments, some ear treatments, baths to get rid of matting etc. We all went, but came back empty-handed."

I looked at Watts. "How long has this been going on?"

Riley purred.

"At least three months. Weird, don't you think?"

"Very," I responded. "We never needed to go to the vet when we were here, so we had no idea. You all never talked about it."

"No reason to discuss it. We figured that's the way it was."

Riley shrugged as I asked.

"Think there's any proof of that?"

"Don't know. Maybe in the accountant's office. It's the third door on the left from the main entrance. Says Monica Wilson on the door…"

"Watts, let's grab a bite and then go back and figure out what to do next. May need Bruiser's help again."

Watts smiled at that thought. "For such a big dog, he sure is a sweetie."

I went back to the dumpster with Watts. "Let's grab some lunch to go. Maybe we can find something for our buddy."

They must have just done inventory and date checking. Found some outdated cat treats and a rawhide bone. I let Watts carry the bone back. Maybe if Watts gave it to him, Bruiser wouldn't think of it as a bribe.

CLAWS FOR JUSTICE

CHAPTER FOUR

We walked over to Bruiser's lair. None of the other canines spent any time with him and they sure would not try to take anything. We saw Bruiser lying on his side. He looked a bit bored. If he needed excitement, he was going to get some.

He lifted his head when he saw us approach and wagged his tail. The wag became stronger when he saw Watts carrying a rawhide bone. New or used, bones always got the same reaction.

"Hey, Bruiser, how's it going?"

Bruiser looked up. "Better, now that you're here. I was a little sad thinking about my owner, Harry. He was old and had to walk with a cane, but I didn't mind. He walked at a slow pace and I walked with him. I knew how much he loved me. One day, he couldn't breathe. His son rushed him to the hospital. Never saw him again. He loved me, and I know he would never leave me on purpose. His ugly son Marcus refused to take me in even though Harry told him to take care of me when he couldn't. I overheard Marcus tell the maid he wanted to take me to the pound. I'm a big guy. We usually get adopted last.

"Harry would never have wanted that, so I ran away from home. Every now and then, I go to the hospital and wait by the entrance, but no luck finding Harry."

His story tugged at my heart.

"Sorry to hear that, Big B. I guess we all share the same kind of story. Some humans think we are toys to play with and discard when they tire of us. They don't want commitment, or the responsibility a cat or dog brings. Your human is probably still in there and loves you very much. Our humans didn't want us anymore. They told the shelter they were tired of taking care of us.

"On a brighter note, did you know that Susan is fighting for our shelter to become a 'no-kill'? She told Amy she is preparing her presentation for the county commissioners. Hope they grant her wish. That would be good for all of us. We wouldn't have to always be afraid and ready to run. The county below here has a shelter like that. If it wasn't so far, I'd wander down there myself. Anyway, I digress. Watts has something that might cheer you up. Show him what you have for him."

Watts lifted the bone in the air as much as he could and then dropped it. Bruiser got up all cheery-like.

"For me? Thank you. Harry used to get one of these for me every week."

Bruiser picked up the bone and lay down next to us to chew.

"Picked up some outdated cat treats. You're welcome to some if you like."

Bruiser kept chewing, so I thought it was a good time to brainstorm.

"We went to the shelter to see if the other cats found out anything more about Robby. They said that they overheard him tell Jinx that the vet was billing the county for services not rendered. Robby told the accountant, Monica, that he found one such bill on her desk, but she said she would take care of the matter. The only way we can find out is to get into her office and mess up all the vet bills on her desk to call them to Susan's attention.

"But first, we must pay a visit to the vet to see if any of her sick or boarding animals heard or saw anything. Jinx said he overheard Amy saying the last text Robby received was from the vet who asked him to stop by and pick up some meds for him after work.

"Anyway he never got them, so we have to find out why. First piece of the puzzle. Now, what do we do?"

Bruiser looked up. "I went there once when I was a puppy. For some reason Harry, didn't like her, so he took me to Dr. Kelsy, whom I really liked. Anyway, at the county vet, Dr. Mond, you can't converse with any cats. They're all locked up inside. We'll have to deal with the dogs. That's where I come in. You stay in the background, and I'll find out what I can. Let me bury this bone for later, and we can go there now and see if anyone knows anything."

Bruiser did just that, and the three of us left for Dr. Mond's.

o0o

He was right. The boarding dogs were in their runs. No one was watching them. Watts and I hid in some nearby bushes while Bruiser approached the runs. At first, they all started to bark. Bruiser barked back telling us later he told them to be quiet because he needed their help.

"Okay. Hush up. I have a few questions about Dr. Mond. My human friend was killed recently, and this was the last place he was supposed to have gone. Anyone seen or heard anything?"

The dogs looked at each other. A pretty Dalmatian named Kitty responded first.

"Not me. I just got here today. My, you are a big boy, aren't you?"

Spot, a brown and white wired hair terrier, jumped in. I couldn't help thinking how stupid humans can be with names.

"I've been here three days. The first night, from my run, I saw a young, tall male human with brown hair enter. He seemed nice and talked to each of us as he looked for the vet. He told Dr. Mond he was there to pick up some meds, but she wanted him to look at a tabby, Fluffy, who was boarding and really pretty…the cat's meow. He went over to her cage and picked her up. She liked him and purred like a kitten. My kennel is directly opposite the exam room, so I could see everything that went on. Humans must think we're really dumb.

"I watched the man caress Fluffy, when, out of nowhere, Dr. Mond popped up behind him holding a needle. She stabbed him on the side of the neck. He dropped to the floor at once. Dr. Mond whistled, and another lady I never saw before came out of the bathroom to help move him. I heard her say 'We'll take him to my car and put him in the trunk.' The other woman was not happy. She commented on how heavy he was. The two dragged the human out and that's the last I saw of him.

"The whole thing seemed strange, so I went out to my run, but couldn't see anything. I was on the wrong side of the building. I heard moans and groans coming from the two women and a loud thud. That's probably when they put him in the doctor's trunk. Hope that helps. That's all I saw."

Watts's mouth was wide open. I tried to keep my cool. Bruiser was amazing. He's a true German Shepherd. No wonder they are police dogs.

Bruiser continued asking questions, as if by instinct.

"Did anyone see what happened to the needle? That could prove to be our best evidence."

"I did. Oooh, I did." A Jack Russell named Rusty jumped up and down as he answered. "I'm right next to Spot, and I like to jump. I saw Dr. Mond put a needle in a funny tall can of potato chips she likes for snacks. She took the red can and put the lid back on and put it in a brown paper bag. She then put it in her pocket when they were dragging your human out. They haven't picked up the trash yet. It may be in the green dumpster on this side of the building. The red one is for medical waste and is sealed. If the doctor wanted to hide it, plain sight is the best route."

A cocker spaniel named Ted said, "I'm on the end. I saw her put something in the green one. They dropped the human for a few minutes and slid the dumpster door open. She had a brown paper bag, and hid it right in plain sight."

"You are all so right." Bruiser commented. "Thank you all for your help. Hope you have a great vacation."

They all howled.

Bruiser walked back to where we hid.

"Did you get that?"

We nodded. Watts gave the kudos. "Great police work. You missed your calling."

I added, "I'll do the dumpster dive." Watts looked concerned.

"Be careful opening that brown paper bag. The poison may have leaked."

"No worries, Watts. I'll be careful."

The three of us walked over to the green dumpster. No one was outside. The plan was that Bruiser was to scare any humans away while I got the can. I dove in and rummaged through trash. I found one bag with leftover chicken salad sandwich in it. Under normal conditions, I would have feasted on it, but not with such lethal poison around. Old soda cans, empty containers of pet food, until—Bingo—a second brown bag. I opened it slowly to find the red potato chip can inside. My paw twisted it open and I looked in. There it was …the needle that killed Robby. I twisted the lid shut, closed the bag, and threw it over the side of the dumpster. Didn't want to put it in my mouth.

When I jumped out, I saw Watts and Bruiser grinning ear to ear. I took charge.

"Let's get this back to the shelter, we have to figure out how to get the humans to notice the needle."

CHAPTER FIVE

We brainstormed as we walked to the county shelter. Watts thought he and I should run in as fast as we could, go directly to Monica's office, and scatter all of the bills on her desk on the floor. Susan would see us, and follow.

That sounded good to me and Bruiser, who volunteered to keep the bag with him. After Susan saw the bills, she would most likely call the police. When Officer Rooney arrived, Bruiser would deliver the bag, drop it near his feet, and bark. Our plan complete, we kept going hoping it would work.

Bruiser carried the bag under his neck since it was dry and he wore a thick leather collar. He hid in some bushes near the main parking lot and waited while Watts and I stayed out of view in a nearby jasmine bush. We knew we had to wait for someone to open the side door nearest Monica's office. Finally, a new attendant came outside for a smoke. We scampered in before he could close the door. He yelled, "Heads up! Two cats just entered the building."

He put his cigarette out just as we made it to Monica's office and jumped on her desk.

"Scatter them everywhere," I yelled to Watts as he threw bills every which way. "Remember, Robby said the unpaid bills were on the top of her desk. Somewhere in there should be the vet bills."

It would have been more fun, if we didn't have such a serious purpose. We had papers flying to the floor in all directions. "Keep going!" I cried.

Susan heard the ruckus and came running in.

"Shurl and Watts? Up to your old tricks I see. I'll get you. You two are not as fast as you think you are."

She had the dogcatcher's net ready to fling over us, but we were too fast.

I thought, "Bet we are!" and signaled for Watts to follow when I heard Susan say, after picking up one of the vet bills, "What's this? Samoa never even went to the vet."

Susan put the net down to look closely at that one bill that remained on Monica's desk. We hid behind the open door as we watched her pick up bills from the floor. She picked them up, one by one.

"Electric bill, water bill, but look at all of these vet bills. I'm going to separate them and while Monica's out sick, I'm going to compare them with my computer records of which animals I ordered sent to the vet. Something strange is going on here, and I'm going to get to the bottom of it."

Susan raced out of the office with armloads of papers. She called Amy into her office.

Amy saw us but she was so happy to see us, she didn't report us. Susan didn't miss a trick. She caught Amy looking at us.

"Never mind finding those two trouble makers. I'll deal with them later. Besides, if they didn't have a party on Monica's desk, I never would have seen these bills. Did Robby mention any concerns he had about the vet to you?"

Amy paused. "Not so much about the vet, but he *did* say he saw a bill for a cat he never took there. He confronted Monica, but she told him not to worry about it, she would take care of it. Didn't she contact you about it?"

"No. she didn't. There are thousand s of dollars here being paid out for nothing. Her actions constitute fraud. I'm going to call Deputy Rooney right now and report this. Those two smarty cats wanted me to see these."

Susan picked up the phone. We heard her dial out as Amy came and picked us up.

"No worries my two little buddies. I won't let anybody hurt you. You two are heroes in my book."

We overheard Susan tell Rooney about the phony bills and how she believed the vet and Monica were in cahoots to cash in on thousands of dollars. "Don't know how long this has been going on. I believe Robby went to the vet before he went missing. We may have more than fraud on our hands. You're on your way? Great. I'll be in my office."

Susan then came over and petted us. We heard a car screech in the parking lot. Amy put us down. As we all walked outside, we saw Bruiser walk out of the bushes with the bag under his chin. He dropped it at Rooney's feet, danced around it in a playful fashion, and barked. Rooney looked at it.

"What's this boy?"

Bruiser gave a loud bark in response.

"You want something. Want me to look inside?"

Bruiser went ballistic. The deputy took some clear plastic gloves from his pocket and put them on. He carefully picked up the bag.

"Potato chips. Want some? Looks like you haven't had a good meal in a while. Looking a little thin, there, boy."

Bruiser danced back some more. He nudged Rooney's hand until the officer looked inside the can.

"Well, lookee here. A needle. I'm taking this back to the crime lab. We'll test the can for prints as well as the contents of the needle. Robby may not have had heart problems after all."

Rooney took the bag back to his car and took out a large evidence bag. He put the can and bag inside and marked it "Robby."

He then looked at Bruiser. "Got a home, lad? Doesn't look like you do by how thin you are. Hop in. You were brave to come to the shelter and bring the evidence even though you risked getting caught.

"I always wanted a police dog of my own. I'm going to ask the captain if I can take you in for training. After I tell him what you did to help crack the case, I'm sure he'll approve." Bruiser put his chest out like he was about to receive the Congressional Medal of Honor. Rooney walked over to Susan to take the invoices and a photo copy of her records.

"Think it's all right to take the dog or do you have to keep him first?"

She smiled. "Fine with me, as long as he gets a good home."

"He'll come home with me every night. My wife'll love him."

Good for Bruiser. He had a tough break in life, but that's about to change.

Susan then turned to us. "Now for you two outlaws. Amy's gonna clean you up and give you a good meal. Tomorrow, we're having an open house for adoptions and celebrate the fact that the county commissioners voted unanimously to make us a no-kill shelter

"Don't worry. I'll make sure you two stay together. I'll even invite Rooney and his new German Shepherd. Now, go get yourselves presentable for tomorrow."

Amy took us and did just that. She unmatted my snarls and towel dried Watts. It felt so good. Then she fed us fresh cans of cat food like we used to get.

The next morning, from our cage, we could see balloons and party signs go up. There were donuts and coffee and pet items for new pet parents donated by local merchants. Humans poured in to see the pets. Susan put us up front as the pets of the day. We hoped somebody would take us home, but if not, we knew we were safe and loved here.

Then, we heard a familiar bark. We looked over to see Rooney and Bruiser enter the shelter. Bruiser looked clean and happy. He was wearing a blue police collar.

Rooney thanked Susan.

"He is one great dog. Molly loves him and the captain gave him his blue training collar today. We couldn't have begun to solve Robby's murder without him. He starts tomorrow, because I wanted to bring him to the shelter today to show people how great homeless pets can be."

Susan asked, "Did you name him?"

"Yep. Caesar. He's strong and regal-looking."

We'd all helped the shelter and the police to start investigating Robby's murder. And the three of us were happy to be safe again. We meowed for Caesar to come over, and the three of us celebrated together.

About the Author—Mariah Lynne

Ever dream of traveling through time? Mariah Lynne does. She takes her readers along on exciting journeys to distant times and beautiful places with strong-willed independent heroines whose memorable tales entertain with twisted plots dabbling in the paranormal and sometimes even murder— *Shadows Across Time, The Love Gypsy, The Duchess' Necklace,* and short story, *Love At First Flight.* Mariah lives on a beautiful Florida Gulf Coast Island; Southwest Florida takes center stage in all her stories. When she is not writing, she enjoys swimming, traveling and spending time with her husband and dolphin hunting dog, Max.

Website: www.MariahLynne.com

Twitter:@mariahlynne1

https://www.facebook.com/pages/MariahLynne/295721153858612

Who Let the Cats Out?

Faye Rapoport DesPres

No one messes with the Jane S. Dooley Cat Shelter.

There are two things I've never told anyone. But before I can tell those two things to you, I must tell you the rest of the story. Then, maybe there's a chance you'll believe me. Let me back up a few months so I can start with what happened on the day right after the fire.

I was standing alone in the old Victorian house that had once belonged to Jane S. Dooley. It was hard to remember what the living room looked like before the fire had engulfed it the previous night. The morning sun streamed in through the bay window, which looked out over the front yard and the neatly trimmed bushes that separated the yard from the sidewalk. But everything inside–the mantel above the fireplace, the wallpaper patterned with delicate flowers, the wood floors, the furniture, the shattered flower vase–was charred and stained, blackened and peeling, covered with ashes.

I had no idea if I would be able to recover the key, and for reasons I couldn't have understood at the time, this thought inspired a feeling of panic. The floor-to-ceiling bookcase had fallen over during the fire and cracked into several pieces. Dozens of sodden books, wet from the hoses of the firefighters, were scattered across the floor. Some had lost their covers and were partially burned; others had singed pages that curled toward the bindings.

I spotted one edge of the old hardcover beneath what remained of the wooden coffee table. The cover of the book had been a prominent red, making it easy to spot in the sunlight. I kneeled on the floor, pulled the book from underneath one of the table's legs, and brushed a light layer of ashes off the cover. The book was the only thing in the room that had been mine: *Crime and Punishment* by Fyodor Dostoyevsky. I opened it and saw that the key was still there, taped inside the front cover. I sighed with relief. Then, I loosened the tape, removed the key, and slipped it into my pocket.

"Adalyn?"

Slamming the book shut, I stood up so quickly that I slipped on the debris that covered the damp floor. My assistant, Billy, stepped through the doorway and caught my arm before I fell. I thanked him with embarrassment, clutching the book to my chest with one hand while I used the other to wipe the soot off the knees of my cargo pants.

"It's a mess, isn't it?" I said, looking up at Billy, who was eight inches taller than me.

Billy smiled sadly. The apartment had been his home for nearly a year, since he'd accepted the job of Assistant Director of the Jane S. Dooley Sheltering Home for Cats. A rent-free apartment came with the job. The shelter's office was at the other end of a hallway outside the living room door, and three upstairs rooms served as living space for ten cats waiting for homes with local families. Another twenty cats, the ones who got along well in a larger group, were housed cage-free inside a spacious cement Cat House that had been built behind the old Victorian at the end of the driveway.

Loose jeans and a black T-shirt hung on Billy's slim frame, and his short hair, dyed jet black, was messy or spiked with some kind of hair product, I could never tell which. One of his eyebrows was pierced, and he had somehow found the time–even on a morning like this–to apply the touch of dark eyeliner that always made his blue eyes stand out. When people first met Billy, especially people who lived in a small Vermont town like Pineville, they usually raised their eyebrows and assumed all the wrong things. They never suspected that Billy had a heart of gold and also was a musical genius. He could play Mozart as well as he belted out the grunge rock tunes he performed with his band, "Black Buzzard," on Friday and Saturday nights. The job at the shelter was just a way for Billy to make money and have a free place to live while he finished his master's thesis in music education.

Now that free place to live, the apartment inside the house that Jane S. Dooley had left to the town as a cat shelter a hundred-and-fifty years before, had been torched.

Billy glanced around the room. I knew that he'd weathered times worse than this; his mother had died when Billy was young, leaving his father to raise Billy and run their horse ranch on his own. It was one of the things Billy and I had in common even though, at thirty-four, I was ten years older. We were both raised by single fathers. I had returned to town two years before to be with my dad before he died, thinking I'd only stay long enough after he was gone to close up the house and sell it. My life had been at a crossroads at the time; I'd been living in Colorado and the software company I worked for as an office manager had been sold to a larger company. When the director of the Jane S. Dooley Cat Shelter announced that she was getting married and moving out of town, I decided to stay and apply for the job.

"You're taking this pretty well," I told Billy, trying to convince myself that I also spoke for me. At exactly the same time, our eyes strayed toward the piano that Billy had moved into the apartment with the rest of his things. It had been a shiny brown upright with gleaming black and white keys, but now it was covered with soot. It had visible water damage, and a large dark spot was burned into the side that stood closest to the window. The burning rag soaked in gasoline had landed next to the piano when it crashed through the window, which the firemen had temporarily boarded up.

"It's insured," Billy said with a shrug. "I'm safe, the cats are safe, Michelle is safe. That's all that matters." Michelle, a local nursing student whose smile lit up the shelter whenever she came by, was Billy's girlfriend.

o0o

It's not as if we didn't know that a certain element in town had been grumbling about the shelter. That element consisted mostly of Doris Nelson, the woman who had moved into the house next door five years before. She was joined in her disapproval by the town's mayor, Henry Carbunkle. Mayor Henry, as I called him, because he hated what he referred to as my "unbelievable impertinence," had, over the previous year, made it his personal mission to shut the shelter down. I had no idea why; Henry, who is in his mid-forties, had lived in Pineville all his life and had been mayor for the last ten years. He'd never had a problem with the shelter before. We suspected that it had something to do with Doris, who complained about everything from Billy's piano playing, which she claimed she could hear from inside her house, to what time we rolled the garbage bins out to the curb every Sunday and whether or not our driveway was plowed in the winter. She had installed a tall wooden fence between her driveway and the shelter's, and that was fine with us. The less we saw of Doris Nelson, the better.

Unfortunately for Doris and Mayor Henry, most of Pineville's small population loved and supported the shelter. Many local families found beloved pets at Dooley, or turned to us for help when an elderly relative passed away and left a cat in need, or when someone found a hungry stray by the side of the road.

"Should you be in here, Addy?"

Billy and I both turned at the sound of the familiar voice. Mayor Henry was standing in the doorway from the hall into the living room. I wondered why he felt he had the right to walk into my office, never mind down the hall to the apartment.

"Tom said we could come in," I said, referring to the local fire chief. I stood up a little straighter and made sure my voice was firm. "Why are *you* here?" I asked.

He ignored my question. "I imagine this place is a goner," he said, raising his eyebrows as he looked around the room. He was six foot four and, in my opinion, an overgrown bully. He wore a cowboy hat and boots as if he thought he lived in Texas and was a sheriff instead of a mayor.

"Actually," I said, "only this room was damaged by the fire. There's just water damage in the kitchen and bedroom. The office is fine, and the upstairs is fine." He shrugged. Getting angry, I added, "And I'm sure you'll be happy to hear that Billy saved all of the cats who live upstairs. You do realize that Billy was in here last night, when someone threw a flaming rag soaked in gasoline through the window. He could have been killed."

I noticed a flash of surprise in the mayor's eyes. "I thought you played with your band on Saturday nights," he said.

"Oh, you did?" I asked, suddenly suspicious. I took a step toward the mayor and Billy put a cautioning hand on my arm. "Why were you keeping track of Billy's nights out, Mayor Henry?"

I might stand five-foot-two and weigh all of a hundred-and-fifteen pounds, and my mane of brown curls might make me appear somewhat childish, but everyone in Pineville knows I'm no pushover. Once, in the tenth grade, I punched a kid in the face when he made a snide remark about a boy who didn't have a lot of friends. My father promised the principal I would be punished, but when we got in the car so my dad could drive me home, he held up a hand and gave me a "high five."

"I'm only saying I had no idea Billy was home last night," the mayor said, involuntarily taking a step backward. He had recovered from his surprise and was back on the offensive. "Had I known, I would have asked if he was alright."

"Right, just like you asked about the cats," I said. "Whoever did this, even if they thought they were doing it when Billy was out, must have known they were going to kill ten innocent cats."

WHO LET THE CATS OUT?

The mayor's face turned to stone. "Well, *whoever did this* might not have even known this place is a cat shelter," he replied smoothly.

"And where were *you* last night, Mayor Henry?" I asked. "Your life's mission for the past year has been to shut down the shelter."

"You have to be kidding me!" he said, furious now. "I'm the mayor of this town and I have better things to do than to try to burn down someone's house or a cat shelter. I spent the entire evening with my wife, in fact, at Buddy's Grill and the cinema center in Layton."

"Will the police be able to find out who did do this?" Billy asked, interrupting our heated exchange. He gestured toward the piano. "There's been a lot of damage, and the truth is, sir, that I *could* have been killed, and the cats could have been, too."

The mayor shrugged again. "It was probably some teenager on a dare," he said. "I'm sure Sam will do his best to find out." Sam Reynolds was the local police chief. Sam and Henry were thick as thieves; I had no doubt that if Henry Carbunkle was behind this fire, his buddy Sam wouldn't do anything about it.

"Well, good luck to you," Mayor Henry said before turning on his boot heel. He walked back down the hall and out of the house. The office door slammed.

Billy turned to look at me. "Look, Addy," he said, his voice sounding tired, "I appreciate the invitation to stay at your house while this gets sorted out, but I'm perfectly happy to sleep on the floor of the office."

"No way," I said. "I'm going to sleep in that office tonight and every night until they find out who did this, and until we get the apartment back in shape."

Billy nodded and walked toward the entrance to the bedroom, where he could pack up some clothes to take to my house. But before he left the living room, he stopped and turned toward me.

"Addy," he said, "there's something I should tell you."

"What?" I asked.

"Last night, before the fire, something woke me up."

"What?" I asked again. "Did you hear people talking, or a car outside the house?"

Billy hesitated. "No," he said, "it was the piano. Someone was playing the piano."

"*What?*" I asked for the third time. "Who?"

"I don't know. But I heard the piano, just a few notes. The sound woke me out of a deep sleep, and then I heard it again. I got up and came in here to see who it was, thinking maybe Michelle had come over. But when I got here, there was no one. The piano was just sitting there. And then a few seconds later I heard a crash and that burning rag came flying through the window." He shook his head as if he still couldn't believe what had happened.

"The flames moved so fast," he said apologetically. "The curtains caught fire. I tried to pull them down and stomp on them, but it didn't work. The fire just kept spreading. I ran into the kitchen and grabbed the fire extinguisher, but by the time I got back here half the room was up in flames, so I grabbed my cell and called 911 while I ran upstairs to get the cats."

Billy hesitated again before continuing. "And it was weird, Addy, someone had opened all the doors upstairs and let the cats out of their rooms. All ten of them were in the hall near their carriers. I think that's why I was able to save them all." We were both silent for a moment, remembering the hours that had followed that call: the sirens, the chaos, the worry about the animals still locked in the Cat House. The terrible fear that comes with loss.

I was still holding my copy of *Crime and Punishment*. I patted my pocket subtly, feeling for the key. It was still there.

"That's strange," I said. "Maybe some jokester snuck into the house before lighting the place on fire. It doesn't really make sense. But if he–or she–comes back, I'll be waiting."

o0o

The Jane S. Dooley Cat Shelter was established in 1863 by an elderly Pineville resident who had inherited her father's fortune and had no close relatives on whom to bequeath it. She had been married as a young woman, but her husband died of a terrible fever and she never re-married or had children. According to local legend, Jane used to stroll up and down Main Street on warm summer days, delighting the town's children by handing out candy. She started a women's book club at the tiny town library and gave generously to neighbors in need. But her passion was animals, especially cats, and when she died at the ripe old age of ninety-seven, she left her entire fortune, including the large Victorian house she had called home all her life, in a trust for the establishment of a sheltering home for cats.

The residents of Pineville, mourning their elderly neighbor, founded the cat shelter that Jane had envisioned. And no one had ever had a problem with the arrangement until Doris Nelson moved next door and began her insidious campaign to close the shelter down. Of course, Doris was the first person I

WHO LET THE CATS OUT?

wanted to blame as flames threatened to devour Jane Dooley's house. I had demanded that Dave Miller, a local policeman who was keeping neighbors away from the fire and whom I knew I could trust, knock on Doris's door to find out if she was home. But Doris, it turned out, was visiting relatives in Boston. She couldn't have started the fire.

The alarm clock I had placed on the floor of the office glowed in the darkness. 1:04 a.m. The office was cold, and I was huddled on the floor in my sleeping bag, wide awake. October nights can be frigid in Vermont, but I didn't like to turn up the heat. I was dressed in a sweat shirt and sweat pants inside the sleeping bag.

I had spent the evening working in the office, sorting through the paperwork that would be required to file a claim with the shelter's insurance company. At 10:30 p.m., I had attempted to turn in because my eyes were hurting and I could no longer concentrate. I pulled on my jacket and went outside to do a final check of the Cat House. All twenty residents were sleeping on cat beds in the specially-designed windowsills, nibbling at the kibble that had been left out in bowls, or chasing each other around the floor in the dark. When I left, I made sure the door was locked, and then I paused next to the shed that backed up to the fence just outside the entrance. The moon was almost full, and the back of the shed was in shadow. It was there, behind the shed, that I had found Jocko on that terrible night.

Jocko. He had been a handsome, scarred, gray-and-white tom cat when he appeared in the driveway a few days after I started my job at the shelter. He was huge–twenty pounds–and tough judging by his ears, which were all chewed up, and by the scar on his upper lip that turned his expression into a permanent scowl. It was clear that he had been living on the street for a long time. But he must have decided that he'd had enough, because he marched straight up to the office door and strolled inside that day. And he proceeded, over the next two years, to become the shelter mascot and the most beloved feline on the property. He spent his days lounging in the office and his evenings sleeping peacefully on Billy's bed after I convinced the Board of Directors to let me hire Billy and move him into the apartment.

Jocko was protective of the cats who arrived at the office hungry, scared and in search of a new home. He nudged and groomed young kittens if they cried. Every morning when I arrived at work, Jocko left Billy's apartment, jumped up and unlatched the door from the hallway, sauntered into the office, and sat down in front of me, hoping to be petted.

Jocko was wearing a collar with a tag when he showed up, but no one in town claimed ownership, even though neighbors reported spotting the big cat roaming the streets near the shelter for years. The tag he wore was fancier than normal cat tags–it was thick and heart-shaped and made of silver. So I was sure he must have belonged to someone. But whenever I tried to remove the collar so I could look more closely at the tag, Jocko hissed, bared his teeth, and unsheathed his claws–behavior he never exhibited at any other time. So, the collar remained around Jocko's neck until the tragic events of July 4th.

It was 6:30 a.m. and raining when Jocko raced past my legs and out the door when I arrived at the office to do some work I had planned to finish on the holiday. He ran down the driveway and behind the shed, and before I could get to him I heard something that sounded like a terrified dog yelping. The next thing I knew, I was frozen in horror, because a coyote had emerged from behind the shed. The animal ran right past me up the driveway toward the street, and I raced behind the shed, calling Jocko's name. I found him lying on his side in the dirt behind the shed with blood seeping out of his neck. Next to him was a tiny white kitten, not more than a few weeks old, cowering against the shed, untouched. I realized in an instant what had happened: Jocko had attacked the coyote to save the kitten. I fell to my knees and begged Jocko to hold on so I could get him to the emergency vet. But he took a few last breaths, heaved a sigh, and died right there in my arms.

The death of any cat breaks my heart, but I had never taken a loss as badly as I took Jocko's. Billy found me sobbing with the cat in my arms, and we buried him later that day in the yard in front of the Cat House. Before we laid him in his grave inside his favorite bed, I took off the collar that he'd never let me touch. As I fingered the tag, I noticed that it had a seam and might even open like a locket, but I didn't have the heart to look more closely in my grief. The next day, I bought a small gold box and locked the collar inside it. I never told anyone about the box, which I placed in the bottom drawer of my desk at the office, or about the key, which I taped inside the cover of one of my favorite books, *Crime and Punishment*. I then stored the book on the bookshelf in Billy's apartment so I would have access to the key if I ever decided to open the box.

After the fire I realized how close I had come to never being able to find out what was inside the cat tag. So after Billy went to my house, I removed the key from my pocket, pulled the box from the drawer, and opened it.

The box was empty.

Sleep continued to elude me. I couldn't stop thinking about the fire, about the fact that Billy could have been killed, about the cats who had been helpless upstairs, about Mayor Henry's visit. I went over and over our conversation with the mayor in my head, trying to pick out anything that would indicate he was responsible. And finally, when my thoughts had raced in circles for so long that they had to land somewhere, I thought about Jocko's empty box, which was now sitting on the floor next to the alarm clock. Twenty minutes had passed since I'd last looked at the clock.

And that's when I heard it.

Plink, plink, plink.

At first it was one note, then two, then a slow crescendo as someone ran his or her fingers up the piano keys. I grabbed the flashlight and struggled up and out of my sleeping bag. Trying to control my ragged breath, I crept on my tip-toes through the door that led to the hallway and made my way toward the apartment. The door to the living room was open, even though I was certain I had closed it after Billy left. I clicked off the flashlight and moved quietly toward the doorway, guided by a sliver of moonlight shining through it.

Peeking into the room, I looked toward the piano, but no one appeared to be there. The piano sat silent in the empty room, which was cast in a bluish light by the moon. I walked into the apartment and over to the bay window, listening for footsteps or any other sound, and keeping my flashlight off. Nothing. No one. Confused, I stared out the window.

Something moved behind the bushes near the street, and suddenly I saw what looked like a human being running down the street, away from the house. I dashed into the foyer, unbolted the front door, and raced down the walkway to the sidewalk, forgetting that it was freezing outside and my feet were bare. Staring in the direction that I had seen the person running, I saw nothing but darkness past the streetlamp on the corner.

Whoever it was had disappeared.

o0o

Two weeks later on a Thursday night, the meeting of the town council was a mob scene. Every seat in the Town Hall meeting room was taken, and men, women, and children were lined up along the walls and milling around the hallway just outside the double doors. Mayor Henry rapped his wooden gavel hard against the podium in a vain attempt to quiet the angry crowd. His wife, Anne, was sitting in the front row with their two children, twelve-year-old Jimmy and ten-year-old Janine. She stared straight ahead, and the children hung their heads and looked at the floor.

The mayor had just announced that the Jane Dooley house was condemned. The insurance company had mysteriously turned down our initial claim, saying they suspected that the fire had been a ploy to get money for the shelter by collecting on the policy. I was outraged at this implication, which, in any case, made no sense. But to make matters worse, the mayor had decided that because there were no other locations in town suitable for a cat shelter, the shelter would have to be shut down. Rumors had been circulating for days that this was his plan, and supporters of the shelter had vowed to pack the meeting and make their feelings known.

"What about the cats?" someone yelled from the middle of the crowd.

"They'll be sent to shelters in nearby towns," the mayor said, "and if any are left without a place to go, they'll have to be put down."

There was an angry roar from the crowd. I was shaking with rage, and Billy and Joanne Watkins, one of our most loyal volunteers, each pulled at one of my arms as I stood at a microphone stand that had been placed in front of the audience, shouting.

"What do you mean, *condemned*?" I shouted. "One room has smoke and fire damage. The rest of the building is sound. What are you talking about? You'll harm one hair on one cat over my dead body!"

"According to the town inspector–" the mayor began, but his comments were drowned out by more shouts from the crowd.

Billy dragged me back to my seat on the end of the seventh row, where I collapsed into my chair, uncertain if I would be able to stop the angry tears that were springing to my eyes. I couldn't believe what was happening.

"Who set the fire?" someone yelled from the crowd, and the question was echoed by a chorus of other voices. "They need to be held responsible!"

"And who got into the house and let the cats out from their upstairs rooms?" Someone shouted from the back of the room. "Who knew that the fire was going to be set?"

The mayor banged his gavel on the podium again until the noise had subsided just enough for him to say, "The police have not found a suspect in the fire. It is the assumption of the insurance company that someone involved with the shelter did the deed to make money, which would explain why the cats were let out." Anything he said after that was drowned out by angry objections.

o0o

Back at the shelter an hour after the meeting, at least twenty volunteers

Who Let the Cats Out?

gathered under the outside light that hung above the door of the Cat House. They were wrapped in jackets, gloves, and hats. Everyone was still angry.

"There's no way we're going to let this happen," Joanne said.

"It's crazy, anyway," said Emily Leblanc, owner of the local breakfast spot, Toffee Coffee, and a long-time volunteer at the shelter. "Why shut the whole place down even if the house is condemned? The Cat House is still fine, and we could always rebuild."

"There's absolutely no reason to condemn that house," said Eric Horner, a local handyman who did repairs at the shelter and who had recently built an outdoor enclosure for the cats. "The structure is fine. Heck, most of the house is perfectly fine. This is a conspiracy if I ever saw one, and when we find out who started this and who set that fire, there's going to be hell to pay."

I had been sitting in the office, exhausted from my fury, trying to figure out what to say to everyone. When I finally joined the group, Joanne turned to me and said, "If the insurance company won't pay, we can fix the house ourselves."

"There's no way we could raise enough money," I said. The last few hours had drained my fighting spirit, and the reality of what we were facing had kicked in. "Our operating budget doesn't include a line item for repairs, and this is a major job. The shelter is barely making ends meet as it is."

"I'll give up my salary," Billy said. He was shivering, and his hands were stuffed in his pockets. Michelle put her arms around him and leaned her head against his chest.

"That's sweet of you, Billy," I said, and I was surprised that my voice cracked when I said it. My throat felt tight, and I forced myself to take a deep breath. "But I would never let you do that—and it wouldn't be enough, anyway. Believe me, I would give up my salary, too."

A young girl standing in the group started to cry. Her mom, Audrey Benson, leaned down and gave her daughter a hug. "It's okay, honey," she said. "Let's go into the Cat House and visit Pepper."

The girl sniffed but looked up hopefully. "Can we take Pepper home now, Mom?" she asked.

Audrey looked at me and I smiled weakly. I knew that her family already had three cats. "Yes, sweetie, I think so," Audrey said. "I think it's time for Pepper to come home."

I nodded at Billy. He unlocked the door of the Cat House and followed them inside.

After everyone left, I climbed once again into my sleeping bag in the office and finally let myself cry. Occasionally, I heard the swish of a car as it passed by the house on the street. As always, I'd closed all the window blinds. There was no moon that night, and the room would have been pitch black if not for the red neon numbers on the alarm clock. The first time I looked over at them it was midnight. By 1:00 a.m., I had exhausted myself by crying and my tears had dried. By 2:00 a.m., I was falling asleep.

Plink, plink, plink.

Three notes on the piano. My eyes flew open.

Plink, plink. Two more.

I was out of my sleeping bag in seconds, the flashlight in my hand. I crept down the hall toward the living room, and again was surprised that the apartment door was open. When I reached it, I stepped right into the room, sweeping the beam of my flashlight from one wall to the other. Finally, I pointed it toward on the keys on the piano.

Nothing. No one. But then, I heard something: footsteps from somewhere past the foyer. I sighed with relief, thinking Billy must have decided to sleep in his room one last time. I crossed the room and entered the foyer.

The front door to the house was wide open. I must have forgotten to bolt it shut that morning when I'd been arguing with the fire inspector in front of the house. Suddenly on guard, I looked toward Billy's bedroom on the opposite end of the foyer and saw what looked like a hooded figure moving around in the shadows. I held my breath, hoping whoever it was hadn't seen or heard me. Then I heard a quiet click and saw a small flame burst to life, illuminating a man who was standing near the bed. It looked like he was holding a rag in one hand.

"Hey! Stop that!" I yelled, turning on my flashlight, and the man dropped the rag and took a few steps out of the room toward me, trying to shade his eyes against the light.

I stared in surprise. The man in the hood–a hooded sweatshirt, it turned out–wasn't a man at all. He was a twelve-year-old boy named Jimmy Carbunkle.

"Jimmy?" I said in surprise. The boy dropped the lighter and dashed toward the front door, but I caught him by his hood and he slid and fell backward.

"What are you doing here?" I asked while he struggled to break free. "Are you here to...are you the one who...did your father put you up to this? Did you come back to finish the job?"

"Let me go!" Jimmy sobbed as he tried to wriggle out of his sweatshirt. A police siren had started wailing and was getting closer to the house, and by the time Jimmy got the sweatshirt off and broke loose from my grasp, a squad car with revolving lights had pulled onto the curb. Dave Miller, illuminated by the street lamp on the corner, leaped out of the car and raced up the walkway. He stopped short when he saw Jimmy standing at the front door.

"I parked at the end of the street after the meeting," Dave said when he saw the confused look on my face. "I was worried there would be trouble. I thought I saw some movement a few minutes ago, so I drove a little closer, and when I saw the flashlight go on inside the house I put on the siren and pulled up." He looked at Jimmy. "So, who do we have here? Jimmy Carbunkle?"

The boy, who was shaking now, continued to sob. Dave stopped me with a gentle hand when I reached down to pick up the lighter that Jimmy had dropped. "Evidence," he said, and I left it where it was.

"As for you, young man, it looks like I'll be giving you a ride down to the station."

Jimmy wiped his eyes with one arm and started to hiccup.

"Wait," I said. "Before you go…" I turned toward Jimmy, who refused to look at me. "Jimmy, tell me why you did this. Why would you want to hurt the shelter and the cats we keep here? I know your father doesn't like Dooley very much, but why would you get involved?"

Jimmy sniffed and stared at the floor. Dave and I waited. Finally, the boy said, "Mom and Dad keep arguing about this place. Dad says he wants to get rid of it because that new lady, Miss Nelson, promised to help him get re-elected if he did. My mom was really upset. She said she was tired of my dad pan…pan…"

"Pandering," I said softly.

Jimmy hiccupped again. "Yes, pandering to people who he likes and who can help him, or something like that. She said she knew that my dad was in love with Miss Nelson and she was sick of it all and going to leave him. She's said she would leave him before, but this time, I think she meant it."

"But why would you try to burn down the shelter?" I asked.

"Dad said some bad things about Billy, about how he was a poor role model for the kids in the town anyway, and how he played with some kind of crazy band on the weekends. He made jokes about his hair and his makeup and stuff. I just wanted it all to go away. I wanted it to stop, for everything to go back to the way it was before Miss Nelson and Billy moved here. I figured since Billy was out of the house on the weekends I could just…just…" his voice faded.

"I think you'd better save the rest until we call your father and he meets us at the station," Dave said. "Let's go." He led Jimmy down the walkway toward his patrol car. Just before they reached the sidewalk, Jimmy turned back to look at me.

"I didn't know there were cats in the house," he said. "I thought they were all out back. I didn't know. I never meant to hurt them. I'm sorry!" And he started to cry again. Dave put a firm hand on his shoulder and opened the back door of the squad car before ushering Jimmy inside. They drove off into the night.

It wasn't until after they were gone that it occurred to me: if Jimmy hadn't known there were cats upstairs, he hadn't been the one who let them out of their rooms.

o0o

A week had passed since Jimmy made a full confession. Ann Carbunkle had packed her bags and left her husband, who had been keeping a very low profile. The local paper printed at least twenty letters to the editor calling for the mayor's resignation–not because his son had been implicated in a crime, or even because of the whispers that he had been having an affair, but because an investigation had unearthed a conspiracy to close down the shelter between the mayor and the town's police chief and fire inspector.

Still, our problems weren't over. The insurance company had agreed to review our claim, but the appeal process was going to take months. We had to repair the main building so that Billy could move back in and there could be 24-hour supervision at the shelter, a town requirement. Our volunteers had put up donation boxes in every store they could think of and were brainstorming about organizing fundraising events. But I couldn't think of any way we could get the money we needed in the short time we had to save the building and the shelter.

I had continued to sleep on the floor of the office so we would be complying with the town's 24-hour requirement. I just didn't feel right making Billy do it. But my back was beginning to hurt, winter was getting closer, and I knew I couldn't sleep there forever. I lay awake in my sleeping bag late almost every night trying to come up with a solution. But as the days wore on and no answer presented itself, I began, in my exhaustion, to consider whether it might be best to focus my energies on finding homes for our remaining cats and preparing to close down—at least, temporarily.

WHO LET THE CATS OUT?

Late one night, I was running through the names of the cats in my mind as the light of the returning moon peeked through the blinds. *Dave might take Midget,* I was saying to myself. *Joanne might open her home to one more. I know she loves little Simba.*

And then, I heard it again.

Plink, plink, plink.

I thought I might be dreaming in my half-asleep state; but this time, the notes kept coming. *Plink, plink, plink, plink, plink,* up the piano keyboard and down again. It was 3:00 a.m. I crawled out of my sleeping bag, picked up my flashlight, and walked through the office into the hallway and toward the apartment.

The door was open again.

I closed my eyes, shook my head a few times, and looked again. Yes, it was open. And this time, I could still hear the piano. *Plink, plink, plink,* faster and faster.

"Billy?" I called out. Silence.

"Who's playing this joke on me?" I said in a loud voice as I walked hesitantly into the room. The music stopped, and it took a moment for the beam of my flashlight to find the piano. I thought I saw something move. Was it a shadow from the branch of a tree outside? Or was it the flick of a tail? I walked over to the piano, but the window was closed and no one was there. Then, I stopped dead in my tracks. Something was lying across the piano keys.

Jocko's collar.

I stood motionless for a moment, barely able to breathe. Finally, I moved forward and picked up the collar. It was time. I opened the locket, and something small and shiny glinted in the beam of light.

It wasn't until the diamond was appraised two days later that I was able to announce that the Jane S. Dooley Sheltering Home for Cats had been saved.

o0o

Here are the two things I've never told anyone. The first one is this: before I placed *Crime and Punishment* on the new bookshelf Eric built when the apartment was fully renovated, something fell from the middle pages onto the floor. It was an old photograph of Jane S. Dooley. When I looked closely at the picture I noticed she was wearing something around her neck. It was a thick, heart-shaped locket, probably silver.

The second thing is this: when I left the apartment on the night I found the diamond, I paused at the door and looked back into the room. I swept the beam of my flashlight from one wall to the other, letting it rest first on the piano and then on the floor. And there, for the first time, I saw something in the soot that I had never noticed before. There were paw prints leading from the door to the piano and back.

And then, I recalled that on the night of the fire, I had also seen paw prints—on the staircase leading to the upstairs rooms.

Both times, the paw prints were gone by the next morning.

About the Author—Faye Rapoport DesPres

Faye Rapoport DesPres is a lifelong writer whose fiction, nonfiction, reviews, interviews, and poetry have appeared in a variety of literary journals and magazines, including Ascent, BOXY Magazine, Connotation Press: An Online Artifact, Eleven Eleven, Fourth Genre, Into the Arts, Superstition Review, and the Writer's Chronicle. She earned her MFA at the Solstice Creative Writing Program at Pine Manor College. Her first book, a personal essay collection/memoir titled Message From A Blue Jay, was published by Buddhapuss Ink in 2014. Faye lives in Massachusetts with her husband and rescued cats, and is an Adjunct Professor of English at Lasell College.

The Calico

Brandy Herr

Will Larry's new cat be a blessing...or a curse?

The popular superstition says that you will have terrible luck if a black cat crosses your path. But for me, that wasn't the case. What brought about my downfall was a calico.

It began late on a Monday evening. Earlier that afternoon, my wife of twelve years had stormed out the door, carrying a hastily packed suitcase, screaming at me for not listening to her...or something.

That night, I found myself sitting alone in my ragged recliner, staring blankly at the television, tuned to some program about dysfunctional marriages. In my left hand was an empty glass. In my right hand, I held an almost empty bottle of whiskey. I decided to bypass the frivolity of mixing it with cola this time and simply get straight to the point.

I had just finished the last of the bottle when I heard the distinct, "Mew!" come from the front porch. I rolled my eyes and ignored the call, desperately attempting to extract just one more drop from the dry bottle. "Darn neighbor cats," I thought. "Probably that stupid tomcat. I should go out there and show it the underside of my boot."

The mewing graduated steadily to loud, plaintive meowing, and I became convinced the cat was not about to leave anytime soon. I heaved a sigh as I pushed my body up out of the armchair, then trudged to the door, determined to put an end to the racket one way or another. I flung open the door, my foot at the ready, but I paused in mid-kick.

Sitting on the doormat, looking up at me, was not the mangy old tomcat that constantly yowled outside my bedroom window, always looking for another cat in heat. Instead, I looked down to see a beautiful little calico cat. The brown and black splotches contrasted brilliantly against her snow-white backdrop of fur. What stopped me cold, however, was her piercing gaze. She stared knowingly at me, looking deep into me, with bright, emerald green eyes. I didn't know what else to do, so I stepped lamely to the side, holding the door open as the cat walked casually inside the house.

The calico followed me into the kitchen and jumped onto the table, watching me expectantly. "You hungry, girl?" I asked. "Sorry, I don't have much in the way of cat food around here, but, wait... Francine did always take a liking to tuna. Maybe I can find some of her stockpile in the pantry."

I dug through the shelves and finally came up with one dusty, slightly dented can. I used the handheld can opener, and then dumped its contents into a dish. The cat stared at me, blinked once slowly, and then licked her lips in thanks before diving head first into the bowl and devouring the food. I watched her eat, still somehow mesmerized.

When she finished, making sure to leave a few morsels of food behind so as not to appear desperate and pathetic—as proud cats are so prone to do—she jumped off the table and sauntered into the living room, with me following. I lowered myself back down into my recliner, while she curled up neatly on the couch, her eyes on the television. I wasn't all that invested in the TV program anyway, so I switched it over to the nature channel so she could marvel at her brethren.

Looking at her sitting comfortably on the couch, I couldn't help but laugh, in spite of the earlier events of the day. Francine had always wanted a cat, sometimes even begged me for one, but I wasn't interested. "It would give me someone to talk to, someone to listen to me when you're too busy watching your sports," she would plead.

"Francine," I would tell her, "if I wanted to invite something into my home that pukes up hairballs and poops in a box, we might as well have your mother move in!"

With that, she would usually curl her lip in a disgusted look, give a haughty sniff, then turn on her heel and storm from the room.

"Look at that!" I said to myself from the recliner. "It took Francine leaving for me to finally give her what she wanted. If she could see this now, she would have a fit!" Then I was suddenly struck with a thought. "That's it! That's what I'll call you. *New* Francine! That's a nice bit of karma for that broad. I like getting the last laugh!"

On that thought, I chuckled again and leaned back in the chair. New Francine slept soundly on the couch. Lulled by the soothing voice of the documentary narrator, I soon fell into a deep sleep myself.

o0o

The sun made its way through the blinds at 7:30 the next morning and shone directly into my eyes. I woke up groggily, wiping the drool off my chin and shoulder, and stood slowly, stretching off the stiffness from a night spent sleeping in a chair. My throat felt like sandpaper, and my stomach was gurgling sickly from the hangover that was only just starting to rear its ugly head. I knew I needed something in my system to stave off the worst of its effects, so I trudged into the kitchen to start the coffeepot and pop in a couple of pieces of toast.

While I waited for the toaster to release my breakfast, I heard a faint and unusual sound from below. *Wap, wap, wap, wap.* I looked down in surprise, and then smiled when I discovered the source of the noise. The little calico cat had followed me into the kitchen and discovered the twist-tie from the bread bag, which she was now batting enthusiastically around the floor.

"You like twist-ties, huh?" I said to her. "Here, how about this?"

I pulled open the nearby junk drawer and grabbed a fistful of the twist-ties that Francine liked to collect for God-only-knew what reason. I held my hand in the air above the little cat and opened my fist, letting the small bands float down in a rainbow of colors around her, much to her obvious delight. New Francine went crazy, batting at everything that moved and hopping in a circle, determined to hit all of them.

"It's not like Francine's going to be here to yell at me for not using twist-ties anymore! Might as well get some use out of those ridiculous things," I said to myself as I spun the newly opened bread and placed it on the counter, tucking the open end at the bottom.

The next two days passed without much incident. New Francine and I were getting used to each other, learning the boundaries and setting up our own routine. I actually managed to scavenge a few more cans of tuna, which meant I didn't have to leave the house to go to the store for a while, and that made me happy.

Early that Thursday afternoon, I was sitting in the recliner with New Francine on my lap when the doorbell rang. I groaned as I pulled myself to a standing position, New Francine sliding gracefully to the floor. I continued to grumble to myself as I made my way to the front of the house and flung open the door. "What do you want?" I snarled.

"Hi, Daddy!" cried the beautiful nineteen-year-old blonde as she threw herself into my arms and planted a kiss onto my cheek. She pulled back quickly in disgust. "Ugh, Dad, gross! Toothbrushes. Ever heard of them? They're not expensive."

I chuckled with astonishment and joy, ignoring the insult. "Candice! What are you doing here?"

Candice pushed past me into the living room. "Aunt Charlotte called. She said Francine left and you were having a rough time. I'm on Spring Break now, and I had some spare time, so I thought I would come spend a few days with you and see how you're doing! I have to leave on Sunday to get back to school, but Aunt Charlotte will be here then to stay with you. She can't get here any earlier than that; her cat sitter isn't available until then."

I rolled my eyes. The only thing that could dampen a spontaneous visit from my daughter was the thought of my nosy spinster sister invading my house and ordering me around. She had been hinting, and not very subtly, about wanting to move in here, since there wasn't much room for her and her seventeen cats at her tiny rental home. "She'll take any opportunity she can to weasel her way in here, won't she?" I thought to myself as I watched Candice float around the kitchen, picking up discarded beer bottles and microwaveable dinner containers.

"Oh, my God, Dad, when did you last clean this place? Here, why don't you run upstairs and get a shower, and for the love of God brush your teeth! I'll stay down here and tidy up. It'll make you feel better!"

Candice had a point, so I made my way up the stairs to the sound of her cleaning and dusting below. I turned on the bathroom faucet, and in a few seconds I was stepping into a steaming shower. She was right: I was already starting to feel better.

Candice had always been a sore spot between Francine and me. The two of them never quite got along. Francine, for some reason, did not like to think about the fact that she was the second wife, and Candice was a constant reminder of the life I lived before her. Francine always tried to create excuses for why Candice couldn't visit, but she was my daughter, and God help the person who tries to stand in the way of me seeing my daughter.

I stood under the water until I felt the first hint of cold rain down. I reluctantly turned the faucet off and stepped out of the tub, making my way over to the sink. I wiped a streak through the fog on the bathroom mirror and took a close look at my face, releasing a sigh at what I saw.

Dark brown eyes, bloodshot from all the beer and whiskey I had been consuming as of late. Dark brown hair, with more gray at the temples than I remembered. Still no crows' feet yet—thank God for small favors. But the dark stubble on my chin and the deep frown lines flanking my lips made me appear much older than my forty-two years.

I grabbed at my toothpaste and toothbrush and scrubbed as hard as I could at the layer of grime coating my teeth. Once I got all I could, I spread foam across my face and carefully shaved with my dull razor. After patting my face dry with a towel and slapping on some aftershave, I took another look into the newly fog-free mirror. I offered up a tiny smile to see a small glimpse of the young man I once was, before Francine and I started going downhill. "You clean up rather nicely, old guy," I whispered to myself.

I finished drying off and pulled a t-shirt over my head, the first clean shirt I had worn since Monday. Stepping into a fresh pair of sweatpants, I padded barefoot down the stairs to the kitchen, where I found Candice sitting at the table, petting the calico.

Candice turned as she heard my approach. "Look at you, Daddy! Looking good!" she squealed.

I kissed the top of her head. "Thanks, darlin'. I guess your old dad still has a few good years left!"

Candice stood up to ruffle my hair, and then turned to do the same thing to the cat. "What a sweet kitty, Dad! When did you get her? I thought you didn't like cats!"

"I didn't. I don't. She just showed up on my doorstep Monday night after your step-mother left— and I don't know, I just felt like I needed to let her in. I've named her New Francine."

"*New* Francine?" Candice lifted her lip and stuck out her tongue in a grimace. "Dad, that's kind of sick. You're using a cat to replace your wife?"

"You've been watching too many indie movies, sweetheart. I just thought it would be funny: now that Francine's gone, I get the one thing she always begged me for *and* I name it after her? It's about time I get the last laugh!"

"I guess..." Candice conceded, still with her lip curled. "It still just seems weird to me, though. But at least it's good you have someone to keep you company now! Well, besides me and Aunt Charlotte."

I groaned inside. I had almost forgotten about Charlotte's impending arrival.

"Let's head into the living room and have a chat," I said, changing the subject. "Bring a couple of beers for the two of us, and we'll put a saucer of milk down for New Francine, and you can tell me all about what's going on at school."

"Daddy, I'm only nineteen!" Candice protested.

"Yeah, and I happen to know your college has been ranked one of the top party schools in the state. You mean to tell me you haven't already had a beer or two?" I teased.

"We-ell, I guess you're right..." Candice looked sheepish as she snatched two bottles from the fridge and headed to the living room, with New Francine close on her heels and me with the milk following behind.

"So? How's school?" I asked as I settled into my recliner.

Candice perched on the sofa next to New Francine, who happily lapped up her milk. "School's great, Daddy! I'm taking some really interesting classes this semester. I'm almost done with the basics, so now I'm starting to get into classes that actually relate to my major!"

"Imagine that," I said with a sarcastic grin. "Only a year-and-a-half and $20,000 later, you're finally getting to learn what you wanted to learn in the first place!"

"I know, right?" Candice nodded. "It's all a big scam. Anyway, there's this really nice guy I met in my biology class…"

"Oh, no, I don't think I'm ready to hear this!" I interrupted as I playfully clapped my hands over my ears.

"Daddy! It's not like that!" Candice threw a sofa pillow at my face, which I caught with ease. "He's a great guy, so nice and smart, and he's pre-med, just like me! He wants to be an orthopedic surgeon. His name is Jimmy, and we've been seeing each other for about three weeks now. I would love for you to meet him sometime, I think you'll really like him!"

"Okay, darlin', if you say so," I said with an exaggerated sigh. "I'm sure he's a perfectly sweet guy with no ulterior motives. Just let me know when you want to bring him around to meet me, and I'll have the shotgun ready and loaded."

"Oh, Dad, you are just the worst," Candice stuck her tongue out at me again and grinned.

We settled into an awkward pause, the only sound to break the silence being the low vibration of New Francine's purr as Candice gently stroked and scratched her head. It should have been a lovely moment, but something about watching the two of them interact left me with a gurgling sensation of unease in the pit of my stomach. Or maybe it was just the last remnants of my latest hangover.

"So, Dad…" Candice began apprehensively. "Do you, you know, want to talk? About Francine or…whatever?"

I slumped in the recliner. "Not much to talk about, really," I muttered out of the corner of my mouth. "She screamed at me, I screamed at her, she packed a suitcase, and then she left. Same stuff, different day, you know? And that's the last I heard of her."

"You haven't tried calling her? It's been three days. Hasn't she always come home before now? You don't think she's gone for good this time, do you?"

"Nah, I haven't tried calling her. I'm not about to go crawling to a woman on my knees. I tried that with your mother and I'm still looking for my dignity from that after fifteen years. If she's gone for good, then it's good she's gone." I snorted and took a big gulp out of my bottle.

Okay, so maybe that was a little bit of a lie, but Candice didn't need to know about my weakness. I did try calling her once, late Tuesday afternoon, after the haze of Monday night's date with the bottle of whiskey had a chance to clear a bit. It went straight to voicemail with not even a single ring, so I slammed the phone down on the receiver and vowed not to resort to such stupidity again. If she wanted to talk to me, she could darn well turn her phone on and call me herself.

The little calico cat sat on the couch next to Candice, staring at me with her head tilted to the side, as if she could sense the little white lie I had just told. Or maybe she could. She was, in fact, in the room when I attempted the call, and I suppose cats are probably more perceptive and intelligent than we give them credit for. Still, though, I wished she would quit staring at me like that. I shifted uncomfortably in my seat as memories of Monday afternoon came flooding back to me.

Francine and I had been on the rocks for some time. The first few years of our marriage had been great, filled with love, passion, and romance. Then, old habits started creeping back into my life: first the beer, then the hard liquor. Francine took my drinking in stride at first, but it slowly took a toll on her as my increasingly constant inebriation became harder to ignore.

It didn't help matters when Candice hit puberty and began blossoming into the stunning beauty she was to become. This only compounded Francine's jealousy of my daughter. The years and our marriage were playing a part in her looks, and Francine's fiery red hair became a dull orange. Body parts began to sag and others expanded as the tumult of our relationship drew lines on her face. She was still a lovely woman, at least in my eyes, but women are always the most critical of themselves, especially when in comparison with a perky blonde co-ed. Her growing hatred of my daughter only succeeded in driving a wedge further between us, and I began retreating to the comfort of televised sports to complement the alcohol, leaving Francine alone in a house with no one to talk to. Not even a cat.

The fight on Monday had been the worst. Francine came home from her women's empowerment group, or whatever they're calling it these days, to find me in my natural environment, leaning back in the recliner, bottle of beer in hand, football on the television. She stood in the darkened doorway, hands crossed tightly over her still ample breasts, and stared hard at what she could see of me illuminated from the glowing television screen. Several minutes passed before a commercial break began and I became aware of her presence.

"Good Lord, Francine!" I yelled out with a jolt. "How long have you been staring at me like that? You trying to give me a heart attack?"

"I think you're doing a pretty good job of that yourself," Francine replied with her disgusted sniff. "All that alcohol and sitting around is going to come back to get you one of these days."

"Oh, good, apparently they're teaching medical science at your group along with all that feminist garbage. Keep it up, and in a few years after Candice graduates, we can have *two* doctors in the family!" I sneered at Francine and turned back to the television as the football game resumed.

"Don't you dare call my group garbage!" Francine screeched. "Those women have done more for me in the past month than you have in the past six years!"

"And just what have I *not* done for you, Sweet Thing? Have I not worked hard, providing you with a paycheck that you can spend on crystals and metaphysical whosits and whatsits and all that other self-help nonsense you seem to think will fill this imaginary void in your life? Have I not remained faithful to you all these years, even through our increasingly expanding dry spells? So what have I not done for you, huh?"

"Oh, please," Francine dismissed my last statement with a wave of her hand. "If you had half as much energy for me as you do for drinking and sports, we wouldn't be having *any* dry spells!"

"What is *that* supposed to mean?" I countered, really getting irritated. This was an important game, a playoff! Why did this nagging shrew not understand that? "You saying I'm not a man?"

"I'm saying I don't know *what* you are anymore," Francine replied, deflated. "You're certainly not a friend, a companion, or a lover. We're just sharing the same space, and barely at that. I just don't know; I think we need to talk to some-"

"*Go, go, go... Touchdown! Yeah!*" I jumped from the recliner, beer still tightly in my hand, as I raised my arms toward the television in victory.

"Are you *serious*?" Francine resumed her screeching. "Are you seriously more interested in your stupid game than you are in our life together? *That is it!*"

Francine stormed up the stairs, and within seconds, I heard the sound of frantic scurrying up above in our bedroom as she opened the closet and pulled out her suitcase again for what seemed like the hundredth time. I rolled my eyes and continued watching the slow motion replay.

Minutes later, Francine blew down the stairs like a hurricane, lugging her suitcase at her side. "I'm done, Larry. I'm done! I'm leaving, and I'm never coming back until I take this house from you! Do you understand me? *We are through!*"

"Yeah, yeah, yeah, don't tempt me with a good time!" I retorted.

Francine whipped around, showed me her finger, and flung open the front door. The last I saw of her as she blazed past was a white shirt sleeve hanging out of the back of her suitcase, waving at me as if in defiance. I stared after her for a second once the door slammed shut, then shrugged and turned back to the television. It was the fourth quarter, and I'd seen this charade before. She'd be back.

I came back to myself to see both Candice and New Francine staring quizzically at me from the couch. Their almost identical looks of concern forced a laugh from my lips, which only served to deepen Candice's frown. "Dad, you okay? I thought I lost you there for a second!"

"Yeah, I'm fine, darlin'. Just got lost in my thoughts. Hey, I got an idea. How about I go put on some real pants and we go out for some ice cream?"

Candice's frown turned into a grin. I knew she could never resist ice cream. "You got it, Daddy! It's a date!"

After two cones of Rocky Road and an invigorating walk in the park, Candice and I returned home to see the little calico cat waiting expectantly at the door for us. "Sorry, girl," I told her. "They were all out of tuna-flavored ice cream!"

New Francine sniffed at the air and then did an about-face, walking away stiffly with her tail straight in the air, giving it a slight twitch in rhythm with her stride. I rolled my eyes and looked at Candice. "Cats can be so sensitive, can't they? They're a lot like wives!"

Candice giggled, punched me playfully on the arm, and then continued on into the house.

The next two days with Candice were some of the best days I'd had, as of late. We spent a great deal of time talking and catching up. I got to hear all about her classes and her friends, and even more about this new boyfriend of hers. She opened up to me in a way I hadn't seen since she was thirteen and I married Francine. We had always been close, but now I was starting to see her as my friend and not just my daughter.

While we talked, Candice was constantly on the move, flitting from one room to the other with a trash bag or a dustpan, making sure every corner of the house was spotless. "Just because a woman doesn't live here anymore, that doesn't mean it can't look like it's got a woman's touch!" she would gently chide me.

"Hey, now, don't forget, a woman does live here!" I grinned and pointed at New Francine.

Candice bent at the waist to give New Francine a pat. "Well, until she starts pulling her weight and learning how to run a vacuum, I guess someone else will have to do it!"

Similar exchanges went on throughout Friday and Saturday. Saturday night was especially lovely. After dinner, we retreated to the living room, Candice and New Francine taking their respective places on the couch. I, however, remained standing. "Since this is your last night here, I thought we would celebrate," I said with a grin.

Candice cocked an eyebrow in question. New Francine blinked slowly. I turned to the closet in the hallway and made a production of digging through the stacks of junk buried in there. Finally, I found what I was looking for, nestled among the multitude of winter coats and empty clothes hangers still waiting for their phantom sweaters: Candice's old Super Nintendo system. I pulled out the gray box and blew the dust off the top.

Candice yelped with joy and excitement. "Oh, Daddy, you still have it! I can't believe it! I haven't played with this in years!"

"Wait up," I told her. "I think I still have some of the old games in here, too!"

I dug around some more and finally came up with a black shoebox filled with game cartridges. "Aha! Here we go!" I handed the box to Candice. "So, what game shall we start with?"

We settled on the classic *Donkey Kong Country* and spent the rest of the night fighting our way through the jungle, playing well into the early morning hours. New Francine simply slept curled up on the couch, lightly purring, her tail twitching on occasion, either content or bored, or somewhere in between.

I awoke the next morning very reluctantly. Though the brilliant sun streamed through the window onto my bed, I struggled with the resistance to keep my eyes closed. Candice was heading back to school that day, just as we had really started to bond, and I held the misguided hope that if I prolonged my waking, it would somehow prolong her leaving. Eventually, I knew I could put it off no longer, and I swung my legs over the side of the bed, pressing my feet to the cold hardwood floor.

Candice had beaten me to the punch and was already in the kitchen frying up some bacon and eggs for our last breakfast together. She smiled sweetly at me as I descended the staircase and kindly avoided making any cracks at my disheveled appearance. New Francine was on the table, enjoying her breakfast of tuna mixed with a scrambled egg.

"You're going to spoil my cat, you know," I grumbled unconvincingly at

The Calico

Candice.

"Well, someone has to! You better get used to doing so yourself. Cats tend to expect a certain level of luxury. It dates all the way back to the Egyptians, when they used to be worshipped for their alleged metaphysical attributes."

I groaned. "You, too, with the metaphysical mumbo-jumbo? You're starting to sound just like Francine. Anyway, can we postpone any more of the history lesson until after I've had my coffee? I just don't think I have the brain power to focus on much of anything right now."

Candice rolled her eyes and turned back to the stove.

After breakfast, Candice retreated upstairs to begin packing for her trip back to college. I sat sullenly in the living room, wishing I could prevent the inevitable. Soon, the only company I would have left was my cat, and, God help me, my sister Charlotte.

As if on cue, the doorbell rang. "Aw, man, no, she's here already?" I moaned to myself. "I was hoping I would at least be able to say good-bye to Candice before that harpy showed up!"

I made my way slowly to the door and opened it unwillingly, my eyes cast downward, just waiting for the nagging and the lectures to begin. They always began rather immediately the moment Charlotte showed up. However, with my eyes trained on the floor, I noticed something different. I did not see Charlotte's practical brown flats. Instead, I saw shiny black boots. The type of boots normally worn by...

"Excuse me, Mr. Cochran?" the police officer asked.

I looked up to see a solemn, yet kind-looking young officer holding a badge, his eyes full of sympathy and regret. Puzzled, I cleared my throat. "Ye-yes, that's me. Lawrence Cochran."

"Husband of Francine Cochran?"

I was now on full alert. "Yes, that's my wife..."

The police officer briefly shifted his eyes downward, as if he had to gather the strength to say what he was about to say next. "I'm sorry to tell you this, sir, but your wife is dead."

The news hit me like a blast of heat from an erupting volcano, and I was physically pushed back a step. "Dead? How? When?"

"May I come in, Mr. Cochran? I'm afraid I have some rather upsetting things to tell you."

I grudgingly stepped aside, allowing the officer to enter the living room. New Francine stared at both of us intently.

"Mr. Cochran, my name is Officer Williams. Your wife's car was found this morning in the ravine below the cliff that runs past Old Latham Road. Your wife was still in the car when we found it. I'm sorry but…there was nothing we could do for her when she was found."

I swallowed hard, and then asked what I needed to know. "How…how did it happen?"

Officer Williams lowered his head a moment before raising it to meet my eyes. "There were no signs of skid marks and no signs of a struggle. I'm afraid we are having to rule this…a suicide."

This pushed me another step back. Suicide? I knew she had trouble with depression in the past, but I thought she had been doing so much better. Wasn't that what those infernal women's club meetings were supposed to help her with?

My voice came out barely above a whisper. "When did she die?"

Officer Williams slowly sucked in his breath as if to steel himself for this next answer. "Well, Mr. Cochran, I'm afraid that is the difficult part. From what the coroner could tell from his initial investigation, he has time of death estimated at Monday around 4:30 p.m., cause of death a severe blow to the head from the windshield. The toxicology report has been sent off and won't be back for a few weeks. And, in any event, I'm afraid—"

"Please, stop stalling and just spit it out already!"

Officer Williams coughed and took a deep breath to steady himself. "You see, sir, when the responding officers answered the call that a car had been found in the ditch, there was a rather large feral cat colony in and around the vehicle. I'm afraid…I'm afraid there wasn't much left of your wife for the coroner to autopsy."

My room started to spin and my knees buckled. Had I not thrown out a hand to catch myself on the back of the recliner, I just might have collapsed at the officer's feet. "Please leave," I told him feebly. "I really need to be alone right now."

"Yes, sir, Mr. Cochran, I understand and I am very sorry for your loss. There is just one more thing." Officer Williams reached into the small case he had been holding. "When the officers found your wife, they found this clasped in her hand. I thought you might want to have it."

I looked down at the object the officer had just handed me. It was a well-worn, slightly crumpled photo of our wedding day. Tears sprang to my eyes. "Thank you," I whispered, as the officer discreetly showed himself out and shut the door behind him.

Staring at the photograph, I sank into the recliner. Gone. She was truly gone. I couldn't believe it. Yes, times were rough these past few years, and

THE CALICO

there were times that I couldn't stand the sight of her, but deep down, I'd never stopped loving Francine.

I couldn't take my eyes off the happy couple in the photograph, beaming widely at the unseen photographer. God, but Francine was beautiful. Clad in her mother's heirloom wedding dress with the high lace collar, her fiery red hair cascading in waves around her face, her piercing green eyes, her dazzling smile. And now, she was gone forever. I put my head in my hands and began to weep.

"Mew." The noise came softly from the other side of the room. "Mew."

I looked up to see the little calico cat sitting on the couch, staring at me. "Mew," she said again.

A dawning realization struck me at that moment. Her time of death was thought to be Monday around 4:30, not long after she walked out of my life, and only a few hours before this cat entered. There had not been a sign of a struggle. Francine had always loved cats and would go out of her way to avoid harming one. There were feral cats all over the area where her car had been found.

"You," I uttered in a low growl. "*You* did this. You ran out in front of her car, causing her to swerve! You killed my Francine!"

I lunged at the cat, who darted from the couch with a loud screech. I chased the demon into the kitchen, where I grabbed the first knife I could find.

"You killed her!" I screamed. "Why did you do it? *Who are you*?"

The animal escaped my attacks with the ease known only to cats, disappearing from the corner of the cabinet, and then reappearing on top of the kitchen table. I knocked over pots, pans, and chairs in my lumbering attempt to exact revenge on my wife's murderer. I took a giant swing at the table, and she disappeared again.

"Daddy!" screamed Candice in horror as she hurried into the room. "What are you doing? Don't hurt the cat!"

Startled, I swung around to face my daughter and began to walk toward her. At that moment, I felt soft, tickling fur pass across my shins, toppling my balance and sending me sprawling, the knife flying out of my hand. I heard a sickening crack as my right ankle twisted and snapped, the pain shooting up my leg and instantly becoming unbearable. I landed on the floor with a thud, heaving and gasping as I attempted to catch my breath through the pain.

"Agh!" came the cry from across the room. There stood Candice, eyes wide in disbelief, clutching desperately at the knife that protruded from the middle of her chest in a growing stain of blood. "Daddy...?" Her eyes rolled back into her head, and she slumped to the floor, lifeless.

"Candice! No!" I reached helplessly for my daughter, knowing there was nothing I could do for her.

Sitting on the floor, just far enough out of my grasp, was the little calico cat. She simply stared at me, almost smirking, peering into me with her piercing green eyes. As I stared back into her eyes, my room once again began to spin.

They used to be worshipped for their alleged metaphysical attributes.
I'm never coming back until I take this house!

Francine with her never-ending love for cats. Francine with her new, almost obsessive interest in the metaphysical. Francine with her piercing green eyes. Oh, my God.

"You," I said once again to the cat. "You...you didn't kill Francine, did you? You *are* Francine!"

The cat blinked at me, looked deliberately over at Candice's body, then back at me, again with that almost smirk on her face. She had finally come between me and my daughter. She had won. With a twitch of her tail, the calico skipped gracefully out of the kitchen.

"Come back here, you wretch! I'm sorry I ever loved you!" I screamed after her, attempting to belly crawl my way into the living room. The pain was so immediately intense, all I could do was lay my sweat-soaked forehead onto the linoleum and sob in despair. "I love you, Candice. Daddy will always love you."

The doorbell rang. Knowing I couldn't answer it even if I wanted to, I ignored it, praying they would go away. Moments passed before it rang again.

"Knock, knock!" a singsong voice lilted into the house. "I rang the doorbell but no one answered. You know, it's really not safe to leave your front door unlocked..."

The sentence was interrupted by a bloodcurdling scream as Charlotte stepped into the kitchen. She looked from Candice, to the knife in her chest, then to me with a look mixed with shock and disgust.

"You monster!" she shrieked. "How could you murder your own daughter? Did you think in some sick way that this might win Francine back? How could you?" She raced from the kitchen to the telephone in the living room.

"Charlotte, no! Wait! You don't understand! It was the cat!" I called after her. But it was no use. There was no way she would ever believe me.

I heard the frantic murmur of Charlotte on the telephone from the other room, explaining the situation to the police. "Come quick!" I heard her yell before she slammed down the receiver. Once again, I knew all I could do was lower my head to the floor and wait.

Within minutes, the sound of sirens filled the street in front of my house. Paramedics rushed in with two stretchers, one for my beloved Candice, who was quickly covered with a sheet, and one for me. Officer Williams himself handcuffed me to the railing while he read me my rights, the whole time staring at me as if I was a disgusting slug he had found on the bottom of his shoe. I only half-listened, resigning myself to my fate. After all, my wife and daughter were both gone. What was left for me now, anyway?

As Charlotte stood by to watch the circus in my kitchen, the little calico cat slipped into the room and jumped into her arms. "Ooh!" she cried out in surprise with a coo in her voice.

"Hi there, little girl! Ohhh, you must be so upset and scared with all this excitement. And now your daddy is going away for a very long time, and you're worried no one will take care of you. Don't you worry, little sweetheart. Auntie Charlotte will stay here with you, and she'll bring all her cat friends with her, so you'll always have someone to talk to!"

As the paramedics wheeled me out of my house toward the ambulance, I stared into the piercing green eyes of the little calico cat one last time.

I'm never coming back until I take this house!

I guess Francine was the one who got the last laugh.

About the Author—Brandy Herr

Born in the Dallas/Fort Worth, Texas area, Brandy Herr attended the Pennsylvania State University where she received her Bachelor's degree in public relations. Her book, *Haunted Granbury*, was released in February 2014 by The History Press. She is also the co-founder of the Granbury Ghosts and Legends Tour and is a member of Research and Investigation of the Paranormal, with whom she has participated in many ghost hunt investigations. Brandy has a passion for animal welfare causes and currently lives in Granbury with her husband, their two rescued dogs, and two rescued cats.

Angel

Angela Crider Neary

Don't get too close to Angel or you might get burned!

Chapter 1

    She had been given so many different names over her nine lives that she couldn't keep up with them all. She recalled a few, although they weren't very original: Snowball, Ivory, Pearl, Frosty, Powderpuff, Angel. She had white fur, you see, and was also very transient, so she had had many owners/caretakers over the years. She was partial to Angel. She thought it suited her best, so that's who she thought of herself as, no matter what she was called.

    Angel was a brilliant white color with a medium to long fur coat. She had a pert, pink nose and large, sapphire-blue eyes, making her irresistible to cat lovers—and even non-cat lovers, in most instances. She had the moves down, and could purr, frisk, and frolic when the need arose to impress someone. She could also gaze intently at someone, reflecting a sadness and need in those big, blue eyes, causing the hardest heart to melt into a puddle and making the target putty in her paws. She had learned quite a few survival skills during her life. Angel was generally a stray, since the fire that took her mother and entire litter when she was a mere kitten. Her mother had been a stray, herself, and, when she was heavily pregnant with Angel's litter, had been taken in by a kind-hearted old man who had traveled around in a trailer and lived wherever the moment took him. Mel, the old man, was a lonely sort who happily welcomed the pregnant cat and was ready with a cozy box and warm blankets when she gave birth.

    After they had had several weeks of nursing, Mel began providing canned food and water for the kittens, as they were gradually weaned from their mother. Mel surprised the kittens with little toy mice to play with, and they gamboled and romped all over the tiny trailer together, hunting for these mock foes. "Now, ain't y'all a bunch of cutie-pies!" Mel would always remark, with a big smile on his craggy face.

Although Mel was kind to all the cats, Angel decided that she was his favorite. Maybe it was because of her glistening white fur and large, blue eyes that set her apart from the other kittens in the litter, who were mostly gray or orange tabbies with green eyes. He let her sit in his lap while he rocked in an old ruby-red recliner. The springs were sticking up through the worn fabric of the chair's seat, and the lever that released the foot rest barely worked anymore, unless you put the right amount of juju on it, but Mel knew how to do it—and he loved that old, red chair. He would rub Angel's ears, neck, back, and belly until she purred with delight. Mel would rock back and forth rhythmically while listening to old George Jones albums and smoking his favorite cigarettes.

Angel didn't know that this was considered a disgusting habit—the cigarettes, not the George Jones albums—and the smell of the cigarette smoke comforted her since, to her, it was the smell of Mel.

One smell Angel didn't particularly appreciate, although it was also Mel's smell, was the odor that emanated from Mel after he cooked up and consumed his favorite culinary specialty, beanie-weenie. "Okay, kitties," he would announce, chuckling, "who wants me to cook up a batch of delicious beanie-weenie?" He was never discouraged by the fact that the cats just turned their heads and pretended not to understand. They preferred to stick to the kitten food.

Mel got up from his recliner one night after making one of his beanie-weenie announcements and started bustling about the kitchen, turning on the pilot light on the gas range, getting out his pots and cans of beans and weenies. He also liked to throw a little Tabasco sauce into his concoction for flavor and a nice little kick. He was parked in Louisiana, after all, so he liked to pay homage to the state's spicy sauce.

Angel saw the signs of what meal was about to be prepared, so she jumped up onto a storage shelf above the kitchenette cabinet, and then leapt out one of the skylights, the screen to which had long since fallen out and been discarded, to get some fresh air. Mel didn't let the kittens outside without supervision since they were still so small, but Angel would sneak out now and then to explore the trailer park area. The skylight was just barely open a few inches, and when Angel leapt out, she hit it with her back and it banged shut, barely missing her tail, so she didn't know how she would get back in. Maybe she would have to mewl at the door until Mel heard her and came to her rescue. She knew he could never get mad at her.

oOo

Mel poured the aromatic ingredients into the pot and stirred it around real good. "Mmmm, mmmm, mmmm," he mumbled, breathing in the flavor, his eyes closed and a smile on his face. He then went to heat up his succulent supper on his tiny stove, his stomach starting to growl and rumble at the anticipation of the treat that was to come. To his surprise, however, there was no flame. "Well gol-darnit!" he said, tilting his head to the side and peering at the burner. "I thought I turned this danged thing on." The range was ancient, and it often took a while to get it to light. He set the pot on the counter and decided to have a cigarette before messing with it anymore.

Mel puttered around the trailer, looking for his smokes. "Now where did I put those things?" he asked no one in particular, except maybe the cats, who never answered him. Mel could never remember where he left his cigarette pack the last time he had a smoke. He often thought he might just quit the habit one day, simply because he couldn't find his cigarettes. To further complicate things, the cats would often bat the pack onto the floor and then under the table or couch, making it even more difficult for Mel to locate it. When he couldn't find it on the dinette table or the side table next to his recliner, he knelt down to try to look for it on the floor and in any nooks and crannies it could have gotten to. He was a little hesitant to do this since there was always the risk these days that he wouldn't be able to get back up. He wasn't as spry as he used to be, back in the day, when he had been a pretty hot number, if he didn't say so himself.

Just when he was about to give up and go back to tinkering with the range, Mel spotted the white and silver package of addiction in the back corner under the couch. He sat up on his knees and looked around the room for something to use to retrieve the cigarettes. He noticed the broom, luckily within reach, and used the handle to fetch out the smokes. He slowly stood up, using the broom and the couch to get fully and creakily to his feet. Was it really worth all this? he wondered. Well…yeah.

When he finally steadied himself, he patted the almost-new pack of cigarettes on the heel of his hand several times, withdrew one of the cigarettes, and inserted it between his lips, ready to suck in some yummy toxins. "Now, where is that darned lighter?" he asked. The cats did a collective eye roll, but Mel didn't notice. Mel repeated the whole process of searching for the lighter, and finally located it, surprisingly right where he had left it. As Mel put his thumb on the lighter and pressed down to flick the switch, an enlightening thought that must have been hidden in his subconscious while he looked for the cigarettes popped into his head, but it was too late. His fate, and that of his feline charges, was already set in motion.

o0o

Angel had meandered over to an area of the trailer park that contained a sandbox for trailer community kids to play in. She encountered a pretty impressive sand castle made with stacked pails of sand that even had mini American flags flying from the turrets. Angel decided this would be a regal and refreshing place to do her business. Mel kept a litter box in his trailer, but it had to be shared by all the cats and Mel wasn't too fastidious about cleaning it out. And besides, it wasn't very private, and a girl needed her privacy every once in a while. There was no one around the sandbox at that moment, so it was the perfect opportunity. Angel was just squatting down in the moat to enjoy some open-air relief when she heard and felt the explosion that rocked the entire trailer park like a comet ripping through the atmosphere.

Angel immediately and instinctually sensed the immense loss, and galloped as fast as she could toward the ball of fire that used to be her home and sole source of comfort and happiness. She ran as close as she could to the flames that jumped higher and higher into the sky and licked out at her like serpents' tongues, searching for Mel and her feline family, hoping that one or more of them had miraculously escaped, but no such luck. Although she could not really comprehend what had happened, she knew in her heart that she would never see Mel or her cat family again. At that moment, something shriveled up and died inside her, her heart turning hard, cold, and black, crumpling like the burning shards of Mel's trailer. Angel finally gave up her fruitless searching, and just sat staring at the golden flames, their light reflecting in her glistening blue eyes, strangely drawn to the fire that had just taken her joy and life as she knew it.

Chapter 2

"Come 'ere, Earl!" shouted Birdie, excitement in her voice, after most of the smoke and ash had cleared and the fire trucks had finished with their bleak business, slowly and sadly rolling out of the trailer park to leave behind a soaked and blackened hole where their neighbor's trailer had been cozily nestled only hours before. Earl and Birdie had recently retired, Earl after finally selling his small-town dental practice, and Birdie from working the counter at the Bad Moon Diner—nothing but Creedence on the juke box, 24/7—Earl's favorite lunch spot and the place they had met 38 years ago.

Earl had wanted Birdie to quit her job at the diner after they had married and maybe work in his dental practice doing the books, or some secretarial work. But Birdie had refused, as she was the outgoing type and enjoyed the socializing and people watching that the Bad Moon offered in spades. She had come by her nickname, Birdie, as a child. Her parents noticed that she chattered nonstop, like a cardinal, they said. She still wore the little red cardinal pendant her parents had given her every day, as a totem by which she remembered them.

After Earl finally took the plunge and sold his dental practice, they agreed to purchase a motorhome and travel the country, to have some adventures and see all the things they had missed while working all their lives and raising kids.

"Lookee here, Earl!" said Birdie, waving her arm and fruitlessly trying to get Earl's attention, but he was chatting with the other trailer park denizens, speculating as to just what could have happened to cause poor old Mel's trailer to ignite into an inferno. Lucky for the other folks at the park, Mel's trailer had exploded out the front and back sides, where no other trailer was immediately parked. The trailers in close proximity to Mel's, however, were a bit scorched on the exteriors, but it was nothing that a good power washing couldn't fix.

"That poor bastard," said one of the men, referring to Mel. "He was a nice fella and didn't deserve something like this happening to him."

"He was obviously irresponsible with his gas lines and probably lit himself on fire smoking one of those infernal cigarettes he always had hanging out of his mouth," said one of the less compassionate residents. "He coulda killed all of us!"

ANGEL

"Here, kitty, kitty, kitty," coaxed Birdie, ignoring all the trailer park chitchat. She had discovered a stunning white kitten roaming the periphery of Mel's former trailer, its white fur singed and black in areas. The kitten looked over at her with irresistible blue eyes, looking shell-shocked, but refused to let Birdie come too close.

"Earl, I think this must be one of those kittens from the litter of that pregnant cat that Mel took in," said Birdie to the still-distracted Earl. "I thought they must have all gone up in flames, but this one must have survived. Bring me some of that tuna we had left over from lunch!" Birdie looked up and realized that she still didn't have Earl's attention. Sighing, she said, more to herself than to Earl, "Never you mind, Earl. I'll get it myself."

Birdie quickly retrieved the tuna from the trailer fridge and put the bowl down on the ground in an effort to entice the cat. The cat wouldn't make a move toward the bowl, however, until Birdie moved about a half a dozen feet back. Then, slowly, but surely, the cat crept toward the bowl—what cat could resist tuna? When the cat was fully ensconced in scarfing down the tuna, Birdie made her move. Not too aggressively, she inched slowly and quietly toward the elegant, traumatized feline. When she was finally close enough, she knelt down and began to stroke the cat's head and back. The cat finished the tuna, looked up at Birdie, and blinked those enchanting eyes several times, as if to hypnotize her prey. She then rolled over onto her back, paws in the air, and let Birdie rub her silky belly, already able to sense that she had this human right where she wanted her.

Earl, finally tearing himself away from the gossiping neighbors, came upon the scene at just this moment. "Oh, golly, Birdie!" he said, shaking his head. "Don't you even think about it!" He knew about his wife's propensity to be a sucker for any wayward animal in need, especially one as bewitching as this one appeared to be.

"Come on, Earl," said Birdie. "Can't we keep her? She's an orphan now, all alone in the world."

Earl looked down at the intriguing animal and into her seductive eyes. His heart immediately melted. "Well, since you put it that way…"

oOo

The temperature was below freezing in Opal, Wyoming. Earl and Birdie had continued their journey across the U.S. in their motorhome, stopping to see the sites along the way, like Cadillac Ranch, Camel Rock, a barbed wire moose, and the world's largest jackalope, all the while with Angel in tow. Only, they called her Sugar. Angel didn't cotton to this, of course, but had no way of expressing her opposition, aside from ignoring the name when she was called, which is what most cats do, anyway, so no one knew the difference.

Angel had never grown close to Birdie and Earl, no matter how much they spoiled her. Earl vaguely sensed something missing in the cat's demeanor, although he couldn't put his finger on what it might be, but Birdie never noticed a thing wrong and treated the mysterious little creature as if she were her own child.

Angel would purr and play like any other adorable kitten, but the usual bond or connection experienced between a pet owner and a pet was somehow missing. She would sometimes nip, bite, and claw a little more aggressively than what was called for in normal kitten play. Birdie just chalked it up to her earlier trauma from the explosion and ignored it.

The only time Angel seemed to respond with anything resembling happiness was when Earl and Birdie would make a small campfire at night outside their motorhome and let Angel wander about on a little kitty harness. She would jump and frolic with delight as the flames sparked and crackled, and stare into the fire, the light glinting in her huge eyes, mesmerizing her. Birdie often thought Angel just might jump into the flames if they didn't tie her harness far enough away, and would always have trouble tearing Angel away from the fire at the end of the night. Earl thought this behavior was a slight bit demonic, but didn't say anything since he knew how much Birdie loved the little animal.

Earl and Birdie had been enjoying their retirement and their road trip across the states so far, but had made a strategic, rookie error in judgment by coming up to Wyoming this time of year when it was hit or miss whether the weather would be nice and spring-like or still at risk for a winter spell. Just hours before their arrival, an arctic storm had blown in, bearing snow, sleet, ice, and whiteout conditions.

"I told you we should have stayed down in New Mexico a little longer," said Birdie, shivering as they rolled into the Crimson Estates Mobile Home Park, even though they had the heat cranked up high.

"Oh, it'll be fine," said Earl, trying to look on the bright side of things. "We never let a little bad weather get in our way before. We'll just have to cuddle up a little closer," he said, waggling his eyebrows up and down. Birdie laughed and slapped him on the arm. "Oh, Earl," she said, "always the charmer."

Angel detachedly watched this exchange from the fluffy cat bed Birdie had bought for her along the way. It was currently reinforced with a couple of warm blankets, which Angel was glad for since even her thick, white coat was not keeping her too warm in this frigid weather.

After they got parked and organized, Birdie asked, "Okay, so what's the plan for not freezing to death? Besides cuddling up real close, of course."

"Well, you know we have those space heaters for just such an emergency. Those oughtta do some good," said Earl.

"Sounds good to me," replied Birdie. "Anything to take the edge off this wintriness and avoid frostbite sounds like a plan. I think I'll put on all the clothes I have with me. You think we can get sweet Sugar to sleep with us? I don't want her to turn into a catsicle."

"You know she doesn't like to get too snuggly, but we can try," said Earl, thinking there was no way the cat would sleep in the bed with them, even in these polar conditions. Earl secretly hoped she wouldn't, since she had been giving him the creeps lately, with her strange attraction to and trancelike stares into the fire.

While Birdie was busy squeezing into her sixth layer of clothing, Earl dragged out the antiquated space heaters, and worked at untangling their cords and getting them plugged in. When he finally got that done, he placed a heater at each corner of and facing the bed, hoping to get the most heat possible directed toward it.

"Well, that oughtta do it," said Earl, brushing his hands off, a look of satisfaction on his face. He turned to look at Birdie and bask in her approval, but did a double take at the sight he beheld. She slightly resembled a rotund snowman, and even had a couple of knit hats on her head topped off by a coonskin cap she had picked up at some sort of theme park they had passed along the way.

"What're you lookin' at?" she asked, insulted by the befuddled and amused expression on Earl's face.

"Oh, nothin'," said Earl, chuckling. "Just thinking you might not be able to sleep very well in that get-up, much less do any cuddling. In fact, that'll keep you a couple of feet away from me at the minimum!"

"Well, at least I'll be warm," said Birdie with a huff, "which is more than I can say for you." She scanned Earl's handiwork with the heaters and said, "I'm not sure about those old things. Do you think they're safe?"

"Of course they're safe," said Earl. "What could happen with just you, me, and the cat in here?"

"All right, I guess," said Birdie, not looking too convinced. She then switched her attention to the cat.

"Come here, Sugar," Birdie said, trying to lure the cat into the bed. Angel just ignored her and hopped down to the floor when Birdie tried to lift her and her cat bed and move them onto the foot of the larger bed. Birdie put the cat bed, minus Angel, up in the big bed, patting it to encourage Angel to jump up into it. No dice. Angel just curled up between the two heaters without her comfy bed and blankets, and sulked, staring at Birdie from the corner of slitted eyes.

"Just leave her down there and come to bed," said Earl. "Maybe she'll get cold and come up here."

Birdie occupied herself by reading a book, which was no easy task while wearing ski gloves, and tried to out-stubborn the cat. After only a little time had passed without the cat having given an inch, she couldn't stand it any longer. She got up from the bed and placed the cat bed and blankets on the floor where Angel was lying. Angel immediately hopped in and curled up. Birdie adjusted her between the heaters so that she wouldn't be too close to them, but would still benefit from their warmth. Soon, notwithstanding the frigid temperature, everybody fell asleep.

o0o

Angel didn't sleep well that night and only cat-napped, in and out of dreams of Mel and the trailer fire, which haunted her. At one point, she dreamt of herself as having flames instead of fur, and walking around as if she were a feline fire ball, setting ablaze everything in her wake. In her periods of wakefulness, she found herself entranced by the electric glow of the space heaters that were furiously pumping their heat in a failed attempt at keeping the trailer warm. The serpentine coils of the heaters throbbed with incandescent fever.

Finally, able to sleep no more, Angel got up, stretched, and walked dangerously close to one of the heaters. She stared at the heater, a molten glow in her eyes, and began to reach an ivory paw toward one of the scarlet coils. Just as she was about to make contact, she pulled back, and quickly slid around the heater. As she walked away, the heater fell forward onto one of the blankets Angel had been sleeping on. Within seconds, silvery wisps smoke began to emanate from the blanket, quickly followed by sparkling, popping embers.

Angel watched as the cozy blankets she had been sleeping on only moments before alit and flickered into flames. She noticed that the frolicking flames did not seem to awaken Earl and Birdie, and she did nothing to remedy this, paralyzed as she was by the conflagration. As the fire engulfed the bed, licked at the ceiling and walls of the trailer, and began to surround her, Angel snapped out of it. She jumped up onto the dining table, slid a side window open with her paw, butted the screen out with her head, and jumped out. She crept into the hoary night, never once looking back.

Chapter 3

"Do you suspect arson, Sheriff?" Jim-Bob McCullough asked Frank Tagger, the sheriff of Winter County, Colorado.

"It's hard to say at this early stage of the investigation," answered Frank as he worked a toothpick around in his mouth—his eternal habit. It helped him think. He stared up at the blazing mid-day sun, taking his hat off to wipe the sweat that had puddled on his brow with his handkerchief, revealing his shock of red hair.

Summer had come early to Winter County that year, and it was not what you would call a "winter county" at the moment, with the temperature approaching 90 degrees in only early May. Frank was distracted for a moment by a white, fluffy cat that approached him, and was now rubbing and slithering in and out between his legs. Frank gently nudged the cat away with the toe of his boot, but it would not be dissuaded, and proceeded to roll around on its back in the dirt at his feet. Frank carefully stepped over the cat and knelt down at the edge of the burned-out mobile home that had just recently ignited into flames that had been extinguished by the local fire department.

"When we get the arson investigator's report, I'll let you know," Frank told Jim-Bob, "but I'm guessing it's just an accident like all the others. Unfortunately, people are prone to be a bit careless when handling flammable materials." Since Frank's jurisdiction included several mobile home parks that had experienced three fires in the last several months, his investigation had led him to the discovery of a rash of trailer park fires over the last several years in different parts of the country. Although the amount of trailer fires in such a short period of time was suspicious, there appeared to be nothing to link the fires, other than the fact that they all involved mobile homes and killed the unfortunate souls who happened to be inhabiting the homes at the time. This time, it was Joe and Eileen Ferguson who had been meandering across the U.S. from their home state of Florida. All of the arson reports Frank had managed to get his hands on, however, ruled the fires an accident caused by things such as a negligence with a space heater or poor handling of matches and a gas stove.

"Well, you need to hurry it on up," said Jim-Bob. "We need to know if there's a maniac fire bug on the loose." Jim-Bob was a permanent fixture at the Cozy Hearth Trailer Park, and had, understandably, become a little spooked by the rumors of all the recent fires.

"As I've told you, Jim-Bob, the other fires have been ruled accidents," said Frank, trying to assuage Jim-Bob's worries.

"Hmph," said Jim-Bob. "Those investigators do shoddy work, if you ask me. Just trying to hurry up so they can take an early lunch, lazy government workers. Ouch! What the heck?" Jim-Bob said, pulling up his leg and rubbing at his foot. Without his noticing, Angel had approached and given him a good bite on the ankle. She wasn't normally that affirmatively aggressive, but this Jim-Bob person was getting on her nerves. Frank failed to stifle a laugh.

"Hey!" Jim-Bob said. "Get your dadburn cat outta here or I'm going to sue your butt. I'll probably have to go get a rabies shot, now."

"It's not my cat," said Frank, "and I would advise you to control your outbursts directed at the law, or you might have more trouble than rabies on your hands." With that, Frank walked to his patrol car and got in, leaving Jim-Bob all in a huff, agitatedly rubbing his ankle. Before Frank could close the car door, Angel had jumped in and situated herself neatly in the passenger's seat, as if she belonged there, looking at him with her big, sapphire eyes. Frank laughed again. "You're braver than any deputy I've worked with in a long time," he told her, "so I guess you can ride along for now. Buckle up."

oOo

Frank hadn't meant to keep the cat as he was somewhat of a loner, bachelor type, but she had stuck with him and had become a normal fixture in his office and house. During his interviews with the trailer park occupants, he had learned that she had belonged to the recently deceased Fergusons, so he had felt bad for her and tolerated her company more than he might normally have done. The sheriff's office was less than a mile down the road from the trailer park where they had first encountered each other, and Frank lived in a small, rustic cabin in the woods right behind the office. They mainly just coexisted, although sometimes enjoyed each other's company. When Angel wanted a treat or some food, she knew how to turn on her "purrful" charm, and Frank couldn't resist giving in. Frank, however, wasn't generally sentimental about animals, and just let Angel do as she pleased for the most part, although he fed her and took care of her basic needs. There was an old doggie door in the cabin that Angel could use to come and go as she pleased, so there was no need for a litter box.

About a week into their relationship, the weather took a drastic turn and became cold and snowy, which was also rare for May. That was okay with

Frank, as he preferred the brisker temperatures. He liked to light a nice, wood fire in his cabin and study his cases on the couch in front of the crackling fire. Angel, of course, liked the fire, as well. Frank found it curious how Angel would gaze into the fire for hours, enraptured. At first, because she would sit so close, he was worried that she would light her fur or tail on fire, but after a while, he stopped worrying, as she seemed to sense how close was too close.

On work days, Angel would follow Frank back and forth between his office and the cabin, which caused a bit of snickering among the sheriff's office personnel, but Frank didn't pay it any mind. Angel easily made friends with everyone at the office and they liked having her as an unofficial sheriff's mascot. She livened up the place a bit and kept the random field mouse that would venture in at bay. They named her Creampuff, one of Angel's least favorite monikers she had been given, but luckily Frank had not adopted it and just called her kitty, cat, or darlin'.

When Frank finally received and reviewed the arson inspector's report, he said to his deputy, Ben, "Just like I suspected. The fire's been ruled an accident due to damaged wiring." Frank looked at Angel and gave her a scratch on the head. "You were lucky to get out of there alive, little darlin'," he told her. "I'm surprised you weren't sleeping along with those poor Fergusons." Most of the trailer fires had occurred in the dead of night, when no one had much of a chance of escape since they were most likely sleeping soundly. Angel just turned her head and licked her backside, seemingly paying no attention to Frank's observation.

"You know what's kinda curious?" Ben asked Frank.

"What's that, Ben," said Frank, rolling his ever-present toothpick from side to side in his mouth.

"Well, I seem to recall one of the other fire investigation reports mentioning that the folks who died also had a white cat. I think it was the one outta Silver City, Idaho. Pretty coincidental, huh?" said Ben. "And look here," he said, rifling through some papers on his desk, finally picking one up and shaking it at Frank. "This report says the man who burned up in Chalky Butte, Montana, also had a white cat."

"I usually say there's no such thing as a coincidence," responded Frank, "but in this case, that's gotta be one." Frank looked at Angel and asked her, "There's no way you were all the way out in Idaho and Montana, is there?" Angel just stretched and yawned, feigning indifference, and hopped off Frank's desk where she had been resting. She walked over and pushed open the screen door with her two front paws, letting herself out into the chilly afternoon. "No, I didn't think so," said Frank, although the thought knocked around in his brain awhile. The cat really did seem fascinated with fire. But that was silly to think there was any connection. He shook the thought off and concentrated on chewing his toothpick.

o0o

On her walk back to the cabin, Angel experienced a chill, and it wasn't from the nippy temperature. The things Frank and his deputy had said made her feel unsettled, although she didn't understand exactly why. It was just a funky feeling, like her fur didn't fit quite right. She had grown used to Frank's company, if not very close to him, but today had changed things.

Angel went back to the cabin and entered through the doggie door. She didn't take her usual six-hour nap that day, but roamed around the cabin, feeling restless and agitated. Frank came home at the normal time and cooked himself a hamburger on a skillet on the stove, after making sure Angel was fed. After dinner, Frank settled into his normal routine of lighting a hearty fire and pulling out some files to go through on the couch. He treated himself to a bottle of beer while he retrieved the files he had brought home from his backpack. Tonight, he wanted to go through more of the materials he had gathered on the trailer park fires.

Angel took up her normal spot on the hearth to watch the fire, this time sitting up on a stack of old magazines Frank had placed there, meaning to take to the recycle bin. Frank flipped through his files and sipped his beer, looking up at Angel with a quizzical look every now and then. This made Angel feel a bit apprehensive, although she didn't know what Frank was thinking about. He could have just been admiring his cozy fire and graceful cat, for all she knew. Angel stared back and forth between Frank and the fire, observing how the fire's light glinted in Frank's hair, making it an even deeper red.

After a couple of hours and several more beers, sleep overtook Frank, and the file he was reviewing slid off of his lap and onto the floor. The beer bottle he had been holding fell from his hand, but it was empty, so there was no spillage. Angel had been snoozing, too, but the *kerplunk* of the dropping file and bottle startled her into consciousness. She gazed into the fire and back toward Frank, and then at the file that had fallen from his lap. Those files made her anxious. She gazed into the fire for a while as if concentrating, then leapt off of the hearth to the floor below, the slick pile of magazines slipping and skidding beneath her paws as she jumped.

Angel went over to her food bowl and took a few bites of kibble as the magazine that had slid into the edge of the fireplace ignited. As the fire moved onto the larger pile of scattered magazines, Angel took one last look around the cabin. She had the fleeting thought that she might actually miss this place. She exited through the doggie door as the fire engulfed the large area rug in front of the fireplace. By the time the fire's rosy fingers reached out to encircle Frank's sleeping figure, she was halfway back to the trailer park. In Angel's experience, the trailer park was the only place she felt assured that she would fare well in this world.

Chapter 4

Emily Ash pulled into the Cozy Hearth Trailer Park at the end of a very long day. She had driven all the way from Fairmont, Nevada, and was ready for a good night's sleep. Emily had grown a little weary of the life her mini trailer offered her, and had begun to second-guess her decision to chuck everything from her prior life and downsize, although she knew that she did not want to return to what she had had before.

A year ago, she had held an executive position in a Silicon Valley high tech company. Her 12-hour days were spent in meeting after meeting, and her nights were spent entertaining clients and at company parties in swanky Bay Area venues. These places were usually so hip, only those "in the know" were even aware of their existence—kind of like the speakeasies of the past, where a person had to have a password or special knock to gain entry.

It was all so very exciting in the beginning when she was younger and fresher, but had been surprisingly unfulfilling to Emily, and had eventually worn her out, both mentally and physically. So, she had cashed in her stock options, sold her sought-after Peninsula property, and purchased the trailer, hoping to see the country and decompress from her decade and a half of corporate life. She felt that she could always go back and find her dream job, or she could even retire early with what she was able to make and save during her tech career.

Emily got her trailer parked and connected, and then freshened up a bit. She decided to go out and explore her surroundings a little before it got too dark. Although chilly outside, Winter County was beautiful country that she hated to miss a minute of while trapped inside her tiny home. Emily had not anticipated how cooped up and lonely she could sometimes feel in the small trailer. Just another thing she had learned about herself on this journey of self-discovery.

Her stressful job had made her somewhat negative about human nature, and she had been happy for the solitude at first, but she now realized that she missed regular human contact. Of course, she spoke to people almost daily at the mobile home parks where she stayed, at the diners where she ate, or at the landmarks and parks she visited, but it wasn't the same as the relationships one developed with friends, colleagues, and family. That's what she had missed most lately. Maybe it was time to make a change.

Emily bundled up, opened her trailer door, and breathed in the crisp, twilight air. As she stepped down, she almost tripped over a splendid white cat. The cat blinked up at her with sparkling, sapphire eyes, and began to rub her sleek body on Emily's shins. She was taken aback by the beauty and friendliness of the cat. She had never had time for a pet when she was working eighty-hour weeks, and was not what anyone would mistake for a "cat person", but this one immediately disarmed and charmed her. Maybe it was her own loneliness and need to bond with another living being. Emily knelt down and stroked the cat, who responded by purring and rolling over on her back, allowing Emily access to her soft, fluffy belly. Emily was enchanted.

"You must belong to someone," she said. "You're too pretty and refined to be a stray." She felt around Angel's neck for a collar and some identification, but found nothing. She looked around to see if there was anyone who might know about the cat, and spotted a man walking around the corner of the trailer next door.

"Excuse me," Emily said, waving to get the man's attention.

"What can I do you for, Missy?" said Jim-Bob McCullough.

"I was wondering if you knew who this lovely little creature belonged to," said Emily, indicating Angel.

"Oh, that mean old thing?" responded Jim-Bob. "I heard tell it belonged to those poor folks who died in the trailer fire here recently. Not sure where it's been taking up since then." Jim-Bob said, and then, cutting a wide berth around Emily and Angel, walked on.

"Mean old thing?" Emily said to Angel. "Who could he be talking about? Not you, I'm sure. And it looks like you're on your own, just like me. Trailer fire! Such a horrible experience. You better come inside and have a snack," she said, holding the trailer door open for Angel who hopped right inside and made herself at home. It didn't take more than a moment for Emily to decide that she would keep the cat. "I think I'll call you Angel," Emily told her.

o0o

For the next few days, Angel observed Emily with fascination, somewhat akin to the way most people regarded Angel. Angel was intrigued by Emily's white-blonde hair and alabaster skin. And the fact that Emily actually called her by the name she had adopted for herself inspired a contentment inside Angel that she barely remembered experiencing unless she reached back into the far recesses of her memory.

One day, while Angel was sleeping in a cupboard that Emily had left open and fitted a fleece blanket into for Angel, she was awakened by an eerily familiar scent. She blinked her eyes several times and saw rings of smoke floating in front of her eyes. She then noticed Emily sitting at the dinette, smoking a cigarette while flicking the ashes into a crystal ash tray, and she spied the familiar silver and white packaging of the cigarettes. "Sorry, Angel," Emily said. "It's a nasty habit, but I just can't seem to kick it. I'll open a window so you won't have to breathe too much of this in." But Angel didn't mind, and was so comforted by the smell that she fell back into a deep and dreamless sleep.

That night, Emily lit a campfire and told Angel that she would be making S'mores, one of Emily's favorite childhood foods, apparently. According to Emily, this treat was likely to make her fat, but she didn't mind since they were well worth a few extra calories. Angel didn't care much about the S'mores, but was excited about the campfire, and ran around animatedly under Emily's feet as she prepared the kindling.

Emily let Angel roam around outside the trailer freely since she had noticed that Angel never strayed too far away. Angel lay down by the fire to warm herself, but the blaze didn't hold the same attraction for her as it had in the past. She noticed a steadily increasing warmth inside her that seemed to replace her old yearning for the glimmering flames.

"All right, Angel," Emily said after a few hours spent lounging by the fire and Emily enjoying the decadent, gooey, marshmallow and chocolate goodies. "Let's go in and have some tuna and wine." She laughed and said, "My diet has really been suffering since I set out on this expedition. Who knew I would go from champagne, caviar, and *foie gras* to tuna, box wine, and S'mores?" She pondered on it for a few seconds, then said, "I kind of like it better, if you wanna know the truth, but don't tell anyone." She extinguished the fire, and Angel stared at it for a few moments like a long lost friend that she used to love, but really didn't know any more.

Emily played some jazz music on her phone and fed Angel some tuna. She poured some wine for herself and lit a few lavender candles for relaxation, as she attempted to hum along with the music. "Now, this is all anyone really needs, right?" she asked Angel. "Cheers!" she said, and clinked her wine glass against Angel's tuna bowl. Emily sprawled out on her bed to read her book—a mystery about a good-natured sheriff out in East Texas. She eventually yawned, said goodnight to Angel, and turned off the lights, neglecting to blow out the candles, a mistake she had made several times in the past and would always chastise herself about in the morning.

Angel wasn't tired, and sprang up onto the dinette table where one of the candles was sitting, casting its glistening glow against the walls of the trailer. Angel tried to conjure up her usual infatuation with the flickering flames. She thought back to the first fire she had experienced that had taken Mel and her family away, remembering the hard coldness she had felt inside that had remained with her for most of her days. She placed her face dangerously close to the candle's flame, causing it to cast an evil, bloodshot shadow over her face. She reached toward the candle with her paw and began to push it toward the edge of the table. She pushed it again and again, watching as it got closer and closer to the edge of the table and only a short distance from the wicker mat on the floor below.

Just as the candle reached the edge of the table, Angel looked over at Emily, sleeping soundly in her white, billowy comforter and pillows, almost as if she were sleeping on a snowdrift. Angel turned back to the candle, then abruptly leapt into her cupboard. She kneaded her cozy, fleece blanket, as if she were a kitten again, preparing to nurse from her mother, and drifted off to sleep.

About the Author—Angela Crider Neary

Angela Crider Neary is an attorney by day and writer by night. She is an avid mystery reader and especially enjoys reading novels set in interesting locales. She was inspired to write her first mystery novella, Li'l Tom and the Pussyfoot Detective Bureau (The Case of the Parrots Desaparecidos), by one of her favorite areas in San Francisco, Telegraph Hill. Angela is a native Texan who relocated to the Bay Area in 2008. She currently lives in wine country with her husband and their extremely spoiled cat.

The Easter Cat

Bill Crider

Never give the Easter Bunny a ride.

Let me give you a little piece of advice: Never stop to help the Easter Bunny change a flat tire. I would never have done it myself except that it was obvious that he was totally incompetent and no one else was even giving him a second glance. Besides, I thought I recognized him.

So I drove on by and coasted to a stop by the curb about half a block in front of the Bunny's pre-war Chevy. It was the same model as mine, in fact, a 1940 model, but mine was in better shape. The Bunny obviously wasn't a very good driver.

I got out of my car, stretched, and took a deep breath. It was a beautiful California day, all blue skies and sunshine, low humidity and the smell of oranges drifting in from one of the groves that still remained nearby. If I'd had any sense at all, I would have kept right on driving. But then, no one ever accused me of having any sense at all.

I walked back to the Bunny's Chevy. The passing cars ignored both of us. We were out near the studios, and you don't have to live in Hollywood for very long to get used to some pretty strange sights out there. Or anywhere else, for that matter.

The Bunny was trying to loosen a lug nut. He was down on his knees, straining so hard that his long pink ears were quivering. As I watched him strain, his hands slipped off the lug wrench. He keeled over on his side and hit the pavement.

"Damn," he said, which I thought was pretty strong language for the Easter Bunny, and I told him so.

"Yeah? And who the hell asked you?" He didn't bother to get up. He just lay there on his side with his puffy white tail sticking out toward the traffic.

"Nobody asked me. Nobody asked me to stop and help a bunny in distress, either."

He sat up then, and turned to look at me through eyes narrowed against the sunlight. He was who I'd thought he was, all right, Ernie Wiggins, dressed out in a bunny suit. Rabbits' noses were supposed to be pink, I think, but his was a bright shiny red.

"Ferrel?" he said. He put a hand up to shade his eyes. His eyes were a little red, too. "Bill Ferrel, private dick?"

"It's me, all right," I said. "And better a dick than a bunny rabbit. You got a part in something?"

It was a natural question. Ernie Wiggins was a has-been comic who'd started out with a couple of bits in Leon Errol shorts and then done one with the Three Stooges. Someone at Gober Studios spotted him in that one and gave him a try as the comic sidekick in a Rick Torrance jungle epic, *Johnson of Java*, I think, but it might have been *Benson of Borneo*. I can never remember which one came first.

Torrance and Wiggins hit it off, and Ernie had been funny enough to get a couple of good mentions in the trades. Not only that, but the box-office take was a little better than Torrance's last picture. So naturally, they put Ernie in another movie with Torrance, *Johnson* or *Benson*, whichever, and it looked like Ernie was on his way.

He was on his way, all right—on his way *out*. As it happened, he was a lush. Now, that's no big thing in Hollywood, of course. If they fired all the lushes tomorrow, every studio in town would close down. But Ernie was the wrong kind of lush. He started showing up drunk on the set, forgetting his lines, and missing his marks. Even that might not have been so bad on some pictures, but Rick Torrance's directors weren't exactly top of the line. They preferred the methods of William "One Shot" Beaudine. So, after one more picture, *Andrews of the Amazon*, Ernie was out on the streets.

And not only that. Now, he was dressed like the Easter Bunny.

Ernie stood up, none too steadily, and brushed haphazardly at the knees of his bunny suit. He didn't say anything about having a part. What he said was, "Can y' gimme a hand wi' th' tire?"

Even the exhaust fumes from the passing cars couldn't disguise the fact that he'd been sipping on the Old Overholt, or whatever he favored. Did I say "sipping"? He'd probably slugged down a fifth of the stuff by now, and it was only a little after noon. He'd never get the tire changed by himself.

So, fool that I was, I said, "Sure."

I took off my hat and jacket and laid them on the hood of Wiggins' Chevy. Then, I picked up the lug wrench and got to work. Ernie stared vacantly off into space and leaned his back against the car as if he needed a brace to help him stand up. While I worked at getting the wheel off, he slid slowly down the side of the car, an inch at a time.

I got the wheel off, put on the spare that Ernie had left lying in the street behind his car, and tossed the flat into the trunk. By that time, Ernie had slid all the way down the side of the car. He was sitting in the street, his back to the Chevy, snoring heavily.

I jacked down the car, tightened the lug nuts, and threw the wrench and jack into the trunk with the flat tire. I slammed down the trunk lid as hard as I could, hoping the noise would wake Ernie up. It didn't.

I wiped my hands off on my handkerchief, then put on my hat and jacket and looked down at Ernie, who was still snoring. He'd drawn a bunch of little black lines straight out from the sides of his nose. Whiskers, I guess.

I kicked one of his feet. Gently. I'm not some tough peeper like Bogart in *The Maltese Falcon*. "Wake up, Ernie," I said.

He opened one eye. "Ri'. Wakey, shakey. Gotta job."

If he had a job, it wasn't at Gober Studios. I'm on retainer to Gober, the big cheese himself, and I know the casts of every picture on the lot, which is how I got to know Ernie in the first place. Wayward starlets, over-sexed leading men, pregnant ingénues—I'm the one who tries to keep them out of trouble—and when that fails, to keep their names out of the papers.

In fact, I was on my way to do a little job for the studio at the moment, or I was supposed to be. I didn't think Mr. Gober would appreciate my helping out the Easter Bunny.

"Where are you working?" I asked Ernie.

"Rick's place. Kid's party. All I can ge' 'ese days."

He shut his eye and began snoring again. I hunkered down beside him and slapped him on both cheeks, gently. That didn't work, so I shook him. Gently, of course.

"Stop," he said. "Stopstopstopstop."

"Not until you wake up."

"Can't wa' up."

He slumped forward into my arms, and I shoved him back against the car. He opened one eye again. "Gotta ge' to Rick's. Gotta be bunny a' party."

I couldn't just leave him there, so I dragged him around to the passenger side of the car and held his head up by the ears to keep it off the street while I opened the door. Then, I tried to get him inside. It was like working with a very heavy dummy filled with flour dough, but I finally managed it. Of course, his feet were in the seat and his upper body was in the floor, but at least he was in the car. His head was practically up under the dash.

I shut the door and looked down the street at my own car. It would be all right where it was for a while. I could drive Ernie to Rick's house. Maybe he would sober up on the way.

Sure he would.

And maybe MGM would call me to replace Robert Taylor in some big-budget foreign intrigue film because I was so much better-looking than he was. My nose has been broken twice, I'm going bald on top, I'm a little overweight, and my eyes are too close together. You figure the odds.

I sighed, walked around to the driver's side of the Chevy, and slid in. As it happened, the little job I was supposed to do was at Rick Torrance's house. It seemed that there was some kind of dispute going on, and Mr. Gober wanted me to settle it. He hadn't said what it was, which is why I wasn't in much of a hurry. It apparently wasn't an emergency, and I didn't like settling arguments. That wasn't my idea of what my job was all about.

But I was going to do it. That's what I got paid for.

o0o

Rick Torrance lived not far off Sunset in Beverly Hills. I'd been to his place once before, when some starlet had nearly drowned in his pool, where she'd fallen after being goosed by a chimpanzee that had wandered in from Rick's private jungle.

The house was a big three-story stucco job, painted pink and set back from the street behind a pink stucco wall on a couple of acres of ground, only a little of which was given over to a well-manicured lawn and a drive lined with bougainvillea bushes. The rest was covered with the jungle: three or four kinds of palm trees, banana trees, creeping vines, climbing vines and a few varieties of exotic flowers.

God only knew what the water bill was, but it didn't matter to Rick. The studio paid it. The jungle was good publicity, giving the place the semblance of the kind of terrain Rick Torrance was supposed to prefer.

Anyone familiar with Rick knew that he actually preferred the terrain of a nice shady bar to a jungle anytime, but most of the ticket-buying public didn't know Rick at all. Instead, they read about his private jungle in the fan magazines and had fantasies about him running around among the palm trees with his shirt off. Most of his pictures didn't require big wardrobe. He never wore a shirt if he didn't have to, and I didn't blame him. If I had pecs like his, I'd go shirtless, too.

I stopped Ernie's Chevy at the gate in the pink wall. The gatekeeper, an

THE EASTER CAT

old geezer with bifocals and white hair growing out of his ears, recognized me from the last time I'd been there. He was willing to let me inside, but he wanted to know who was in the floor.

"The Easter Bunny," I said.

The geezer wasn't surprised. "Oh, yeah, him. He's late. Mr. Torrance and Mr. Gober are having a fit."

"He's a little under the weather," I said. "You say that Mr. Gober's here?" I hadn't realized that Gober was calling from Rick's place.

"In the flesh," the gatekeeper said. "He's the kid's godfather, or something. He's fit to be tied because the bunny hasn't showed up. If I was you, I'd do something about your buddy, there, and get him ready. Mr. Torrance and Mr. Gober, they don't want the kid to be disappointed."

I didn't want the kid to be disappointed, either, and I didn't want Ernie to get into any trouble. But I didn't know what to do about it.

The gatekeeper had a suggestion, however, which is how I wound up in the bunny suit, walking up the drive with a basket of colored eggs in each hand. The eggs and baskets had been in the Chevy's back seat, and now and then, I stopped along the drive to hide an egg or two in a bougainvillea bush.

I was careful not to wander off into the jungle. There was no telling what was in there. I thought I could hear spider monkeys calling to one another, and then there was that chimp. So I stuck to the drive.

The gatekeeper and I'd had a hell of a time getting Ernie out of the bunny suit, and I was having a hell of a time wearing it. It was hot, it was too tight, and it smelled a lot like Ernie. I wasn't a happy bunny when I hammered the brass knocker against the front door of Torrance's house. Ernie, lying asleep in the gatehouse in his underwear, was considerably happier than I was.

No one answered my knock on the door, so I tried the knob. It was open, and it swung back into the house.

I looked inside just in time to see a familiar-looking man hurtling down the hallway toward me. He had a cat in his arms, a huge tabby that was dark and light gray on top, with a lot of orangey gold mixed in, and a solid white stomach. It was colored almost like an egg—sort of an Easter cat.

I thought maybe it had something to do with the party, and I was trying to get a better look when there was a thunderous explosion and the door frame shattered above my head.

Maybe the little dispute Mr. Gober had called me about was more serious than I'd thought.

I looked around for a place to run, but before I could move, the man from the hallway crashed into me. I'm pretty sturdy, but I don't think I slowed him down much. It was hard to tell. I couldn't see very well because I was lying flat on the tiles in front of the door. There were colorful hardboiled eggs all around me.

There was another explosion and I raised my head cautiously. I could see Rick Torrance back in the hallway. He had an elephant gun to his shoulder. At least, it *looked* like an elephant gun. Maybe it was only a .30-.30. Pistols, I know a little bit about; rifles are something I don't generally have to deal with.

I squirmed out of the way before he could run over me, too. He ran past me and headed down the drive. Then Mr. Gober, who must have been behind him, came outside. He stopped and looked at me.

"You're not Wiggins," he said. Studio heads have to be perceptive.

"No, sir. I'm not."

He recognized me then. "Damnit, Ferrel, what are you doing in that outfit?"

He always says that. *"Damnit, Ferrel,"* I mean. I'm thinking of having my first name changed, since he can't seem to call me anything else.

"I'm taking Ernie's place," I said, standing up.

I started gathering up the eggs. Most of them were cracked, but I put them in the baskets anyway.

"Damnit, Ferrel!" Gober said. "You're not supposed to be playing with Easter eggs. You've got to stop Rick. He's going to kill somebody if you don't."

"What about the party?" I asked. I didn't want to disappoint the kids, not after I'd gone to the trouble of getting dressed like a bunny.

Gober, however, didn't care about the kids. He was more interested in his star. "Forget the party. The kids have waited this long; they can wait a little longer."

"Where are they?"

"They're in the back yard. Peggy's with them. They're fine. Now, get going!"

"I need to know what's going on here, first," I said.

Mr. Gober took a deep breath and tried to control himself. Patience wasn't his strong suit. "The guy that ran you over is Lawrence Berry. Rick's going to kill him."

I didn't think so. It was widely known that Rick was a terrible shot. But I was curious. "Why?"

"He got Felicia pregnant, that's why. Now—"

I interrupted him. "Felicia? I thought Rick's wife was Penny Turnage."

Gober's face was turning a truly amazing shade of red. It was almost the same color as Ernie's nose. I wondered if Gober had been drinking. He took another deep breath.

"Felicia's the cat," he said. "Rick's cat."

"And Larry Berry got her pregnant? Illicit pregnancy is one thing, but bestiality? And cross-species breeding? Wow! Wait till the fan mags get hold of this one! Not to mention *Scientific American*!"

Berry was a well-known womanizer who generally played the villain's role in films. He'd been in a couple of Rick's pictures, playing an evil white hunter in *Kent of Kilimanjaro* and a murderous guide in *Clive of the Congo*. Or maybe he was a guide in *Kent* and a hunter in *Clive*. As I said, it's easy to get confused. The pictures are a lot alike. Plenty of shots of Rick with his muscles showing, and lots of stock footage of crocodiles sliding off sandbanks into rivers—things like that.

"Not Berry, you idiot!" Gober yelled. "He didn't get Felicia pregnant! His *cat* got her pregnant! Berry lives next door, and the cat comes sneaking over the wall to assault Felicia."

"Was that his cat Larry was holding?" I asked.

A rifle boomed.

"Yes! Now are you going to do something to earn your retainer, or do I have to turn things over to the Continental Agency?"

I handed him the Easter baskets. "Hold these," I said.

oOo

As an Easter Bunny, I was more of an urban-type of animal. I didn't really belong in the jungle.

For one thing, my ears kept getting caught on the vines that dangled from the palm trees. It wasn't so bad if I realized what was happening in time to extricate myself, but once or twice, I'd nearly jerked my own head off.

For another thing, the ground was squishy and wet underfoot. Rick had some kind of irrigation system for all the plants, and it was doing a very efficient job. Water dripped down out of the palms and soaked into my fur.

And for still another thing, I didn't like the noises, especially since I didn't really know what kind of wildlife Rick Torrance had stocked the place with. There were rumors in the fan magazines that monkeys weren't the only things in there. Pythons had been mentioned more than once. And boa constrictors.

Of course, snakes don't make noises. That's one of the things I don't like about them. They're very sneaky, snakes are. But lions make noise, and one article had hinted that Rick had a lion on the property. I wondered if lions liked to eat rabbits.

Even though I wasn't exactly an old jungle hand, it was easy to follow along behind Rick and Larry. They were crashing along like a couple of rhinos in rut, and now and then, Rick would let off another volley with his cannon.

When he did, a screeching like nothing I'd ever heard in real life would arise, and the trees above me would come alive with terrified monkeys. They weren't any more terrified than I was. I was afraid that if Rick saw me, he'd shoot me. He probably didn't have any rabbit heads mounted on his trophy wall.

Larry was probably even more frightened than I was. Rick was actually trying to kill him, which he'd done often enough in the movies, but never before in real life. It was pretty stupid considering the circumstances; but then, Rick probably hadn't taken the time to think about that. Maybe it wouldn't have made any difference, even if he had.

There was a sudden frenzied fluttering off to my right, and I jumped about five feet straight up. I was a credit to the bunny clan. It wasn't a lion, however; it was only a bunch of colorful birds that were no doubt as scared as I was. They were cockatoos, which reminded me of my last case for Gober. That one had involved a cat, too. I was beginning to think that everyone at Gober's studio was nuts, though even that wouldn't be big news in Hollywood.

I looked down at my shoes, which I'd managed to force onto my feet over the bunny costume. They were ruined, naturally. I'd put them on the expense account, but I was still upset.

What with the noise and my shoes, I momentarily lost track of Rick and Larry, but then I heard something that sounded the way Tarzan might yell if he pulled a hernia. When I looked up, Larry was swinging toward me on a thick vine that he had gripped in his right hand. He had his multi-colored cat cradled in his left arm.

This time, I was able to get out of his way, but I didn't really have to. From somewhere in the jungle a rifle roared, the vine parted, and Larry splatted on the wet ground, flat on his back.

He didn't fall far, but he was stunned. He lay there in the dappled shade with his eyes rolled back into his head. His cat, demonstrating the loyalty for which cats are renowned, took off for the tall timber.

Rick Torrance came crashing through the undergrowth, his rifle at the ready.

"All right, you son of a bitch," he said when he spotted Larry, "say your prayers."

"That's more like a Monogram Western than a jungle epic," I said.

THE EASTER CAT

Maybe Torrance had seen me on his stoop, or maybe not. At any rate, he seemed pretty surprised to see a six-foot bunny in his jungle.

"Jesus Christ," he said, and I didn't bother to reprimand him for it. It seemed appropriate enough, considering the season.

What *didn't* seem appropriate was the barrel of the rifle that he had leveled at me. It might not have been an elephant gun, but the bore looked big enough to stuff a python into.

"Who the hell are you?" Rick asked.

"Bill Ferrel, private bunny."

He didn't laugh. "What're you doing in that outfit? I thought Ernie was supposed to be here."

"It's a long story. Why don't you give me that rifle and we'll talk about it?"

"Forget it." He aimed the rifle at Larry's head. "I'm going to plug this varmint."

"Monogram again," I said. "Or maybe Republic. Have you ever starred in a Western?"

"No, but I like to watch 'em. Now, why don't you just get out of here and let me do what I have to do?"

Larry's eyes were no longer rolled up in his head. They were wide and bulging as he stared into the rifle barrel. I think he was holding his breath. He'd looked into plenty of rifle barrels in his movies, being a villain most of the time, but he wasn't used to them when he wasn't acting.

"Killing Larry would be bad publicity for the studio," I said. There was no need to bring morality into it; stars don't understand morality. So I was appealing to his practical side. "And bad publicity for you, too. What about that picture you're working on now?"

"*Manfred of Madagascar*? What about it?" He moved the rifle, pointing it at the wet ground, and Larry let out a slow hiss of air.

"Think how it would look to the fans if you murdered your co-star," I said. "Larry's in the picture, isn't he?"

"Yeah, he's in it, but I wouldn't call him a 'co-star.' He's just the bad guy. I don't have co-stars."

"Right. But it still wouldn't be a good idea to kill him, not over something as silly as a pregnant cat."

The rifle barrel came up. Now, it was pointing at me again. Right at my pink bunny stomach.

"There's nothing silly about a pregnant cat," Rick said. "Especially not about Felicia. She's a pedigreed Siamese, really expensive. Very classy. I've got all the papers on her. And now, she's been polluted by alley trash."

"You should've kept her up. That's what people usually do."

"She was in the back yard. She likes to get out a little in the daytime. Get some exercise. There's a fence, so she should have been safe. Besides, Berry's the one who should have taken precautions."

Torrance turned the rifle barrel back toward Larry. I have to admit to feeling a guilty twinge of relief. But I can never resist asking questions when I shouldn't.

So I said, "What precautions?"

"He could have had his alley cat fixed."

"I thought about that," Larry said.

His voice, always firm in his movie roles, quavered just a little. Not that I blamed him.

"But I just couldn't do it," he continued. "If I had a wife, she could probably have had it done, but I just couldn't."

It was clear that Larry had certain psychological problems that we weren't going to be able to resolve for him. Or, it was clear to *me*. Rick seemed to think he could resolve them easily enough.

He pointed the rifle in the general direction of Larry's reproductive organs and said, "I could fix *you* right here, and take care of the cat later."

While Rick was focused on Larry, I made my move. I'm not generally a very quick guy, but maybe the bunny suit inspired me. I jumped to Rick's side and grabbed the rifle, trying to twist it out of his grasp.

He didn't want to give it up, and he twisted back, which caused both of us to fall to the squishy ground. Luckily, I landed on top.

We thrashed around for a while, but neither of us could get the advantage. Rick's muscular chest wasn't just a movie illusion, though. He managed a powerful roll that turned the two of us over and put him on top. Then he began slowly wresting the rifle from my grip.

I thought that if I could hold out long enough, Larry would get up and help me out, but I was wrong about that. You can never trust a villain. I heard the frantic rustling of palm fronds, and I knew that Larry was leaving the area. Possibly, he was extremely worried about his cat and wanted to find him as soon as possible. More than likely, however, he didn't really care what happened to me, just as long as it didn't happen to him.

I could tell it was going to be up to me to rescue myself, so I resorted to low bunny cunning.

"Rick," I gasped.

He didn't stop trying to get the rifle, but he said, "What?"

"Are there any tarantulas in this jungle?"

"No." He sounded a little nervous, which was good. "Why?"

"Well, there's a couple of big hairy black spiders on your back. I thought maybe—"

"Spiders? *Spiders?*"

Rick let go of the rifle and jumped to his feet, brushing wildly at his back with both arms.

"Did I get them? Where are they? Step on them! Step on them!"

I stood up, holding the rifle. My formerly fluffy white tail was soaking wet, and it dragged down the seat of my suit. I was willing to bet it wasn't white anymore, either.

"The spiders are gone," I said. "They probably weren't tarantulas, anyway."

He seemed happy to hear that, but he kept looking around anxiously until he noticed who was holding the rifle.

"You son of a bitch," he said. "You're going to let Larry get away."

"He probably won't leave without his cat," I said. "Let's see if we can find them."

It didn't take long. We found Larry at the base of a tall palm tree, trying to coax the cat down with a toy mouse. I didn't bother to ask where the mouse had come from. Larry probably carried it around in his pocket.

Rick and I stood quietly behind a banana tree until Larry had the cat safely in hand. Then, I took over.

o0o

We marched back to the house with Rick in front, Larry and his cat behind him, and me bringing up the rear. A guy wearing a bedraggled bunny costume and carrying a rifle. I felt like an escapee from an Abbott and Costello set.

To add to the fun, Rick and Larry yapped at each other all the way to the house.

"You'll regret this Berry," Rick said. "I'm going to get you and that cat if it's the last thing I do."

"Fat chance. As soon as I leave here, I'm calling my lawyer. I'm going to sue you for every cent you've got. You'll be living in a jungle, all right—a *hobo* jungle!"

Stuff like that. I didn't try to keep them quiet. I knew someone who could do that for me when we got to the house.

And he did. Four or five words from Gober, and they were sitting in a pair of leather-covered chairs, as quiet as a couple of rocks. Larry's cat was spread out all over his owner's lap, sleeping calmly.

"That's better," Gober said. Then he looked at me. "Damnit, Ferrel, you've got to settle this. I can't have two of my stars running around trying to kill each other."

"I didn't try to kill anyone," Larry said. "It was Rick. He—"

"*Shut up!*" Gober roared.

Larry shut up.

"Larry's no star!" Rick said. "*I'm* the star. I—"

"*You too!*" Gober thundered, and Rick was quiet.

Gober turned to me. "What about it, Ferrel? You're a fixer. Fix it."

One of my ears kept flopping over my eye. Probably got broken by one of those stupid vines. I pushed it out of my face and said, "Well, Mr. Gober, I think we can take care of things. The way I see it, there's been no crime committed here. Rick got a little excited, but that can happen. He didn't hurt anyone, after all. And I'm pretty sure Larry's cat isn't guilty of anything."

Rick jumped to his feet. "The hell he's not! He...he *raped* Felicia! He—"

"*Shut up and siddown!*" Gober shouted.

Rick shut up and sat.

"I can't swear that Larry's cat—by the way, what's his name?"

"Slim," Larry said with a straight face.

I didn't smile, either. "I can't swear that Slim didn't have his way with Felicia. But I'd be willing to bet my month's retainer from Gober Studios that he didn't get her pregnant."

Rick jumped up again. "That's a lie! He—"

This time Mr. Gober didn't say a word. He just looked at Rick, who sat back down. I wished I could look at people like that.

I went on as if I hadn't been interrupted. "I'd be willing to bet that Slim didn't get anyone pregnant because I don't think he's capable of it."

Larry was incredulous. "Not capable? Are you kidding? Look at the size of his b—"

Gober glared. Larry shut up.

"It's not the size that matters," I said. "The truth is, that cats with as many colors as Slim are usually females. And when they're male, they usually can't reproduce. They're sterile."

"Is that really true?" Larry asked. I guess he had a suspicious nature.

"Of course it's true," Gober said. "Ferrel knows his cats. Isn't that right, Ferrel?"

I didn't really know all that much about cats, but I nodded. I'd heard

The Easter Cat

something like that once, and it might even have been true.

Rick looked as if he believed me. Or if not, he believed Gober.

"So, who knocked up Felicia, then?" he asked.

"I don't have any idea. But if you think a fence is going to keep male cats away when a female's in heat, you're crazy. You may have caught Slim with her, but you missed the others. And I'd bet there were plenty of them."

"I did hear some howling out in the back yard earlier," Rick admitted.

"So, there you are," I said. "If you want pedigreed kittens, you'll have to make the proper arrangements. And if you want no kittens at all, you'll have to keep Felicia up or get her spayed."

It took a little more persuasion, but Rick eventually admitted that everything was mostly his fault, not that he ever came right out and said so. He even apologized to Larry, sort of, for trying to kill him. And then, he asked him if his cat could stay for the party. With Felicia safely put away in the house, of course.

oOo

The party was a success. I looked pretty crummy, even for a fake Easter Bunny, but the kids didn't care. I'd hidden the eggs, and that was all they really wanted. They ran down the drive looking for eggs in the bougainvillea bushes, yelling happily every time they found one.

But the real hit of the party was Slim, who was billed by Rick as the Easter Cat, the Easter Bunny's special guest and helper. Slim had the coloring for it, all right, and he wasn't a nervous type. Even after all the excitement he'd had, he let the kids rub him and scratch behind his ears and under his chin. I could hear him purring from ten feet away.

When the party was over, I went back to the gatehouse. I took a couple of hardboiled eggs with me, a blue one and a pink one. I figured on having them for dinner. I might as well get something out of my day's work.

Ernie was awake, but still in his underwear. He was drinking coffee with the gatekeeper and looking right at home.

"Damn," Ernie said when he saw me. "What did you do to the bunny suit? It's rented, you know. You're going to have to pay for having it cleaned."

I gave him a look. It wasn't as good as one of Gober's, but it was a pretty good one.

"Ernie," I said, "I've never killed a man before. But I've never worn a bunny suit before, either. There's a first time for everything."

Ernie smiled weakly. "Oh. Yeah. Right. I see what you mean. I'll take care of the suit. Did you get my check?"

I reached inside the suit, pulled it out, and handed it to him.

He gave it the once over, started to stick it in his boxer shorts, then thought better of it and just held it in his hand.

"Great," he said. "Thanks, Ferrel. I mean it."

"Sure," I said, and I started peeling myself out of the bunny suit. "You're welcome."

"You know," he said, giving the gatekeeper the elbow, "you look pretty cute in that outfit, Ferrel. You ever think of getting into the movies yourself?"

They had a good laugh at that one, and while they were guffawing, I reached down and got the pink egg from the basket. It would have made a nice dinner with a little salt and pepper, but I had a better use for it now.

Holding the egg behind my back, I walked over to Ernie and said, "Open up and say 'Ah.'"

For some reason, he did it, and I shoved the egg into his mouth, slapping away his hands when he reached for it.

"M-m-m-m-m-m," he mumbled.

"Happy Easter, Ernie," I said.

About the Author—Bill Crider

BILL CRIDER won the Anthony Award for best first mystery novel in 1987 for *Too Late to Die*. His story "Cranked" from *Damn Near Dead* (Busted Flush Press) was nominated for the Edgar award. His latest novel is *Between the Living and the Dead* (St. Martin's). Check out his homepage at www.billcrider.com or take a look at his peculiar blog at http://billcrider.blogspot.com.

Made in the USA
San Bernardino, CA
03 October 2015